WET
PAINT

Gwynn Popovac

WET PAINT

Boston 1986

Houghton Mifflin Company

Library of Congress Cataloging-in-Publication Data

Popovac, Gwynn.
Wet paint.

I. Title.
PS3566.0628W4 1986 813'.54 86-10470
ISBN 0-395-38222-X

Printed in the United States of America

S 10 9 8 7 6 5 4 3 2 1

The author is grateful for permission to quote from the following songs:

To Vladimir

CONTENTS

PROLOGUE

Rough Sketches

Shelters

"I think you might be frightening them," said Marleen. Henry glared at her. One quick look from Henry was enough to make Marleen clamp her mouth shut.

Henry pressed his palms together and continued, "When that siren goes off I don't give a damn what your teachers say, you get the hell out of there. I want you to hightail it home." He made one hand take off like a rocket. His daughters were so startled they jerked back away from him.

Flora pictured their practice drills at school. The last Friday of every month. Everyone down on the floor, drawn in like turtles. "Clasp your hands behind your neck," said her teacher, "and I want perfect silence." There was always some snickering. The teacher could never tell who was doing it, because all of her students were under their desks. Flora thought about all the children like herself, hidden under all the desks in so many classrooms, in so many schools everywhere, and all the teachers talking calmly to empty chairs, and she couldn't stifle her amusement.

"You think it's funny, do you!" Henry pinned his eyes on Flora. "The light will blind you, the heat will fry everything in sight. All the windows will be blasted out and metal will melt. There's nothing in that school that can save you."

Daniel grimaced at his father. At the age of five he already fretted like a fifty-year-old and wondered whether to trust anything that Henry might say. Deep in play in the back yard Daniel talked to himself and tortured his collection of plastic soldiers. He hung them from tree branches and melted them with matches. He had seen World War I and World War II on TV. He eyed Henry suspiciously.

"I don't think the bombs are funny," replied Flora. She was straining to show her father the most sincere and serious expression her face could produce.

Julia, the baby, whimpered, and Marleen joggled her on her lap and kept kissing her on the top of the head.

"All the gates are locked during schooltime," challenged Janice. She was Henry's oldest, a bright eleven-year-old who enjoyed asserting herself.

"I don't care how you get over that fence, but get over it." Both of Henry's hands were clenched into fists. He looked down at his notepad. "OK," he said after a moment, "Marleen, you will get the boxes of canned food. Janice, you will grab the blankets from the hall closet. Flora, you will get the tools out of the garage. And Daniel, you will help her—the axes, the saw, the scythe, the metal toolchest, the shovels . . ."

"What will you do?" asked Janice.

Henry gritted his teeth, stood up, and leaned forward, his fingertips still touching the table. "I'll be getting the guns," he said coolly. "Then I'll hitch the trailer to the car." He stepped over to the stove. In order to simulate an air raid siren he twisted the dials on the stove clock until the buzzer went off. "All right," he said, "everybody get going!" and then he tore out of the kitchen as if he were being chased. Julia laughed.

A couple of years later they really did leave, only not so fast because no siren had gone off. Henry said it was time to get out of there. To all the cold weather clothes and cooking utensils, soaps and cleansers, dried food and first aid supplies already packed into the trailer, they each added their assigned goods. Julia, carrying nothing, fell off the front porch and scraped her knees on the concrete steps. "I don't want to go to Cuba," she cried.

Henry hitched the trailer to his new eggshell-blue Plymouth station wagon, put two rifles in the trailer and a pistol under the driver's seat, leveled the flip-down seats, and pulled foam rubber mattresses in over them. All set, he hoisted the tailgate and heaved it shut. In the dark of the night he drove his family away from Los Angeles. They went over the Grapevine and sped past a sleeping Bakersfield. The crescent moon followed them along the nearly deserted highway, cutting across the sky like a very keen sickle slicing through thin clouds. The odor of ripe crops—beets, beans, tomatoes, onions—whiffled in through the windwings. The children lay awake on the mattresses, heads propped against the wheelwells.

In a motel somewhere they spread their sleeping bags on the floor and crawled into them. Flora listened to the occasional cars and trucks that passed by and smelled the dust in the carpet. The damp autumn air seeped in through the slightly open window at her head. Mixed in with ripe crops was the scent of wild and dying leaves—sycamores and cottonwoods and willows. She thought of the classes, of the people, she would be missing tomorrow and maybe forever.

She listened to the separate tossing and turning of her parents' bodies, to the creaking of the metal bed they were lying in. Metal that might melt at any unknown moment.

When she slept she dreamed that an earthquake was splitting the earth open. Volcanoes erupted and lava chased her and she ran faster than her feet could possibly go until she came to a crack that was too wide to leap. Her family called to her from the other side but she could not get across. Lava was rushing down upon her and her nightgown was being ignited by flakes of flying ash.

She woke in a silent sweat and felt all the padding around her. She was wearing jeans and a sweater, not a nightgown, and she and Janice were constricted in a sleeping bag. Janice's back, pressing against her own, felt like a hot bolster. She felt stifled and yet she stayed put. She wished she knew where they were.

Henry got everyone up before dawn, and they climbed back into the car without eating breakfast or washing their faces. "This is no vacation," he said, hand on the ignition key. "Are all the doors locked?" He had his jacket collar turned up, either from the chill air or from the seriousness of their venture. Flora wondered which. She punched the lock at her elbow and lay back on the mattress. Stretching out in the station wagon made it seem like a hearse. Janice and Daniel and Julia were lying still. What was the use of running away? she thought. When all of the fun had been taken out of being alive.

They rode like that for most of the day, and then for three days they stayed in a trailer park along a river. The entire park was vacant so they had their choice of any camping slot. Henry cruised around and around on the little paths and finally unhitched the trailer in a space surrounded by quaking aspens. The leaves shook night and day with the menacing rhythm of a shaman's rattle.

Marleen fixed meals in the cramped trailer and did a laundry in the dank laundry house. Henry fiddled with the kerosene lamps, cleaned his guns, and sharpened the axes and scythes.

Marleen was tearful and nervous. Daniel walked sullenly around the empty park kicking at the picnic tables, the faucets, and the posts fixed with electrical outlets. Janice complained of missing classes. Julia fetched seedpods, leaves, and rocks that nobody was interested in.

"Think of it as a vacation," said Henry. He tested the edge of the axe with his thumb, picked his sharpening stone up off the picnic bench and gave the blade several more strokes. Leaves rustled and rolled over the yellow grass. It wasn't like a vacation. The air was cold.

Flora went down by the river and sat on a rock. The stiff wind coming down the river seemed to be telling her to go away. *Go away,* it said. *This place too will be destroyed. Fluorescent mint green waves of heat will blast over the mountains, boil the river away, and burn everything along with it, everything in sight.* Chilly little ripples chewed in anger at the pebbly banks.

She went back up to the park and tried to play shuffleboard with Janice, Daniel, and the mongoloid daughter of the park owners. They shoved the pucks up and down a court littered with cottonwood leaves. It was nearly impossible to tell when points had been scored. Only the ageless mongoloid clapped her hands and rahed whenever a puck came to rest. She was happy to have children to play with so far out of season. She jumped up and down and the raw wind whipped her hair every which way.

While Flora was away from school, her closest friend told everyone they both knew that Flora was hiding from atomic bombs. When she came back a week later, they called her "The Survivor" and asked her how heavy the fallout had been up in the mountains.

Every time her father took the family on Sunday drives he pointed out, even stopped the car and investigated, potential bomb shelter sites. Every culvert, every gulch, every natural sandstone cave or manmade drainpipe beneath a road became a place to duck into at a moment's notice.

The landscape was spoiled. The playgrounds of her childhood were spoiled. There was a deep fissure between her and her schoolmates. And America hadn't even been bombed.

They had stayed. She had run. She was a deserter.

Now she was wordless and waiting for it to come into view. She went back to staring out the side window, and Marleen resettled herself in the front seat.

The houses that had been flying by seemed to slow down, and she recognized the neighborhood. She spotted Jericho; she didn't particularly care for that as a street name. Little plum trees had been planted all up and down their block at the curb; Plum Lane would have been better. She braced herself by screwing her heels into the floor mat and peered straight ahead. She had the same fearful feeling she always got when she was in an airplane that was about to touch down.

From Wingtip to Wingtip

Henry thought everything should be perfect now that he had a prestigious, well-paying job as a crew member for a major airline and could come home to his own house, which was in a good neighborhood in a beautiful valley in the most desirable state in the best country in the world. But he didn't sleep well. Whenever he went to bed, whether he was in a hotel room in Paris or New York or in his own room in the valley, he lay there between drowsiness and sleep while thin metal fingers quivered and whirled inside glass gauges filled with glowing numbers, and tiny red indignant lights blinked and beeped in front of his face. Or else he saw the pages of his logbooks: page upon page of schematics and diagrams for circulating and supplying water, oxygen, heat, fuel, electricity to all the planes, every model, and every change in every model, the pages flipping and fluttering in front of his face, demanding to be understood and memorized.

When he finally fell asleep he'd have a dream: all the long jagged lines of the circuits, the wiry maze, would loosen up and become silky threads that flowed along smoothly and evenly, like a stretch of river devoid of rapids. He'd float along in the current, feeling ecstatic and relieved and totally relaxed. Suddenly the lines would knot up into a nettling mess and he'd be thrown into a panic. He'd mistake the satin fabric that trimmed the edge of his blanket for the tangled wires, and try frantically to smooth them out.

When he had this dream at home, instead of in a hotel room in some far-off city, Marleen would be wakened by his groans and cries, and she'd see him rapidly petting and clawing the blanket that lay in confusion across his chest. She was thankful that he bit his fingernails, because when she tried to wake him, or help him straighten his blanket, he often directed his clawing at her. In the morning she'd ask him what his nightmare had been about, and he'd say he didn't remember. He said he never dreamed.

If he didn't have that recurring dream, he'd have another one. One, two, three, and then four propellers would spin down to a dead stop. All the while he'd be grappling with levers and poking buttons. He'd grab the throttles, and he'd be gripping them even as the plane darted into the black Atlantic. He'd wake up sweating. During this one he was too busy to cry out, so Marleen slept through it. He'd look over to her and she'd be breathing deeply, her chest rising and falling like the gentle swells on a quiet sea.

He had this dream over and over, and every time he'd drown himself along with a new fold of passengers, all fast asleep and dreaming of the same destination, or all awake and screaming.

They all went down together every time.

Henry could never return to sleep after this dream. It wasn't just that he didn't feel up to reliving it twice in one night. He felt an anguishing guilt for having failed to save all those people; he needed to dismantle the ship, tear it apart from wingtip to wingtip, from nose to tail, if he had to, in order to discover what had gone wrong and how he had missed it.

Henry felt the pressure of these dreams all the time. During the day it formed a film in front of everything he tried to look at. He couldn't even see his children clearly on account of these nightly horrors. It was like being made to wear thick eyeglasses when his eyes didn't need them.

Whenever he had a night flight to someplace like New York or Chicago ahead of him, or an overseas flight, he tried to take a long nap before going to the airport. Marleen trained the children to tiptoe down the hall and go into their rooms only to fetch necessities. This way Henry didn't have to listen to or look at anyone for a while. Whenever Marleen peeked in at him, he had the sheet pulled over his face. With the door closed he stared at the bedroom ceiling and at the light fixture that was centered there. He thought that its three tiny ball chains were too flimsy to keep it from falling. The frosted floral design of its glass bowl was marred by a dark, blurry cluster of dead flies. He had pointed out the mess to Marleen more than once. She was ashamed of what she saw when she looked up. He was sure she cleaned it, but it seemed there were always dead flies there.

Marleen thought dreams were wonderfully whimsical, nice things to relate at the breakfast table. Henry ate his toast and eggs in silence while she told her daughters about the dream feasts she sat down to but could never eat because they'd disappear as soon as she picked up a fork or a napkin. Flora told her mother about the black panther that kept leaping at her just after she got to sleep, about the bright marbles she saw in the far corners of her eyes. "That's just your eyes seeing themselves," explained Janice.

At dinner Henry told his children about the romance of flying and about the peculiarities of far-off places. He had Jayne Mansfield on his flights every so often and she was always very gracious. The French go pee-pee in pissotières, which look like American voting booths in rows along their streets. "Even in the plushest hotels in Cairo," he warned them, "only order whole melons and split them yourselves at the table. It'll save you a lot of trips to the toilet and maybe even your life."

He told them about the close calls, like the time a window broke on the emergency exit next to the galley and all the passengers would have found themselves without oxygen and someone might've gotten sucked out the broken window. But he thought very quickly and dunked a towel in a sink of melting ice cubes in the galley and spread the wet towel over a plastic serving tray, then slapped it up against the broken porthole. It immediately froze and sealed the jagged hole, stopping the gush of precious oxygen.

At this point his children could breathe freely again, and they sighed in appreciation. It gave Henry relief to see the dazzled eyes and slack-jawed faces of his children. When the dinner was over no one could have recalled how the food had tasted, not even Marleen, who had cooked it.

She herself felt slightly frightened by Henry's stories and hoped they were no more than fabrications from his imagination. She secretly hoped he never had to be a hero in the air, or on the ground. She just wished for her family to be safe and have pleasant dreams.

What Henry didn't tell his family was that he had witnessed a real plane crash. Marleen apparently had not heard any news report about it, and he was glad of that. It was just after sunup. Frost, like a gray mold, coated the wings of the waiting planes. He was on the ground in New York, checklisting a plane he would be taking off in shortly. Another plane taxied onto the runway. He watched it pick up speed, and the next thing he knew, it had nosed over. Just like one of his daughters on a tricycle: one minute she's pedaling along smoothly, and the next thing you know, she's dumped herself onto the pavement and she's squalling. Sirens set up a wild cry. Henry jumped onto the running board of one of the fire trucks, and they rushed for the plane, which by now had come to rest on its side with one wing folded partially under itself. Before they could reach it, a giant balloon of fire burst from the broken wing, followed soon after by an even greater blast. Henry felt the powerful whoosh of heat, as if a dragon had breathed on him, and then the entire plane was sprayed with flame. The fire trucks pulled in as close as they could, and Henry saw one of the side exits drop open. A stewardess in her sky-blue uniform tumbled out. A bunch of passengers clinging to one another fell after her, and they all landed in a pool of burning fuel. Henry had no wish to recall it like this, but there was no getting away from it: they were burnt to a crisp in a matter of seconds, like pieces of bacon in popping grease. There were other sights, too: a man with his back on fire sliding belly-down on the charred wing of the plane. And faces screaming in the tiny square windows. A few people leaping from an exit in the tail of the fuselage, landing ridiculously, like cloth dolls. Someone yelled for Henry to grab a stretcher, and he did.

Looking back on it, Henry thought it was so strange: this crash was more like a bad dream than a bad dream.

When it was time for Henry to get out of bed, he pulled his sheets and blankets up under his chin and shook them until they were all smoothed out. Carefully he'd pull his legs up and out from the top, pivot around sideways, and spring clear of the bed. Then he quickly batted his pillow into a flattened formality and swept the bedspread up over the entire thing. It was a way of never having to look at his bed while it was unmade. He wanted to forget he had ever been in it, struggling to sleep or trying to fly without crashing.

Dirt Cheap

There was nothing special about the outside of the Jacksons' house. It was a typical single-story tract dwelling of pastel stucco walls with a low-pitched shingled roof, a small, unusable porch and a prominent garage. It looked much like the other houses on the block, of unswerving design, like bird nests of a single species.

Inside, the Jacksons put down hemp squares instead of wall-to-wall carpeting. They furnished the living room and the den with rattan sofas and chairs that looked like saltless pretzels. The cushions were upholstered in a napless fabric printed with unfurled hibiscus blooms, pale pink on a background of dark green. Their picture window was curtained with the same kind of fabric. The closest match they could make for the hibiscus pattern, however, was a network of vermilion bird-of-paradise flowers against the same shade of green. When the evening sun shone at the window, the flowers glowed and the dark green became a mesh of chartreuse light. The living room was lent a tropical, humid atmosphere—an unforeseen effect.

Lean alabaster gazelles from Rome leapt in place on the end tables. On one other table, in a corner of the room, stood a manzanita branch from the Malibu Mountains. Clumps of dried chartreuse moss from Yosemite were affixed to the tips of the twigs. Henry made this tree. He'd seen a similar one at the bonsai exhibit at the Los Angeles County Fair. Beneath it lay an unused oval ashtray, looking like a reflection pool without water. It was made of glazed porcelain with a bird of some sort, a pigeon, painted in it.

Woven leather hassocks and brass vases from Egypt were gathered around the brick hearth. Over the fireplace Henry hung an original oil painting: a hard-packed dirt street bordered by nearly windowless mud-and-straw houses, all baking in the heat of day beneath a glaring turquoise sky. The scene is devoid of life but for one woman, no Cleopatra but a working woman, draped from head to brown calves in a veil the same color as the sky. She is retreating, balancing a large egg-shaped water jug on her head.

To Henry this painting represents poverty, drudgery, and filth. He bought it dirt cheap in a Cairo market and had it put in a gilded frame. To Marleen the painting is a beautiful shade of turquoise.

Thinking back, Flora couldn't recall ever discussing this painting with anyone. The rest of the family seemed to regard it as a patch of well-established wallpaper. Whenever she looked at it she wished the woman would set the jug down and rest for a while. The painting made her thirsty, and it aroused a strong yearning in her for something, besides water, that she couldn't name.

If Henry ever got it into his head to remove the painting, Flora was going to beg him to rehang it in her room. But he never did. It hung there over the mantel for years until its surface cracked like plaques of clay on a dried-up pond.

Henry took charge of most of the changes in decor, or rather, he made most of the original decisions, and the household abided by them over the years. Only an occasional earthquake or a reckless child jarred his arrangements. Marleen consented to everything, even the green and yellow tile, instead of the cream and turquoise, that went onto the kitchen and bathroom counters. That was what the tilers had on hand the day they were supposed to tile, and Henry said it didn't make any difference. Marleen bit her lip.

Henry also selected the new refrigerator and the new range where Marleen would keep and cook the food. He seemed to be well informed as to their good features, and to Marleen they looked unbelievably immaculate and shiny. Henry chose all the lamps and lampshades. He even chose the brown and yellow plaid curtains and bedspreads of Janice and Flora's room. Marleen thought this was his way of saying he was expecting a son or two, someday.

Most of Marleen's touches to the house, such as vacuuming and meals, were short-lived. On a Monday, with masking tape she would stick a cardboard-and-felt Snow White, encircled by the Seven Dwarfs, on the wall over the dresser in the girls' room. Dwarf after dwarf lost his grip until by Saturday Snow White stood alone. Even she occasionally lost her grip and fell down between the wall and the dresser. It became a habit of Marleen's to catch them up on the nozzle of her vacuum cleaner and stick them up again with some fresh masking tape.

Marleen was an excellent housekeeper. The beds were always changed before anyone could tell what soiled sheets felt like. The linoleum floors were glossy. No one in her family thought linoleum could look otherwise. Henry didn't think it could ever wear out. No one ever saw any dust on the end tables. Henry couldn't find any dust on the top of the refrigerator or the door frames. Henry thought that the San Fernando Valley was not only frost-free, it was dust-free. That was one of the jokes he used on Marleen when he saw her looking sad or remote.

In the master bedroom (which is what Henry always called it, despite the fact that it was no larger or grander than the children's room), there was a dresser, too big for the room, and a dainty vanity. Arranged at one side of the vanity mirror were cut crystal powder jars, a burlwood jewelry box, a mother-of-pearl compact and matching lipstick dispenser, balanced on the other side by a row of empty marble bud vases. All these things and more Henry had brought back from his flights to Rome or Paris or Cairo. The skirt on the vanity and the spread on the bed were a dusty rose floral print, in satin, from Sears.

Sometimes Marleen would sit at the vanity, gazing at herself threefold in the triptych mirror, and get a little queasy at the thought of being responsible for so many fancy things. She fingered the smallest of the vases. She figured she couldn't possibly keep fresh flowers in so many vases. Henry kept bringing them home—brass, marble, crystal, alabaster. Everywhere she turned, there they were, the vases and the statuettes and the candleholders, sitting on dressers and shelves, tables, windowsills, the mantel. They could be found everywhere except in the children's room.

Whenever she looked at the gazelle that stood on Henry's nightstand, with its spindly legs no bigger around than pencils, she couldn't help but remember what had happened to the other one of the pair, which had once stood on her nightstand. She had put Flora down for a nap in the master bedroom. At the sound of something clattering on the floor, she and Henry had come bounding into the room and found Flora holding the white legless body of the gazelle in one hand and one of its long thin legs in the other. Henry grabbed the fragments from her and flung them against the clothes closet. Then he grabbed her by the hair and jerked her out of the room. He kicked her down the hall, from one side to the other, back and forth, until Marleen herself cried out louder than Flora. Henry stopped and turned to her. "What is the problem?" he asked, but Marleen was too distraught to say anything, so he gave Flora a final kick and told her to get up and get in her own room. Janice must have gotten up from her nap, because she was bumped in the forehead when Flora pushed their door open. They cried in unison for a while; then there was silence. They stayed in their room all afternoon, and Marleen couldn't go to them because Flora, at least, was being punished.

They were only four and five years old then. Marleen wondered why she remembered that incident so clearly. Lots of things got broken, mostly toys. Maybe it was because it was one of Henry's things that got broken that time, and also because it was the first time she had ever seen him thrashing out violently. She was pregnant at the time, too. That evening, after she had read Janice and Flora their bedtime story, they wanted to listen to the baby. They asked her if he kicked hard. "Not too hard; he just wants to let us know he's here." She gave her belly a gentle pat. They put their ears down against her and listened.

Less than two weeks later, Marleen miscarried. She had hit the dashboard of their car. It was an intersection accident, very close to home. She saw another car crossing in front of them and Henry was moving forward too. She had started to say something, but by then it was too late.

Flora couldn't remember if she had been in the car at the time or not. Janice said she remembered getting thrown against the back of Henry's seat and hearing Marleen say, "Oh! Oh! Oh!" Flora couldn't come up with any such details. She did remember a night long ago when they were driving Henry to the airport. The door of their Chevy flew open as they were coming around a hairpin curve and Flora was flung out. Not much harm was done: an abrasion from the soft shoulder, and some scratches from the scrub oak. Nobody but Flora had any recollection of this incident.

A year or so later Marleen gave birth to a son, and a couple of years later to another daughter. Henry named his son Daniel and his daughter Julia. Janice and Flora were shifted into the den and Daniel and Julia took over the girls' room. He said they'd have to move the television, which used to be in the den, into the living room, and Marleen nodded her approval. He also decided to trade the old Chevy in for a family-sized car. He drove off in the Chevy and came home in a brand-new blue station wagon.

At about the same time, Henry redid the living room. He stored the rattan pieces in the garage and brought home a black Naugahyde couch and two easy chairs—one coral pink and one turquoise. They reminded Flora of dented cupcakes that had been rolled in shredded coconut, like things she had sometimes found in her lunch sack.

Canned Plants

On his days off from flying, Henry landscaped the yards. He planted the back yard in dichondra and rimmed it with peach, apricot, and nectarine trees. In the front yard he planted palms, sycamores, evergreen shrubs, and a eucalyptus. In both yards he planted oleander, acanthus mollis, and a variety of other plants that his own father would never have been able to identify, much less grow in the Midwest, such as bougainvillea, rubber plants, paper trees, pampas grass, a monkey tree, guava, mock orange, even a banana tree, which, however, never produced bananas and finally died of a frost after surviving for ten years. He also planted a yucca and an array of cactuses and succulents. He liked to leave the nursery tags on all of his plants and have his children read off the Latin names as he made inspection tours of the yards. Henry bought so many plants the Roseway Nursery loved to see him coming. What they didn't know was that many of the plants he took home with him never got out of their cans. Everywhere around the back yard there were rows of canned plants—all stunted, on the verge of drying out, with tufts of roots protruding through the drainage holes.

One day, after pruning apricot trees until his body ached, Henry came into the house and found that his two oldest daughters, like mushrooms in moonlight, had grown. They were longer and leaner than he had thought, and they were lounging around on the living room furniture, overflowing it. They were wearing lipstick, pale pink lipstick that seemed to erase their lips, and soot-black mascara. And they were wearing nylon stockings with runs from soiled toe to garter clasps, or else wide horizontal snag lines that were threatening to run. They looked too big for the furniture, too big for the house. One stretch and either one of them might easily thrust a foot through the picture window, or up the chimney.

"Enjoying the cartoons?" Their father's voice came as a surprise. Daniel yanked his thumb from his mouth, Julia stopped twirling her hair, Janice quit picking at her toe (the one that poked through the hole in her stocking), and Flora stopped chewing on her fingernail. They all turned their heads toward the hallway, where Henry was standing.

"They're boring," said Janice.

"Then why are you flopped out in front of them?"

"They're the only good thing on," said Daniel. He was sitting on his hands.

"What's wrong with the outdoors?" asked Henry. A tremor of disgust had crept into his voice.

"That's boring too," said Janice, staring back at the TV set.

"Well, there's branches all over the back yard. I want them all bundled up and put over the back fence before trash pickup tomorrow." Henry turned and drifted back down the hall.

His oldest daughters had ceased babbling freely and happily like children. They were as silent as clams. Or else they were asking for keys to the front door, or begging for hours away from home, hours over and beyond school hours. They wanted permission to be taken away by strange young guys in loud cars to hell knows where, and they sulked when they didn't get their way. The only thing they never asked for was help or information.

Henry longed to be home more. He had enough seniority so that he didn't have to fly overseas flights anymore, and he was thankful for that. But now, even the flights to New York seemed like too much to bear.

Marleen had taken on a job as a secretary. It seemed to him that she was gone most of the time. It looked like she was going to be late getting home today. When she did come through the front door, she received a quartet of *Hi, Mom*s. In the bedroom she found Henry laid straight out on his bed with his yardworking clothes on. He had his hands folded over his chest and he was staring at the ceiling again.

"Remember when we threw cold water in their faces, and then they'd straighten up just like that." He snapped the fingers of one hand. Marleen slipped her shoes off and started hanging up her work clothes. She thought for a moment he was talking about his plants; then she realized he was complaining about the children again. She couldn't remember ever throwing water on them. She had no idea what to fix for supper.

"What would you like for supper?" she asked.

Deadheading

Marleen loved beautiful writing—calligraphy, that is. As a schoolgirl she took pride in her penmanship. She took great pains to write neatly and gracefully. It was an inexpensive way to bring elegance into her small-town Missouri upbringing, where all too often things around her looked faded, ragged, makeshift. As she matured, her strokes remained obedient to her early handwriting manuals. If anyone were to compare a letter she wrote now with an essay she had written then, they would be hard put to find a difference in her handwriting.

Marleen also loved spelling bees. Almost without fail she had been the last one left standing at the blackboard, a little bowlegged, bangs cut straight across her brow, wiping her chalky hands together in a futile effort to do something besides just stand there being the best speller again. Her favorite words were descriptive words of three syllables or more. She didn't need a dictionary to spell words like *lachrymose, pugnacious,* or *punctilious.* She wished her boss would sometimes dictate words like these; she would have enjoyed typing them. Except when she could insert them into a crossword puzzle, she rarely found a place for them.

Her family could depend on her spelling abilities, and did, as if there wasn't a large dictionary in the house. Henry, when he was writing a business letter, would ask her again and again how to spell the same words. Usually, after telling her to repeat herself more slowly and clearly, he'd challenge her version and go to the dictionary. He'd end up slamming it shut as if it were a bashed trash-can lid and would return to his letter mouthing the word every which way, none of which sounded right to his ear.

Marleen didn't believe that Henry's difficulty with words had anything to do with how smart he was; the things he had to study in his logbooks looked extremely complicated. Rather, she figured it must have something to do with his left-handedness. Everything had to go into and come out of his brain in an odd way—maybe the long way around. When he first saw Flora using her left hand for schoolwork, he bellowed, "Oh no you don't!" as if she were reaching for some forbidden fruit. He wadded up her paper and told her to start over with the right hand. She had nearly finished a full page of practice lettering, upper- and lower-case *p, q,* and *r.* Now she had to start over. It was as if she were using an artificial limb and watching herself write in a mirror, with the added task of wiping tears off her paper before they soaked in.

Henry told Marleen she was the one who was going to have to see to it that Flora got straightened out. He wasn't home enough to make sure the job got done right. When he looked down at Flora, she was writing with her left hand again. The switch had occurred without anybody knowing it, not even Flora. When Henry whacked the pencil out of her hand she looked dumfounded. It took her a moment to realize what was wrong. Marleen fetched the pencil off the kitchen floor and ventured to say that maybe it wasn't possible to make a person change hands. She looked up and Henry was gone. He returned with an ace bandage, which he wrapped firmly around Flora's left fist until it looked like a club. Flora was wailing by now. "Henry," said Marleen in a beseeching tone. Henry pointed his finger at Flora and said, "Do whatever you want, but if you're going to write like that you might as well go through life walking backwards." He himself backed out of the kitchen. Marleen covered her mouth with her hands because she had no control over the expression on her face.

Still, Marleen had an unquestioning confidence in the way Henry did most things, whether it was decorating the house, disciplining the children, or exchanging his career with the airlines for that of a realtor and land developer. She wanted to stand by him. She didn't know why he wanted to quit his job. Maybe it was just because he wanted to trade clouds for solid ground—something more manageable than air currents. Whatever the reason, she didn't question him. She just hoped everything would go smoothly, like a new zipper.

More and more he bid flights to New York, or to some other city back East, and then deadheaded home. When she drove to the Los Angeles airport to pick him up, he'd insist on driving home. Before pulling out of the parking lot he'd spend several minutes readjusting the driver's seat and the rearview mirror. Sometimes he got out of the car and looked under the hood, even in the dark. He usually seemed irked.

On what would turn out to be the very last time Marleen met Henry at the airport, he seemed no more or less irked than usual. On this particular Friday night Marleen dared to express an idea: maybe, since she had a job now, too, and needed to drive herself to work, it would be a good idea if they became a two-car family. That way, he could drive himself to and from the airport. Henry nearly went through the roof of the car.

"Don't you understand anything?" he shouted at her. "What makes you think we can live so high on the hog?" Marleen smoothed her skirt over her knees. Julia, who had come along for the ride, wished she had stayed home with her sisters and Daniel and watched *The Twilight Zone.*

Tomorrow Henry would be poking and peering at everything. He had always been in the habit of doing this when he returned home from a flight. But in the old days, after he'd been gone for almost two weeks, there'd be an air of joviality about his inspections. They would seem like a ritual, and even though he was sure to find several things out of place or neglected, he didn't seem to be too disturbed, and so neither was Marleen or the children. And chances were he had brought them some exotic gifts—a doll from Switzerland, a hand-embroidered shawl from Madrid, a vase. Now he just brought himself home, in his uniform, or more often now in his suit, which smelled heavily of cigarette smoke. Henry himself complained about the smell. And though he had been gone for no more than two days, the fault he found around the house was sure to be great.

Marleen sat in silence as they swerved down the main boulevard, down into the valley. She watched Henry sniff the sleeves of his coat and shake his head. She dreaded tomorrow. What fault would he find? That there was another chipped plate in her set of starburst dishware? She had tried to coach her daughters to check a dish for chips before setting it at Henry's place on the table.

Henry screeched to a stop at a red light. As he waited for it to change, he had a huge shiver. He reached across Marleen and checked the lock on her windwing.

Last time he had come home, he had thrown Janice's gym shoes out in the back yard because she had left them on the service porch floor. And he had rubbed a bar of Lava soap in Flora's face because she said Janice wore just as much makeup as she did. Why did he have to find fault? Why did he have to? Marleen's eyes got very wide, and then she squinted with the strain of an idea. It was as if the sun had popped back up and shed light on everything. Now it made sense: Henry *had* to find things wrong when he got home. If everything remained perfectly neat and orderly while he was away, that would mean he wasn't needed. She felt like leaning over and hugging him.

Henry came to an abrupt stop in their driveway. Without a word, he got out and opened the tailgate of the car. He got his satchel full of logbooks and carried it to the garage. Marleen saw Flora part the picture window curtain just a crack and then whip it closed. Henry put his satchel in the garage. He actually skidded it across the cement floor with a shove from his foot. That was strange. He usually brought it with him into the house. He plodded up the porch steps. Marleen felt Julia shoving at the back of her car seat.

"I wanna get out," she demanded.

"Can't you use your own door?" said Marleen.

"The lock's stuck," whined Julia. Marleen reached around and pulled up the lock button for her.

They followed Henry into the house. Alfred Hitchcock's profile was being traced on the TV screen. Henry walked through the living room, right past his daughters. There was a light on in the kitchen. He looked in there. Daniel was seated at the kitchen table twirling the propellers on a silvery-gray plastic airplane model. He started to hide it under the table when Henry appeared, but it was no use. There were other bits and pieces lying on the table, and also the box it had all come out of. The cellophane wrapper was on the floor. Marleen held her breath as Henry dropped the car keys into a little marble vase on the kitchen counter. He went over to the table and lifted the folded instruction sheet out of the box without looking at Daniel.

"Just couldn't wait until we could work on it together." Henry said this not as a question but as a conclusion. Daniel set the plane down carefully and bent his head.

Henry picked the plane up and turned it over so that it was belly-up in his hand. He thumped at the wheels; one flew off and bounced on the wall.

"Where are the landing flaps?" he asked. Daniel searched around for them. He even looked under his chair. "When are you going to learn to read and follow instructions?" Daniel picked up a small sheet of decals. "That's all you think there is to it: slop it together and slap some decals on it." Henry shook the plane.

"Look," said Marleen, "he made sure the propellers would go around." She reached over Henry's arm and tapped one with her finger. Henry jerked the plane away from her.

"It's a mess," he said, and with that, he dropped the plane on the floor and stepped on it slowly so that it sounded like cornflakes crunching inside Marleen's skull. Daniel's face showed no emotion.

He just stared at Henry. Marleen knew Daniel didn't put it together perfectly, but he did do a darn good job for a nine-year-old.

"Maybe next time you'll follow directions," said Henry. Daniel gathered up some pieces on the table. "Clean up this mess, too," added Henry, pointing to the floor.

"I will," said Daniel, nearly voiceless. Marleen couldn't bear it anymore. She left the kitchen.

She went to sleep thinking what a cruel person Henry was, and woke up to the sound of his voice. It drifted in through their bedroom window, sounding overly gentle and persuasive. It reminded her of when he was proposing to her, telling her how he would take care of her and cherish her, and what a wonderful life they would have. Henry's voice seemed to be coming from the garage. No one was answering him, and so his monologue went on and on.

"Looks like it'll be a perfect day. Weather report says not a cloud in the sky. It won't be just fighters. There'll be planes you might never have a chance to ever see again. And a crop-dusting exhibition, and the Silver Wing Flying Circus." There was a steady swishing sound. Marleen couldn't resist. She crawled over Henry's bed and peeked out the window.

Daniel was sweeping leaves off the driveway with the big pushbroom. Henry was standing in the garage holding a rake. Marleen sat on the edge of Henry's bed and listened.

"We won't have to get up too early. If we left by nine we could be out there before noon. Just the two of us. What do you say?" Henry was really asking this time. There was silence.

"This air show is like a birthday: it only comes once a year." The sound of sweeping started up again.

The Clothesline

Henry stopped flying altogether. He was at home most of the time: resting, doing yardwork, or sitting at the dining room table toiling over survey maps. While he eased his way into the real estate business, Marleen continued her job. They needed the monthly income because Henry was sinking their savings into parcels of land. She hated being away from home so much, especially when her children were returning from school. She loved them with an intensity she had never felt before. They all looked strong. They all ate well. She had them all vaccinated, down to the last booster shot. But she still worried about them all the time, even when they weren't sick. At night when they were asleep she cried for them. They had accidents, they made mistakes, they said things, they went places they weren't supposed to, they broke things. But they were good, their intentions were good. They were good in their hearts. Actually, this was how Marleen felt about all people on earth.

Around the time Henry started being home more, Marleen started having a dream, the same one at least once a week: She'd be taking a load of white sheets out of the washer and putting them in the laundry basket. When she lugged the basket outside, it got unbearably heavy. She kept spilling it, or the ends of the sheets would fall loose and drag on the ground. When she finally made it all the way to the clothesline, she struggled to get them pinned up. The sheets braided themselves together; they twisted and got tangled, coiled and uncoiled as if they were alive. When they finally allowed her to spread them and smooth them over the line, she saw that they were covered with soiled spots and streaks of dark lint.

Why did things have to be so difficult? Marleen wished there was a way to convince Henry he didn't have to be so hard on the children. Daniel and Julia looked dismal, like puppies in a pound. They were learning to run and hide from their father, but they couldn't always get away quickly enough. He was still using on them, when he could, the same thing he had used on Janice and Flora: a yard-long knotted loop of clothesline, a nylon cord covered with plastic, the kind of soft plastic some baby dolls are made of. With it, he left long red welts on the backs of their thighs. And when it wasn't in use, it hung on a hook in the broom closet so that they all had to look at it every time they went for the broom.

Marleen hated the sight of it. After the fourth child, this clothesline whip seemed so bizarre, so uncalled for, but she had nothing very convincing to offer him as a replacement. She wished it were as simple as exchanging a harsh, ineffective laundry detergent for a milder, brighter one. "Are you tired of getting dingy results for your hard labor?" A housewife on TV stops wringing annoying suds off her hands and looks up. "Then toss out that ol' . . ." Easy for someone else to say, thought Marleen.

In her most painful moments she knew it wasn't the whip but Henry's pure anger that really threatened the well-being of her family. When he forgot to go for the clothesline and used his hands and feet instead, that's when she really got frightened. Such as the Sunday morning of the air show when he yanked Daniel out of bed and started whacking him on the head because Daniel had said he'd rather stay on the block and play with his friends. That's what could keep her awake at night.

What made Henry think he had to be so rough? She'd lie there in bed and start going over what she really knew about him. She discovered she didn't know much about his childhood. Night after night she'd return to a story he had told her and the kids over and over again. It was about the time he had been raising piglets, five of them, all summer long, and one day while he was off at school, his father sold them. "Any money anyone earns in this family is family money," his father said as he pulled a wad of money from the chest pocket of his overalls. When Henry started to protest, his father walloped him across the face with the back of his hand and broke his nose. She'd look around and see her children holding their noses. That story was as bad as a recurring dream.

There was another story too, about the Christmas his mother actually filled his stocking with coal and wouldn't tell him why. Marleen thought that sort of thing happened only in fairy tales, but Henry nearly lost his temper when she expressed her disbelief. The story didn't end on such a bleak note, however. He said that later in the day he had found a box containing a little felt Saint Nicholas at his place at the dinner table.

Marleen tried to picture Henry's mother shoveling coal into his stocking. She might've done it. Whether indoors or out, Mrs. Amy Jackson was full of purpose, scurrying and scratching around like a hen before a blizzard. Marleen had been invited to the Jackson house for Sunday dinner several times when Henry was courting her, and Amy never once sat down to a meal. She was always dishing up, or worrying over the stove, or scooping a second serving onto someone's plate. With a washrag clutched in her nervous little hands, she darted around everywhere, sometimes peering out of the kitchen window like a weasel behind a fallen log—a quick little head popping up and down. Back then Marleen had thought Amy was peculiar. She seemed less so after Marleen herself had been married for a dozen years.

Marleen never heard about, or saw, any show of affection between Henry and his parents. When they came for a visit there was only a rapid round of pecklike kisses and then the problem of where to put the suitcases.

All of the Jackson offspring, Henry and his three sisters, had swept over the Great Plains and on over the Rockies like milkweed fluff in the wind. They had all seeded themselves in California. Amy and Jacob somehow, for some reason, managed to uproot themselves annually and make a tour of California, visiting for a week at each of their children's homes. By the time they left, Henry always looked tired and bothered.

Marleen sighed late into the night. She concluded that Henry felt unloved. But it didn't seem to her that she could be of any help. Whenever he rolled over into her bed, try as she might to relax and accept him, she couldn't. She felt herself hardening up like a block of alabaster. She knew he could tell he had taken something from her she hadn't really felt like giving, because as soon as he was finished he crawled back under his own covers without saying anything. She had been more open to him when there had been babies to make. But now, with that phase of life behind her, she seemed to have lost her desire to be physically close to Henry. She could do without that part of their marriage. Henry, on the other hand, acted hungry or desperate. Something about his touch made her feel like a scared child. She didn't know what to do.

PART ONE

Life Drawing

Gullies and Lizards

All over the school there were concrete gullies, and wooden footbridges with wooden handrails spanning the gullies. Between classes and during lunch hour groups of boys perched on the railings and graded the girls who passed over. They hooted or whistled, or stuck their feet out to lift the hem of a skirt.

Flora took a detour and jumped over a gully. She dropped her lunch sack and it rolled toward the muddy rivulet that ran along the bottom. A dark-haired boy was standing on the other side, and when he saw her sack fall he leapt down and retrieved it.

Flora said, "Thank you," but he didn't say anything. He just squinted at her with one eye as if he had something, like an eyelash, stuck in it. She watched him leap up the other side of the gully. His hair was smooth and straight and carefully cut. It reminded her of the wing of a crow. He moved agilely and suspiciously, like a mature Siamese cat. He did an odd thing. Instead of walking over to the nearest stairway and going into the Long Hall, he seemed to vanish in the open space. Then he reappeared over by the wall. He looked as if he was merely skimming over the asphalt—not a cat anymore, just the shadow of a cat. He stayed close to the wall until he came to the stairs; then he swung himself up over the railing and with one bound was at the doorway. He glanced back at her and then disappeared into the hall.

Flora was not a newcomer. She had already gone to Hazelton High for over four years. This was the second day of the winter semester, and she was glad for the change of classes. She didn't mind being at school; like anyone who has had to spend a long time in one place, whether a dump or a palace, she had grown attached to it. She thought of the buildings as a large family of pale pink stucco lizards basking themselves in the San Fernando sun. They sprawled out over acres of flat land: long spines of halls, and attached to these, shorter halls, like arms and legs; appended to these, classrooms made more of windows than of walls. She had grown attached to the cardboard walls—bruised and busted, gouged and defaced by rough and hopeless students. She had grown attached to the parched crabgrass lawns and to the rows of huge, dusty, sulky eucalyptus trees, the asphalt paths, the footbridges, the ramps leading from the halls. She liked the school's labyrinthine quality, so many angles and turns. She appreciated the dim side halls where she could straighten a slip or let out a sigh without being seen or heard.

The central hall of Hazelton High was the Long Hall. All the other halls fed into it. On a rainy day it was so packed with students, it was like a snake that had eaten a snake. Flora always brought an umbrella so she could walk outside on those days. On the usual dry days the Long Hall was a good place to parade for those who wanted to parade. It bordered the lunch area, so most students passed through it one way or another to get to lunch. Flora and Tess, her closest friend, shared a locker there. As a seventh grader Flora had been assigned a locker in the hall close to the Main Offices. All students in the lower grades were given lockers in more remote halls and gradually worked their way up to the Long Hall.

Though the student body was immense, it was not big enough to fill all the corners and crannies of the school. There were rooms that supposedly no one, not even the custodians, had set foot in; their doors were stenciled in black enamel paint with the words OFF LIMITS. All sorts of frightening and unsavory stories were circulated about what those rooms contained: the bubonic plague, the creeping crud, amputated limbs, decomposing bodies, demons, old vice principals, the murderer with the hook for a hand.

Whatever Hazelton High was now, it hadn't always been. It had seen even worse times. Originally it was a receptacle for the maimed—an army hospital built in 1941.

The music hall used to be the hospital chapel.

The student store used to be the morgue.

The gym dressing rooms used to be warehouses.

The ramps and bridges were for amputees and paraplegics.

The classrooms were sick wards and operating rooms.

Flora had the secret notion that the walls or floors of the rooms still gave off an anesthetic, an ether, or something like it. After sitting in them for a while, she nearly always became drowsy, dreamy, or silly to the point of wanting to laugh at anything.

Flora's tenth-grade year hadn't gone so well. There had been an influx of new students, graduates from the rich kids' junior high in the Hills. From among them there was one by the name of Floyd who Flora liked. They had never dated each other, but they had shared an English and a biology class. He was always twisting around in his seat and whispering to her, such funny things about the teachers, the subjects, the other students, themselves, that Flora had trouble containing herself. She covered her eyes with her arms and pressed her face to her desktop to keep from laughing. Then he'd slip a note or a cartoon under her arm. Usually they were just silly things like a drawing of their biology teacher picking algae from his teeth and showing it to the class. Floyd skipped classes a lot. Sometimes he showed up for morning classes and was gone in the afternoon. Next thing Flora knew, he had been expelled from Hazelton High and she never heard from him again.

School wasn't the sanctuary she thought it was. Until Floyd, she had never been close to someone who had gotten kicked out. They had done it so easily. The message she got was that if they felt like it, they could and would get rid of anyone.

Just how far could they really go? She imagined photos of disreputable students lined up on the bulletin boards in the administration building. She snapped a photo of herself inside her head and tacked it up among the others, a front and a profile shot: Flora Jackson, tenth grade, light complexion, green eyes, long wavy dishwater-blonde hair, five feet seven inches tall, skinny, walks with too big a stride (as if she thinks she knows where she's going).

All Flora knew was that she didn't want any more restraints. She got enough of that at home. She didn't want to join any team, league, council, or club, with the exception of Glee Club, but by the time she went to sign up, they already had more than enough voices. She never wanted to try out for cheerleader or march with the drill team. She had gone to a few football games, but it seemed to her that a girl could get excited only if her boyfriend was down on the field, and she wasn't attracted to football players. It seemed to her they stood around the lunch area like inflated punching dolls. She didn't want to be part of the student government. And the vague title *Girls' League* frightened her. Wasn't she already a girl? Who needed a league for that? She suspected they worked for the administration. She didn't fall in with the gangs at the back gate, either. They had their own ranks of ringleaders and followers and battled among themselves and against the administrators. Flora didn't see where she was supposed to fit in.

Flora and girls like her were an enigma to Mrs. Baines, the Girls' Vice Principal. Flora got top grades but could be seen associating with the problem kids, the ones who lost their report cards, who forgot to bring their textbooks or even themselves to class, who talked back and swaggered—all those students that the administration lumped together as the losers.

Flora found herself attracted to those students. They seemed self-reliant, not defiant, and entertaining in a harmless way. One of them, a guy named Chris, who everyone called by his last name, Dalavantes, had bet Flora he could sit in every one of her classes except gym without being detected by any of her teachers. Flora agreed not to give the slightest hint he was in the room. He got through the first half of the day easily. After lunch he sat in the vacant desk right next to Flora with a tag pinned to his jacket that read, I'M LOST. PLEASE CALL MY PARENTS. And Flora cracked up.

Flora thought school would be boring without this restless portion of the student body: they were bright in an ungradable way, jokesters like Floyd. She never thought of them as losers. And despite the company she kept, she rarely missed a day of school or a class, and she was always carrying around a load of books as if she had never been assigned a hall locker.

It was at an open party that Flora first met Tess. Tess was one of the rich kids from the Hills and a grade ahead of Flora. The main thing they had in common was that neither of them dated any one boy in particular. They were also enrolled in the same dance class —Intro to Modern Dance. Tess had joined the class late after quitting the girls' swim team. "I like swimming," she said, "but racing is for speedboats." When dancing Tess tended to move in a series of abrupt poses as if she were a mannequin in the hands of a finicky boutique keeper. Nonetheless, Flora admired her self-assurance. Tess always looked as though she were draped in silk.

Henry approved of Tess. He thought she was classy, like Jayne Mansfield. When she first came to the house, she told him he had a sexy voice, and he blushed. He was impressed when he found out she had been to charm school. He thought her parents were very successful because they owned a catering service, a house in the Hills, and a Mercedes-Benz. If it was a matter of Flora going along with Tess to a school dance, Henry had no objections. "Keep your eyes open and stay out of trouble" was all he said, addressing himself to both of them.

He didn't like any of the boys Flora went out with. After a while she felt she was accepting dates with different boys just to see if she could come up with one her father would say something nice about. But in his eyes they all had major flaws. They were dumb looking and inarticulate. They didn't know how to address an adult in a respectful manner. Or they were surf bums. Their hair was too long. Or their cars were too loud. They smoked—they were just waiting to get out the door so they could light up. Or they didn't seem to know for sure where they were going for the evening. Or they didn't open the car door for her. Flora was sure to hear his objections at the breakfast table. Finally she asked him, "Well, what kind of a guy am I supposed to go out with?" and he said, "If you don't know the answer to that question, you have no business going out at all." She looked to Marleen for help, and Marleen gave her a discouraged look. Flora went away from the table doubting her own judgment. She felt unsafe. Maybe she had been stepping out too far? She imagined her evenings ending in disasters: car accidents, raided parties, dates turning into brutes, abandonment on dark distant roads . . . She decided to stay home more. She confined her outings to places where she and Tess could go together. Tess figured Flora must have a crush on someone and wasn't saying who. Now all the boys who came to the Jacksons' door asked for Janice, and Henry acted as if he didn't notice the change.

At school Flora started getting summoned out of class at a predictable time—during her geometry class, which came directly after lunch. The door at the head of the class would whine open and in would come some girl, usually the same one, wearing the same plaid skirt. She had tightly pursed lips and very straight posture. She moved toward the teacher's desk with mincing steps, as a way of excusing herself for the intrusion, deposited a yellow slip of paper in front of the teacher, and, smiling curtly and malignantly at Flora, exited by the same door. Flora wondered why this girl carried on as if she knew her.

What got to Flora was that her math teacher would stop midsentence, in the middle of the story of how the line was going to make a tangent to the circle, drop his straightedge and his chalk, and pick up the slip of yellow paper. Then he would walk down the aisle and let it fall on her desk without a word—not one word of concern or regret, not even a questioning glance. Flora liked this teacher, and she thought he liked her too. Either he was following the rules mindlessly, or else he simply resented these intrusions.

She read the slip of paper as if she didn't already know what it would say:

SUMMONS FOR: Flora Jackson
TO APPEAR AT: Mrs. Baines, G.V.P. Office
WHEN: 5th period

And then the date, whatever it was, and Mrs. Baines's signature, which looked like a big bulbous *B* followed by a couple of tiny knots.

Flora got up and left, and the class resumed. Actually it started resuming even before she got out the door. She thought it strange, and wrong, that they went on without her. This must be the way a dying person feels, she reflected as she walked down the empty hall. Her tennis shoes made a ridiculous squeaking sound.

The first time Flora entered the vice principal's office, she was told to get down on her knees, and she did. Mrs. Baines leaned over, which was a chore for her, and saw that Flora's skirt did not touch the floor. Her face swelled up until it looked like a blister. When she straightened up again, she informed Flora that there were certain citywide dress standards that must be upheld. When she spoke, the fleecy yellow hair on the top of her head quivered. "Your skirt must come no higher than the middle of your knees. We don't want to attract undesirable attention to ourselves, my dear. And that's a fair warning." Mrs. Baines's blueberry eyes seemed to be watering from the strain of it all.

The second time Flora was summoned, Mrs. Baines shook a seam ripper at her and said she had no recourse but to call her mother in. Flora thought to tell her that her mother worked during the day and probably couldn't come in, but because Mrs. Baines was carrying on so, Flora remained mute. Her silence seemed to make Mrs. Baines fume all the more. "This is a disgrace," she said. "A young lady like you shouldn't have to be told twice." Flora couldn't believe the situation she was in. She just wanted to be an anonymous tenth grader. Yet now Mrs. Baines was acting as if she knew something awful about her that she herself wasn't even aware of. It was as if Mrs. Baines had sources of secret information which, when all added up, could prove she was a bad person. It was a fearful notion. Finally Mrs. Baines handed her the seam ripper and told her to take her hem out. Flora went around school for the rest of the day with frayed seam-binding dangling about her calves.

A few weeks later a summons slip was dropped on her desk during one of her morning classes. She snatched it up and was halfway to Mrs. Baines's office before she noticed that it was from the Girls' Dress Board. She hadn't known there was such a thing. They wanted her to appear in Room 101, the Student Council Hall, at the beginning of lunch period. When she went there what she found was about twenty girls sitting behind long tables that had been arranged in the shape of a U. They were all eating their lunches out of sacks. There seemed to be three judges and a recording secretary. The rest of them looked like witnesses of some kind. The girl with the tight lips and the plaid skirt was there, and so was Janice. Flora stood before them, shocked. They criticized her appearance and gave her suggestions for improving herself. But she didn't actually hear anything they said, and she didn't make any response either. It was as if they had called in one of the deaf-mutes from the student body and she wasn't able to read their lips.

What a way to spend a lunch period, thought Flora. She kept glancing at her sister. Janice never looked up. She seemed to be reading her own sandwich in between taking bites out of it. At home Flora waited for Janice to say something about this unexpected encounter, but Janice never did.

Eventually Marleen was called in for a conference with Mrs. Baines. She couldn't believe how red the woman's face got just over the length of Flora's skirt. She dreaded trying to explain all this to Henry. In front of Mrs. Baines she asked Flora to try to wear longer skirts, and then realized with dismay that it was she herself who had sewn most of them. It seemed as if Flora's legs would never stop growing out from under her skirts. Thank goodness she had always made allowances for a generous hem.

Marleen and Flora spent several evenings redoing the hems of Flora's favorite skirts. In the mornings Flora stood before the mirror on the back of the bedroom door and regarded her long skinny figure from all angles. She pondered her proportions, took hold of her skirt at the waistband and carefully rolled it up until it was the right length for her own particular body—about two inches above code. She gathered up her books and as she was going out the front door she called good-bye to her parents, who were still sitting at the kitchen table. If Henry called her back for an inspection, she could pretend she didn't hear him and keep on going.

Tess rolled her eyes when Flora pulled her sweater off in the gym locker room and revealed a woolen skirt that was rolled up a couple of notches.

"You're just asking for more trouble," she said, but Flora gave her a demonstration of how quickly she could unroll it and told her she was keeping an eye out for Mrs. Baines and learning to spot Mrs. Baines's snitchers, too.

"Wouldn't it be easier to wear them at the right length?" asked Tess.

"They are at the right length," said Flora, "as far as I'm concerned." Tess rolled her eyes again. Flora pulled a wad of black leotards out of their gym locker and handed Tess hers. Flora pulled her own on and tried to distribute it evenly over her body. But it was no use; it always ended up looking as shriveled as the skin on a raisin. Tess wore her dresses and skirts well below the dress code limit. She had a different body. Her clothes looked good at that length. She had shapely legs and an easy gait that made all her skirts swish nicely about her calves as she moved down the halls. And no matter how carelessly Tess put on her leotard, she never ended up with crinkles.

Rocks and Faces

Flora got through the first half of the eleventh grade without being summoned. At the start of the new semester she felt in some ways a little smarter, or at least more wary. She also felt more alone.

When the school day was over she dreaded going home. Henry was nearly always there, in the master bedroom pretending to be asleep, or else sitting at the dining room table with a pile of topo maps. She knew he was waiting for her and Janice and Daniel and Julia to get home. He seemed so anxious to have them all together under one roof. She could see it in the way his gray eyes darted around. They reminded her of minnows in a river pool, scurrying about in search of cover. If anyone walked in the door a few minutes past due, he wanted to know why.

He didn't want Daniel and Julia to stay after school to play on the playground. "I've seen it," he said. "It's not properly supervised."

"But . . ." whined Julia and Daniel, wrinkling their faces, not knowing what else to say. They could see kickball and handball games going on without them, other hands swinging on the rings.

"Besides, there's plenty to do around here." If they asked to go back out and visit a friend, he'd assign them chores. He'd tell Daniel to go water the plants that were in cans, and Julia to sweep the patio and the front porch. If they finished too quickly, he'd find something else for them to do, such as picking up all the trash that had been spilled around the trash cans in the alley. Eventually they stopped asking to go anywhere.

"All you want to do is run off, just run off. That's all you're interested in."

"Can we invite someone over?"

"No, your mother doesn't want strangers in the house when she gets home." They turned away with skeptical, screwed-up faces.

He was as frantic and as inflexible as Mrs. Baines, only with him it was worse because once anyone came home there was no way to get away from him. Their house was just too small. Flora could lock herself in the bathroom for only so long before it began to look suspicious or someone else really needed to use it.

She sat in there for a while eyeing all its features, imagining what it would be like to live in the bathroom, make a bathroom her home. There were several sources of running water, a place to eliminate waste. She could make a bed every night in the tub and heat food over the electric heater. There was a mirror where she could keep track of her face and several cabinets where she could stash some essentials, even a shelf for art supplies, and one frosted window that could be cranked open on nice days with a sill wide enough to eat off of. One door. The room was compact and complete, simple. She could see herself with a bag of groceries unlocking the door to this bathroom, this bathroom placed somewhere else.

What she really wanted to do after school was go straight to her room, kick off her shoes, and collapse on the bed. She always needed to take a nap. But nearly always, as she was lying there waiting for the knots in her muscles to loosen, her breathing to slow, there'd be a token knock on the door. It would swing open, and there he'd be, leaning against the door frame. She felt like screaming. She wished she had it in her to frighten him away with one long shrill rasping scream, like the warning song of a large jungle bird. However, she just leaned her elbows back against the bed and listened to him while he went on and on, usually beginning with some cutting remark about her dress habits.

"No girls wear black and puke-green." Flora took a cautious glance down at herself. She was wearing an olive-green corduroy skirt, a black blouse, and a forest-green mohair vest. It made her feel like part of the forest, and as soft, as cushiony as moss. She dared wiggle her toes and discovered a hole in her stockings. Not again today, she thought, frowning. He went on about the pack of kids she ran with, who were looking for trouble, not for fun as she might suppose; her last-semester grades, which weren't all A's like Janice's; her hair, which was parted down the middle where it shouldn't be; the expression on her face, which was unbecoming and disagreeable; and all the chores that needed to be done immediately, before her mother got home.

Before retreating he'd always point out something, some graphic example of her lowly ways; this time it was grime on the door frame. He examined the smudge so closely that Flora thought he had to be looking cross-eyed at it. "Probably some of that soot you smear around your eyes," he said as he finally pulled the door shut.

Flora took an index finger and wiped along the lower edge of her eye. Then she regarded her finger. There was a shadow of mascara there, or was that graphite from a drawing pencil? "I don't 'run' with anyone," she muttered to herself. "And I haven't been called into Mrs. Baines's office for ages. What more does he want? I'm not even going out with any boys."

She rolled over on the bed and wrapped her arms over her head. In doing so she knocked against the rocks in the windowsill. One tumbled onto the bed; she picked it up and gave it a close look. She could almost see her reflection in it. It was like looking from a lighted room through a windowpane into a black night. The rock was a fist-sized piece of obsidian, something she had brought back from Hot Creek, a campsite the family vacationed at ten years or so ago. She dared not rub her finger too hard along its choppy edges. They didn't look blunt. She put the rock back in the windowsill and picked up another one. She couldn't name this one. It was a clump of two or more minerals colliding and swirling together, some kind of wonderful accident.

She had two boxes of rocks stored beneath the bed. Her favorites, however, were always sitting in the windowsill, waiting to be held. Even the rougher ones looked glossy from her handling of them. Each one had a unique, complicated, mysteriously stable personality. She knew where she had met each one of them—a certain river bottom, a certain hillside. She couldn't help wondering how they had got there. She hated to do it, but sometimes she couldn't resist taking a few of them out on the back patio and cracking them open with a hammer. They rarely revealed a secret to her in this way, only which ones gave off sparks, which were hard and which were soft and which were in between. All she saw were their ragged interiors, unpolished, unaccustomed to rubbing against other rocks.

Once she set a very round, softball-sized stone down on the patio and gave it a good solid whack with the hammer. The stone split open too easily, and two bowl-shaped pieces spun around on the cement. Each was lined with chartreuse crystals, like moss growing on the inside of a rock. She picked up the fragments and went running to find her father.

"That's a geode," he said as he took the halves from her. He looked at them more closely. "They're probably worth something." He thought for a moment. "We ought to take them to that rock shop in Topanga." Flora took the halves away from him and tried to screw them back together again.

After that she stopped cracking rocks apart. She was content with their surfaces. She licked and rubbed them and gazed at their miniature patterns, their intricate designs. They reminded her of the faces of people she knew, of the faces of strangers, of flowers and food, of other planets, paint palettes, mazes, maps, skies, landscapes, some lush, others barren, cultivated, or austere. Rocks could be as thick as a storm cloud, as scaly as a lizard, as crumbly as cake, as chippy as old paint, as smooth as glass, as transparent as a dragonfly's wing. When she stood knee-deep in a river holding a cupped handful of glistening stones, she was caught by their endless variety. A person could keep picking up rocks forever and never find one that looked like another one.

She could recognize and name a dozen of the common kinds, and she knew the names of some of the precious and semiprecious ones, stones she never expected to find lying around. But always there for the taking were the exciting nameless ones. Sometimes she wished she could carry an entire strand of beach or stretch of river back home with her. On some of the last trips the family had taken together, camping along the Kern or Kaweah rivers, she'd go off by herself, up or down the river a ways, and toward the end of each day she'd come back, jumping along over the boulders with a bucket of jangling stones and a head filled with the sound of running water. Dazed, untroubled, perfectly balanced, nearly flying, she felt like a shorebird.

It wasn't just the stones themselves, but all they could evoke. Whenever she took them out of the windowsill and held them, she could imagine the dragonflies that rested on them, the moss and algae that grew on them, the crayfish and trout that hid under their ledges, the water that washed them, the driftwood that snagged up in them, the willows, cottonwoods, sycamores that shaded them, the patches of sand they held away from the river's current, the heat they held after sundown. The rocks in her sill were like steppingstones that led to a place where everything seemed to touch and be touched.

Like rocks, any face she had a chance to look at for a while would suggest something else to her. Janice's face reminded her of vanilla ice cream licked smooth. Sometimes when Henry spoke she thought of cracked cement. The woman who lived next door had a face of finely meshed wrinkles, like gauze. She seemed to be afraid of smiling, as if her skin might easily tear. The man who ran the laundromat had a face as pink and puffy as bubble gum.

Faces could look as if they were made of nearly any substance: satin, rubber, cardboard, sponge, suede, tree bark, cheese, tissue paper, veined marble, frost, metal, lace. But they also had the power to do something rocks couldn't do—change their shape. She saw a cashier at the supermarket who talked so far out of one side of her mouth it seemed to have been placed on one cheek, and yet whenever she stopped talking it swung back to perfect center. She had a teacher once who was so unkind to his face that whenever he spoke he pawed at his cheeks as if they were made of clay and he wanted badly to remodel them. Floyd had an elastic face. He could wad it into a grimace or stretch it out to a look of sheer attentiveness quicker than the twist of a teacher's head. When Flora was small she crawled into bed with her mother around dawn and watched her face while she continued to sleep. Her eyes moved around beneath her closed lids like children burrowing beneath their bedsheets. At times they bounced up and down or swung back and forth. Was she vacuuming in her dreams, or changing beds, hanging clothes on the line, watching her children swing on their swings? Her cheeks and forehead reminded Flora of the rose quartz in her windowsill. Her mother's skin rippled and shimmered, went taut and loosened; it never stopped moving. Flora felt like she was watching a face through several inches of clear running water.

When Henry and Marleen bought a modern dresser and mirror

for their room, Flora and Janice were given the little white vanity with the spindly legs, satin skirt, and three-paneled mirror. It was a marvelous new toy. Flora would push aside the jewelry boxes and knickknacks and fold the mirror into a triangle, leaving an opening just wide enough to wedge her face into. Sometimes she and Janice would do it together, squeeze both their faces in there at once. They also tried dolls and porcelain figurines, jewelry, rocks. Anything they could think of that would fit, they'd stick inside the magic triangle and shift around into reverberating patterns. They used to ooh and aah at every little change. But they were older now and only Flora entertained herself by making and remaking faces in the mirror. She used her fingers to coax her eyes and mouth into a certain expression. She could easily make Janice's disdainful look with the lips gathered into a knot and drawn up tight. She practiced Floyd's way of smiling with one corner of his upper lip, and Tess's habit of fluttering the lashes of only one eye. She thought she could get the blank blurry look Henry got when he lost his temper.

Once Janice walked into the room and caught her at it. "Vanity, thy name is Flora," she said. Flora looked around, surprised, and then laughed.

"I'm just looking at all my faces," she said.

"Isn't one face enough?" asked Janice. "You get into enough trouble as it is."

Flora shaped one more face and then opened up the mirror and offered Janice a turn. "Want to do it?" Janice wrinkled up her nose and shook her head.

When Flora woke from her nap she found she still had a rock in her hand, one of the unnamed ones, one she was glad she never ruined with a hammer. She turned it over and over, and wondered when Henry would knock on the door again. It was still a mystery to her why he had sold the geode. He couldn't have gotten more than a couple of dollars for it, so it couldn't have been for the money.

One evening the entire family was watching a news report about a man on death row somewhere, who was about to be executed and still insisted he was innocent. Photos of the man were flashed on the TV, and Henry said, "It's obvious he's guilty. It's written all over his face; just look at him." Flora wished so much could be told so easily.

Sometimes when she and Henry were working together, she'd stop whatever she was doing and watch this man, this stranger clawing dead leaves out from under a bush with his bare fingers, or exhaling his damp breath onto chrome and rubbing insect specks off with his thumb, and she couldn't figure out who he was. It was as if she had been anesthetized and kidnapped and she had just come to. When he looked at her with his tense face, with its stone-gray complexion, his eyes would be asking her why she had stopped what she was doing, and so she would begin again. What she really wanted to do was ask him who he was and what he wanted.

This feeling didn't just go away. It would turn on her so that she was left feeling strange and remote. She was the one who had come home to the wrong house. Maybe she belonged several doors down, or on another block even. She was a fugitive coming around, asking for shelter.

Wide Open Spaces

Flora stepped out of the Long Hall and looked around for Tess. The same tall, black-haired boy, the one who had fetched her lunch sack the other day, was sitting on the stair railing. It startled her to see him again so close up. Before she could look away, he slowly winked one of his obsidian-black eyes. He acted as if they shared an important secret.

Flora hurried on down into the thick mass of students. Always at the beginning of a new semester, the lunch area was more crowded than usual, and the students were restless, like bees in a hive on the verge of a swarm. The snack lines were long and undulating, the cafeteria was packed, but no one seemed to be eating. Everyone was busy finding out, one way or another, who had what classes and when. Flora twisted her way through the crowd, looking for Tess. After a while she gave up. She couldn't sit down at a lunch table because then everybody would know she was alone, so she clutched her lunch sack and kept walking. She circled the lunch area several times, pretending to be on her way somewhere, until finally the bell rang.

In the Long Hall she stopped to drop her lunch sack in her locker and found a note:

Flora,

Where were you! I looked everywhere. Guess what, I switched my classes around so I got Pazetti's dance class before lunch with you! See you tomorrow. No, see you in a while, that is if you decided to take Timpanelli's Life Drawing class? Guess who's going to be the model!!!

XXX Tess

On her way to Timpanelli's she felt excited and apprehensive, as if she were on her way to give a performance. When Henry found out she was taking an art class, he would be mad. She would tell him that in order to get the best chemistry teacher, she had to arrange her schedule this way (not entirely a lie), and besides, she was required to take an elective, and the only ones she could take after lunch were art, ceramics, horticulture, and auto repair. Ceramics and horticulture were full, and auto repair was offered only to boys. He'd eye her suspiciously, but he'd tend to believe her, and maybe he'd forget about the art class for a while.

Timpanelli was one of the few teachers at Hazelton High who was not only tolerant of, but in league with, students who felt the need to express themselves in a freer way. Sometimes she even tore up summons slips, or at least held on to them until the end of the period. All the students who for one reason or another felt like misfits could find sanctuary in her room. She got the nearly homeless, some of the truants, the solitary, those who were incapable of reading or writing, those who'd rather draw than try to write, those who loved to draw, those who wanted to learn how, the deaf, the nearly blind, the mentally retarded. All these students, and more, were in Timpanelli's class sooner or later, and a few of them seemed to be in her class all of the time.

All Timpanelli asked of them, whether they were listed in her rollbook or not, was that when they were within the boundaries of her room, they try not to harm anyone or destroy anything. "And," she added, "if you feel the urge to create something, by all means do." She stood behind her desk with her hands clasped tightly together. "And if you don't feel like drawing, don't hinder or annoy anyone that does, or I'll kick you out." She surveyed the class with her teeth bared in a silent growl.

Flora dropped her pencil, and most of the class looked toward her as she picked it up. She didn't recognize anyone in the room. Timpanelli said, "The model didn't show up, so today you'll have to draw each other's faces or else whatever hand it is you don't use to draw with." Flora thought for a moment, and then looked down at her own right hand. It was shaking a little. A hum started up in the class as Timpanelli sat down and started thumbing through a magazine. Flora looked at her hand again, and then at the sheet of paper on the easel before her, and then out the open window next to Timpanelli's desk.

By some quirk, or perhaps as a result of some clever planning by the administration, Mrs. Timpanelli's room was in plain view of the Main Offices. However, it was not within hearing range, and so whenever Mrs. Baines or someone like her emerged from the offices, some self-assigned vigilante stationed next to Timpanelli's desk, by the only window whose blinds were kept open, would yank the alarm. The alarm was a confusion of plastic doll limbs, cans, and palette knives tied to a rope that hung from a hook in the ceiling. The awful clanking sound it could make would bring all questionable activity in the class to a halt, so that by the time Mrs. Baines was lurching along the path that would bring her close to Timpanelli's room, all she would hear was the sound of Venetian blinds jingling lightly. And if she decided to drop in for a visit she wouldn't catch The Cat sticking her easel with a penknife, or several students in the washroom painting the walls, or Mrs. Timpanelli taking sips from the earthenware vase that always sat on her desk without any flowers in it. Everything would look as normal as could be expected for an art class.

Mrs. Baines thought it was ridiculously quiet. Several times in the past, she had tried to ban the use of bikinied models. If nothing else was going on in there, it was at least obvious that a nearly nude person was flaunting herself before an entire class of goggle-eyed pupils. The other art teachers came to Timpanelli's aid over that one. "It's nearly impossible to observe muscles through clothing, even leotards," they said at a board meeting. They also suggested that perhaps the school swim team, which was number one in the city, ought to be made to wear suits that were less revealing, or, if that was not possible, maybe the team should be disbanded altogether.

Timpanelli's repeating students could cite times when Mrs. Baines had stood at the threshold and addressed the model on the table directly. "Young lady," she'd call out, in a harsh and trembling voice, "I want to have a word with you in my office." Nowadays, she could pick on only a few small things as she retreated. She wanted to know what that junk hanging from the rope was supposed to be. Timpanelli didn't have to open her mouth. A chorus of students told Mrs. Baines that it was a "construction." They sounded so sure of themselves she dared not question them any further about it. But she also wanted to know why most of the blinds were closed on one side of the room. They asked her if she had ever tried to draw in glaring light.

Whenever Flora drew or painted, even at school, she could always feel her father frowning down at her, casting his shadow of disapproval across whatever it was she was working on.

When she was still a small girl and Henry was still flying, once a month he'd spend an entire evening at the kitchen table going through his flight manuals, inserting new pages and letting the obsolete ones glide to the floor. Flora would be under the table waiting to gather up the discarded sheets. Most of them were printed on both sides. These she threw in the waste paper basket. But several dozen out of every batch had one clear side, and these she took back to her bedroom and put in a drawer along with a supply of watercolors, crayons, and colored pencils.

The pictures she drew on these pages—the imaginary beasts, the leaping gazelles, the birds in flight, the amusement parks and the utopian villages—she could never share with her father. He didn't want to be reminded that she spent so much time hiding away in her room bent over a drawing. He had a sneery way of referring to her drawings as "pretty pictures." "Flora's in there making pretty pictures again. Wasting her time, when she could be doing something useful around here." He'd say that loud enough so that she would be sure to hear. Or he'd peek his head in the door and twit, "Get any fresh air today?"

He thought painters were a sorry lot. He told her about the ones he saw in Paris. "They practically live in the streets. They call themselves artists, but what they really are is beggars. You can't go for a walk without getting paintings shoved in your face. And you know how they all end up? Do you want to know? Heaps in the gutter. They die without enough money to bury their own remains. And while they live, most of them never have enough money to buy a baguette or a bottle of wine. That's all they ever eat, and they can't even afford that. If that's the kind of life you want, have at it, but don't come crying to me."

Julia would start to cry and Daniel would ask what a baguette was. "A long bun French people are always carrying around with them," Henry said. "And why are you crying?" He gave Julia a disgusted look and she covered her mouth with her hand. When he told his stories at the dinner table there was no predicting who would take his words to heart. He let up when he saw that Flora's eyes were watery, too.

Sometimes he could spoil it for her, but she never quit drawing. Though there were only one or two drawings taped to her closet door, she had a box full of them on the closet shelf.

After lunch on the third day of the new semester, Flora was sitting on a high stool in front of an easel, staring at another blank sheet of sketch paper. She didn't think she was going to be able to draw anything in such a big room with so many people around. Three years back she took a crafts class from Mrs. Timpanelli and had no trouble getting to work. They had made mobiles, color scales, linoleum mosaics, tissue paper collages, balsa wood constructions, wallpaper designs, papier-mâché animals. But when it came to drawing, she was used to crowding her private visions onto a space eight and a half by eleven inches and hunching over them to keep them safe even from Janice's prying eyes. The sheet of paper in front of her now was three times that size. It might as well have been as big as a billboard. Then too, this was Life Drawing—the importance of it made her tense. She looked over to Timpanelli. Tess was sitting beside her wearing nothing but her string-tied bikini.

Timpanelli told Tess that if she wanted to be the model, she'd have to wear her hair up. Normally she wore it falling loose over her shoulders like a gauzy black veil. She spent the first five minutes of class braiding, coiling, and barretting it to the back of her head. Completely at ease, she slipped through the oval of about thirty easels and, using a chair, stepped up onto a large table. Her turquoise bikini had faded to aqua, but her January tan was nearly as deep as the one she had at the end of summer. After a moment of moving around as if she were in an elevator all by herself, she struck a pose with a hand on one hip and her head bent down toward a projected foot.

"That's fine," Mrs. Timpanelli called out. Tess smiled from beneath a fallen strand of hair. She enjoyed showing herself off. From over the tops of or around the sides of their easels, everyone looked at her, regarded her shoulder blades, her hipbones, the toes she couldn't keep from wiggling. As they all looked, they scribbled and scratched away with their pencils—all, that is, except for a few talkers clustered around Timpanelli's desk, a deaf boy and girl signing to each other over by the supply cabinets, Flora, and one other person. Through the space between Tess's legs, Flora spotted the raven-haired boy with the dark eyes, and he was staring back at her.

"Flora, get to work!" cried Timpanelli. "You've only got twenty more minutes." Flora hid her face behind her easel and tried to draw something. "You too, Matthew, before I kick you out of here!"

Timpanelli enjoyed yelling at her students, and she never wanted to kick anyone out of her class, especially not for staring. She always said, "Observing well is the first step to drawing well."

When the bell rang Flora quickly took down her unfinished drawing, folded it into a small rectangle and stuck it inside her notebook.

On her way to algebra class she looked back. Matthew was a dozen or so paces behind her, sauntering along, whistling a sad tune and looking up sideways at the sky. Flora felt embarrassed by these unexpected appearances of his. Planned or coincidental? She couldn't tell. She walked on as fast as she could without looking like she was in a rush.

For the last period of the day, she had signed up for a Spanish class in a room at the far side of campus. It was a light room, like a sunporch, made mainly of windows. It faced a chain-link fence, one of the boundaries of the school. Through that, one could gaze at a field of dirt and clumps of weeds. Flora took a seat and divided her attention between the field and a colorful travel poster that depicted something like a pyramid poking up out of a jungle and a border of fruit and birds. She thought it would be impossible to learn another language. English was bad enough. She hoped this would be the easiest way to fulfill the language requirement. Mrs. Moore, the teacher, had a reputation for being kind-hearted, speaking slowly, and asking that only ten sentences be memorized per week. Sometimes they were as short as "¡Hola! ¿Qué tal?"

Mrs. Moore had arranged the desks very neatly with rows on one side of the room facing rows on the other side, leaving a spacious aisle down the center. She stood at the head of this aisle now, slowly and clearly reading off the names in her rollbook. When she located each student, she nodded and smiled. Her high plucked eyebrows, prim mouth, and hair pulled back from her temples with combs gave Flora the impression of an alert and cheerful parakeet. The girls answered with either "Presente" or "Aquí," and the boys would say "Aquí" or "Here" or merely raise their hands and then let them fall back on their desktops with a thud. No one answered to the name of Matthew Cartier. After looking all around, just in case he was a totally silent one, Mrs. Moore remarked that she would just have to erase Señor Cartier's name. As she was raising her pencil to do so, Matthew entered the classroom. He walked up the center aisle, turned in at Flora's row, walked past her without a glance, and slipped into the vacant seat behind her. He heaved a big sigh. Flora felt a tingle at the back of her neck.

"And who might you be?" inquired Mrs. Moore. She leaned back against the edge of her desk and folded her rollbook over her lap.

"Cartier," said Matthew, with a hint of dignity. Flora felt prickles race back and forth across her shoulders as if he were tracing his name there.

"I suppose you had to come a great distance?" Mrs. Moore asked with a smile. Half the class laughed.

"Yes," answered Matthew. He was bouncing the eraser end of his pencil lightly on his desk.

He slipped out of class several minutes early, right in the middle of "Me gusta mucho," when Mrs. Moore had her back turned to his side of the room. Flora felt her own back relax a little.

That night, while Janice was out of the bedroom, Flora searched through her notebook for the folded piece of sketch paper. She unfolded it cautiously, as if she weren't sure what it would contain. She stared at the dark eyes for a long time, refolded the drawing, and put it in one of her dresser drawers. He was bold, at least his eyes were bold. Yet the way their paths kept crossing had seemed merely accidental. Except for the way he looked at her, his demeanor was casual. He had just slipped into that seat behind her, but then, it was nearly the only empty seat left. And he hadn't even given her a side glance. She was bothered, maybe even a little frightened, by his strangeness.

A Headless Venus

"Can't you see him standing over there?" Tess nudged Flora in the arm.

"See who?" said Flora.

"Phil Ridley, the new guy I was telling you about." Flora's apparent blindness both amused and annoyed Tess. She put her hand on one jutting hip and pivoted toward Flora. "How long are you going to pretend you're not interested in the opposite sex?" Flora looked in the same direction Tess had been looking, but she couldn't see anyone who looked especially new.

"He doesn't know anybody yet, except Stan, at least that's what Stan says." Tess looked back to where she had been looking before.

Flora saw Stan. He was leaning against the cafeteria wall talking to a blond-haired boy. The blond boy had his hands in his pants pockets and was staring at the ground in front of his feet. "Is that Phil? The one with his hands in his pockets, the madras shirt, and the tanned arms?"

Tess raised her eyebrows and smiled broadly at Flora.

"I can't even see his face," said Flora. She watched Tess's mouth warp from a smile to a pout in a split second.

"What a turnoff you're being," moaned Tess.

Before the end of the lunch period Tess shoved Flora ever so slightly as they were passing Phil. After bouncing off each other's chests, Phil and Flora found themselves face to face.

Stan said, "Hi, Flora," and then he nudged Phil with his elbow, said, "See you later," and walked off with Tess.

On Friday, not long before dusk, Flora was standing at her front door introducing Phil to her mother while her father listened from the kitchen. As Flora hurried down the driveway, Phil kept pace with her. She could almost hear her father getting after her mother for having failed to ask them where they were going.

Despite the crisp air they headed for a drive-in movie. During the series of halts and lunges that were bringing them closer to the ticket booth, Phil finally turned toward her and said something.

"Are your eyes really turquoise or do you wear contact lenses?"

"I don't wear contact lenses or glasses and my eyes are green." Flora had a sour feeling in her throat. She couldn't quite determine what was maddening about what he had said. She looked straight ahead through the speckless windshield, right into the rays of the setting sun. It was teetering on a distant ridge of hills, ready to fall off the far side.

Phil accepted two tickets from a slender hand displaying several jangling bracelets and long red nails. "I was just joking," he said as he put the tickets in his shirt pocket.

Flora softened a little. If he was trying to make a joke, she supposed she shouldn't be upset. When he glanced at her she gave him a smile. He had the perky bulbous nose she associated with wittiness. Maybe he could be funny.

"Front or back?" he asked.

"Front or back?" Flora frowned with disbelief. She took a quick glance over her shoulder. The back seat was hardly bigger than a suitcase.

"Do you like to be up close to the front or back in the back, in front of the snack bar or behind it?" He gripped his steering wheel and chuckled.

Flora took a deep breath and thought for a moment. "I think I want to be in the same row as the snack bar."

Not much else was said. After several minutes of watching a car speed down a narrow mountain road with a valley swinging into view at unexpected curves, Flora asked Phil where he lived. She wasn't surprised when he said, "Up in the Hills." They were sitting in an imported sports car of some kind. It had comfortable leather seats and a varnished wood dash. Phil laughed out loud at the movie several times and made some amusing digs. Flora tried to laugh along with him. She wasn't watching the movie closely enough to respond. Maybe she wasn't the sort of person who had the urge on a first date to divulge everything she had ever heard, seen, or imagined, but tonight she felt as if her mouth were taped shut. Out of the side window the moon kept catching her eye. Its scant crescent shape bothered her. Over and over in her mind she traced its faintly visible rim, completing the circle.

Sometime well into the movie, Phil put his arm around her and a minute later gave her an abrupt kiss, one that had a definite beginning and a definite end. He drew away from her, and with his hands still clutching her shoulders he stared at her. Flora felt he wanted a comment, something about how good it had been, so he could begin again. She didn't know what to say. She felt as if she'd need until morning to think of something. So she just leaned forward and gave him a reciprocal kiss.

They continued to kiss as if their lips were suctioned together. To Flora, Phil's arms and hands felt like numb and useless appendages clinging to her body at odd locations. She wondered if her hands felt the same way to him. She carefully lifted one hand off his ear and was wishing hard that he would remove his fingertips from her right clavicle when the movie screen flashed to titanium white and engines started revving up all around them.

That night in bed Flora went back over the time she had just spent with Phil. Nothing much had happened. The espionage film was forgettable. Aside from gazing at the moon she must have been gazing at his dashboard, too, because she could still see every knob and dial on it. The silver light from the movie screen had made Phil's blond hair glow. She could still feel the stiff, almost rough texture of his madras shirt. She could still smell his cologne.

When she smelled it again, she heard herself saying yes, she would go out with him Friday night. That was in the parking lot before classes began on Monday morning. Later, during modern dance class, Tess said, "Look over there," and pointed her thumb toward the open doorway at the far end of the dance room. Flora looked over her shoulder in midleap and saw Stan and Phil standing there with grins on their faces. Pazetti, the dance teacher, looked over too. "Would you two boys like to join the class?" she asked in a melodious voice, and they disappeared, but not before Flora had done a flop on the cement floor.

"Do you always move so well?" Stan asked as Tess and Flora approached their table during lunch. He and Phil were sitting backward on a bench, slouched, with their elbows propped up on the table. They looked smug and on the verge of a laughing fit.

Flora blushed and then recovered. "Only when there are clowns in the audience."

"Do you always go where you're not invited?" added Tess, lowering her eyes at them. She and Flora walked away before Stan or Phil could retort.

Back in Timpanelli's class, Flora struggled to loosen up and draw. She tried not to look to the other side of the room. Whenever she forgot and looked beyond Tess, she saw Matthew, or rather a portion of Matthew, leaning close to his easel, working intently. Once she saw him standing back from his work, regarding it with his head tilted sideways.

He never said a word in Spanish class, but she could hear him shifting behind her, and sometimes he stretched his legs out until his feet were underneath her chair.

Marleen said that Phil looked like a nice boy, very polite and good looking. Henry complained that Phil broke the speed limit when he came down Jericho. "He screeches and skids his car up to the curb like he thinks he's making a pit stop." But Flora knew that her father approved of Phil for the most part. "What kind of a surgeon did you say Phil's father was?" He had asked her that twice since she told him Phil's father was an orthopedic surgeon. She also told him that Phil intended to go to medical school. She figured this was why she was allowed to go out with Phil. Or maybe Henry was even glad to see her dating again.

After two more weekends and five dates, which consisted of another night at the drive-in, a foggy Sunday at the beach, a dinner at a fancy restaurant, and two Saturday night parties, one held at Stan's parents' guest house and another one that was seemingly hostless, Flora felt a certain softness toward Phil, maybe because of the way he held on to her as if she were an irreplaceable stuffed animal. He was awkward with his hands but bright in the head. He sometimes made her laugh with his wit. He had a way of looking sorrowfully and affectionately at her, a way of slumping into a blue-eyed pout that invited her to hug him. But she didn't think she could ever fall in love with him, and she never felt like sitting in his car with his cock in her hand and his hand on her small breasts.

Still, she kept on going out with him, and soon she had a place for herself, beside him, at a special table in the lunch area. The arrangement was accepted by everyone else there. It was assumed that she would be going out with Phil and only Phil.

The group at the table consisted of other couples and some boys who didn't have specific girlfriends, but rarely would a girl sit there without a boyfriend beside her. Tess dated Stan sometimes, and sometimes she would sit down next to Flora and across from him. But after several minutes she'd get restless and jump up. "See you in Timpanelli's." She'd tap Flora on the shoulder, and take off. "There goes the tease," Stan would say, trying to sound jocular, but Flora could tell he wished he had more control over Tess.

Flora sat there with her arms crossed on the table and Phil's hand on her leg, hearing the surf reports and the plans for parties and asking herself how they had gotten so tightly linked so quickly. She watched Tess join up with two other girls and the three of them weave and swerve their way among the clusters of students—gesturing coyly, flouncing, and flirting with teams of roving boys.

Watching them, she realized one advantage of staying put: she was less likely to be spotted by members of the Girls' Dress Board or by Mrs. Baines herself, who often patrolled the lunch area. Flora could take some comfort in the notion that this table was a safe niche for her. Those at it didn't conform, and yet they broke no written rules. Best of all, no one paid them much attention.

When a summons slip was dropped on Flora's desk during algebra, she was stunned. She didn't recognize the girl who delivered it:

someone fawn-eyed and slender with a ravel of thread at the hem of her pleated skirt which clung to and let go of, clung to and let go of, her calf as she stepped lightly out of the room. Flora let her own skirt down a notch by flipping over its waistband, got up and walked numbly out of class.

She had thought this wouldn't be happening again, that they wouldn't be bothering with her anymore, but no, it was happening again. The pink stucco buildings in her peripheral vision and the black asphalt beneath her feet were a blur. She trudged up a ramp and turned into a hallway. She thought she saw Matthew, or someone who looked a lot like Matthew; he was way ahead of her and walking toward her. Suddenly he ducked out of sight. She heard footsteps coming up behind her, and when she turned around, the Boys' V.P. passed her at a gallop.

She didn't know what Matthew was wanted for, but whatever it was, he wasn't going to get caught. She turned aside. Instead of going to the Main Offices she headed for the nearest restroom. "I'm not going to keep stepping in their snares; why should I?" she muttered. She was in tears as she blundered through the swinging door.

She stood there in the silent, inert air of that used and deserted room and looked at the pale green floor tiles. They were scoured dull by the scuffing of feet; the grout was black with ground-in mud. She scanned the metal doors on the row of toilet stalls. The creamy pink enamel had been chipped and scratched with initials. At the other end of the restroom, sunlight, no more than a milky haze, passed through the panes of frosted glass. Beneath the window, wads of paper towels were clustered around a dented trash can. She walked over, squatted down and started grabbing handfuls of the used towels and stuffing them in the trash can. She worked faster and faster, then all of a sudden sank down against the side of the can and held on to its rim. "Why can't they all just leave me alone!" she said aloud, beginning to cry. "I just want to be left alone." Then she cried without words. The crying slowed to a whimper, and the whimper to an occasional shudder.

Hearing a dripping faucet, she pulled herself up and went over to it. She started to wash her hands, then stopped and looked at herself in the mirror. She bent closer and saw two terrified eyes. "What am I doing in here, like a stowaway?" Her face was distorted and miserable looking. "I don't have to do what everybody tells me to do." She pounded her fists on the rim of the sink, sending a hollow vibration through all the plumbing.

 By the time Flora got to Spanish class, the tardy bell had rung and everyone else was seated. She approached her desk by walking in back of the rows and coming past Matthew from behind. That way he wouldn't see her face. She sank into her seat and opened her book. "Buenas tardes, Señorita Jackson," said Mrs. Moore. Flora only nodded. She didn't trust her own voice yet. She looked at the pages in front of her. Her head was throbbing, and the words jiggled painfully with every throb. She could feel Matthew behind her. He was breathing deeply and evenly as if he were asleep. She wished she could go to sleep. She waited for someone to arrive waving a fresh summons slip. To her amazement, no one did. In the meantime she hadn't heard a word of the Spanish lesson.

She swore she would never allow herself to get caught. She would roll down her skirts. She would improve her peripheral vision. She would duck out of halls. She would not get caught. And she would not do something just because someone told her to.

When she entered her house after school, she felt like turning around and going back out. But where to? The air was still and cool inside. The whole house was quiet except for a slow drip at the kitchen sink. The curtain was drawn on the kitchen window. She went into the living room. The curtains were drawn on the picture window, too, as usual. It was as if the house was supposed to hold in some precious secret.

She went down the hall and peeked into the master bedroom. Henry was there, with the bedspread pulled over him, halfway over his head. He was fast asleep, maybe. Daniel and Julia had undoubtedly taken this opportunity to run off to some friends' houses. Maybe even Janice had come and gone already. She stepped into their room. No, Janice was asleep too, sprawled belly-down on the bed.

Flora slumped down in the chair at their desk. She didn't know what to do with herself. She pulled open her art supply drawer and looked in it. All the pads of paper Marleen had bought her had been used up weeks ago. She scrounged around in the desk drawer for a sheet of writing paper and a pencil with a good eraser on it. She picked up Janice's physics book to use as a drawing board. Janice was still lying motionless on the bed. Her slip was twisted and binding in one place, lying in loose whorls at another, draped in graceful waves over the backs of her thighs. One of Timpanelli's suggestions had been to get someone to pose for you at home. Janice moaned, flopped her face away from Flora, sighed, and went on sleeping.

Flora did just barely enough drawings of the model to satisfy Timpanelli. She wished she could move her easel way back into a corner of the room. She still felt uncomfortable working out in the open, and she hated the results of her efforts. For a drawing of a human body, her lines were too stiff and angular; they were more suitable for tree saplings or marsh reeds. Timpanelli never commented on that. She did point out that the arms on her figures were often too short. When Flora looked again at the drawing before her, the defect stood out as an obvious deformity. It was embarrassing. She crumpled up her paper and began again.

When the assignment was to do quick sketches as the model changed positions every couple of minutes, Flora felt harassed. She couldn't keep up with the pace and left class on those days feeling depleted and more dissatisfied than usual. She preferred the days when the model maintained the same pose, or nearly the same pose, for the entire class period, and the assignment was to do a careful, detailed drawing—the very days Tess groaned about.

On one such day Matthew picked up his drawing board, walked halfway around the room, and set it up again on the empty easel next to Flora.

"I don't want any funny business over there," warned Timpanelli. But when Flora, with a distressed look, turned her head, Timpanelli made a face that said, It's your problem, not mine.

Matthew flipped his pencil in the air so that it turned over and over in two easy somersaults and landed back in his hand with the point aimed at his new easel. Then he leaned forward and started drawing as if less than a breath had passed since his last stroke.

Flora felt stiff before. Now she felt petrified in the bones, the muscles, and the flesh. Her forearm, all smudged with graphite, had been resting in a nearly upright position against her drawing; now it felt like it was stuck there. There was some consolation in the way it shielded most of what she had done from Matthew's view.

Matthew, however, was not looking at her drawing. He was working on his own, and Flora couldn't keep her eyes away from it. Finally she had to stare at it. What she saw was a wonderfully sinuous female form, complete in every way except that it lacked a head. Aside from that, every curve and crease was there. He worked on one small area at a time, making delicate strokes. He held his pencil at all angles to soften a line around some curve or to make it more distinct in some crevice. His hand never stopped moving.

Flora looked up at Tess. Tess had a good figure, she thought, but not that good, not that sensuous. Watching Matthew draw was a new experience. She slowly moved her pencil and began shading in a portion of the outline she had been working on.

That same day, as Flora was walking to her locker, Matthew suddenly appeared on the path beside her. His head was cocked to one side. He seemed to be scrutinizing her arm.

"What are you looking at?" Flora heard the annoyed tone in her voice. He had caught her off guard again. It was too bad the first sentence he ever heard her speak had to sound like that; she couldn't help it.

"Your book cover," he said, quite simply. He slipped her algebra book out from under her arm and turned it around and around. Then he handed it back to her and said, "You do very nice calligraphy." She put it under her arm again and thanked him. Her book cover, made from a brown paper bag, was swarming with lettering in different styles: "Algebra" in Arabic script, "Sixth Period" in Hellenic Wide, and variations of the name Phil—"Phillip," "Felipe"—amidst abstract designs. It was something she did with a ballpoint pen during classes.

After taking several steps in silence, Matthew made a lighthearted attempt at more conversation. "He owns you, doesn't he?"

"Who?" Flora felt defensive and baffled.

"You know—Phil. He owns you, doesn't he?"

Flora made a quick sucking sound with her tongue set against her teeth and looked away from him. But Matthew was no longer there. He had turned off on another path and was loping toward the parking lot.

Flora lingered at her locker. Where does he get all his information? she wondered. Is nothing private? She shoved her book in the locker and saw Phil's name all over it. She was still upset, but not at Matthew. He had spoken to her frankly. She had watched him draw. He was not so mysterious anymore. She wished she could go home with him, see where he lived.

Matthew entered his empty house and walked down the hall to his bedroom. He flung his books so that they skidded across the carpet and rattled against his closet doors. He fell back onto his bed, lay motionless, and let the cool winter breeze bully him. He never closed the window next to his bed, summer or winter, day or night, unless a rare rain was blowing in, and even then he'd let it spray in for a while before cranking the window shut.

The curtains sprang at him, sucked back, and then went lifeless. He reached over and pulled them shut. Then he looked upside-down at one of his own creations, taped on the wall over his bed: a large pencil drawing of a naked female. This figure had a head, but her face was turned away demurely. Her legs were squeezed together, and her fingers were spread out gripping her own thighs. Matthew unzipped his pants and began rubbing himself. He saw Flora's hips moving slowly up and down, and he saw her wide green eyes. Then everything became a hot blur.

The next day Matthew took his place next to Flora as if it had been his assigned seat since the beginning of the Life Drawing course.

Flora was feeling slightly looser. She looked at Tess's shoulder and made a nice swooping line. She drew the curve of her clavicle and made several light strokes for the tendons on her neck. Since yesterday she had been plagued by the words that had gone back and forth between Matthew and herself. For the time being she wanted to put them aside. The thought of Matthew working away, focusing intently on the same subject she was, made her feel weightless. As she and Matthew spun around a common center, everything else dissolved.

She tried to imagine Tess's breasts beneath her bikini top and drew several swift lines to represent them. Her pencil was dull; its point was worn down to the wood. She could no longer put off a trip to the pencil sharpener. When she returned, there were two carefully shaded nipples added to her drawing. Matthew was hard at work, as usual, on his own drawing.

Flora looked over to Timpanelli. Timpanelli was taking a sip from her earthenware vase and thumbing through an art journal. "You have a lot of nerve," mumbled Flora without looking at Matthew. She erased the nipples. She hated to do that because she liked the way they looked, but it was a matter of dignity. No one had the right to tamper with another person's creation, not while it was still being created. But she felt confused. She liked his attention to her drawing, and he was a better drawer. Did that give him the right to touch her work? Timpanelli never put her pencil to anyone's drawing.

During Spanish class that day Matthew took his pencil and played with several strands of Flora's hair, lifting them slowly, drawing them out, and letting them fall on his desktop. Flora got a shiver.

"Please don't do that," she whispered irritably. She looked around at him for the first time since he had taken that seat behind her. Her father had taken the family to see a silver mine once. Matthew's eyes looked like mine shafts—narrow, deep, and glinting, like light reflected off metal.

"It was lying on my desk," he replied in a barely audible voice. Flora took the entire mass of her hair and brought it over her shoulder so that it lay across the side of her chest like a pale fur stole. Matthew made what sounded to her like a mock sigh. He left class several minutes before the bell rang.

That night Flora recalled the words her mother had neatly recorded with a fountain pen in her satin-covered baby album. "Flora's first words: Don't Do Dat!" She had said just about the same thing to Matthew. She moaned and pulled her blanket up over her head.

Jellyfish

Phil had not been in school for a week. Stan told Flora that he was sick with something.

"Sick with what?" asked Flora.

"How should I know, I'm not a doctor," said Stan.

"You wouldn't know if you were one," said Flora.

On Friday after school, while Henry was out in the back yard planting camellias, Flora went into the kitchen and stood by the phone. She picked up the receiver and put her finger in the dial. She kept hesitating; calling a boy was taboo. But he's sick, she told herself. She quickly dialed his number, let the phone ring five times, and hung up. She peeked out the kitchen window. Henry was still working out there. It looked as if he was actually taking a plant out of a can.

She sat down at the kitchen table and stared at the phone. Why couldn't somebody call her when her father was out of the house? A minute later the phone rang; it was Tess. She said her parents would let her have the Mercedes to go to the school dance, and that there was going to be an open party not too far from school. If Flora wanted to go, she'd have to be ready by seven-thirty. If Phil calls now, thought Flora, I'll tell him I've already told Tess I'd go with her tonight.

Someone's parents had gone to Palm Springs for the weekend. In the back yard, the pool lights were on. A sickly green glow hovered over the surface of the water like swamp gas and illuminated the crowd of people standing around the edge of the pool. Flora stood on the back porch with her arms folded against the chilly night. Must be heated, she thought. A moment later a girl was pushed in and a boy leapt in after her; others followed. There was shrieking and laughter as fully dressed bodies thrashed about. A jellyfish, no, a pair of panties sloshed around at the shallow end.

Flora stepped back into the house. Tess was dancing with the tallest, lankiest boy Flora had ever seen. When he flung his arms up, he nearly jabbed the ceiling. The walls were throbbing with the Rolling Stones doing "Mercy Mercy." A row of boys were doing impressions of Mick Jagger's swiveling sidestep. The sofas were covered with sprawling bodies. Beer cans were scattered everywhere, wobbling on the arms of the sofas, tipped over on the mantel, stacked in the windowsills, rolling around on the carpet. A guzzling contest was under way in the hall. All the bedroom doors were closed.

It was a moonless night, difficult to see who was arriving and who was departing. Tess and Flora had been out back and inside, and now they were standing at the curb debating whether to go or stay. They knew of no other parties, so their only alternative was the school dance. They were about to walk to Tess's car when a large black one pulled up next to them. The rear door swung open and Matthew got out. Before Flora could say anything he had taken her by the arm and pulled her into the back seat.

She got a glimpse of Tess standing on the curb with her mouth hanging open making steam. She wanted to say something to Tess, but Tess was already far behind. Matthew was holding Flora on his lap with his arms wrapped around her arms and waist. His fingers gripped her in the ribs. She couldn't tell if it hurt or tickled.

Some frizzy-headed guy Flora had never seen before was driving. He punched in a cassette tape and the Stones sang "That's How Strong My Love Is." Flora's head cried out that this was outrageous, but she said nothing. Matthew held her tighter. He was giving directions to the chauffeur, navigating with confidence. She didn't know where they were going. Finally she made an announcement to the blurred lights and the speeding darkness: "I'm supposed to be at the school dance." The driver said nothing.

"Who wants to be at the school dance?" Matthew whispered in her ear and tightened his hold on her.

They drove up a long driveway where the leaves of overhanging trees were even darker than the sky, and came to a stop at the side of a house. There were no lights on anywhere. Matthew lifted and pushed her out of the back seat without ever losing his hold on her. The house looked like a dark red mountain to Flora, a steeply sloped mass of iron rising up before her. Matthew, still clasping her around the waist, kicked open a door where she hadn't seen one. It whinnied in response, and she winced as if the kick had been meant for her.

As soon as they were inside the house, Matthew let go of her waist and took her by the hand. He called back to the guy in the car that there was beer in the icebox. Flora was led down a pitch-black hallway, and she didn't pull back and she didn't scream. This was Matthew holding her hand, the one who shared two classes with her. A classmate, a fellow student. "Where are we going?" she asked.

From a window next to Matthew's bed, the night cast a darkness less dark than the inside of his room, and in this paler darkness he pressed her down. He held her hands in his, placed them beside her head, and laid himself down on top of her and pressed and pressed while all those hot, lonely afternoons rose up inside him.

Flora couldn't see his face. She couldn't tell if he was frowning or smiling. She kept crying, "No, don't, please let me go, you mustn't"—phrases that sounded like ones she had read in paperbacks her parents stored high in the hall closet. She saw a hefty woman in nothing but a brassiere and a garter belt pushing away two men who were molesting her—a grainy black-and-white photo. She struggled to get out from under Matthew. She felt his mouth breathing heavily at her neck, and the buckle of his belt denting into her belly, and the hardness between his legs pushing between her legs. And she heard him saying, "Please, Flora, please."

But he never unzipped his pants and he never pulled up her skirt, and finally he got up and told her she could go if she wanted to. Then he remembered that he was the one who had brought her there, so he took her hand and helped her up off his bed. He guided her back down the hall. Flora felt as if she were on one of those grotto tours where they turn out the lights for a while just to show you how dark dark can really get. The lights would go on again in a moment. If you were afraid, you were supposed to hold on to someone else's hand. Matthew's hand felt clammy, like dew on a stone.

The chauffeur was sitting at the kitchen table, tipping a half-finished beer bottle back and forth between his fingers with an easy rocking motion. A candle in a brass holder burned without a waver in the center of the table.

"Would you mind taking Flora and me to school?" Matthew's voice sounded tired and a little shaky.

"No, not at all," drawled Matthew's friend as if he were delivering a line he had rehearsed many times. He scraped the chair on the floor and got up slowly.

The three of them went outside and got into the front seat of the car. Flora sat between them, and Matthew didn't hold on to her. During the short drive from his house to school, he put his hand on her thigh once and gave it a quick squeeze. Then he let go and clasped his hands in his lap.

Flora felt a heaviness and an aching throughout her body, especially beneath her rib cage, not because of the way Matthew had thrown himself upon her, but because he was no longer pressing against her. The sadness and the loneliness were like a pain that drove all the air out of her. She dared not brush against his arm for fear of irritating him.

He glanced at her once and looked away out the side window. They sat silently in the parking lot, the motor still running. Flora knew he was waiting for her to say something.

"Would you please let me out?" she said. Matthew jumped out and held the door open for her, and as soon as she got out he jumped back in. She watched the car swerve out into the boulevard and disappear.

In the parking lot, engines were revving, headlights were flashing on, car doors were slamming. The dance was obviously over. Tess was walking toward her.

"Well, what was that all about?" said Tess as she planted herself in front of Flora. Flora couldn't answer; she just shook her head.

"I guess you're lucky I decided to come back to the dance," said Tess in a huff. Flora nodded. Tess waited.

"I'm sorry," said Flora. It was against the rules to desert a girlfriend anywhere, especially at an open party. It didn't matter if that girlfriend had her own transportation or not. It was a matter of loyalty and security. Flora felt like crying. The blur of lights, the noise of the traffic, Tess's accusing face, and the damp chilly air drifted away from her like weightless particles. She felt herself standing there detached, collapsing in on herself.

That night as she lay in bed, with her back to Janice, she thought about Matthew. Had that been a show of force or a sample of affection? If he had wanted to, he could have ripped her clothes off, and his own too, jumped on her, and done whatever it was that he had wanted to do. But he didn't.

He hadn't even kissed her.

On Monday Phil was still out of school with mononucleosis. Flora didn't feel like staying in the lunch area. She didn't want to face anyone at their table. Tess had snubbed her during dance class, and she didn't feel like being snubbed again so soon. If she could get past the hall monitors she would go to Timpanelli's. Timpanelli always kept her room open during lunch hour and sat at her desk eating her lunch out of a paper bag.

While one monitor was gazing out a window, Flora tried to cross the Long Hall. The monitor spun around and yelled, "Hey, where do you think you're going?"

Flora had a line ready. "I forgot my lunch," she said. She hid her sack behind her back.

"Do you have a pass?"

"No, but my doctor says I'll faint if I don't eat." He flagged her on.

When Flora got to Timpanelli's room she found two kids, the deaf couple, working at the same easel, and a boisterous group around Timpanelli's desk. Timpanelli looked up. She was smiling, amused. "Thought you might sneak up on an easel?"

Flora gave her an embarrassed smile. "I guess so."

"Well, you know where the paper is." Timpanelli waved a half-eaten pretzel toward the supply cabinets.

Flora sat down on the stool in front of the easel she used during Life Drawing. What she really wanted to do was sit next to Timpanelli and have a private talk. But the other students were binding Timpanelli in, like hoops around a barrel of laughs. A private talk was out of the question. She took a cheese sandwich out of her lunch sack, took a bite, and eyed the supply cabinets, then put her sandwich back in the sack and went to get a sheet of sketch paper and a soft-lead pencil. Once the paper was tacked on the easel, she started to draw.

It was a drawing she had never thought of doing before, not even by the light of a flashlight after the rest of her family had gone to sleep. She could have been beneath a tent of blankets, or at the beach, or sitting on a rock in the middle of a river—it didn't matter. For the first time, it didn't matter to her that there were other people around. Only each convex or concave line concerned her now. A network of shading, like thick cobwebs, appeared in any space where the two bodies for anatomical reasons could not meet. She was far away from the asphalt patches and cement ditches of the lunch area. Timpanelli had told them to regard negative space, the shape of the spaces where nothing seems to be. Flora remembered the sight of Matthew at the other side of the room framed in the triangle of Tess's open legs. He was closer to her now. For the first time she felt the muscles moving between two people as if they were dancing a close dance. And as she felt them, she drew them. She gave special attention to the hands, and then to their thighs. She carefully drew the woman's breasts and the profiles of both faces. Finally, she moved back a little and looked at her drawing. It wasn't great. The proportions, for one thing, were off: the arms were too short, or else the legs were too long. Nevertheless, there was some feeling in it, even without the features on the faces, even without the eyes. She imagined Timpanelli saying, "Well, it's so-so. Try again."

The bell marking the end of the lunch period sounded. Most of the people around Timpanelli's desk got up and left. They were replaced by a trickle of Life Drawing students. Matthew was among the first to appear. He went directly to the supply cabinets and got a sheet of paper. He brought it to his easel without rippling it. Without looking at Flora or saying a word to her, he began drawing. This is somebody else, she thought. Somebody separated from her by a one-way mirror. There was a racket of people talking and shuffling their stools and easels. Matthew went on drawing, and she felt hot and tense in her head. Her fingers were cold and sweaty; they slipped down to the nub of her pencil and rested against her drawing.

Timpanelli came up behind Flora and stood there silently regarding her drawing. Flora sat perfectly still, as if she were waiting for a mosquito to land so she could smack it. Timpanelli gave her a sharp little pinch in the back of the arm and continued on around the perimeter of the class. That was Timpanelli's way of saying, "You've got something there." Flora started drawing again.

Midway through the period, when she had to leave class to go to the restroom, Matthew leaned over and this time erased the pointed nipples from her figure. When she returned and saw the smudges, she didn't say a word. She took the thumbtacks out of her drawing, folded it up, and stuck it in her lunch sack. She looked over to Timpanelli. Timpanelli hadn't been watching.

Flora spent the rest of the period staring back and forth from Tess's frozen figure to the new blank sheet of paper before her.

After Spanish class, Matthew stepped up beside her.

"I'm sorry," he said. His dark eyes glittered like slivers of pyrite. "I didn't mean to ruin it for you."

Flora raised her chin toward him. "That's all right," she said, "I was finished with it." She lied.

"Then maybe you won't mind if I keep it?" He held up the lunch sack she had forgotten to take with her as she rushed out of art class. The warm cheese was making greasy spots through the brown paper.

"If you want it, you can have it." Flora tried to sound exasperated.

Matthew clutched the sack to his chest with exaggerated devotion. Instead of flinging it into the nearest trash can, as Flora expected, he kept holding it there as they walked together down the hall. Flora gave him a doubtful glance, which he didn't see. The hall was nearly deserted and quiet except for the sound of their footsteps. She was afraid he might say something about Friday night. If he said anything, she might apologize for the way she had acted, for the way she was acting now. The silence between them was making her ears ring.

He said, "I'd ask you if I could carry your books, but somebody else's name is on them." He gave her a wry smile. Flora gave him a laugh that sounded half like a cry, and he grabbed her by the arm and pulled her out of the hall.

"No, please don't!" she cried.

He pushed her against the stucco wall outside the door and motioned to her, with his fingers on her lips, to keep quiet. He stood perfectly still with his other hand pressing her shoulder. Flora held her breath. Then she heard the clicking and clomping of a heavy-footed person, someone in high heels who was just trying to get from one place to another with no concern for grace. A few seconds later, Mrs. Baines scudded past the doorway and passed on down the hall. She was in a rush to complete her end-of-the-day rounds—seeing to it that there were no loiterers, that the school was being properly emptied of its students.

"I didn't want to watch her stick her fat finger in your pretty gold earring and pull you all the way back to her office." He gave the ring piercing Flora's left ear a little flick with his finger. He turned on his heels and took off down the ramp.

"Thank you," Flora called to his retreating figure. She lifted her hand unconsciously and felt the gold ring she had forgotten was there.

As Flora walked in the front gate of school the next morning, she spotted Phil's car in the parking lot. He saw her and beeped his horn. She walked over and got into his car.

"Did you miss me?" Phil's voice sounded playful, but Flora could tell by his eyes that he sincerely wanted to know.

"Yes, of course I did." She tried to match his tone, but she had hesitated and now he was wrinkling his brow. Her own head felt wobbly. She tried to recall something she knew about him, something she could focus on.

"You never called me," Phil challenged her.

"Yes I did, on Friday, but no one answered." She was feeling guilty. Then she saw his tanned hands gripping the steering wheel. "You don't look like you've been sick."

He saw her eyeing his hands. "I laid around the pool a lot." Suddenly he put his arm around her shoulders and took one of her hands in his. "I missed you, Florey." He pressed her hand into his lap and gave her a pleading look. "Couldn't we . . . now, before class?"

Flora hated to hear him plead like that. She was glad the tardy bell rang a second later so she could jump out of his car.

"I'll see you at lunch," she called back over her shoulder. As she ran up the path to her first class she saw Matthew out of the corner of her eye. He was leaning against a post at the edge of the parking lot, watching Phil get out of his car.

Flora sat with Phil at their usual table beneath a sparse mimosa tree. Stan was going to have a party the following Friday night. His parents had told him he could use the guest house if he promised not to destroy it. Phil squeezed Flora on the leg and told her he'd pick her up at seven. She said, "All right," nodding and gathering fallen mimosa leaves into a small pile before her on the table.

Halfway through the lunch period she told him she was going to go to her art class and work on some drawings. Phil said, "What?" But she was already on her way. She had a written pass from Timpanelli now and didn't have to lie to the hall monitors anymore.

Several weeks later, on Jericho, on the opposite side of the street from Flora's house and four or five houses down, a moving van was parked at the curb, a rare sight on that street.

When Flora turned the corner on her way home from school, the movers were still unloading. Two men in gray dungarees shouldered a mattress and carried it up the path and through the front door of the shabbiest house on the block. She wondered who would be moving in there, a place with peeling paint and no trees in the front yard. Matthew was leaning against one of the porch posts. She pretended she didn't see him and quickened her pace until she got to her own driveway. Then she looked back, feeling certain she would see someone who only looked like Matthew, not Matthew at all. All week long she had been mistaking other people for him. Matthew waved at her from his new front porch: a casual wave, like one longtime neighbor to another.

Flora looked up and down the block; several neighbors were standing in their front yards looking in the direction of the movers. People on Jericho didn't accept newcomers easily. When the Zelenoviches first bought into the neighborhood there seemed to be a conspiracy to make them feel unwelcome. The old residents used the Zelenoviches' driveway to turn around in, parked their cars at the curb in front of the house, let their kids ride bikes over the lawn, and otherwise ignored them. Gossip went around about the Zelenoviches being immigrants from New York City who lived in a tenement and probably wouldn't know how to take care of a house. When Mrs. Zelenovich's camellias were about to bloom, someone snipped the buds off during the night. The Zelenoviches got so exasperated they started calling the police every time a kid kicked a ball onto their lawn.

That night after dinner Flora and Janice were in their room studying, with the bright ceiling light on as usual. The windows look more like mirrors than windows, thought Flora. She could see herself sitting on the bed wearing nothing but a blouse and underpants. Suddenly she leaped up and pulled the shade down below the bottom of the windowsill.

Janice turned around from the desk and frowned at her. "What did you do that for?"

"Remember when we used to imagine that the boogeyman was standing outside the window?" Flora pretended to shiver. Janice huffed a sigh of annoyance and returned to her physics book.

Later that night, when all the lights in the house had long been shut off, Flora lay with the blankets spread smoothly under her arms and her hands crossed over her chest. She watched the shadows of the papertree leaves, like large hands, waving patterns on the wall, fingerpainting the closet doors. It was a windy, moonlit night and she was keenly awake.

Fact really is stranger than fantasy, she thought. If she had told anyone that the person she was dreaming about had moved down from the Hills, down to the flats, right smack onto her block, they wouldn't have believed her. Why would anyone move onto Jericho? She tried to imagine Matthew back at his home in the Hills, his father laying a hand on his shoulder and giving him the news: "The business"—whatever it might be—"just isn't bringing in what it used to, son. So I've sold the house. We're going to be renting one for a while." Matthew's mother would be wringing her hands. But Matthew wouldn't be too disturbed; he would agree with his father that they weren't home that much anyway. But then Matthew's parents would go out somewhere, leaving Matthew to sit alone on the sofa in the living room of the house he would be leaving soon, and he'd look around at everything he'd be leaving behind.

Flora thought back to her own predicament. From now on Matthew could watch Phil Ridley pull up in front of her house, watch her get into Phil's car voluntarily. In fact, if he wanted to, he could see her open Phil's car door for herself—a thing that irked her father—and drive away with Phil. She didn't even want to get into Phil's car anymore. And from now on, everybody on the block would watch that tall boy with the long black hair come and go, and they would gossip. And her father would hear things. She couldn't get to sleep.

The next day, in Life Drawing, Tess was changing positions every few minutes and Flora was trying to keep up with her. When Tess was doing something that looked like drawing water from a well, Matthew scrawled some words at the edge of Flora's paper: "Was that you I saw walking down Jericho?"

He tapped out a few beats with his pencil on the ledge of his easel.

Under his words Flora wrote, "It might have been."

Matthew sharpened his pencil on a little square of sandpaper, and wrote a third line: "Well then, how about dropping in on your way home from school?" Flora was too surprised to respond.

"We could play house," Matthew added, and winked. He went back to work.

Flora looked at his paper. It was filled with undulating legs and curving spines, arms outstretched and wrapped over heads—Tess's poses woven together into one drawing. It looked like the dance of a person who could do anything she felt like doing. Flora had a burning feeling in her chest. She scribbled "Impossible" in tiny letters at the margin of his paper. He didn't seem to notice her response. He kept right on drawing.

Not too many nights later, at the dinner table, Daniel mentioned that some new people had moved into the house up the street. Flora heard her mother start eating faster and saw her father's face grow tense as if he were experiencing pain somewhere in his body. Julia added cheerfully that the boy was tall and had pretty eyes.

"And hair floppin' over his neck," Henry chimed in angrily. He gave himself a series of quick karate chops at the back of the neck. "And a drunk for a father!" There was a moment of silence. Henry looked as if he might eat something off his plate, and then didn't. "And do you want to know?" he said, lowering his voice to a harsh whisper as if someone might be eavesdropping. He eyed everyone at the table, including Marleen. "There isn't a mother in that house. Some kind of a setup that is!" He jabbed his fork into his mashed potatoes. "The first house ever to be rented on this block, and you could just bet it'd be rented to a couple of no-gooders."

Flora knew he was really going to give himself indigestion over this one. She tried to look as though the topic didn't interest her. She hated being trapped in the corner with the table and the walls wedging her in and her father sitting across from her. She glanced at him and he pointed his fork at her.

"If I ever see you, if I ever hear of you, even being *near* a jerk like that, you'll wish you'd never been born." His eyes were glazed over with anger and the fork he held was vibrating.

Flora looked down at her food. She felt a dam of hot tears at the back side of her eyes burning to break loose. After a couple of minutes of silence, marred only by the tinkling of stainless steel against plates, Marleen braved a mild criticism in the form of a question.

"Don't you think you're being a little harsh?"

Henry raised his brows at her. "A word to the wise is sufficient."

His voice was slow and steady; he had restored himself to a dignified calm.

That night Flora went with Phil to a drive-in. The movie was *Performance* and Flora wanted to watch it, but Phil spent almost the entire show trying to convince her that sexual intercourse would be good for their health. He even turned on a flashlight and read several pages from a psychology paper a college friend of his had written. It was meant to support his argument, but page by page Flora felt increasingly isolated and claustrophobic. She hoped he wouldn't feel as awful as she did when he finished reading and found she wasn't at all moved. As an epilogue to the evening she put her hands around his cock and did the best she knew how, and Phil didn't say, or read, another word.

Matthew didn't show up at school on Monday. He wasn't there on Tuesday either. Flora kept glancing at the vacant easel beside her and wanting him to be there.

The Zelenoviches, who lived next door to the Cartiers, told a neighbor, who told another neighbor, that they smelled smoke coming from the Cartiers' house, marijuana smoke. It was being sucked in through their air conditioner and was stinking up their den, poisoning them.

"What are the Zelenoviches doing using their air conditioner in the wintertime?" asked Janice. Henry gave her a threatening look.

"What do you expect from a hippie?" He was ignoring Janice and testing Flora. Flora kept eating her supper as if she didn't expect anything from anyone. It was obvious that he wanted her to know he knew the word *hippie.* He seemed to be more concerned with that than with Matthew's alleged use of marijuana. She didn't dare ask him what he thought a hippie was; he would have spewed on about the degeneracy of her entire generation.

On Wednesday Matthew still wasn't in school; at least, Flora hadn't seen him leaning against a post in the parking lot that morning. She hadn't gotten a glimpse of him anywhere—down a hall, or out a window.

At the beginning of lunch period Phil came up to her while she was at her locker and told her he wanted to go with her to the art room. She tried to dissuade him. "I'm only going there to work on drawings, and how can I work if you're there?" He could take that as a compliment if he wanted to.

"I won't bother you," he promised. He looked so prim, so blond and well scrubbed, it was a wonder her father didn't come right out and say that Phil was the perfect one.

They went to Timpanelli's room together and he sat next to her, on Matthew's stool, and ate his lunch while she did some anatomical drawings of the bones of the shoulder and arm. She kept referring to a large textbook that was lying open on a stool on the other side of her. She labeled the different bones as she drew them. This was an assignment that Timpanelli required of all her Life Drawing students, to do labeled drawings of every muscle and bone in the human body. It was an assignment that almost everyone put off until the last days of class or never did at all.

When the lunch bell rang, Phil followed Flora into the washroom. Flora held her hands under the water and rubbed away the pencil smudges. Phil stood beside her with nothing to do but watch. "I don't see what's so exciting about coming here for lunch," he said. He was truly baffled.

Flora turned toward him and held on to the edge of the sink. "It's something I like to do, and I can't do it at home. Maybe it's a bad habit of mine." She turned around and jammed the faucets off.

Phil smiled. He was thinking of her rolled-up skirts. He didn't have to look at her legs; he knew they were long and lean. She didn't know it, but she could probably outrun him in a sprint on wet sand. The tardy bell rang and he gave her a hard, quick kiss on the lips and left the washroom.

Matthew wasn't in class on Thursday or Friday either. Flora had a feeling of dread stalking her around school. It followed her through the halls and sat down behind her in class. And it followed her home, too. She tried to study, but she spent more time worrying about Matthew's behavior, Matthew's health. Had he been expelled, or was he sick, she wondered. Either way, she was a little mad at him, and sad, too.

After school on Friday, Tess slammed their locker door shut and said flatly, "It must be nice not having Matthew around to do touch-up work on your drawings."

Flora arranged her books under her arm. "Oh, he doesn't bother me that much." She tried to sound as nonchalant as she could. She hoped Tess wouldn't go on talking about Matthew.

"Can you believe those drawings he does of me?" said Tess as they walked down the Long Hall. "It's embarrassing. He must be such a pervert." She glanced at Flora, and Flora wouldn't agree or protest. "He's always walking around alone," she added, looking out one of the hall windows as they passed it. "He's got a nice build, anyway. I wonder why he's not on the swim team, or something."

Flora shrugged her shoulders. "Have you seen that little earring he wears in his ear?" She squinted around at Flora.

"I don't think so," said Flora, shifting her books from one hip to the other and then back again.

"He's got to be weird." Tess's voice shut down on a note of peevishness.

That night Flora went with Phil to an open party in the Hills. She wasn't in the mood to be with or see anybody, but she didn't want to stay home either. Phil sensed her touchiness and reacted by not holding on to her anywhere. As they climbed a long flight of winding stone steps, his hand barely touched the small of her back. When she looked around, he beamed at her. His face looked radiant.

"Do you know whose house this is?" she asked.

"Stan knows. It's somebody he's known for a long time." He opened a giant-sized oak door and they stepped into a marble foyer. It was deserted until Stan came rushing in from the center hall. A glass full of something sloshed in his hand.

"Is this swanky enough for you?" Stan said as he rolled his eyes up and around at the high vaulted ceiling. Phil looked around.

"What have you been drinking?" asked Flora. "Water?" Stan looked at the glass in his hand and gave it a jiggle.

"Vodka on the rocks, the best."

He led them into a broad, brightly lit room filled with people—not just people their own age, but older people as well. A woman in a liquid silk gown, holding a drink in each hand, approached them with a squinting smile of sheer ecstasy, then drifted on past them and out another door.

"That's his mom," said Stan.

"Whose mom?" asked Flora.

Stan gestured toward an ornately carved mahogany bar that was nestled below and between two curving staircases. "Clinton's," he said, cracking a piece of ice between his teeth. "He likes to be bartender." Flora looked at the guy mixing drinks behind the bar. It was the same person who had driven her and Matthew to and from Matthew's house. She was certain: the square, too-serious face, the bulky build, the wild, fuzzy red hair that stood out all over his head.

"Whose house is this?" asked Flora.

"Clinton's," said Stan, sounding as though that should be obvious. He rushed off to get Phil and her a drink. Flora was going to say she didn't care for one, but he was already at the bar. Clinton looked in her direction and she turned her head aside slowly.

"There's a band upstairs," said Stan as he handed them their drinks.

Phil said, "Let's go, Florey," already beginning to guide her toward one of the staircases with his hand at her back again. She set her drink down on a pedestal next to a Chinese urn with a philodendron growing out of it, and they ascended the stairs. Phil kept his hand lightly at her back as they stepped around the leaning and lounging couples. They all looked as if they were holding bizarre and sexy poses for fashion photographers. Flora didn't recognize anyone. She began to feel like an observer or, worse, like an intruder.

They stopped at the entrance to a room filled with dancing people. Three guitarists and a drummer played toned-down rock 'n' roll, their version of "She Was Just Seventeen," from a marble hearth beneath crossed swords and a shield made of pewter. Their amplifiers were set up on low mahogany tables with legs curved like a cat's hind quarters. It was a dimly lit room. Red satin chairs and velvet sofas gave off a hushed light. Flora's attention was drawn to a lamp at one side of the room, a frosted ball of crystal that glowed like a full moon. She looked to the other side of the room. There was another one to match it. The lamp base was an alabaster statuette of a woman wearing a loosely draped gown. Her arms were crossed up over her head and she looked as if she were on the verge of fainting. Matthew sat at the end of a sofa, beneath the pale light shed by this lamp. His legs were stretched out far enough to trip unwary dancers. One of his hands lay across his belt and the other one was carefully stroking the velvet nap on the arm of the sofa. He wasn't drinking or smoking anything.

His eyes were fixed on Flora, steady and unblinking, as stern as stone. A small arc of light glinted off the gold loop in his ear. A couple danced across their line of vision, and then another couple, and another, before the space between them opened up again.

"Do you want to dance?" Phil whispered in her ear, and he drew a circle around and around on her back with his fingertips.

"No," said Flora. She felt her face flushing. "I don't feel like dancing." She tore her eyes away from Matthew. Phil gave her a puzzled look. "This room doesn't feel right." Her voice trailed off. She made a turn around him, leaving his hand stuck out in midair so that he looked as if he were about to shake someone's hand or accept a square-dance partner. He looked around the room.

“I don’t see anything wrong with it,” he said, obviously confused. Flora liked to dance much more than he did, so she knew she had to give him some sort of reason.

“I don’t feel very well,” she explained, moving toward the opposite stairway.

“I’m sorry,” he said. He followed after her.

“It’s not your fault,” she said as they curved down the stairway. He held her by the arm.

When they got to the bottom, he said, “Would you like to lie down in one of the bedrooms for a while?” She pictured trying to battle him off in some plush, canopied bed in a secluded wing of this huge house.

“No, please, would you take me home?” She felt an urgent need to be alone. She hated to see the forlorn look on his face, but she persisted. “Please, I’d really just like to go home and go to sleep.”

Phil set his unfinished drink down on the newel post next to a Chinese urn that matched the one on the other stairway, and they walked briskly through the main hall and the foyer. “All right,” he said, “but I can’t believe you. The first party we’ve been to without flying beer cans, and you want to go home. I don’t get it.”

Flora appreciated Phil’s attempt to understand, but she didn’t dare show him the slightest hint of kindness. “I can’t help it,” she said as they hurried down the stone steps.

Phil skidded around corners and ran two red lights without incident. He drove as if he were on a racetrack, with his eyes pinned straight ahead. By the time he reached the curb in front of Flora’s house, he seemed to have forgotten what it was Flora had said she wanted to do. He kissed her on the ear and tried to reach his hand up under her skirt.

“No, please don’t,” Flora pleaded. She pulled her skirt down. “Not tonight, and especially not in front of my father’s house.” She opened the car door and jumped out.

With her hand clamped over her mouth and the bedsheets over her face, she tried to muffle her crying. She didn’t want to hurt Phil’s feelings and she had this desire for Matthew that she didn’t know what to do with. She struggled her way into sleep, and sometime before dawn she had a dream:

She was holding a summons slip and heading in the direction of Mrs. Baines’s office. Janice joined her in the hall, took her by the hand, and guided her the rest of the way there. “This isn’t anything to worry about,” said Janice. “It’s for your own good.” Mrs. Baines greeted them at the door with her V-shaped smile and her twinkling beady-blue eyes. "Come this way," she said as she placed her hand at the small of Flora's back and ushered her through the office and to another door. Mrs. Baines pushed the door open, and there, in the dimness of a small closet, was Matthew, standing as motionless as a figure in a tableau. His face was too dark to see, but Flora knew it was him. Phosphorescent lavender, Mercurochrome pink, and other luminous hues—colors with no heat—spread in intricate patterns across his chest, all down his arms, even to his fingertips. Someone had painted him. Flora looked at her hands and they were covered with paint. She slumped down on the floor at his feet and cried, "But it wasn't me, it wasn't me . . ." Mrs. Baines said it wasn't ladylike and was pinching her by the ear and trying to pull her up.

Invisible People

At daybreak on Saturday Flora was roused by the clattering of trash cans and the high hum of the garbage truck. Clumps of pampas grass had grown enormous enough to block out most of the view over the back fence, but they had done nothing to muffle the sound of traffic in the alley.

As a child she used to get between the curtains and the window, scoot her rocks aside, and sit in the sill so she could watch the men swing the trash cans over their shoulders and listen to them whistle and joke and sing while the big gray lip of the truck went up and down and ate everything they tossed to it. She used to, until one morning Henry opened the bedroom door while she was sitting there. He called them "jigaboos," as though they were something people blow out of their noses, and threatened to use the clothesline on her if he ever caught her looking at them again. She had been puzzled, and then frightened. She crawled back under the covers and tried to figure out why he didn't want her to look at them, why he didn't like them. Was it because their faces were so black and their smiles so white? Was it because they whistled while they worked? Because they were so strong that no matter what kind of trash you crammed into your trash can, no matter how heavy you made it, they could heave it high in the air and send it flying into the mouth of their truck and cart it away, never to be seen again? They could get rid of anything.

Now Flora listened to the garbage truck working its way up the alley. It seemed to be announcing the start of a dismal weekend. She got up, got dressed, and went out quietly. She had it in her mind to get at the yardwork before anyone else was up. Henry had said for her to clean the front yard. Maybe she could get most of it done before he got out there.

The sycamore leaves were still damp and limp with dew and raked easily. She might have been hypnotized by the strokes of the rake except that all the while a crow that was perched high above her kept ranting. It seemed as if he had been assigned to her for the morning, to protest her presence down below. Ignoring him was a struggle because his caws sounded louder than her thoughts. She took a look up the street and saw a diminutive form of Matthew sitting on his porch steps with his chin in his hands and his elbows on his knees. He seemed to be looking in her direction. She felt better. The dull ring went out of her raking and she worked with more vigor. Even as she slung armfuls of the tart-smelling leaves into a big cardboard box, she tried to do it with grace. Pazetti had told her students, "When you are at home, whatever you're doing, turn it into a dance." The crow heaved himself off a swaying branch, cawing once as if he had been insulted, and with a ponderous flapping of wings, flew away. Flora thought of the words Matthew had scrawled in the margin of her drawing and remembered the villages she had drawn as a child: houses side by side, so full of doors and windows they looked more like happy, open faces. She looked up the street again, hoping to see him still, but he was no longer there.

Henry came out and took a look around. Flora dragged her box to the far corner of the lawn and started gathering up another pile of leaves. He picked up the rake and followed her.

"Aren't you the early bird," he said. Flora kept putting leaves in the box. Henry raked up some strays. "You're going to put the Japanese gardeners to shame." There was a chuckle in his voice.

Flora looked up at him. An uncertain look, a half-smile, hung on his face. "I still have to clean out a couple of flower beds," she said.

"I'll get Daniel out here to finish up. Your breakfast is waiting for you. You ought to eat it while it's still hot."

"All right," said Flora. She hoisted the box onto her shoulder and headed for the side gate. As she up-ended the box in the empty trash can she thought, Doesn't take much to get along with him. Get up at dawn, do whatever he tells you to do, and everything'll go smoothly.

Later that afternoon, when Flora was rinsing scouring powder out of the bathtub, Henry came in and turned off the water.

"That rich brat's on the phone." He looked mad. "Keep it short, I'm expecting a call."

Flora held the receiver gingerly. "Hi, Flora. How do you feel?" It was Phil.

"Better than I was feeling last night," she had to admit. She glanced at Henry. "How are you?" she returned. She knew she should say something decisive, but she couldn't. Henry was leaning against the sink counter drumming his fingers on the tile. It was the sound of bones being bruised.

"Fine." Phil sounded enthusiastic all of a sudden. "Do you want to go to a movie tonight?"

Flora looked down at all of the papers her father had arranged around the telephone—official-looking documents with seals and stamps, and sheets with nothing but columns of numbers on them.

"If you don't mind"—Flora took a breath—"I'd rather not . . ." There was some silence. Even Henry stopped rapping his fingers. She changed her grip on the receiver. Why did its black plastic always feel as sticky as licorice? She tried to soften her statement. "I really don't feel like going out." There was some more silence. "Maybe," she said. She heard a click and then the dial tone. For an instant she had the frightful thought, This is what it's like to go deaf, nothing but an awful buzzing. While Henry busied himself with the knobs on the stove clock (it was never at the correct time), she waited with the receiver still to her ear. Maybe Phil's little sister had cut them off, as she sometimes did. But Phil didn't ring again. She really didn't think he would. Well, maybe he couldn't; she hadn't pushed the receiver button down. She couldn't remember how telephones worked, especially when some people had more than one of them in the same house. "Well, yes . . . No, that's all right. I'll see you at school on Monday," she said into the phone for Henry's sake. "Good-bye, have a nice time." She put the receiver in its holder and in the faintest voice said, I can't help it, I'm sorry, Phil. Henry was still bent over the stove, grinding the gears on the clock and pretending he didn't know she was leaving the kitchen.

* * *

Tess called on Sunday and asked Flora if she wanted to go to Malibu. Flora said, "I'd like to, but I can't." Phil would probably be there, trying to surf on the crowded little waves. She saw surfboards knocking about, skidding riderless up onto the beach, Phil walking alone along the low-tide line, his lips blue from the cold water. "I need to study. I'm way behind."

"You can't fool me," said Tess. "I bet you'd go if you thought there was the slightest chance Matthew Cartier would be there instead of Phil."

Flora thumbed through Marleen's pocket calendar. On the front there was a picture of a crane flying before a full moon. "Why didn't you go to the party Friday night?"

"I wanted to, but I couldn't," said Tess, sighing.

"Why not?" asked Flora. It was so much easier to ask questions than to have to dream up answers.

"Because Stan asked me to go with him, and being there with Stan would be worse than not being there at all. Don't change the subject, Flora."

"I really don't feel like going to the beach today," said Flora. "I think I'll just stay home and work on some drawings. But thanks for asking me."

"You're turning into an introvert," said Tess with annoyance. "One of these days, everyone's going to just give up on you."

After hanging up, Flora considered what Tess had said. She was losing contact, but she couldn't seem to help it. Her desire to be with other people had dwindled down to wanting to be with just one person. She went into her bedroom and closed the door.

Henry had left the house right after breakfast. He said he had to set stakes for the grading of an easement road and wouldn't be back before dark. Janice and Daniel and Julia were away with friends. Marleen sat on the front porch steps with a glass of red wine and watched the sycamore leaves fall like saucers through water. The late afternoon sun made it just warm enough to sit out there. She was glad to have a quiet moment: no job, no housework, no Henry. He hadn't insisted on a family outing for a long time, not even to a new housing tract to look at the model homes. "I'm not going to beg you anymore," he had told them. "I've got better things to do on Sunday than entertain a bunch of ingrates." Marleen got tearful thinking about all the places he had taken them—rodeos, fairs, air shows, fish hatcheries, aquariums, arboretums . . .

She didn't feel like going on any more of his outings, but she wished the children still did. She had never enjoyed the camping trips. When she finally told him she wasn't going to cook any more meals in the trailer, he got mad and sold it. Then he bought those ten acres of brushy hillside in the Malibu Mountains—not to resell. Among his piles of real estate papers he had plans for a house he himself had drawn up. He used to ask her to look at them, but she couldn't get very excited about something she didn't think they could anywhere near afford. Every Sunday, he'd drive the entire family out to The Ranch, as he called it. There was nothing out there, but the children seemed to like it. They ran off into the ravines or disappeared over the hills and Henry'd have to holler them back when it was time to go home. He never seemed to get tired of walking around on the building pad, pacing off his floor plans on the bare ground. He'd expect her to stand perfectly still in one spot or another so he could take compass sightings off her extended arms. And all the while gnats would be flying up her nose. After that she'd go sit on a rock in the shade of a bush while he figured out where the sun would come up and where it would set in every season. She really didn't care. She didn't like the idea of having lizards and snakes all around. She didn't want to change jobs. And what did she need with a big house? Four bedrooms and two and a half baths to keep clean. "Such an angry man," she said out loud. She looked down at the red wine in her glass and swished it around.

Flora opened the front door and found her mother sitting there on the steps. "Where is everybody?" she asked.

"Oh, with their friends, and your father is working on some property." Marleen twisted around and looked at Flora. "What have you been up to?"

"I'm working on a drawing," said Flora.

"That's nice," said Marleen. Flora started to close the door. "Flora," Marleen called her back.

"Yes?" said Flora.

"I was just wondering, do you think your father ever really wanted to build a house out at The Ranch?"

"The Ranch?" Flora frowned. "No, I doubt it. I think he just took us out there so he could boss us around."

"But he had all those plans and everything?"

"So why didn't he go ahead and build it? Who was stopping him?" Flora closed the door.

Marleen took a sip of wine and stared at the driveway. Henry had stopped asking her if she wanted to come along. Then he had gone ahead and planted fruit trees out there, and he put the children to work watering them. They told her they had to sit on the tailgate of the car with a metal drum filled with water between them, and as he drove from tree to tree, they had to put the hose at each tree and turn the faucet at the metal drum on and off when he said so. And they weren't supposed to let the water go down a gopher hole. Even Julia worked. She had a little broom for sweeping out the back of the car, and she helped fix the tree wells with a small hoe. They also rolled fallen rocks out of the roads, filled the ruts that the rain and rodents had made in the banks of the building pad, cut brush for fire control, and scythed the grass, Marleen wasn't sure why.

Her bottom felt cold from the concrete, and the sun had set behind the house across the street, so she went inside. She thought she'd fix herself a cup of coffee and read a magazine, or work the Sunday crossword. On second thought, maybe she should start dinner.

Flora had been in her bedroom all afternoon. With colored pencils and watercolors she drew a street of gay houses—two- and three-story houses with lots of garret windows, chimneys, wide porches, and vines growing all over the walls from one house to the next. There were gates beneath stone archways, cobblestone promenades running in front of the houses and parallel to a river. The river was spanned every so often with curving bridges made of river stone. In Flora's mind there were people coming out of their houses and walking along the promenades, crossing the bridges, visiting one another on the porches, being invited into one another's parlors, but the people were all invisible.

PART TWO

In Color

The Washroom

On Monday a boy from the boys' swim team came out of the washroom wearing his swim trunks. He hopped like a frog onto the table where Tess was already posing, sitting with her arm dangling over the back of a chair and her knees pressed discreetly together. Without moving her head, she looked him over from head to toe and suppressed a smile. He had no pockets to put his hands in, so he crossed his arms and looked over to Timpanelli for instruction.

Timpanelli stood up and said, "The title of this assignment is 'How to Make a Pleasing Composition Out of Two Human Bodies.' " She sat down again, and the girl called The Cat snickered as if to prove she was enjoying some inside joke. She had stationed herself next to Timpanelli and was bending down one of the slats in a Venetian blind and peering out the window.

The boy, who was an expert in four or five swimming strokes and excelled in the butterfly, was far from water now and seemed to feel ill at ease. He chose to stand behind Tess's chair like a tree, and place his hand like a fallen branch on her shoulder.

"You look like wooden puppets!" cried Timpanelli. "Can't you do something that looks more real?" She rolled the *r* in *real* and ran her fingers through her reddish hair. She flipped madly through her art journal. "Pretend you're at the beach or something," she growled.

"Yeah, and your parents didn't bring ya," The Cat blurted. Timpanelli gave her a perturbed look. From all around the class suggestions for all kinds of poses started up like a drove of seagulls, until nearly everyone was laughing and calling, and there was danger that the Main Offices would hear the racket.

Timpanelli finally shouted, "Everybody shut up," and the noise slacked off to a safe level.

Though she was amused, Flora had been silent throughout the episode. She figured Tess was enjoying herself immensely. The position they had finally arrived at was one where Tess was lounging on her side and the swimmer was approaching her on all fours. It was a tableau the entire class seemed to have agreed upon. Everyone was scribbling away quietly. Tess wore a sublime expression. One of her tits looked just about ready to pop out of her bikini top. The space next to Flora was vacant. She felt an ache in the back of her throat. She wanted to cry out. She hated his absence. She tried to make her hand move over her paper but it wouldn't. She kept pleading for him to appear, as if he were the sun hiding behind a cloud. Just as she had sunk to cursing her own wishes, he walked in.

He was wearing his usual white shirt with the sleeves rolled up and his dark blue pants. His corduroy jacket was slung over his shoulder. After speaking in a low voice with Timpanelli for a while, he came over and sat on his stool. He sat there with his uncanny silence, like a stranger taking a short rest on a park bench. Flora was about to say something like "It's good to see you in class again" when he sighed. He took his pencil out of his shirt pocket, held it in his mouth and bit on it as he regarded the scene on the tabletop.

After a minute he jumped up, went to the supply cabinets, and came back with two boxes of oil pastels. He held one of the boxes out to Flora. His offer surprised her so much that she was slow to accept it. He had to place the box in her hand. She lifted the lid and saw a nearly new set. Only the ends of the sticks were rounded off, and none of the sticks were broken. A neat row of colors like a child's xylophone. "Thanks, Matthew." She heard herself saying his name out loud, to him, for the first time. She glanced at his ear. There was no gold ring there. She had left her own at home too.

Matthew transformed Tess and the swimmer into a drawing that was nearly mystical. The colors seemed to race back and forth between their bodies and lift them right up off the paper. He can work in color, thought Flora, not just in black and white and shades of gray. Her own sheet of paper was still blank.

She held the box of pastels in her hand, arranging and rearranging the sticks, reading their labels as if they might provide her with some clue—viridian, scarlet, crimson, orchid. She had an urge to draw clouds. She began making light strokes, and before long she had lost herself in the prismatic colors. After a while she saw figures floating in the clouds. The vague form of two dancers emerged here and there. She feared that at any moment the drawing would become a mess of smudged and tangled lines, and yet she kept drawing.

Matthew leaned over and put his pencil to her paper. She held her breath while he wrote his message. At the same time, pretending he was no more than a breeze skimming by her, she continued to work. When he returned to his own drawing, she took a quick side glance. His pencil marks looked like the claws of a crow clutching at the rim of her paper. She had to take a closer look: "I'd like to brush your clouds away."

She straightened up slowly. She tried to remember some lines of poetry, something from last-semester English. "If you were coming in the fall, I'd brush the summer by . . ." and then something about a fly. Anyway, this was midwinter. Maybe a line from *Heart of Darkness* or *The Tell-tale Heart*? She couldn't come up with anything, so at the margin of his drawing she wrote: "Why? What do you think you'll find?"

Timpanelli called out a singsong warning: "Keep your mitts on your own easel." Most of the class looked up and around, but no one could tell who the culprit was.

Flora had always been a slow writer. At the sound of Timpanelli's voice, she was startled into an upright position on her stool. Then the bell rang.

"Want me to put the pastels back?" Matthew nudged her gently in the arm.

"Yes," she said, nodding, and she gathered several sticks from the ledge of her easel and put them in their proper places in the box. She still felt stunned. She watched Matthew take the boxes back. When he returned, he rolled his drawing into a tube and walked out of class with it stuck under his arm. She rolled hers up too. As she went by Timpanelli's desk she said, "See you tomorrow," as if Timpanelli didn't know she hardly ever missed a day of school. Still, Flora had an impulse to let Timpanelli know for sure that she would be coming back, that she didn't mind being yelled at by her, not at all.

Timpanelli scowled at her. "Let's see your drawing." (She hadn't made the rounds today.) Flora unrolled it and held it up. Timpanelli rested her chin in her hands and slowly nodded her approval. Flora shifted her fingers so that they hid the words Matthew had written. Timpanelli made no comment, so Flora hesitated a moment and then rolled the drawing up again.

"It's excellent," said Timpanelli. "It's what I expect from you."

Flora looked at her, beaming. Timpanelli's eyes were closed. She was massaging her brow with the palms of her hands. "See you tomorrow," said Flora again as she backed away. Timpanelli waved good-bye to her and mumbled something about wild horses.

At the beginning of lunch the next day Flora passed Phil in the hall and he didn't even blink. She didn't blame him. She opened her mouth but closed it without saying anything, and went on to Timpanelli's room. Matthew was already there, working at his easel. The usual crowd formed a barricade around Timpanelli's desk. In addition, there were a couple of former students, graduates who had come back for a visit. They never seemed to have any trouble getting onto the school grounds. They looked smug and relaxed, tipping back with perfect balance in their chairs and even resting their feet on the edge of Timpanelli's desk. One of the boys had brought his portfolio and had it spread open before Timpanelli. She looked like she was reading a large menu.

Flora entered unnoticed. Matthew jerked a little when she came up beside him. That was the first time she had ever startled him with *her* approach. He tilted his head slightly, raised one eyebrow, and gave her the slyest smile she had ever seen on anyone's face, even his. Something had to be amiss. She looked down at herself and discovered she was standing there with nothing to draw on, nothing to draw with. Her hands were empty. She glanced at his work. He had already drawn three views of a hand and was working on a fourth. His own right hand had obviously been the model: turned this way and that, it looked like a fluster of birds on his paper. "I guess I'm not the only one who has more hands than they know what to do with," she said, raising her eyebrows, pretending to be smug. She went to get some paper and Matthew, with a smile on his face, turned back to his sketching.

All the easels in the room were vacant except for the one Matthew was at. She suddenly felt awkward about using the one closest to him. She went to the other side of the room, where all the blindless windows admitted the afternoon sun. How could he ever have left this side? she wondered. She loved to have the sun soaking into her back. She sat there motionless, absorbing it. In her head she saw lizards, spotted and striped, lying on rocks; two were slowly entwining. As she leaned forward to begin drawing, the shadow of her shoulder beat her to the paper and blotched out the bright light. She looked across the room. The sun was glinting off the top of Matthew's head, making his black hair shine like blue slate. He was working intently. He had one hand poised as if to catch something he had tossed in the air. The room, the lighting, her own shadow, everything seemed to be teasing her. It was impossible to draw. She removed the paper from the easel.

Timpanelli was still the center of much attention. She was tipping back in her chair, laughing at something someone had said. Some guy was rummaging through her top desk drawer. He insisted he could make a rocket out of nothing but a foil gum wrapper, a match, and a paper clip. All he needed was the paper clip. Flora went to the washroom and threw her paper in the trash can beneath the sink.

She liked to stand alone in the washroom. It was no Sistine Chapel; it was a mess—and yet there was something sacred about it, something that Mrs. Baines, for one, wasn't able to disturb. For years Mrs. Baines had tried to order its desecration. She wanted its walls ripped away and replaced with new Sheetrock, so the rumors ran. But still the old walls were there, and every year they grew thicker with another layer of paint, free and gaudy patterns applied with and without talent by each new influx of Timpanelli's students. Initials inside hearts, initials without hearts, mottoes, oaths, pledges, and curses were etched in the soft tempera with the nubs of brushes and the points of sharp pencils. It formed a silvery filigree, the final touch. The room looked like an oil slick swirling in the sunlight, or like the inside of one of those big marbleized balloons that might well have been dipped in a pot of whirling paint. It was soothing to Flora in a way she could not account for; ordinarily she could not abide such sloppiness and disorder. In her own room, before she could begin to rest for the night, she'd hop in and out of bed correcting things that were askew or ajar. Janice's teasing was nothing compared to the discomfort of disarray. She could never work well on a messy drawing board and couldn't stand the sensation of holding a paintbrush with a paint-encrusted handle or ferrule. She hated the sight of litter lying on the ground or the floor, especially when it was near a trash can, so easy to dispose of properly.

As she stood there, she felt her fondness for the room growing. It seemed to have a timeless patience, accepting whatever marks were left upon it and all the while silently offering its confusion of tools and supplies to whoever might come along. Tiers of shelves were loaded with paint cans—full, empty, half full, dried up, spilled. She liked the dust, in all hues, which must have come from the careless mixing of powdered paints and which coated everything: the shelves, the paint cans themselves, the jars filled with new, used, and useless brushes in all shapes and sizes. Timpanelli always warned them, "Don't scrub with the brushes!" It was easy to see why. Most of them had obviously been scrubbed with, or at least never properly cleaned. The bristles were bent and broken and fraying out like feather dusters, or else glommed with paint like lashes on girls who used too much mascara.

Flora stood at the big porcelain sink with the water running, washing her hands for a long time. She watched the pale tints of color dissolve from the hardened specks of paint left in the sink, and thought of them as long-tailed comets whirling around. A long creak sounded above the running water. She looked over her shoulder and saw Matthew standing with his back against the door. The afternoon sun was shining on him again. He lifted a new paintbrush out of one of the glass jars beside him and stroked its bristles carefully between his fingertips. He had the air of one who is deep in thought—as if he were a young Michelangelo envisioning the ceiling inside his own head. He continued to stroke the brush in a methodical way while Flora watched him. She couldn't let him get away with this. "Don't be obscene," she said, and yet she could not turn her eyes away from him. They felt fixed, like stones in a setting.

"All right, I won't be," Matthew responded with prompt obedience. He dropped the brush back in its jar. "What would you like me to be?" he asked. He didn't seem to be joking, though he might have been; Flora had a hard time telling. Joking and being serious were well blended in Matthew, as easily as blue and red joined to make purple. But the distinction didn't really matter to her now. She forced her eyes back to the swirling water. The color continued to feather away from the tiny specks and flow into the drain. "Maybe . . ." There was a clog in her throat.

"Maybe what?" Matthew urged.

"Maybe somebody to love." Her own words had escaped, and she was glad they were finally free.

"Somebody *who* could love?" asked Matthew, as if she hadn't said enough already. She glanced at him. He hadn't moved from the door. She took a deep breath and looked out the window opposite from him. "Somebody *I* could love." She pronounced each word slowly and precisely.

Matthew carefully drew the latch shut. Flora heard the click and felt him move up behind her. He wrapped his arms around her waist and pressed himself against her backside. She took hold of both faucet handles, first turning them the wrong way so that the water came gushing out wildly, and then the other way so that the water stopped abruptly. In the silence, she heard his breathing, and even through two layers of clothing, his and her own, she could feel the heat from his chest. It pounded against her like quick waves breaking on a steep beach. His lips touched the side of her neck. And down below, through all their other clothing, she could feel that hot, hard part of him she had fought against so long ago. She contracted and relaxed with a pleasurable shiver as if she had sunk into a tub of hot water, and held on to his arms. She wanted to remain that way forever, but as soon as that thought was complete, she switched to an opposite sensation. She felt stuck, and backwards, like a toppled turtle.

Matthew backed away and drew her around so that they were face to face. He looked like a dreamer dreaming with his eyes open. He unbuttoned her blouse while he gazed into her eyes. Flora didn't need to look at his hands. She knew they were long and smooth. She had watched him drawing often enough. He caressed her breasts as if he were drawing new paintbrushes into perfect points. She felt a painful tingling all through her body. Somehow, even when he seemed to be dreaming, he looked mischievous. She could see it in his eyes, and when she saw it on his lips she wanted to kiss it. His mouth was wetter and stronger than she had imagined. She put her arms around his waist and held him tighter.

Then, as if she were floundering in an uncontrollable dream, she felt him slipping away. She couldn't catch hold of him. She was sure she had lost him. But no, he was only gliding down onto the floor. She was glad the custodian had mopped it. She saw the dark green linoleum shining, and Matthew's white shirt flung aside and his smooth, pale chest rising and falling. He undid his pants and let his cock stand up bold and vulnerable. The colored dust of the washroom turned denser to Flora's eyes. She held her breath and felt a streak of hunger pass up through her, not a painful growl from her belly, but a shrill, silent cry from farther down. "Oh," she groaned and knelt down. Matthew put his hands under her skirt, her cumbersome skirt, and pulled her underpants down. He ran his fingers lightly up and down her thighs and over her belly until she felt like a full rain cloud. She longed to lower herself down, but he wouldn't let her. He held her away, at a certain distance, and waited. He narrowed his eyes at her and she remembered the night she had struggled against him, that cleaving instance of blackness. "Please," she whispered. Their tips touched and there was a sudden discharge of energy, like a summer electrical storm. He let her come down, ease down. She felt a great pressure as he moved slowly up inside her. All she could think was that she wanted him to go deeper, and she wanted to keep him there, but he pulled himself out of her. She felt sad and crazy with desire for him.

Matthew smiled up at her. In the midst of the gaudy afternoon light, his eyes were like the deep, dark water of quarry pools. They tempted her to dive straight down from a high ledge. She wove her fingers into his black hair, kissed his lips and his neck, and hid her face there. She didn't want him to look at her face when her desire for him was so strong that it made her feel like crying out. She pressed down around him with all the weight she had and he pushed back up inside her with more force. She looked beyond him and saw the windowpanes wink and turn black, and then turn to mirrors. She saw herself sinking and rising, her back bending and bowing. She and Matthew made a rhythm together that beat away every bad sensation she had ever felt. She watched hummingbirds probing fuchsias, deliberately, in and out, on a hot, humid day. She saw cadmium red light squeezed out of a tube of paint—a glistening coil, never to return. Blazing fuchsia filled her head and its heat spread throughout her body with one long throb followed by a strand of shorter throbs. Matthew sighed as if all the air were being sucked out of him. "Flora." Her name sounded like a flood, not a name, and a warm fluid filled her deep inside. All the banks caved in. Quarry stones toppled from their sills and sank into the pool below. She pressed her cheek against his ear and squeezed her eyes shut.

Matthew took her head in his hands. "You're my baby now?" He looked into her eyes and searched around. She felt every little pulse in his body, and she saw the hope and the need and the love in his eyes. Then she heard her father's taut and angry voice: "You'll wish you'd never been born." Her father's words fled out of the washroom like a fearful bird; they went right through a windowpane without shattering it. She had never felt happier in her life, so glad to be alive. She kept staring into Matthew's eyes. The bell sounded outside in the hall. Matthew winced inside of her. Feet scuffled and tromped by. The drinking faucet wheezed on and off. A foot accidentally kicked the door, and voices called to one another. She kissed him lightly on the lips and then on both of his eyelids. "Yes, I am . . . I want to be." A sob rose from her.

"I'm in love with you, Flora. I hope you're crying because you're happy." He nipped her on the ear. She rose up abruptly and almost cried out, like a dreamer startled out of a dream who hasn't found her voice yet.

"I am," she insisted in a whisper. She sat on his hips and rubbed her ear on her shoulder.

"Am what?" Matthew insisted. He squeezed her hands in his. He wanted to hear her talk in full sentences.

"I am very happy," whispered Flora. "I can't keep from loving you." A couple of tears dropped onto his chest and she released her hands from his and tried to wipe them away. He gripped her by the wrists.

"Please don't ever try to." He sounded serious. He sat up and gave her a long, hard kiss. Then he sighed deeply and looked past her to the door. She looked around at it too.

They got up together. Matthew picked her underpants off the floor and handed them to her. He zipped up his pants and buckled his belt. I don't want to go out there, thought Flora. Matthew stood behind her and smoothed back her hair as she looked down and tried to rebutton her blouse. She wanted to make sure she got every button in the right hole. Someone pounded on the door. More feet went by, nimble ones and slow, shuffling ones. Matthew fixed his own shirt and ran his fingers back through his hair. His mouth turned down at one side; he tipped his head toward the door. Flora could almost hear him say, This is the way it is, the way it has to be. He pulled back the latch and sidestepped out of the narrow opening. She quickly straightened the rest of her clothing; then she doused her face at the sink and patted it dry with a paper towel. She reentered Timpanelli's room, trailing behind the last arriving students, and headed straight for the supply cabinets. She had enough presence of mind to know that she would need a clean sheet of paper for the hour ahead. She didn't dare look at Timpanelli. Like a homing pigeon, she joined Matthew at their usual site.

Tess, without the swimmer, was already posed on the center table. She had her head flung back and her hands on her hips. She cast a dreary eye at Flora, and Flora hid her face behind her easel. Matthew was sketching Tess as if he had never seen her before. He was using an ordinary yellow writing pencil. Flora saw no point in drawing. She stretched her eraser, kneaded it into a ball, and stretched it out again. "Don't worry," said Matthew in a reassuring undertone. Flora put her eraser down and began sketching Tess just as she was posed, adding nothing, taking nothing away. Her mind was still back in the washroom. She glanced over to Matthew. She wondered how he felt. He seemed to be concentrating on what he was doing.

When the period ended, Timpanelli called out clearly over the commotion of departing students, "F and M, I want to see you after class—now, in other words." Tess, as she jumped down off her stage, threw Flora an expression of disdain, a quick curl of the lip, and Flora caught it. Her heart held still for a couple of counts and then pumped wildly.

After everyone else had left the room, including Tess, she and Matthew approached Timpanelli's desk. "I like what you're doing for each other's creativity—on paper," she said, raising her brows high above the rim of her glasses. "But," she continued, "if you ever lock that door again and carry on, it's—" She finished this whispered warning by drawing her finger, like a rubber knife, across her throat. Then she took a long sip from her vase, eyeing Flora and Matthew all the while.

Flora felt feverish with embarrassment, and then chilled with fear. What if someone besides Timpanelli knew what she and Matthew had done? It could cost Timpanelli her job. She wanted to ask Timpanelli for forgiveness, promise never to do it again, but ended up only nodding faintly as a sign of agreement and contrition. She felt Matthew shift his weight from one foot to the other.

Timpanelli tapped her pencil on her desktop with nervous rapidity. The tapping stopped abruptly, and after a minute of silence, she said, "All right, you two star-crossed lovers, get out of here." She waved them off with a lazy flick of her pencil. "I'll see you tomorrow," she added.

They had been spared for the time being. Were they really star-crossed? Flora wondered. They set off down the hall together, and just when she thought they might keep on going in a straight line forever, he gave her a gentle squeeze on the arm and took off down a side ramp. Now she felt like a planet traveling without a sun, or a moon without a planet. She watched him retreating and suddenly remembered that he lived on her block, in her father's domain, *not* at a safe distance.

Somehow she landed herself in her next class, but once there, she only wanted to rest her head on her desk. She needed time to relive their time together—Matthew's heat, his strength, his words. It was hard to believe what had happened. He had said, "I'm in love with you, Flora." She wished he had said, "I love you, Flora." But he had wanted to know if she was his baby. He had said that she was, he wanted her to be. His baby. She sat up straight, but her math teacher's voice was no more intrusive than the sound of a drinking faucet squeaking on and off. She couldn't picture Matthew sitting in a regular class. It was easier to think of him roaming around between the buildings or down the halls, keeping on the move like a cat at night.

He didn't appear in Spanish class. She didn't really think he would. She was there because there was no other place she knew of going without making trouble for herself. She actually found herself listening to Mrs. Moore's melodious voice. It was a relief to hear another language, to hear the sound and not the meaning of the words. If Mrs. Moore sang, her voice would be alto, and her songs would be lullabies for babies who had to go to bed without enough to eat.

When Flora opened her locker she found Tess's books piled on top of her own. She tried to pry several books out from the bottom but they kept catching on the metal rim. Finally she took all of Tess's books out, set them on the floor, and got what she thought she needed. She replaced Tess's books and slammed the locker shut.

She was halfway home before she thought to check her books: she had her Spanish book instead of the algebra book she needed for tomorrow's test, and she had mistaken her Shakespeare book for her history book. She stopped in her tracks and groaned. Just when she was thinking she ought to go back no matter how long it took, a car pulled up to the curb beside her. She started walking again and didn't look at it. Men wearing suits and ties, different men each time, sometimes leaned over and asked her if she needed a ride.

"Do you want a ride?"

She whipped her head around. Matthew was holding his hand up over his eyes and squinting at her.

"Sure," she said without hesitating. She stepped over to his car and took hold of the door handle.

"You'll have to climb in," he said. "That door doesn't work." Flora looked down and saw that it was tied shut with a rope. She climbed into Matthew's roofless car and sat down in its one good bucket seat. Matthew was seated on a sawed-off chair—a straight-backed, weather-worn dining room chair—looking as though nothing were odd about that. He glanced down at the stack of books in her lap. "Got some studying to do?" There was a hint of mockery in his voice.

"Yes, a little . . ." Flora started to say something about a book she needed for a test, but studying didn't seem so important just then. It had never occurred to her that Matthew might have a car, a faded indigo-blue Thunderbird. The sun glanced off its hood and shone in her eyes. She looked out at the familiar houses they were passing. It was a smooth ride. Matthew started to whistle a tune as if to accompany the humming engine, but the breeze in his face hushed him up. He glanced at Flora and turned the corner of the street that ran perpendicular to Jericho.

Flora panicked; she grabbed him by the arm. "I can't let you take me home!"

"Then let's go somewhere else." Matthew sounded decisive.

"No, Matthew, I mean please pull over." She tugged at his arm. He eased to a stop at the curb and waited for her to explain. "I mean, I can't be seen with you."

"You mean we're neighbors who don't know each other?" He watched Flora while she searched for words. "You mean I have to be invisible?"

Flora stared into the gleaming slits of his eyes. "Please, let me tell you." She hesitated, straightened the books on her lap. "My father doesn't want to see me near you." She had to warn Matthew. She had to protect herself, and him. "I guess," she added uneasily, "I'm the one who should be invisible."

Matthew didn't seem to hear her last words. "But he doesn't even know me," he said and looked up into the sky. "We've never even met." He closed his eyes and clenched his teeth.

"He's seen you and that's all he thinks he needs," said Flora, blinking away a tear. She watched him put both his hands on top of his steering wheel. He's afraid even to touch me now, she thought.

"Try not to let it bother you," he said. His eyes opened and he gazed down the street. "We'll work it out."

He sounded valiant now. He looked valiant. Flora leaned over and was about to kiss him when she spotted Janice way up ahead just turning the corner onto Jericho. She didn't dare touch Matthew. She climbed quickly out of his car. "Yes, I'll try. We'll work it out," she said, whisking a tear off her cheek and smiling. She stood for a moment on the curb as Matthew pulled away. She wanted him to look back and see her standing there looking confident, but he didn't.

She felt like dropping her books in the gutter. On the rainy mornings of her grammar school days, before the storm drains had been dug, the streets were flooded with muddy water. She wished she could see those torrents lapping over the curbs now; they would match her mood and maybe help to wash it away.

She broke away from the curb and headed down the sidewalk. She didn't want to go home. Matthew hadn't gone home. He had driven right on past Jericho. When she was younger, her father used to say, "When the real air raid siren goes off, don't crawl under your desk like a nitwit, run home as fast as you can." She was sure now that she would never run home in the event of a nuclear attack. She didn't want to die at home. She'd rather die in a gutter somewhere.

She walked slowly up the driveway and entered the house by the back door. This was one of her father's rules: children must enter by the rear entrance. He was standing with his back to the kitchen sink, gulping a glass of milk. He clanked it down on the tile when she came in. "Just a minute," he ordered. After another gulp, he said, "Where have you been?"

"What?" Flora stood stark still.

"You heard me. Where have you been?" He glowered at her. "Janice has been home for ten minutes already." Flora envisioned Janice sprinting down the street with a great urge to get home.

"I go slower," she dared say. She stepped sideways through the service porch and went on down the hall. She expected to see Janice in their room looking indifferent, but the room was empty. She lay back on the bed and waited. Sure enough, after a minute or so the door was pushed ajar and Henry stood there with his head bobbing slightly as if he had forgotten what it was he wanted to say. Finally, he steadied his eyes upon her. An intense anger mounted in him.

"I warned you not to go near him!" he roared.

Flora thought she was about to be ripped to shreds. She wished she could fly out the window, unscathed.

Henry sucked in air. "You're grounded until I say you're not." He spit that out and pulled the door shut with such force that a puff of cool air was dragged through the window behind Flora.

She sank back and rolled her head from side to side against the bed. "What am I going to do? What am I going to do?" she chanted.

 She remembered her sister and sat up. "And where's that fleet-footed Janice now?"

Half an hour later Janice finally showed up. Flora was still on the bed. "How was your day?" Janice asked pleasantly.

"Fine," returned Flora, flatly, "in some ways." After a long pause, she added, "It took you a long time to get home from school, didn't it?"

"So-so," said Janice, thumbing through one of her textbooks, which had been lying on the desk.

"It looks like your books got home before you did," said Flora.

Janice looked up and saw that Flora was frowning at her stack of books. "I have two sets," she said defensively, patting them. "One for home and one for school."

"Isn't that against school rules?" inquired Flora. She hated being beside the point.

"What's it to you?" said Janice, putting her hands on her hips. "Since when do you follow school rules? Anyway, I don't have to tell you anything."

"That's true," said Flora. "And you never do." She rolled over on their double bed and faced the wall. "I don't have to tell you anything either." She chewed her lip in frustration.

"Whatever," said Janice smugly. She flung open her side of the closet and started hanging up her clothes. "When you're the top honor student"—she was speaking to herself, almost—"you get what you want." She yanked a hanger onto the clothes rod and peeked around at her sister. She got no response. Flora seemed to be dead to the world.

That night, as Flora lay awake beside Janice, she kept thinking she'd give anything to be able to exchange Janice's body for Matthew's: Matthew in a soft bed, between sheets, beside her, on top of her, inside her. She got up and in the dark took care of some unfinished business: she gathered up her books, removed their brown paper covers as quietly as she could, and threw them away—Phil's name, calligraphy and all.

A Mugger

It was a gift, Flora thought, the way Timpanelli kept her classroom open during lunch hour, a gift Flora wasn't sure she now deserved. She was standing several paces from the open door, overcome by uncertainty, her lunch sack in one hand, her hall pass in the other. She felt so foolish. She had intended to have a talk with Timpanelli, confide in her and make some sort of apology. She had imagined it would all go smoothly. Now she couldn't even bring herself to enter the room. She crept up to the doorway and peeked in. She saw no one at the easels, no sign of Matthew. When she dared look toward Timpanelli, she found her engaged in a quiet conference with two boys who looked so young they must have been seventh graders.

As she moped her way to the lunch area, she let the hall pass she was holding, with Timpanelli's signature on it, brush along the hall lockers and deflect off every handle, row after row. She wondered how Timpanelli managed to make contact with so many different people. She thought back to the first class she had taken with her. She'd been given the last available desk, right alongside Timpanelli. To the other side of her was a double desk, and two retarded boys sat there. One was fat and one was thin, and they were both so funny, and serious, and inept. Timpanelli had said, "Don't they remind you a little of Laurel and Hardy?" One had a knack for cutting folded shapes out of tissue paper and making collages, and the other one was tireless in his production of crayon sgraffiti. Flora helped Timpanelli help them. And Timpanelli never said anything bad about any of Flora's efforts. She even praised her junk jewelry mobile and her papier-mâché gazelle. When Timpanelli leafed through her art magazines she showed Flora things she thought were funny, and once they laughed themselves silly after achieving a colorblind rating on a test called "How Sensitive Are You to Colors?" They had worked on it together and in earnest. The test, it turned out, was phony, designed to show how optical tricks can distort color perception. Flora laughed a little even now, remembering. Those were times when even wrongs came out right. Flora continued wandering around the lunch area until the hour was up.

She entered Life Drawing with a crowd and eased past Timpanelli's desk, still too embarrassed to look at her. Timpanelli drew her mouth down like a bulldog's and followed Flora with her eyes. Matthew was still not there. Flora tried to convince herself that it didn't matter; he'd show up when he was ready to. She halted as if she had been lassoed and turned back a little. "Mrs. Timpanelli, may I talk with you after class?"

Timpanelli, with her face back to neutral, nodded slowly and emphatically.

Flora looked to the center of the room. Tess and the swimmer were posing apart. The swimmer was straining to hold the pose he would take on a starting block as he waited for the smack of the gun. Every so often the muscles across his back trembled. Flora sketched a male on the verge of leaping at an unsuspecting female. Tess was turned away. She maintained a striding pose with her face lifted toward the sunny windows. She had the stoical aspect of a figurehead. When the bell rang, she plunged feet first off the edge of the table and walked out of class.

Flora thought she might lose Tess for a friend if she didn't manage to talk with her soon. They hadn't gone anywhere together or had a long talk since the night Matthew whisked Flora away. They avoided each other in dance class, art class, and elsewhere. She would have run and caught up with Tess now, but she needed to talk with Timpanelli too. She looked over at Timpanelli, and Timpanelli widened her eyes. Flora came over clutching her drawing and sat down.

"Let's see your sketch," said Timpanelli right away. Flora hesitated and then unrolled it and handed it to her. Timpanelli held it open at arm's length. "The muscles across the back are well done. There's a strong feeling of spontaneity." She paused. "Looks like someone's about to get mugged, or raped?" She looked at Flora with a screwed-up, questioning face.

"I'm sorry," said Flora. "I feel so sorry about yesterday." She had been saving these words for Timpanelli, out of reverence for her, for a day and a night. She wished she could erase everything that had happened.

"Matthew forced you?" Timpanelli frowned at the drawing and then at Flora.

"No, no, not at all," insisted Flora. Yesterday's embarrassment came back full force. "I mean, I'm sorry for causing *you* trouble."

Timpanelli relaxed back in her chair. "It might easily have been trouble, but it wasn't," she said, still looking at the drawing.

"What's really bothering you? Is it your father?" Flora sighed. "Is he still tearing your pictures off the wall?"

Flora looked over to the easel where she had just been working and then down at her lap. "He seems to be after me all the time. I think he's waiting for me to do something wrong so he'll really have something to get mad at." She took a deep breath. "I don't know what he wants." She pressed her fingers to her eyelids. "I only wanted to apologize to you." She hadn't intended to complain about her father to Timpanelli.

"OK, I accept your apology," said Timpanelli. "Now you don't have to come in here cringing anymore." She raised her hands up beside her face, wiggled her fingers, and pretended to grind her teeth. She didn't make a very mean-looking beast. Flora almost laughed. "All I want you to do is draw, and enjoy it." She looked at Flora's drawing again and then ventured a guess: "Your father doesn't approve of Matthew?"

"My father has never approved of any of my boyfriends. He's never even met Matthew and he detests him." Flora's eyes were becoming dangerously hot again. She hated being such an easy crier, like a full kettle of water over a high flame, always splattering on everything. Once she even ruined a nearly completed watercolor with tears. When she tried to blot them up, she made a bigger mess.

"You've talked to your father about Matthew?"

"No, never!" The suggestion frightened Flora.

Timpanelli began to wonder if Flora wasn't slightly delirious. "Then how does your father know Matthew exists?" She stared closely at Flora and realized that she didn't look delirious, she looked forlorn.

"Because," Flora rolled her eyes, "Matthew lives on the same street as I do, several houses away."

Something between a gag and a chuckle escaped from Timpanelli. "Now *I'm* sorry," she said, giving her head a scratch with the eraser end of her pencil. "Such is life; I guess you'll just have to make do." She rolled up Flora's drawing, bopped her on the head with it, and then handed it back to her.

Flora bit her lower lip and nodded in agreement. Timpanelli's statement, despite its vagueness, had made her feel there was hope for herself and Matthew. "I guess so; I'll try to. Thanks, Mrs. T., for your time."

"For what it's worth, it's yours," said Timpanelli.

Flora tossed her drawing in a trash can and ran to her algebra class. She sat down, caught her breath, and took a test she wasn't entirely prepared for. For some strange reason some of the numbers and signs slid into place, and she felt encouraged enough to struggle with the rest of the problems. She managed to finish before the bell rang, and even had time to chew the eraser off her pencil before she handed in her paper.

She was so glad to have the test behind her that she nearly flew down the six steps from the math class. She was on her way to her next class when someone clutched her about the waist from behind and swung her around. Another student, with a load of books, had to dodge her flying feet.

"Put me down!" she cried. Matthew let go of her. He looked pleased with himself.

"What are you doing tonight?" he said. "Do you want to go dancing?" He took her hand and kissed the back of it. "I mean, I'm aware that I cannot come to your door," he added with mock seriousness. "However—"

"Matthew, I can't go out with you." Flora interrupted him with a pained expression. She pulled her hand away from him and started walking.

"I was going to say, I know of a way." Matthew kept in stride with her.

"My father knows I've been near you—*near* you." She looked away from him so he wouldn't see her distorted face. "He says I'm grounded." The anger she had for her father made her feel tight and tearless.

Matthew stuck his hands in his pockets and cast a critical glance at the sky. Small clouds were scattered all about. "For how long?" he asked.

"He didn't say. I guess he doesn't know yet." Flora glanced at Matthew and saw that his jaw was clenched. A moment ago he was swinging her in his arms. Now he had his hands in his pockets and seemed to be singling out a far cloud, looking as if he wanted to yank it from the sky. They were about to cross one of the main paths. She took a look down it and saw Tess walking toward them. Phil was at her side. Flora jerked her eyes away and she and Matthew continued down the path toward their Spanish class.

"Well," said Matthew. He looked at his feet as he walked along. His face had softened. "When your father decides you've been a good girl long enough, I'll send my chauffeur to your door." He winked at Flora.

Matthew was not one to give up. She felt a shiver of happiness mixed with apprehension. She wondered who would act as Matthew's chauffeur this time. She pictured wild-haired Clinton knocking at her front door. "I hope he'll look . . ."—she tried to find the right words—"like someone my father won't be suspicious of."

"Like the boy next door," said Matthew.

The Clay Ballerina

In the Jackson kitchen no one sat at the head of the table. There wasn't room for such an arrangement. If anything, the refrigerator had the place of honor. At dinner on Friday Henry refused to look at or address Flora, as if by ignoring her he could draw her more tightly into the family. They sat across from each other like strangers in a cafeteria.

Flora vowed she'd never say the name Matthew in front of her father. She would not talk to him about anything. She would not ask him for anything. She would not request to be ungrounded. She would wait for him to say she could go out again.

Her love for Matthew put her in a bubble of calm, but it did not seal her from the troubles around her. It magnified them. She saw her mother offering and reoffering food. She saw her brother and sisters squabbling.

Daniel, who was humiliated by the crew-cut Henry had just forced him to get, was scoffing at Julia. "She just took more potatoes when she still has a pile on her plate."

Julia stopped eating, her mouth open wide. She hated coming home when her mother wasn't there. She hated Henry for forbidding her afternoon snacks, for his keen ear and the way the doors on the food cabinets squeaked, for the way he sometimes even stood guard in the kitchen. She was nine years old, but they called her the baby, and that was what she felt like: a big, plump, unfed baby.

"Shut up, bristlehead," she said. "You're the one who drank a Coke on the way home from school."

"I did not," protested Daniel.

"You wanna bet?" said Julia, full of scorn. Her face was as pink as bubble gum.

"Will you two be quiet," snapped Janice. She turned back to Marleen. "I don't know how you could've forgotten. I told you about it more than once." She was exasperated because Marleen had forgotten to give her a check to pay for her class photos and senior album. "I was supposed to have it today!"

Henry finally yelled, "Shut up!" And then in a quieter voice he added, "If you don't have something nice to say, don't say it at all." Everyone had heard that saying so often it sickened them.

"Please," said Marleen, "let's just eat," and she passed Julia a bowl of peas and corn, which Julia frowned at. Marleen was the only one in the family who tried to keep a semblance of peace. Flora wasn't so sure that was a virtue. Sometimes she wished her mother would give up the constant mending and let everything fall apart at the seams.

After dinner Janice made a big show of preparing for the Friday night dance. She stayed in the shower for half an hour and then ran back and forth between the bathroom and the bedroom a dozen times. She even dried herself in the bedroom as if she were trying to rub something in.

Flora refused to feel left out. She had no desire to go to the school dance. She lay back on the bed and watched Janice's performance. There was a long phase of dressing and undressing and redressing. Clothes were flung every which way. She had nowhere to go to get away from this flurry of activity. The phone rang, but someone answered it after one and a half rings.

Janice snatched up her purse, reached down and shoved a dresser drawer closed. Is this a properly dressed Girls' Dress Board member? wondered Flora. She could see Janice's garter clasps when she bent over. Flora couldn't resist; she had to say it: "Don't let anyone look up your skirt." Janice's face gathered itself into an instant snub as she pulled the door closed. Flora thought it had to be her most essential expression, as predictable as the way a sea anemone puckers in when probed by a human finger.

Once alone, Flora wanted only to think of Matthew. The rest of the family must be in the living room, settled into a truce. All was quiet except for sudden bursts of laughter from a remote audience. She got the impression her parents and brother and sister were performing a clever pantomime before an amused crowd. Before there was any final applause, the channels on the TV set were flipped and then she heard the whizzing and blasting of bombs and the hammering racket of machine guns. Henry's favorite Friday evening show was well under way. She got up, turned off the overhead light, and fell back on the bed.

Try as she might, she couldn't get close to Matthew. She had no trouble conjuring up a distinct image of him, but as a picture in still water is disrupted by the toss of a pebble, when she touched him he shattered into a million fragments. She pictured him perched on the rail outside a hall, but as she stepped up to him, he dissolved. She directed him to drive down the street in his indigo Thunderbird while she stood at the curb and waited for him to see her, which he surely would, and pull over. When he passed by, he might as well have been going a thousand miles an hour; he and his car were no more than a streak of blue light. She placed a small figure of him on his own porch steps, too far away to do anything but wave. She waved at him, and he almost waved back, but changed his mind, got up and went into his house.

Flora sighed with frustration, rolled over face down on her bed, and Matthew made a surprise appearance. He was leaning against the door of the washroom, smiling at her. He was so close she stopped breathing. She didn't dare wish to hold him for fear of sending him away. She waited to see what *he* would do. He got blurry, and the harder she looked, the better he blended into the chaotic colors of the walls. She forced herself to look away, and when she looked back again, he was perfectly camouflaged. He might as well have been part of a well-worked palette of paint.

It was no use. Knowing that Henry could fling the door open at any moment, she could not hold Matthew close to her. So Friday night went on and on and she did nothing but lie on her bed and listen to the sounds and the movements of her family: Marleen sorting dirty laundry for tomorrow, the toilet flushing, Daniel complaining that Julia was always shoving his stuff way back under his bed like it was trash. Henry must have stayed in the living room. No one checked on her. She got up once and changed into her nightgown.

When it was pitch black outside, and everyone else had finally bedded down (even Janice had come home and was breathing deeply), Flora began dreading time. She wished the night, the entire weekend, would devour itself and disappear. She wanted to see Matthew again, for real. A cool breeze came in through the window and she didn't crank the window shut. She looked up and watched the pale curtains puff in and out as if they were having trouble breathing. Every so often they parted enough to reveal a sliver of starry sky.

She woke late on Saturday morning. Everybody was up and about and grumbling. Henry was giving out orders for the day. The tile around the bathtub needed scouring. The picture window had to be washed. It was covered with flyspecks. The front door was covered with fingerprints, dirty fingerprints. He toured the house, his own fingers creeping over every surface. Flora could see them moving like tentacles as she sat in her bed amidst a tussle of sheets. Janice had hung up all of her rejected clothes. She was saying, "Yeah, yeah, yeah, when I get around to it," to Henry from the kitchen. Marleen's voice was missing completely. She must have already left for the laundromat. The vacuum cleaner went on. Maybe Henry is pretending I'm not here, Flora conjectured. She dressed quickly and snuck out of the house. Daniel was out back, watering the canned plants. Henry was pointing to a kink in the hose. She got a box and a rake and went to the front yard. At least he couldn't criticize her for the way the leaves fell.

There weren't too many. She raked up two small piles and was bending over to pick up the second one before she snuck a sideways look up the block. She didn't see Matthew. She took a few more glances, but he was never there. She began to feel there was nothing she could predict or count upon. Her thoughts stopped there and she focused on the sight and the sound of her rake ringing in the sparse grass, the way it grasped at and missed, grasped at and caught, the dead leaves.

The side gate clanked and Daniel came around with a smudged and blank face. He walked across the driveway with his empty hands swaying before him like a chimp's and disappeared into the gaping entrance of the garage. Flora got into her half-filled box of leaves and stomped on them. So much for modern dance.

Tess saw Flora entering the front gate on Monday morning and strutted up to her. "What's with you?" she said, more puzzled than annoyed. "I called your house Friday night to see if you wanted a ride to the dance, and your father said you were indisposed. Then he hung up on me!"

"I've been grounded for a while," said Flora. She hoped this would curb Tess's agitation.

"Oh, that's just fine. What did you do, break a dish?" said Tess in her old familiar way. They walked together in the direction of their locker.

Flora didn't want to lie. "No, I accepted a ride home from school with a stranger, and my father found out and got upset. That's all."

"That's all, you say. Really, Flora, you're just asking for it." Tess twisted the combination lock on their locker back and forth and back again with three precise jerks and then flung the door open so hard that it bounced off the locker next to it and shut itself. Flora watched while she did the combination all over again.

Lots of boys asked Tess out and she usually turned them down. She preferred the freedom she had when she drove her parents' car on the weekends. Maybe she's mad, thought Flora, because she can't count on me to go cruising with her anymore. But that can't be it. Tess knows plenty of other girls. She never has to go anyplace alone unless she wants to.

Flora wanted to be Tess's best friend, but that meant sharing secrets, and she was afraid to do that. If Tess had been raised in *her* family, she'd understand, Flora was sure, how a person could be slow to reveal her feelings.

Tess grabbed some books out of their locker and turned around. "I can't believe you dumped Phil for that gypsy jerk!" Her eyes were narrowed.

Flora bumped back against a locker, and Tess stomped away without waiting for a response. Flora recalled how she had come to meet Phil in the first place—an unexpected shove. Maybe she was disrupting some grand plan of Tess's. "I'm sorry, but I never was in love with Phil," she called after Tess, but Tess didn't bother to turn around.

There, Flora told herself, I've confided something to her and what good does it do? Flora was in a foul, choked-up mood. She knew she hadn't really confided anything to Tess; she had treated her like a stranger. She and Phil were like strangers, too. If they bumped into each other in the halls now, they'd say no more than "Excuse me." She wanted both Phil and Tess to be her friends, and they had become nearly the opposite of that. She felt a long, complicated explanation was needed. But whenever she pictured herself approaching them, with so much to say, no words would come out. The words were in there, but it was like trying to shake coins out of the top of a piggy bank.

Matthew was the only person she knew who could get words out of her when he wanted them. He'd never walk away from her and leave himself guessing. Her bad temper fell away. With him words could come forth smoothly, like drawings in oil pastels.

She wondered if it would be so easy to communicate with him

 if they didn't share a love of drawing. She skirted a group of laughing boys and thought of Floyd, of how he used to make her laugh. Then her heart took a sudden dip: Floyd was gone. She walked down the hall and everyone seemed to be coming at her. "A humorous person," Floyd once told her, "is one who is willing to stick his neck out," and he handed her a cartoon of his own face with his neck winding all over the paper, exposing itself to all sorts of peril: saws, daggers, bear traps, train tracks, the jaws of mad dogs, whips, ripe tomatoes, hypodermic needles, and even possible strangulation on account of its own tendency to get knotted up, indicated by an arrow pointing to a bad tangle. Flora took a deep, defiant breath. She resolved to be more open. Anyone passing her at that moment might have thought they had offended her in some way.

She sat down in her first class of the morning, American history. The teacher, a thin woman named Miss Corbie, was myopic, and nearly everyone joked about it. They called her the Bug Woman. She wore thick glasses and almost had to touch her nose to the blackboard in order to read anything she'd written there. You'd think she'd want to encourage class discussions and give oral exams. But no, all her tests were multiple choice, true and false, and fill-ins—blurred and blotchy purple print on slick paper with that sweet poison smell. Flora wondered how Miss Corbie managed to correct them all. She'd even pick up a piece of chalk from the blackboard ledge and hold it in front of her face just to make sure it was really a piece of chalk. Some of Flora's classmates never failed to laugh at this. Even Floyd, who had Miss Corbie the year before and had drawn a Bug Woman caricature, said, "If she'd develop a knack for feeling the identity of things like blind people do, she wouldn't attract so much cruel laughter." Flora was glad Miss Corbie kept trying to use her eyes. She found herself straining to see for Miss Corbie.

Second period, Flora had a class in Shakespeare with Mr. Langtry. He was the only teacher she knew of who had a podium, and with his zest for speaking, he deserved one. He used it so well —tipping and swaying it this way and that, gripping it intensely, shaking it. He looked like a classical bust on a pedestal set in motion. It often seemed that he would topple over, but he never did. Instead of reading along in her own textbook as Mr. Langtry recited, Flora watched him. She found him attractive, strange to say, since his face in itself wasn't all that pleasing to look at. It was deeply cracked, and the skin beneath his eyes looked as though it were crumbling away. And if anyone had a seat to the front and side, as Flora did, they'd only have to take a peek around the podium to see that Mr. Langtry's gray suit pants were wrinkled and the cuffs were too long, soiled at the back edges. His unpolished black boots were worn way down on the outside edges of the heels. Yet his eyes were ablaze with interest and his voice sang Shakespeare. He moved easily back and forth between the characters of Othello and Iago—just one person doing a duet, inviting the class to be the chorus. Even his grizzly head of billowing hair looked charged with inspiration. At night, whenever Flora read Shakespeare, she heard Mr. Langtry's voice inside her head, shaking life into every line.

Her third class of the day, chemistry, left her cold. The teacher, Mr. Whitney, was a tall, slim man with an oily gray complexion and a mustache like a scrub brush. His face looked like a piece of raw asbestos. He often presented himself to the class in a knee-length white cotton coat and stood in front of his desk with one side of his mustache bent upward, smirking indignantly. He spent the first portion of every period insulting his students. He assigned seats not alphabetically but according to some far-fetched system based on the periodic table. After every test he shifted almost everyone around. It was as if he were using them as markers and playing some kind of game only chemists know about. He had recently switched Flora away from a group of students who shared one of the lab counters, a section he dubbed the rare earth elements, to the rear of a row of regular desks, saying, "You are now antimony, Sb, a brittle metal."

As the weeks passed, he selected his elite students and held them in a cluster around his own desk—his inner shell of electrons. They had the refinished desks, the few the custodian delivered to the classroom at the start of each semester. Flora's desktop was so marred it looked like the surface of Mars, scored with canals this way and that. For a smooth writing surface, she used the cover of her notebook. Midway through the last exam, Mr. Whitney stood over her, stroking his mustache with his red plastic ruler. When she looked up, he swiped her test paper out from under her hand and crumpled it into a tight ball. He grinned down at her notebook. "This desk is too rough to write on," she explained. He gave her a look like, What do you expect?, picked up her notebook and tossed it on the floor at her feet, strolled back to his desk, dropped her half-completed exam in the wastepaper basket, and returned with a fresh copy, which he presented to her as if it were a gracious offering. As he strolled back to his desk again, a little acidy voice in Flora's head said, "Thank you, Master Molecule." She was glad she sat at the back of the class, as far away from him as she could be. When the bell rang, she got out of his room as if the real air raid siren had gone off.

Nevertheless, this was the class she studied for the most. Chemistry was Janice's favorite subject, the subject Henry judged their future well-being upon, the first grade he checked at report card time. Janice's grade had always been an A, and Flora's never was. "It's so simple," insisted Janice. "I wish I had it now instead of physics." Before the Christmas break, Mr. Whitney had given Flora her lowest grade, a C–. "C minus, as in Santa Claus on a sled," he said with a swagger of his head.

Before lunch, Flora had Pazetti's modern dance class with Tess and about fifty other girls. Tess and Flora used to work out all of their dances together, the two of them alone or within a larger group of five or six girls. There was never any arguing, any misunderstandings. What anybody had in mind could be visibly demonstrated. Sometimes they tried for moves beyond their ability and fell flat, but alterations were made until finally a dance was pieced together, and then they practiced over and over until they couldn't wait to perform it for Pazetti and the rest of the class.

Pazetti always complimented all her girls after a performance. Every time Flora reached the end of a routine, upon hearing Pazetti's praise, she'd flash back to the same image: a clay ballerina that she had made as a child. She had spent an entire afternoon working on it. At the last minute she embedded transparent seed beads all over the tutu and used them in the eyes too. After that was done, she stuck toothpicks in the toes of the toe shoes and stood the ballerina on a clay pedestal, placed the pedestal on a Little Golden Book, and went from the bedroom to the doorway of the kitchen by taking small shuffling steps. But before she could make an announcement, the ballerina fell over backward and flattened out like a cookie on a cookie sheet. Marleen looked up from her sewing machine and said, "It's just beautiful."

Pazetti, as usual, glided into the dance room, as if on the tips of her toes. She wanted to direct the class in limbering and balancing exercises. She flexed her tight little figure and bobbed up and down, eager for everyone's attention. Flora took a place next to Tess with the intention of saying something nice.

"I'm sorry about this morning," she said, bending toward Tess. "I really don't know what I did that got you so worked up."

Tess acted like she was trying to pull a tendon. She refused to look Flora in the face, so Flora decided to concentrate on her own muscles for a while. Pazetti's voice kept fading in and out.

Matthew leapt into Flora's head as if he had been given a stage cue to appear. He danced around her, behaving like a sprite. Flora found him both alluring and amusing—it was so strange to see him looking like an airy figure from one of his own drawings, or one of hers. When Pazetti told the class to stand up, Flora wanted to remain lying down. She kept hesitating and was out of sync with the others. When she did jump up, her head lagged behind with Matthew. Pazetti gave her a scolding look.

Flora could barely wait to peel off her leotard and get back into her clothes. She was anxious to get to Timpanelli's class. It had been a long weekend, and the morning had seemed to be standing still at times. She didn't bother to roll up her skirt.

Charcoal Slashes

"What's for lunch?" asked Timpanelli. She was, strangely, free of guests. Flora veered over and sat down by her.

"Crayons, I guess," said Flora. She hadn't eaten a crayon in years, and yet she could still taste them.

"You must get a little faint by sixth period," said Timpanelli, resting her chin in one hand. Flora felt herself smiling out of one side of her mouth, the way Matthew often did.

"I eat my lunch on the way home from school." After that she didn't know what to say. She crossed her arms lamely over her lap and looked at Timpanelli's desk. Timpanelli's brown lunch sack was lying there like an unopened baked potato.

Timpanelli didn't say anything. Flora knew Matthew was over there, at his easel. Timpanelli was watching him, daring her to have a look, too. Flora turned her eyes slowly, and then her head. His posture made an elegant profile. He looked so relaxed and at the same time so determined: leaning back on his stool, bracing himself with one hand, with one foot propped on the lowest rung, his drawing arm extending straight out and his head jutting forward. All his attention was aimed, thought Flora, like a beam of light on the line he was drawing. She felt she should leave him alone, not bother him. An unexpected sigh escaped from her.

Timpanelli swayed toward Flora and with a little confidential shake of the head said, "Get to work, Flora. Don't waste your time being intimidated." Flora rose up out of the chair. She felt a hand was at her back, gently urging her to join Matthew. It had been a long time since she'd been near him. He seemed like an outsider, a newcomer, someone she should introduce herself to.

Matthew grabbed her hair at the back of the neck, leaned over and gave her a hard kiss on the lips. Timpanelli opened her roll book and searched the list for students who hadn't turned in their anatomy assignments.

"It's lonely without you," said Flora. She watched the pencil twiddle between his fingers.

"We're big people now, try to keep your pants on." Matthew spoke in the tone of a preoccupied parent. He kept himself from smiling as he lifted his pencil to his drawing.

Flora didn't know how to respond. Even though she was pretty sure he was teasing, she felt as if he had pushed her away. And now he was concentrating on his drawing again as if she weren't even there. She looked at what he was doing: lines, with almost no shading, of two figures, one superimposed on the other. It was impossible to tell who was in front of or behind who, or who was on the top and who was on the bottom. The two figures shared many lines.

"Do you like it?" said Matthew. He continued to draw.

"Well, yes," said Flora. She looked more closely. She wondered if she should tell him she thought it was a bit confusing. She looked up. Tess stood cool and inert, as if she had been sculpted out of marble. She reminded Flora of the story of the statue that came to life, the sculptor loved it so much. Flora shuddered as though the temperature in the room had abruptly dropped. This was the lunch hour. Tess should be out roving around. She was never in Timpanelli's room during lunch—never until now.

"Matthew." She called his name in a whisper, as if he were so far away it would be useless to cry out.

"What is it?" he asked. "Draw me something." He didn't take his eyes off his drawing.

"But Matthew, what is Tess doing here now?" She needed to know immediately.

"Trying to lose weight, I guess," Matthew commented blandly, as if there were nothing unusual about Tess's being there. "You'd know sooner than me," he added and bent closer to his easel. "I thought she was a friend of yours."

"She is . . . I think." Flora saw that there was a clean sheet of paper tacked to her easel. Matthew must have put it there. She looked around the room. Other people were working quietly at their easels. She pulled her pencil out of her coat pocket and started sketching Tess just as she felt Tess looked that very moment. The white winter light spread itself evenly throughout the room and made Tess's body shadowless. Only her curving silhouette stood out against the row of gleaming windows. Flora thought of the alabaster statuette, the base of the lamp Matthew was sitting next to at that party. She had enjoyed recalling this scene, but now she wasn't so sure she wanted to see him sitting in the light of that lamp anymore.

They are never jealous
Because of the cause,
But jealous because they are jealous,
It's a monster begot upon itself,
Born on itself.

When Mr. Langtry had scrawled those lines on the blackboard, Flora had puzzled over them. Now they made perfect sense. When she finished drawing the female statue, she drew a vicious-looking dragon. He swooped down from a high horizon line and swung his scaly body around her feet. His head reared up, and his mouth, crowded with pointed teeth, was open wide as if he couldn't wait to devour her.

Matthew had started a new drawing. He was no longer looking at Tess. He was glancing at Flora every so often, and when he drew, his eyes were nearly shut. They looked like charcoal slashes. Tess, after shifting in and out of several reclining positions, settled into one that looked like a mermaid lazily seated on a stone watching for ships. Halfway through the hour, Timpanelli made a tour of the class. As she approached Matthew and Flora, they stepped back from their drawings. She looked closely at each. "You two are beyond repair." She spoke in a mock mad undertone and moved away.

Flora swiped a glance at Matthew's drawing and was struck by the sight of her own face.

"I hope it doesn't offend you?" said Matthew.

"No," said Flora, "not at all." What she saw was a refined, ethereal version of herself. Her eyes shone in shades of green oil pastel and her wispy hair was singed all around with a lavender aura. She felt he made her look a little crazed, a little too much in love, as if she might leap out at him. "I hope I can live up to it," she said, blushing. Then she remembered her own drawing and wanted to hide the sight of her ugly dragon.

"This is wonderful," said Matthew, bending toward her easel, and then with feigned distaste he added, "but it's not very pleasant."

Flora felt her own face copying his, shifting like his from a frown to a smile. He made her feel it was all right, anything she felt like drawing was all right. As she softened a few lines on her dragon, she envisioned a different scene: wildflowers winding around the base of a statue, a goddesslike figure holding up the ball of the moon.

The bell rang. She wished she could take Matthew's hand and run with him through open fields. Or just walk with him arm in arm, in broad daylight, and let any eyes that cared to, look. But she balked. That wasn't their way. Their love had sprung from concrete gullies and linoleum floors. It took shelter in dilapidated rooms and traveled unseen along the sidewalks between school and home. She laid her pencil on the easel ledge and took down her drawing. It only runs inside dreams and dances on sheets of sketch paper, she thought. It rests like dust on a shelf in the dark.

"I'm not going to Spanish class," said Matthew. "I'll see you tomorrow." He gave the rolled drawing in his hand a quick kiss and waved good-bye to her with it.

Tomorrow, thought Flora. It had a name like Tuesday or Wednesday, but it looked like a dense cloud. She stood there and felt most of herself trail after him.

When she got home she searched through her dresser drawers for the folded piece of paper she had tucked away. "Nothing is safe, nothing is safe," she kept saying, and yet there it was. She unfolded it and saw the dark eyes, the vague outline of Matthew's face, a trace of his lips. "I don't think I can stand it," she said, addressing the drawing in a whisper. He stared back at her with unbending certitude. Not even the paper crease along the right side of his nose and another one over his brows could spoil the expression. She refolded the drawing and slipped it in with the others beneath stacks of old school papers and behind boxes of puzzles on the shelf in the closet.

Henry wasn't home. Where he was she didn't know or care. Marleen was typing in an office somewhere. Everyone else was gone. The clock on the desk made an unkind, electronic click and hummed for a moment. She sank onto her bed and Matthew came to her in such a sharp image it was as if he had lain down beside her. When she turned toward him, he guided her hand and she climaxed abruptly. Then he vanished. His weight and his heat dissolved and she lay still, too much aware of every little sound and sight—the smudges around the light switch by the door, the creak of the electrical lines that were attached to the eaves outside the window. She had never done such a thing before. It was an incredible discovery. But one person alone shouldn't be able to create such a sensation, she thought in protest. It should be able to happen only when two people who are in love join together.

Janice barged into the room with an armload of books. "Hi, Flora," she said as though she were surprised and thrilled to find her there.

"Hi, Janice." Flora imitated her tone.

"You spend more time on your back than anyone I know," said Janice.

"I hope you don't lose any sleep over it," Flora responded carelessly and rolled over on her belly.

"What's with you?" said Janice. She looked helpless.

Over the years, they had practiced insulting each other so often that by now the insults settled easily over every attempted conversation like salty dew on metal. Any politeness they started out with quickly turned mean, and neither of them ever bothered to polish things up with an apology.

After dinner Flora climbed back onto the bed with her thick blue volume of Shakespeare. She flipped to *Othello,* Act II. "Bless'd pudding! Didst thou not see her paddle with the palm of his hand?" Mr. Langtry's voice wasn't coming through easily. "Didst not mark that?" *Rod.:* "Yes, that I did; but that was but courtesy." Her eyes kept skipping off the page, over to Janice, who was hunching over a book, reading with her pointer finger, shuffling papers, erasing madly, scribbling rapidly, as if she were in a race to discover something. This was her own sister; they shared the same room, the same bed even. Janice was the one person in the world she had a real opportunity to share her thoughts with, and yet they rarely spoke unless it was to annoy each other. They had seldom gotten together about anything as far back as she could remember. They couldn't even dress dolls together without bickering.

Janice huffed, slapped one book shut and reached for another. Flora looked back to her book. *Emil.:* "How do you, madam? How do you, my good lady?" *Des.:* "Faith, half asleep." *Emil.:* "Good madam, what's the matter with my lord?" Flora wished she were down the street sharing a bedroom with Matthew. *Des.:* "With who?" *Emil.:* "Why, with my lord, madam." *Des.:* "Who is thy lord?" *Emil.:* "He that is yours, sweet lady." *Des.:* "I have none." But what did she really know about Matthew? What did Desdemona know about Othello?

She turned another page and felt her menstrual cramps coming on: a hot pain that ducked in and out and crept after her like a crazy man in an alley. She knew the pain would throw itself upon her; it was only a matter of minutes. She went into the bathroom to wash off the grime of the day and prepare herself for the onslaught. She saw herself in the mirror. It wasn't what Matthew's drawing of her had looked like. Was there some distortion in the mirror? She looked so wide-eyed and stupid, so puffy and fleshy and painful, like a retarded boy she'd seen get hit with a softball once. Once was enough. She shook her head in dismay and returned to the bedroom, put on her nightgown, and slipped under the covers.

"What?" piped Janice, when she turned around and saw Flora curled up beneath the blankets. "Giving up so soon?"

"I've got cramps." Flora's muffled voice barely sounded through the covers but Janice understood her.

"Oh," she said, and returned to her calculations. It was a simple answer, one Janice could easily accept.

An hour or two later, when Janice finally came to bed, Flora turned over and stared at the gray ceiling. "Have you ever been in love with anyone?" Flora's voice sounded far away, even to herself.

"I'm so tired," drawled Janice.

"Please, Janice, just tell me that."

Janice's yawn turned into an irritated sigh. "Where have you been? I've been dating John Tucker for months."

"Yes, but are you in love with him?" Flora tried to urge her on.

"Are *you* in love with Phil Ridley?" retorted Janice. She flipped onto her back and scrunched up her pillow.

"No. I'm not even going out with him," replied Flora without a note of regret.

"Of course not, you're grounded." Janice felt like she was wasting her sleep time.

"I wouldn't be dating him even if I wasn't grounded." Flora drew her knees up to her chest as a big cramp came over her.

"What are you trying to tell me, Flora?" Janice's voice was awake with its usual sternness. "Would you like to blame *me* for something?" She raised herself up on one elbow. It was too dark to see her face.

"No," Flora protested. "I'm just saying that I never did love Phil."

"Whose fault is that!" Janice flopped back down.

"Nobody's." Flora felt frustrated. She couldn't believe how fast her words had been run into a ditch. "I just . . . Oh, forget it." She pressed her forehead against the cool plaster of the wall. She just wanted to tell Janice she was in love with someone, and she wanted to say who it was. But that was a crazy idea, trying to confide in Janice. It might even be a dangerous idea.

"It's too late to talk," mumbled Janice, and she fell asleep in less than a minute.

Flora propped her feet up on the wall. She stood on her head. She tried the position grammar school children were supposed to take during air raid drills. She got out of bed and curled up on the floor. She crawled around on the hemp squares. She got up and sat in the desk chair and pretended she was Janice, a person who seemed to feel no pain. After a while she got back into bed and listened to Janice snore.

No use. She got up again and wandered into the kitchen. She filled a glass of water at the sink. At the corner of the window the half-moon showed itself, crisscrossed by bare branches. She returned to the afternoon, when Matthew lay breathing beside her. He was solid and she had held him, felt the tendons in his hands.

When the half-moon had risen above the housetops, Matthew took a kitchen chair out onto his front porch, put one foot up against a roof post, and sat there for a long time, tipping back and forth slowly. He watched the moonlight quiver in the limbs of the leafless plum trees and cast shaky shadows across the lawn. He watched lights going off at random up and down Jericho. Finally the Jacksons' house went black. He wanted to go to Flora's room, travel invisibly up the moonlit sidewalk, silently jump over her side gate, come in through her window . . . But that was just crazy thinking. When the damp chill of the night seeped in through his sweater, he got up and took his chair back inside the house.

In the morning Flora didn't feel like going to school. Always before, she had managed to make it, bearing her cramps or her indigestion like a hidden bulging satchel. She had thought it was her duty to go. But this morning she asked herself why. Why should she go? What was the worth of it? She went to the kitchen in her nightgown.

"I don't feel like going to school today," she said flatly.

"What's wrong?" Marleen, in her fright, nearly flung a plate of toast on the floor.

"Nothing, just cramps."

"Oh," said Marleen blankly. She seemed to be recalling something. After a pause and renewed fright, she said, "But what shall I tell your father?" She stood gaping at Flora.

"Tell him I'm bleeding to death," said Flora. She had considered that she would be forfeiting a chance to see Matthew if she stayed home, but she had forgotten who she'd be staying home with.

"Oh, Flora," said Marleen imploringly. She didn't want Flora to mean what she was saying.

Flora slumped down in a kitchen chair. She picked up a spoon beside a bowl and laid it straight. "Forget it," she said. "I'm going to school."

Matthew wasn't in school that day. It's just as well, she thought. She returned home feeling faint and feverish. She sat down at her vanity and pushed her tennis shoes off. She couldn't understand how Matthew could be absent one day and back again the next, acting as if he'd been there all along. He didn't seem to be conscious of his own being, his own whereabouts. As long as he was drawing, nothing seemed to matter to him. Then, just to prove he knew exactly where he was and what he was doing, he'd glance over and give her a wink. Flora looked in the vanity mirror and gave herself a slow wink.

Julia slipped quietly into the room and squeezed herself between the dresser and the vanity so that she was facing Flora.

"Hi," said Flora.

"Hi," said Julia. She gave Flora a careful smile.

"Aren't there any cartoons on?" Flora watched Julia twine the hair at the side of her neck.

"Yes, but . . . um," she said, starting to rearrange the miniature perfume bottles on the vanity, "but, um, I was wondering, will I have very bad cramps, do you think?" Flora's eyes wandered down from Julia's innocent face to her round little belly. "Janice says her pains are a lot worse than yours," Julia added, wrinkling up her nose.

"Oh well." Flora squirmed a little on the vanity stool, and sighed. "Then maybe yours will be a lot less than mine."

"I sure hope so," said Julia. Then she heard the theme song for Felix the Cat and bounded out of the room.

Even though her cramps and fever were gone by the next morning, Flora decided to stay home. As Janice closed the door to their room, she gave Flora a look that said something like, We'll just see how long you get away with this one. Flora wondered why she had ever imagined she could explain anything to Janice.

That night she heard her father complaining deeply as he lay in bed, and then her mother telling him, "Well, she just doesn't feel well. It's female problems."

Henry didn't open Flora's door the next day, or the day after that either, and those two days disappeared as she wanted them to, like dust and lint sucked up in a vacuum cleaner. She studied for the classes that went on without her. For the first time during the semester, she read through an entire chemistry chapter and felt she understood it, in a way. It had to do with oxidation-reduction equations, and she thought of it as pouring a concoction back and forth between two test tubes until they were perfectly balanced.

She would have liked to have gone out for a walk, but she was supposed to be cramped up and not merely depressed. If she had come out of her room for anything other than the essentials, she would have given Henry all the provocation he needed to start harassing her. Instead, she lay on the bed most of the time. She finished reading *Othello,* and did several sketches of Matthew and herself together—very short-lived works that she reduced to confetti and threw away.

Late Friday afternoon, Marleen peeked into the bedroom. Janice was smoothing out a sweater on the dresser top, and Flora was standing on the bed straightening some bird pictures. "I just wanted to tell you, Flora, your father says you're no longer grounded." Flora wondered what she was supposed to do now: levitate until she hit the ceiling; put an ad in the *Valley Green Sheet* for a date? "He says you can go out tonight if you want to," Marleen added, trying to make everything seem pleasant. No doubt she had worked hard to procure this probation for Flora.

"Thanks, Mom." Flora tried to sound appreciative.

Janice couldn't get her sweater pulled over her head fast enough. She gave Flora a scornful look and swung around toward Marleen. "Why would Flora want to go anywhere? She's sick."

"I think we all know Flora hasn't been very happy lately," said Marleen.

Janice snatched her brush from the vanity and started brushing her hair vigorously as if she had fleas. "And I guess everyone else is jumping up and down for joy? We're *all* so happy." She gave her hair a final swipe and pushed past Marleen.

"Where are you going?" Marleen called after her as she tore down the hall.

"To the basketball game. I'm walking."

Janice slammed the front door, and from the kitchen Henry yelled, "Hey!"

Marleen turned back to Flora. "She shouldn't be doing that, should she? It's almost dark out." She looked worried.

"I don't know, Mom. I guess she knows what she's doing."

Marleen sighed and went away.

Flora decided to give their bedroom a cleaning. Mainly she was in the mood to discard something. She looked in the desk drawer for things to throw away. All she found was a fistful of pitifully short, eraserless pencils, some broken rubber bands, several crooked paper clips, and then, way in the back, a crumpled piece of paper. She smoothed it out and through all the corrections she read:

Dear John,

How dare you tell anyone I've got a crush on Mr. Hansen. That's really sick! He's old enough to be my father. Don't you think I've got any feelings?!

This doesn't have anything to do with Jill Buckley. You can go out with her every day of the week for all I care and that won't make me love you any less.

I Love You Forever,

Janice

More words were scratched and scribbled out than were left intact. It looked as though a couple of alley cats had fought over it. Flora crumpled the paper up again. She stuffed it back in the drawer just as she had found it. Her heart was racing. "Geez, Janice," she said aloud.

She went to the closet and pulled down stacks of old notebooks and school folders from the high shelf. She sat on the floor with the wastepaper basket at her side and started sorting through school lessons that went all the way back to kindergarten. Why should she save examples of her early attempts to form letters, she asked herself, such large, clumsy shapes struggling along between wide-ruled lines? MY DOG HAS BIG EARS. MY CAT IS SOFT. She never had a dog. She had a stray cat for a day, but it was so infested with fleas that she tried to vacuum it, and it ran away. Over and over again, she came across her name spelled with the *F* facing backward. What did she need to be reminded of all this for? Why would anyone want to hold on to such incriminating stuff? She stuck the entire pile in the wastepaper basket. She did the same with dozens of book reports that all began with "I like this book because . . . ," first checking the end of each report to see if she had attached an extra-credit illustration. Some of these drawings she placed on a stack with other pictures she had done as a child. She enjoyed looking back through these beginning drawings. They were as simple as the book reports, but they contained no hint of a painful struggle. She discarded masses of exams in every subject; they were only an indication that she had attended school. The only thing that went back up on the shelf was the stack of early artwork, and behind that a collection of her more recent attempts—most of the drawings she had done while standing beside Matthew. She missed him so much she didn't want to think about it.

By the light of the moon, she shouldered the wastepaper basket and went out to the back fence. When she up-ended the basket, all the pages of scribbling landed with a heavy flop on the contents of a half-filled trash can. Then unexpectedly there came a gentle fluttering-down of confetti. These were the fragments of Matthew's body and hers, torn to bits as a security measure. Every little piece of paper bore a mysterious pencil line: a portion of a thigh, a piece of an eye, a small toe. No one would ever know who or what. She laughed once and ran back to the house. She felt very light. Her bare feet never felt the cold grass.

On Saturday she did more cleaning. She vacuumed the entire house, including most of the drapes, and then took the vacuum cleaner to the garage and did the interior of the station wagon. Then she started in on the front yard. She raked all the debris out of the flowerbeds, clawed away with her fingers in hard-to-get-at places, and snipped the suckers off the oleanders. Henry eyed her suspiciously but didn't say a word, and she pretended she didn't know he was watching.

When Marleen returned from the laundromat she was pleased to see how neat the house looked. She found Janice in the kitchen scrubbing the tile. "Flora's full of energy today," said Janice as she wrung her sponge out in the sink. She slapped it down on the counter. On account of Flora, Janice had to work like a maniac just to look like she was doing anything at all.

Sunday night there was a loud smack. Marleen let out a scream and all her children leapt out of their beds and ran to her room. They found her huddled at the head of her bed with her hands clutching her knees. Henry was sitting at the side of his bed with a small gun in his hand.

Marleen reached over and switched on the lamp by the side of her bed. She opened her mouth to say something to her children but no words came out.

Henry looked around at them. "There was a prowler out there." He pointed his pistol at the window.

"And you shot at him?" said Janice with disbelief. Marleen made a tiny mewing sound.

"Not at him," grumbled Henry. "Don't you think I know how to aim this thing?" He weighed the pistol in his hand. "I was just scaring him off." With the nose of the pistol he moved the drapes aside slightly, leaned forward, and peeked out from side to side.

"He'll think twice before he comes around here again, if he has any brains." That was his final statement. He crawled back into bed and laid the pistol on his nightstand.

Marleen saw her children still standing in the doorway, their eyes unblinking, like owls'. "Go back to bed now; everything's all right," she said in a sweet high tone. They backed away. She wanted to pretend that someone had only had a bad dream and that it was dispelled now. She slipped down beneath her covers. "I'll see you in the morning," she called after them, and switched her light off reluctantly.

Flora lay perfectly still and listened for sounds. She heard twigs rattling against twigs, and the back fence creak with a long, low note every time the breeze touched it. She heard a cat yowl as if it were being squeezed to death.

In the morning Henry sat down at the breakfast table with them.

He made no mention of what happened the night before. Instead, he read fragments of articles from the *Los Angeles Times:* vandalism at Hollywood High, a burglary in Inglewood (a man was apprehended as he singlehandedly tried to bring a brass bed through the rear door of a house). Henry whipped the pages back and forth in a flurry to find better examples, something that was right up their own alley.

Everyone snuck glances at him as they ate their cereal and pretended not to understand why he was reading out loud to them on this particular morning. Daniel dropped his spoon on the floor and asked Marleen for another one. She got up, got a fork out of the silverware drawer, and handed it to him. She looked stunned, like a porcelain-headed doll with flat, painted-on eyes.

Henry lowered his newspaper. "Are you going to school this morning, or to a funeral?" He was staring at Flora's black, high-necked sweater.

"To school," said Flora.

"Get up and stand over by the door," he said. There was a great rustling as he wrapped his paper up. Flora squeezed by him with her bowl raised high, placed it in the sink, and then went and stood in the doorway. Being in the doorway was a good place to be—she was almost out. She straightened the pleats of her royal blue wool skirt. She was sure that it came to the bottom of her knees.

"Black and blue—this is the latest in schoolgirl colors, I suppose?" Henry was leaning back in his chair. Janice lifted her eyes from the open textbook before her and then dropped them again. She suppressed a smile. Flora shrugged her shoulders.

"I'd better not get any news from the principal's office," Henry said as he looked her up and down. Janice made a sound like a stifled sneeze, and as Henry turned his attention to her, Flora snatched her lunch sack from the counter and left.

"What are you doing reading at the table?" said Henry.

"I've got a history test this morning," said Janice without looking up.

All the way to school Flora's weightlessness was still with her. It was as if nothing odd had happened since the night she breezed across the back lawn. The pistol shot, Marleen's scream, Henry's calm and crazy voice had gotten tossed way back in her head along with all the other nightmares. She was thinking of only one thing, of seeing Matthew again.

Before lunch she spotted him in the Long Hall, came up behind him and whispered his name. He turned around slowly and leaned against his locker. She wanted to pin him against it, feel the very substance of him, but she didn't. She stood back and said, "I'm free again. I can fly." As proof, she flapped her arms up and down once.

Matthew smiled a deadly sweet smile, as if he would find out how high, how far. He reached for her.

Tess didn't move her head but her eyes often shifted to Flora and Matthew. All week long she watched them. Flora was practically prancing in place with energy for Matthew. And he'd rub himself against her. It was possible to see a bulge in his pants. It didn't seem fair. Phil was walking around as if he'd been socked in the solar plexus. She had to stand on that table, frozen in space, feeling every tingle, throb, tremor, and gurgle inside her own body while the all-star butterfly stroker–dolphin kicker posed no more than a foot from her. And Matthew and Flora were behaving as though they were in a dimly lit booth in the far corner of a restaurant. She watched Flora nuzzle up to him. He lifted her hair and kissed her on the neck. And aside from that, they seemed to be doing touch-up work on each other's drawings, giving each other lessons. The Cat passed behind them once, and when she looked at their drawings she made an awful face, as if she'd taken a bite out of something spoiled.

Tess noticed, too, that Timpanelli was all eyes, but not once during the whole week did she stop at Matthew's or Flora's easel on her tours around class. It was as though they were exempt from criticism. And they weren't even making any use of her figure. She felt a lump the size of a fist in her throat.

At the close of the period on Friday she saw Matthew slip Flora a note, which she stuck down the front of her sweater. Tess expected to see it flutter all the way to the floor, but it didn't.

As soon as Flora got home from school she peeled potatoes, and they were boiling on the stove by the time Marleen got home from work. She helped Marleen with the rest of the meal. Flora didn't like to cook, and she wasn't hungry. She just wanted to get dinner over with as soon as possible.

At the table Henry made disparaging comments about items that irritated him in the morning paper: Japanese industrial advancements, the movement of water around California, Yugoslavian peace proposals for Near and Far Eastern conflicts. His family didn't care about these things, but they were glad he was carrying on so; as long as he was picking on remote problems he wouldn't be picking on them.

Flora was glad no one asked her if she was going out. She went to the bathroom and stripped off her school clothes. Matthew's note had gotten curled up in her slip. She read it one last time: "8:00, David Beauchamp, semi-formal attire, easily removed." Below that he'd drawn two monograms. Turning the *F* in her name backward, he made a girl with long hair streaming behind her who was running away from his name, which was a monster with a long wiggly stem of a *T* for a tail, a saw-toothed back from the *M* and *W*, and an *E* stretched out into a ferocious mouth.

No one will ever get their hands on this, she breathed, crumpling up the note. She flushed it down the toilet and stepped into the shower. As the hot water pounded down on her she hummed "That's How Strong My Love Is." She wasn't thinking about the tune or the words or anything precisely.

Janice came into the bathroom and stuck her head between the shower curtains. "I suppose you're going out tonight?" She sounded a little irked.

Flora clutched a washcloth to her chest. "Yes," she said when she recovered from the fright of seeing Janice's face. "I've been invited to the ball." She flung one hand up above the steam.

"You mean the school dance?" Janice was half asking a question, half setting her straight.

Flora gave in. "Yes, the school dance."

"That's where I'm going. Who's taking you?" said Janice. She was very eager to know.

Flora reached for a bar of soap. "A very respectable fellow." The soap slipped out of her hand, and she felt around for it. "Someone I haven't gone out with before," she said, straightening up again.

Janice seemed to accept her answer. "Do I know him?"

"I don't think so," replied Flora. "Would you please close the curtain? You're creating a draft."

Janice whipped the curtain shut. "Don't take too long," she complained.

"I'm almost out." Flora watched Janice's blurry form leave the bathroom. She got out of the tub, dried off quickly, went back to their bedroom with her towel wrapped around her, and pulled open a drawer. She regarded the jumble of underwear and had a thought: maybe Matthew was only joking. "Janice, is the dance really semi-formal?"

Janice heard Flora's earnest tone and played against it. "You're the one who said it was going to be a ball," she said and left the room.

Flora had to come to her own conclusion—either that or wait to see what Janice put on. She decided the dance would be semi-formal, not the usual after-game affair with the dance floor packed with jocks in T-shirts chugging up and down and their girlfriends prancing around in pastel sweaters and pleated skirts and bleached tennis shoes. She wanted to follow Matthew's instructions, joke or no joke.

But what did it matter what she wore, anyway? She felt a little foolish giving her attire so much consideration. But it did matter—she was going to be with Matthew. She searched through all her white and flowered underpants and came up with a pair of dark blue ones. This was an easy choice. The other side of the drawer was a mess of bras. Different colors and cuts, even a black lace push-up that Tess had given her, insisting it could do wonders. She had wanted to wear a bra, or rather, she had wanted to need to wear a bra. Five years or so ago, a saleslady, a very bosomy one with rougy wrinkled cheeks and skin like the outside of an oyster shell, had stepped into a dressing room with her. She gave Flora a number and a letter and four styles of bras to try on. "You're a 32A: adorable little teacups." And now she was still a 32A. The hope had passed, but the paraphernalia remained. She promised herself she would toss them all out.

She might have worn nylon stockings if she had anything appealing to hold them up with. All she had was this contraption that looked like hospital gear: a white garter belt she had bought with her mother, something to go with her church nylons back in the days when she still found herself sitting in a pew on Sunday morning. She would feel the long strips of elastic on the back side of the garter creeping around, and wait for the moment when they'd spring over her hipbones and leave her feeling as though she were only half harnessed. She'd do without the stockings.

She lifted out a dark blue slip and recalled the dress it had been bought to go under, a dress she had worn only once, to a cousin's wedding two years before. She went to the closet and ran her hand back and forth through the clothes. The same dress fell to the floor of the closet and lay in a small heap. She picked it up and held it against herself as she stood in front of the door mirror. She had always liked the color, a deep turquoise, no, closer to Prussian blue. She slipped her arms through the flared sleeves. The loose fabric, whatever it was, felt good. She regarded her pale body, draped on either side by the dress. Forget the slip, she decided. She tied the sash at the waist.

On her knees, she searched the bottom of the closet, lifting the lid on nearly every shoebox until she found a pair of black patent leather heels. She sat down on the vanity stool and was buckling one of the straps when Janice came in the room.

"Hey, those are my shoes!" She grabbed one of them away from Flora.

"No they're not," said Flora and she grabbed the shoe back.

Janice grabbed it away from her again and looked inside it, tossed it back to Flora, and went to look in her own side of the closet. She came up holding a pair of nearly identical shoes.

"Here they are!" she said triumphantly.

Flora stroked mascara onto her lashes and, after wiping away a stray smudge, felt her earlobe. The gold earring wasn't there. She dug in her jewelry box until she found it. As she put the loop through her ear, in a side panel of the mirror she could see Janice standing at the dresser. She sensed some frustration mounting around Janice, like steam billowing above a shower stall. She turned to Janice. "What's wrong?" She heard her own voice rolling forth without mockery.

"I can't find anything to wear." Janice flung a handful of underwear back in her drawer.

"What do you need?" Flora got up and came toward her.

Janice had something specific in mind, and although she hated having to ask for it, she did. "Can I borrow your black bra?"

"You can have it." Flora pulled open her own drawer and handed over Tess's black lace push-up.

Janice held it up by its straps and inspected it.

Flora went back to the vanity and started brushing her hair while Janice swished through her own side of the closet and finally pulled out a cream-colored dress with a black velvet bodice and a scoop neck trimmed in cream-colored lace. Flora couldn't see where the push-up made any difference with Janice either. But Janice was obviously in a better mood. She was humming a medley of Beatle tunes. I sure do hope Janice has a good time tonight, thought Flora.

"Who are you going to the dance with?" Flora was almost afraid to ask.

"John Tucker, who do you think?" said Janice as she bounced down on the edge of the bed and started putting her own shoes on. "When are you going to be finished there?"

Flora got up from the vanity. She couldn't stand it anymore; she had to make the announcement. "Janice," she said, "I'm going to see Matthew tonight." She watched Janice stroke her yard of ash-blonde hair.

"I figured as much." Janice's voice wavered between disappointment and fear. She stopped brushing.

"Please, *please* don't tell Dad." Flora's face looked stern and rigid. Janice lowered herself slowly onto the vanity stool. "I love Matthew," said Flora. "I don't want anything to be spoiled."

Janice stared at Flora as she absorbed this last urgent whisper. Then her eyes skipped all around the room before coming back to rest on a line with Flora's. Flora's eyes hadn't wavered.

"I'll never be the one to tell," said Janice with resignation.

Flora took her by both shoulders and gave her a shake, more like a gentle shudder. "Thanks, Janice." Janice made a discouraged face, picked up a bottle of perfume from the vanity, dropped it in her purse, and left the room. Flora hoped more than ever that Janice would have a good time at the dance. It could determine her own fate.

At seven-thirty John Tucker pulled up in the driveway and Janice left without much ado. Flora had some thirty minutes to wait. She sat back down at the vanity and began opening bottles of perfume and sniffing them: her own bottle of Heaven Scent, like the one Janice had dropped in her purse, smelled like something mothers would want to smear on their babies. Indeed, Marleen had given them twin bottles at Christmas. There was also a bunch of doll-sized bottles, perfume samplers from a woman who sold cosmetics door to door. One smelled like sour roses. Another one smelled like clover on a muggy day. One called Sleepless Nights smelled like hot sauce and stung her in the nose. Another one called Hors d'Haleine reminded her of the woman who wore a red wig, with rouge and lipstick to match, and worked behind the cosmetic counter at the drugstore next to the neighborhood five-and-dime. One called Mon Abri smelled like a man's aftershave. She decided she wouldn't use any of them, though by now she smelled like a faint mixture of everything.

Every so often fear, like a dying fish, flip-flopped deep inside her. She rested her elbows on the vanity, covered her face lightly with her hands, and made a silent plea to some nameless deity: Please let everything go smoothly.

At ten minutes past eight the doorbell rattled. Years ago Henry had bent the clapper in the metal box over the kitchen door so that the bell wouldn't ring. Only salesmen or new dates used it. Flora pulled on her gray wool coat and headed down the hall.

Marleen had already opened the door. "Hello," she said, like an alert and polite receptionist.

"Hello, I'm David Beauchamp. You must be Flora's mother?"

Flora entered the living room as David was extending his hand to Marleen.

"Yes, I am," replied Marleen. "I've—" She stopped herself. She was going to say, "I've heard so much about you," but that wouldn't be right. She hadn't heard anything about him.

"Mother, this is David Beauchamp . . . David, this is my mother." Flora swayed back and forth awkwardly. She knew they must have just finished introducing themselves, but she didn't know what else to do. Marleen was smiling graciously, and David made a slight bow. He was wearing a dark jacket and dark slacks, and a madras shirt, not exactly semi-formal, but then, his neat appearance would probably make up for the discrepancy in the way he and Flora were dressed. Flora was fairly well hidden beneath her coat. She smiled and buttoned it up. David ran his hand back through his fine brown hair, and for a split second she thought of Phil.

"Have a nice time tonight," Marleen was saying as Henry appeared in the hall door. He stepped forward and Flora stepped aside, saying, after several long seconds of silence, "Dad, this is David Beauchamp. David, this is my father."

"How do you do, sir," said David.

Henry stood back and leaned way forward to shake hands. Flora thought he might fall over, but then he righted himself and, despite her clear pronunciation, struggled with several variations of David's last name: "Bouchan, Bocon, Beechum." David was a stranger to her, not even a blind date, but she blushed as if he were her beau.

"Beauchamp," repeated David, in the Parisian manner, nodding with civility.

Henry rubbed the back of his neck as if it were sore. "Where did you and Flora meet?" He had to take a deep breath before he could ask this question.

David threw a glance at Flora, slightly accusing, and then, smiling, he said, "Didn't Flora tell you?"

Flora took her cue. "He sits behind me in chemistry class." She hoped her voice sounded steady. She thought it did.

"I hope you do better in chemistry than Flora does." Henry had himself a little joke and laughed out loud about it.

"I do all right," David responded casually, as if chemistry were his major. He reached back for the doorknob.

"Where are you going?" said Henry abruptly.

David shot Flora a startled look; he thought he was being challenged.

"To the school dance?" asked Marleen. She was clasping her hands together.

"Yes," said Flora and David in unison.

"Well, have a nice time," said Marleen for the second time.

"We will," said Flora. She was feeling faint.

David nodded kindly and turned the doorknob without looking behind him. The door swung open smoothly. Flora thought guys must practice doing that—opening and closing doors without even looking. Her father was crossing his arms and looking at the floor. She saw her opening and fled.

David escorted her down the driveway with his hand under her elbow. She couldn't believe the service. As he opened the car door for her she said, "I really appreciate this. I hope it hasn't been too much trouble?"

"Matthew says you're worth it." He carefully pushed the car door closed. It wasn't a big dark car. It was a little white Mustang.

After they had turned off Jericho, Flora asked him if David really was his name.

"And Beauchamp, too," he replied.

"You don't go to Hazelton High, do you?"

"No," he laughed.

Flora suddenly felt ill at ease driving along in a car with a stranger. She held her hands tightly in her lap and tried to keep from swaying from side to side every time they turned a corner.

"How long have you known Matthew?" she inquired.

"About eight years. His father and mine used to be partners in an architectural firm, until his mother got killed."

"His father's mother?" asked Flora.

David gave her an incredulous look. "Matthew's mother," he said and revved his engine.

"She was killed?" asked Flora. She watched a light turn red as they crossed an intersection.

"Yeah, in a car accident. Matthew didn't tell you?"

"No," said Flora. She looked at her reflection in the side window and saw herself speaking. "No, I guess I haven't asked him about his mother, or his father." She felt forlorn and frightened.

David pulled a pack of cigarettes out of his jacket pocket, put a cigarette in his mouth, and offered one to Flora. Flora shook her head. "No, thank you." With one hand he bent and struck a match, and in the glow Flora caught a glimpse of his profile. He was beyond high school, closer to twenty. She could only hope her father didn't think so too.

"That was about two years ago," said David. He flicked the match out the window. "Then Matthew's dad started drinking too much and kept forgetting to come to work . . . What am I doing? Matthew can tell you what he wants to, anything you want to know." His voice trailed out the window along with a stream of smoke.

Flora heard the regret in his voice. "I guess you two are good friends?"

"I don't see him that often, but I guess you could say we are good friends." David looked as if he was considering something he hadn't considered in quite a while. He took a long drag on his cigarette and turned another corner. They were near the school now.

"Where do you live?" asked Flora. She took hold of the armrest.

"In the Hollywood Hills. I work as an interior decorator, and go to school part time, in the art department at Cal State." David might have turned out to be a talker, but they had arrived at school. He swung into the parking lot.

Aurora Borealis

"Would you like me to escort you to the auditorium?" He looked over at her and waited for a response, resting his hands on the top of the steering wheel the way Phil did whenever they stopped somewhere. She took it as a sign of impatience. She scanned the parking lot. More and more cars were arriving.

"If you don't mind?" She didn't want to impose on him anymore than she already had, but she didn't want to draw attention to herself by walking alone when everyone else was in pairs.

"Not at all," replied David good-naturedly, and he started to open his car door.

"No, that's all right," she said, suddenly changing her mind. "I can go alone." She got out. "Thank you for the ride, thank you for driving me here, and everything else."

He smiled and gave her a salute.

Flora put her hands in her coat pockets and walked very fast up one of the dark paths parallel to the illuminated hallway. Through the windows she could see other students moving slowly forward in pairs, like passengers passing from one car to another in a long train that has pulled into a station.

She was almost running by the time she got to the main corridor. At the far end, near the entrance to the auditorium, she spotted Matthew and slowed down abruptly. She was relieved to see that he was actually there, leaning against one of the metal posts, staring down at the floor.

He looked like an out-of-towner, like someone who had been waiting a long time for a train to come in. It seemed to Flora that he sensed her approach without actually seeing her. He shoved himself off the post, as if he'd been jabbed in the back, and moved toward her. He wore a dark blue suit and a paler blue shirt and had a long, dark scarf, not a tie, tied loosely over his collar. He looked too good, she thought, too outstanding, to be in this place, this abused and neglected corridor, which did have the atmosphere of a dying train station—a place where strangers watch strangers come and go and depart themselves as soon as they can.

Matthew slipped his hands inside her coat and around her waist. He stared at her, took a big breath, and smiled deeply. Flora felt herself mimicking his smile. All the other couples arriving for the dance—the boys in their sports jackets and the girls in their pastel dresses, some wearing orchids that jiggled on their shoulders as they hurried toward the auditorium—they all faded into the background like floral wallpaper.

"Are we going to the dance?" He squinted at her.

"I don't think so," said Flora. And then she had a vision of dancing with Matthew in the center of the dance floor, a vision of being seen with Matthew as they moved together so easily. "Well, maybe for a while?"

"Whatever you want." Matthew gave her a slight tug in the direction of the auditorium.

After a few paces, Flora realized she didn't actually know anyone she could show Matthew off to. No one that would see Matthew as she did, no one that would care, really. And no one she wanted to see or talk to more than Matthew alone. She stopped abruptly. "No, Matthew, let's not go. Let's not go at all."

The teacher at the door of the auditorium twisted around and looked at them. He continued to stare at them as he handed tickets to a couple just entering. His face didn't register any emotion. It was Mr. Whitney, Flora's chemistry teacher. Beyond him was a blue glow, the rumble of music, and a sea of bobbing heads. Over the door was a banner, a long drooping one, which read BLUE MOON OVER HAWAII.

"Let's leave." Flora wished she hadn't seen Mr. Whitney's face.

"Your fickleness is my map," said Matthew, and he gave her a kiss on the ear.

They turned the corner of the main corridor, and Flora saw people rushing toward them in the dingy light. "Let's walk outside."

"Gladly," said Matthew. At the first ramp, they turned out into the night. There seemed to be no one else on the paths. They walked along slowly, but in Flora's mind they were running away from something, and toward something else. Yet she felt no need to define what was behind them or in front of them. She was content just to be beside him now, listening to the rhythmic ring of their steps on the concrete path. The moon was a bright hole in the sky; the sky, nothing but a black sheet of paper that might easily be torn away, leaving only this bright blue-white light that could blind everyone into a state of happiness. Marleen used to tell her, "Don't stare at the moon. It will make you crazy." Matthew was holding her hand; she was holding his. She stared hard at the moon and felt entirely happy.

Matthew wondered if he could take Flora back to his old home, the one his father had designed, and partly built, for him and his mother. He saw Flora pinned to his bed, struggling to get away. That night had been a mistake, but not a mistake he was ashamed of. He loved her even back then and he hadn't known what else to do. He squeezed her hand.

"Where would you like to go?" He slowed to a stop, and Flora walked a few more paces in an arc until she was facing him. She hadn't been considering where they might actually go. She searched quickly for an answer. Neon signs whizzed by, hot pink signs advertising motel rooms she had never been in. She saw plush hotel rooms from her memory of movies: luxurious and impersonal, maids with stacks of sheets knocking on the doors, bellboys entering with rattling carts, remote-control TV, huge beds like slabs of stone. She saw the beach: the sand already covered with cold winter dew—too far away, and probably high tide anyway.

"I don't know of anyplace. I just want to be with you." She felt distressed. Then she saw the open window beside Matthew's bed, and Matthew above her, holding her down. "I wish you still lived in your house in the Hills."

Matthew put his arms around her and kissed her deeply on the mouth. Then he pulled away from her. "Do you want to go there?" In the parking lot, a car wheeled around and its headlights flashed in Matthew's face. He was making an earnest request.

"Who's living there now?" Flora didn't want to be involved in any more introductions tonight.

"No one, no one living, that is. A ghost maybe." Matthew ran his fingers up Flora's back with a sudden motion, and Flora gasped. Then she put her arm around his waist and they started walking out into the parking lot.

"My father sold it, but the new owners haven't moved in. They live in New York, or back East somewhere. Anyway, they might have bought the house only to sell it again, I don't know."

Matthew opened the door to his car. Flora wouldn't have recognized it. It had a roof. When she was seated she remembered the time she had climbed over the door to get in. Matthew slid into the driver's seat, a car seat, not a sawed-off wooden chair.

"Elves have been working on your car," she said.

Matthew was searching around in all his suit pockets. "I think they stole my keys." For a moment he was perplexed. Then he thought to feel under his new car seat, and found them. "Do you like the new easy-opening door? I didn't want you to get a run in your stockings, but then again"—he ran his hand down her thigh and squeezed her on the knee—"you probably aren't wearing any." He took his hand off her knee and turned the key in the ignition.

"It's very nice," Flora said, smiling, "and your new seat too." When she had seen his old setup she had been frightened by the thought of him flying through the windshield. "And the roof too," she added. She was feeling safe from all harm with Matthew. Then she heard Timpanelli's voice, a hushed sound saying, "Get out of here, you two star-crossed lovers."

Matthew stopped at the parking lot exit and tried to spot a gap in the traffic. Several cars turned in and then Phil's whipped past them. Yes, it was Phil, and it looked like Tess sitting next to him. Is it possible? thought Flora. It never occurred to her that Tess could be attracted to Phil. Matthew and Phil hadn't noticed each other, and the girl, whoever she was, had been staring straight ahead. Flora was glad of that. She didn't want any disturbances, however slight.

Matthew pulled out into the boulevard. "Did you and David make a smooth getaway?" He stuck his hand out the window and motioned for a lane change.

"Yes, considering my father came in to see who I was going out with." Flora shuddered to think back on it. Matthew switched into another lane. "How old is David?" Flora suddenly thought to ask.

"Nineteen or twenty," said Matthew. He winced and swerved away from a passing car. "His father got him a job working for an interior decorator. Then he got intimidated by the interior decorator, and so he decided to go to college." There was a hint of annoyance in Matthew's voice.

"Yes," said Flora, "he told me he was working and going to school."

"He took that job without thinking twice." Matthew seemed to be shaking his head at the traffic. "He could make it on his own if he had any trust in himself." Matthew raised his hands off the steering wheel for a moment and then let them fall back in place. "His talent is beyond choosing lampshades for people."

Matthew seemed to be talking to himself. He pulled to a stop in front of a cluster of stores and hopped out. "I'll just be a minute." He clicked the car door closed very gently with his hand on the top of the window frame, and scooted into a drugstore. Boys are good with doors, thought Flora for the second time that evening. Several people went in and out before Matthew reappeared. Without looking at her, he turned into the liquor store next door.

Flora watched the car lights coming and going on the street. She knew it was crazy, but very rapidly a feeling of being abandoned was creeping up on her. She had a phobia about waiting in cars, which she traced back to having been left in the family car while her mother and father shopped. Once a man had come up to their car and told them to roll down the window. Janice rolled it down a crack, and the man said the car was parked in the wrong place. It would have to be moved. He wanted them to open the door so he could get in. When they refused, he kicked the side of the car and walked away. Flora leaned across Matthew's seat and was about to lock his door when he came sailing back to her. He laid a long dark bottle of wine down on the floor between them and handed Flora a sack. She peeked into it and saw a pair of white candles nestled in a box and wrapped in cellophane.

When they turned up into the hills, the houses were hidden from the street as if they were frightened or shy. Huge live oaks bowed over the car from both sides of the street and blocked out the light of the moon. They swerved up onto some narrower winding roads, with lamplights blinking here and there from posts at the ends of driveways. Matthew shifted gears and pulled up a long steep one. He swung in at the side of a house and shut the engine off. In the abrupt silence, Flora heard a high-pitched whining inside her head. She felt as if she were still racing along.

Matthew led her through a eucalyptus grove, on a path along the house, past a window with many small panes. He tried a doorknob. "Of course it would be locked," he mumbled in a tone of understanding. They walked farther on until they came to a window. Matthew felt it. "It's open," he said, and he reached in and cranked it all the way open.

"I hope you don't mind?" He handed Flora the bottle of wine and leapt onto the window ledge.

"I doubt if I can do it as easily as that, but I know I can do it." She handed Matthew the bottle and the candles, and he took her hand and helped her into his bedroom, or what used to be his bedroom. The dark carpeting was still down, but there was no furniture at all. The moonlight cut a bright rectangle out of the carpet at the spot where Matthew's bed used to be.

Hand in hand, they entered a large room, the room with the big window divided into small panes. Opposite the window was a massive fireplace constructed of carefully set riverstones. The smooth stones leveled off at a wide mantel and then rose again and disappeared through the high ceiling. The only piece of furniture in this room was a sofa covered with a white sheet. It looked like a giant polar bear slumbering in front of the cold hearth.

Matthew said, "Well, at least the couch is still here. When the movers told my father they'd have to take the front door off its hinges to get it out, he said, 'Leave the damn thing here. It won't fit in the other place anyway.' "

Flora looked out the window at the grove of eucalyptus trees, and Matthew came over and stood by her. "My father thinks those are the most beautiful trees on earth, but nothing . . ."—he hesitated —"nothing grows beneath them."

It sounded to Flora as though he was referring to his mother. It must be hard for him to avoid thinking about her here in this house. Flora felt she should talk more. Several leaves trickled down from the eucalyptus trees and lay still on the bare ground.

She took a deep breath. "My father planted one in our front yard, but after it got to be about two stories tall, the lady next door

started complaining about the leaves that were falling on her lawn.
My father told her he'd top it. Top it," said Flora again; the term sounded sadly amusing to her. "He knew I liked to shinny up it, so he told me to climb it with a coil of rope." Flora showed Matthew with her hands how the rope had hung over her shoulder, but he was looking at her face.

"Well, anyway," she continued as she looked back out the window, "he kept saying, 'Higher, higher,' until I was swaying back and forth. I felt like a grasshopper on a tall blade of grass. It was all I could do to tie the rope around the trunk. And then I came down as fast as I could . . . faster than I should have." Flora crossed her arms tightly; she could feel the abrasions again. "My brother and several other boys on the block pulled on the rope until the top of the tree touched the ground. They held it there while my father sawed away at the upper part of the trunk. I just stood back and watched, I guess.

"Then the tree snapped and sprung back and my brother and his friends rolled into a hedge, and my father fell back with the saw still in his hand. No one got hurt. But what a loony thing to do. My father congratulated the boys on a job well done, and the lady next door stepped out of her house and admired the tree. It looked awful—just a long thin trunk with a couple of straggly branches at the top." Flora stopped herself. "What a thing to remember." She let out a brisk sigh, exasperated with herself. The first story she had ever told Matthew and it had to be that one. She didn't want to even mention her father to him, not tonight, anyway.

"I love to listen to you talk," said Matthew. He looked like a tall, shadowy tree. She could barely see his face, but then she felt his arms wrapping around her and his mouth open and pressing against hers. Then he was whisked away as if a wind had pulled him from her. She heard the sound of crinkling cellophane, and saw one candle, and then another, light up on the stone mantel. Matthew lifted up one end of the sheet that covered the sofa and gave it a flick so that it fluttered away. He sank down onto the sofa and untied his scarf with one hand.

"Come around to me, Flora." She came around to the end of the sofa and watched him unbutton his shirt. He got his shoes off by pushing down on each heel with the opposite foot. She unbuckled her shoes and placed them on the floor beside the sofa. Then she took off her coat, folded it up, and laid it over her shoes. She took a few steps forward until she was standing between Matthew and the candlelight. He didn't seem to be smiling or frowning; he was just waiting. She saw his scarf draped over the back of the sofa—a squiggle of silky fabric against something plush.

She wished she wasn't so restrained. If only she knew something about stripping. She and Phil, along with Stan and his date, had driven all the way to Tijuana one evening in hopes of seeing a genuine striptease act. They found out that the really good shows wouldn't begin until after midnight. They drove back to Los Angeles having seen only some girls, younger than Flora, wiggling their hips in bikinis that were less revealing than most styles seen on Malibu Beach. The highlight of the evening, the thing Stan and Phil joked about all the way home, was the scene they thought an old hag with black teeth made when she sat down in their booth. "Hot love for me, strong boy?" she said to Phil, rolling the *r* in *strong*. "Why not?" She winked at him, and some flecks of glitter fell off her eyelids and onto his shoulder. Flora took a sip from her beer and saw Stan's date with her mouth hanging open. "Why you with baby for?" The woman nodded over to Flora and put her hand in Phil's lap. "No thanks," said Phil, pushing her hand away. He chuckled nervously. It never occurred to Flora to protest. The woman got up and strolled to another booth.

Flora fussed with the knot she had tied in the sash of her dress and wished she could just run over to Matthew and help him take his clothes off. But he didn't need any help. She watched him remove both his jacket and his shirt at the same time, in one easy swooping motion. He did everything smoothly, it seemed to her, whether it was leaping over ramp railings, flipping pencils in the air, or removing sheets from sofas.

"I love you, Flora . . . and your beautiful body." Matthew stretched his arms out. "Come and lie down with me." Flora's sash came loose and her dress fell aside. She went over to Matthew and he pulled her down onto the sofa with him.

"The next time we go out, don't bother to wear any clothes. Tell your father you've joined a nudist colony." He pulled her underpants down and kissed her on the belly. All of Flora's body went tense with the joke and the touch of Matthew's lips.

"If you'll promise to stand naked out in front of the school auditorium," she managed to say.

Matthew got up and took his pants off. Then he lay down between Flora's legs. She felt as though her cool body had been covered with a warm wave; all her muscles shivered and then relaxed. She wrapped her arms around him and sighed.

"I don't want anyone else to see my body or yours, naked,"

whispered Matthew. He kissed Flora on the shoulder and the neck and the soft place between her neck and her jaw.

"I don't want anyone else to see us at all," Flora whispered back to him. She kissed him in the same way he kissed her. She always found herself following his example. It felt so good to her, she hoped it would feel good to him, too. "I don't want to *see* anybody else." She was so happy, she felt she might be capable of hugging him too hard. "I've waited so long to be alone with you." She felt the length of his spine from his neck to his tailbone.

"If it's any consolation, I've had to wait exactly the same length of time." He moved down and kissed her where she'd never been kissed before.

Flora gasped. "It's no consolation." She watched the patterns of candlelight on the ceiling. Quaking rings of light from two sources, intercepting one another. Matthew's hands, as softly as water reeds, traced circles on her breasts. She felt like some sort of water creature, an amphibian floating face up in a warm marsh. The entire room was blushing with a pale light. This must be what the aurora borealis looks like, she thought. She felt so lonely. She was holding on to Matthew's arms, but she wished she could hold on to more of him. "Matthew," she heard herself calling to him as another swell of heat rolled up through her, "I want to feel you inside me."

Matthew hoisted himself up. He was a dark form suspended above her and then sinking into her. A foot sinking into the silty bottom of a pond. Matthew was a gentle stepper, like someone who is exploring and observing, trying not to disturb anything. Flora thought he was holding his breath. She held her own. Then he pressed himself deep inside her. Clay, thought Flora. We're molding and remolding each other out of clay. She kneaded his buttocks and felt his warm breathing at her neck. She felt she loved him beyond anything she could ever express, and then she experienced a strange sensation. It was as if she had deserted her own body. She was inside Matthew's body, making love to someone who was lying beneath him, someone named Flora. She heard Matthew say they were together for life, and then the sensation faded and she sank down into her own body again. Matthew slipped around to her side and lay still.

"I wish we never had to come apart. I love you so much." She stroked his dark hair. Matthew said nothing. She felt the sweat on his skin and got up to get the sheet. She pulled it over him and crawled in beside him.

"Thank you," murmured Matthew, and he put one arm around her.

Flora wondered if Matthew had that same sensation, of having swapped bodies for a while. She sighed and snuggled against him.

Flora woke to the sound of the candles spluttering. One and then the other popped and hissed as if they were talking back and forth as best they could, or disputing. The riverstones came into focus. Each one, from the candles on up to the ceiling, was illuminated on its lower edge by the candlelight. The room felt as drafty as a cavern. Just then Matthew placed his hand on her hip. He was sitting up.

"I'll make a fire," he said softly. He pulled the sheet up over her shoulder, got up and slipped his pants on. Flora regarded his figure dreamily. He looked better than any of the classical sculptures she'd seen in Timpanelli's anatomy books. And he was alive besides.

Matthew went out through the far door. Flora heard another door open and shut and then, after a while, open again. Matthew reentered with an armload of logs and a fistful of twigs. He knelt at the hearth and made a neat crisscrossing of twigs and set two small logs on top of them. He found his book of matches on the mantel, and with one match the twigs were ablaze and, soon after, the logs.

"This wood is so dry, it must be as old as I am. We rarely had a fire in this fireplace."

Flora was sitting up with the sheet around her shoulders. She was wide awake now. The sight of Matthew squatting before the fire made her keenly sad for driftwood fires along riverbanks and the warm rocks of her childhood. "It's a beautiful fireplace."

Matthew placed another log on the fire and regarded the stonework for the first time in many years. "It's the one part of this house my father actually built. Maybe he should have been a stonemason instead of an architect." He put another log on the fire and came back to Flora, picking the bottle of wine up on his way.

"Would you like some wine, to warm you up, to celebrate our reunion?" He wrestled a corkscrew out of his jacket pocket.

"For both those reasons," said Flora, "especially the last one."

"I almost bought some glasses in the drugstore, but . . ." He pulled the cork out of the bottle.

"I don't mind drinking out of the bottle." Flora took a sip and handed the bottle back to Matthew. "I was a bottle baby."

Matthew took a drink. "I was breast-fed for three years, or so I was told. I don't remember a thing." He took another drink and handed the bottle back to Flora. He stared at the fire.

Flora took a drink and stared at the fire, too. She saw Matthew's mother's face in the flames. That is, she saw the face of a woman who might have resembled his mother: porcelain-white skin, flowing black hair, and dark eyes. The woman's face fluttered fretfully and vanished. Flora felt Matthew's oppression and dared to state it in a halting voice. "David told me your mother was killed in a car accident."

"Accident," said Matthew. He broke the word carefully into three parts as if he were snapping a dry twig. He took another drink and kept staring at the fire. "I don't know if it was." He handed the bottle to Flora without looking at her. "She was always threatening to leave. I guess she wasn't happy for a long time." He locked his hands together. "It wasn't anything I could do anything about. It was between my father and her." Matthew leaned forward with his elbows on his knees. "Then she drove down from the hills on a rainy evening, and went to stop for a red light. Her brakes locked and she went through the windshield." He paused. "She told my father over and over again she was going to leave. They were always fighting, but he never listened to her. He couldn't stay away from other women even though he loved her. I think he loved her, anyway. He was always telling her he did." Matthew shook his head.

For the first time in her life, Flora felt as if she had a countless number of questions she wanted to ask someone. She took another sip of wine. "Do you get along with your father?"

Matthew leaned back and took the bottle she held in front of him. He took a swig and handed it back to her.

"I guess so. We don't talk much. Every so often he throws money in my direction." Matthew made a gesture as if casting something on the fire. "He's a likable guy. He's just weak, not mean. He wants to have a good time. He's always telling me how short life is. Then he says, 'You're supposed to tell me to order tall beers,' and then he laughs."

A little laugh, more like a hiccup, escaped from Flora. Matthew almost laughed, too.

"He set his drafting table up in the den and sometimes he's in there all night working on his projects or his mansions, as he calls them, but do you want to know what they are?" He glanced back at Flora.

"What are they?"

"They're mazes. Three-dimensional mazes. Once he worked for six months drawing a multilevel maze with stairs and chutes. It reminded me of an M. C. Escher conception, although I suppose there is a solution."

"A solution?" asked Flora. She didn't know who M. C. Escher was, but it didn't seem like the right time to fill in this particular gap in her knowledge. Matthew glanced at her again.

"You know, a way to get from the center to the outside. A way to escape."

"Oh, right." Flora nodded to show that she really did know what kind of puzzle a maze was, but Matthew was already staring at the fire again.

"He's never asked me to look at them. I think I'm supposed to pretend I don't know what he's doing. But the door is nearly always open, and the drawings are always lying on his drafting table." Matthew extended his hand as if holding out a heavily laden platter. Then he shrugged. Flora wished she could see exactly what Matthew's father's mazes looked like, but maybe that was beside the point, as well as impossible.

"But how is he weak?" she asked.

"He always takes the easy way out. If there's a problem, he'll just leave it behind, like this couch." Matthew leaned back and rubbed his hand up and down its velvet arm. "He didn't even fight well with my mother. He'd rather get drunk and make up, or pass out, before the problem was solved or even discussed."

Matthew suddenly looked at Flora. "I'm dumping all this in your lap! I didn't mean to." He put his arm around her. "It's this house, I guess." His eyes roamed around the empty living room. There was a loud snap from the hearth, followed by a high-pitched whistle.

Flora put her hands around his waist and the sheet slipped off her shoulders. "It's the first time we've been together long enough to talk. Together and alone," she added.

Matthew was silent.

Flora forgot all the questions she had wanted to ask him. She could feel him sinking into something without her. "At least your father has enjoyed himself, at times," she said. "My father seems to think that life is one torment after another, and he's out to prove it. In the meantime, wine will never touch his lips." She took a long sip from the wine bottle and regretted having said what she had just said. She watched a eucalyptus log collapse into embers. The loss of a mother seemed sadder to her than the sour behavior of a father.

"My mother is alive, but she doesn't have a life of her own." Flora frightened herself with that notion. "I think I'll put another log on the fire." She handed Matthew the bottle and jumped up.

"Put one on for my mother, too," said Matthew.

"For Matthew's mother," said Flora. She carefully placed one log over the other.

She figured Matthew was watching her, but she had enough wine in her to make her feel she wouldn't shrivel up just because he could see her naked. When she came back to him he grabbed her and pulled her against him. He held her head in his hands and kissed her. Flora put her hands on the back of the sofa and pushed herself away from him. She knelt down and put her hands around his waist. Then she kissed him at the base of his cock, where it sprouted from his body. A thin layer of soft skin and then such a hardness, and so much heat. Whatever Matthew's parents had done, she was glad they had made him. He pulled her up beside him and they moved as easily together as the flickers of firelight on the ceiling. Why, thought Flora, does anyone ever feel they can't get what they want? When they climaxed, it was as unrestrained, as impulsive, as the sparks shooting up the chimney, as exact as the muted crushing of falling embers. She felt his chest, his heart pounding against hers. The logs shifted in the fireplace and the light in the room became brighter for a moment and then dimmed way down. Matthew pulled himself out of her and lay pressed to her side.

"Flora?" He said and then paused. He hoped she wouldn't take him wrong, but he wanted to know. "Have you ever been with anyone else before? I mean, I thought for sure you and Phil Ridley were together all the time. But then when we were together the first time, it didn't seem like you had ever . . ."

Flora pulled herself away from Matthew a little and tried to see his face. Couldn't a boy tell with certainty whether a girl was a virgin? She thought back to the afternoon in Timpanelli's washroom. There had been no blood, no bloodstains. She had given him no proof. She had no proof to give him, only her word. "I never was in love with Phil; I'm glad I never gave in to him." She regretted the phrase *gave in* as soon as she said it. It sounded like a mudslide or a mine disaster. She pulled herself closer to Matthew. "I never was with him," she said. She felt Phil's arms around her and saw his pleading eyes piercing through the darkness. She felt sad, as if she were erasing him for good. Matthew was stroking her hair and gazing at the ceiling.

"At the thought of you and him being together," he said in a voice made more of air than sound, "I got so . . . so jealous." He took a deep breath. "I wanted to fight him. I remember being at a party and seeing you and him. I don't think you saw me. When I saw the way he was touching you, I wanted to throw a lamp at him, and I'm not a violent person." Matthew laughed in a short gasp and shook his head at himself. "I don't even know him," he added.

Flora felt like sobbing and she didn't know why.

"I just felt that you didn't belong with him," said Matthew. "That's all." He kissed Flora on the cheek. "I thought you belonged with me." He hugged her, and she turned to face him.

"I did, and I do. I feel like I've been in love with you even before I knew I was." She didn't like to think of time away from Matthew. Her feeling of sadness deepened.

"When I brought you here, before, I really thought you wanted to come along with me. I couldn't understand why you wouldn't be with me then. You must've thought I was some kind of maniac." There was wondering in Matthew's voice even now. He lifted himself up a little and stared down at Flora.

Flora stared up at him and tried to make out his features in the firelight. "I was afraid of you," she said, and then she took a long breath and made an alteration: "No, I was more afraid of my father. What he would do." A swell of fear passed up through her, up and out.

"Don't be afraid of him, Flora. He can't really hurt you. You have a strong spirit." Flora could see his eyes gleaming at her. "And he can't keep me away from you."

"I love you, Matthew," said Flora. She kissed his lips and felt as if she were receiving all her strength from him. She wondered if that was a fair or safe thing to do.

"I don't want to be without you, Flora, ever." Matthew pressed himself against her and tightened his embrace.

For a moment she thought she saw the dawn glowing over the back of the sofa, through the eucalyptus trees. But no, it was moonlight, moonlight where she hadn't noticed it before. She tensed up.

"What time do you think it is?"

"I'll check." Matthew sat up quickly and reached for his jacket. He took a wristwatch out of a pocket and faced it toward the window, tipping it this way and that.

"Eleven o'clock," he announced with a hint of relief.

"I've got to be home by midnight." It had just occurred to Flora that she hadn't mentioned this important piece of information to Matthew until now.

"I took a wild guess," said Matthew, still staring at his watch as if it were hypnotizing him. "I asked David to meet us around the block from your house at a quarter to twelve." Matthew held his watch against his ear.

"Not such a bad guess," said Flora. She felt at ease.

"The watch stopped. It's been eleven o'clock for who knows how long." Matthew sounded annoyed with himself. He held the watch by its band and shook it slowly. He knew it was ridiculous to try to resuscitate it now. He stuffed the thing back in his pocket.

"I guess we'd better go," he said regretfully. Flora had already found her underpants and put them on, and was picking up her dress.

"It's probably not twelve yet," she said hopefully, but her eyes were drawn to the mantel. The candles had disappeared, and the last two logs, the ones she had put on, were a mat of glowing rubble. She got one last look at Matthew's body before he whipped his shirt on. She tied her sash, put her coat and shoes on at the same time. Matthew picked the corkscrew up off the floor and put it in his pocket. They looked around. The only thing amiss, aside from a residue of wax and ashes, was the sheet. In the moonlight it looked like a glacier slipping down the slopes of the sofa. They took the corners in their hands, made it billow up, and watched it fall gently like a thin, soundless snowfall covering a landscape at night.

Matthew picked up the nearly empty wine bottle. He glanced at the fireplace and then took Flora's hand and led her back down the dark hall. When they came to his bedroom Flora saw that the rectangle of moonlight had disappeared entirely. The moon had floated all the way over the house.

They climbed out the window, and Matthew cranked it shut again as far as he could without squeezing his arm. When they were back in his car, he leaned over and kissed Flora on the cheek. "I'm sorry about this rush," he said.

She touched his thigh. "I'm sorry too," she said. All she wanted to do was sleep all night through with Matthew, but that couldn't be. She had to go home. She felt the tingling in her head that was a prelude to crying, but she managed to focus her eyes straight ahead as Matthew swung his car down the driveway and on down the curving road.

"Matthew, why did we leave by the window? Why didn't we just leave by one of the doors?"

Matthew was silent for a minute. Then he laughed. "I have no idea." He gave Flora a blank look and laughed again. She laughed too.

When they turned onto the boulevard, they found it nearly empty. A few cars were weaving along heedless of the lanes. Matthew and Flora didn't speak. As they approached a liquor store, one that was still lit up inside, Matthew slowed down. There was a large clock on the back wall, like the kind they had to look at in classrooms. The hour hand and the minute hand, it was plain to see, had combined to form one thick finger pointing straight up.

"That's not too bad," said Flora, smiling and raising her eyes. Her time was up, but she wouldn't be so late. Maybe Janice would get home at about the same time.

"Could've been worse," agreed Matthew. He wasn't so sure David would be waiting for them. He sped up. He picked the wine bottle off the floor, held it between his legs and removed the cork. He took a long swig and offered the bottle to Flora. As they passed the school, she tipped the bottle up and the last of the wine trickled into her mouth. All the lights were off. There wasn't a soul in the parking lot.

A Dog Yowled

Along the smaller dark streets, Matthew sped up a little more until he got to the street next to their block. Then he slowed the car to a creep. Halfway up the street, they spotted David's white Mustang. Matthew pulled in behind it and he and Flora got out. David rolled his window down. A cloud of smoke poured out.

"Two more minutes and I was going to go home and go to bed." His voice was a harsh, sleepy whisper.

"Thanks for waiting," said Matthew. "My friggin' watch stopped." He led Flora around to the other side of David's car. He put his arms around her and spoke close to her ear as if he were delivering a secret. "I wish you could sleep with me in my bed tonight, but since you can't—" He kissed her. Flora felt his cock through all their clothes and groaned, more like a hum. She didn't want to move away from him, but time wasn't holding still. David punched in his car lighter and huffed back into a slouch.

"I'll dream of you," whispered Flora, opening the car door. There was nothing else left to do. "Good night," she said as Matthew pushed the door shut. He backed away. David had started up his motor. Already contact with Matthew seemed as cordial and as brief as exchanging greetings with a parking lot attendant.

"How do you like Matthew now?" David's voice sounded bored and lofty.

"More and more," sighed Flora. She didn't want to accept the fact that the evening was over and she was being returned to her usual state: that of being separated from Matthew. They turned onto Jericho and eased up in front of her house.

"I really appreciate all you've done for me. I hope I can return the favor someday." Flora couldn't imagine at the moment what favor she could possibly do for him, but she didn't know what else to say. She was truly thankful and somewhat puzzled by his altruistic behavior.

"I'm dreadfully tired," he said. "Just tell me I don't have to walk you to your door."

"I don't think that's necessary," said Flora. She got out of his car and pushed the door closed softly. "Thank you," she whispered. She ran lightly across the dewy lawn as he pulled away. His car made a low rumbling sound. Flora glanced back and saw him come to a stop at the curb in front of Matthew's house. She fetched her key out of her coat pocket and stuck it in the lock as quietly as she could.

The door swung open as if there were a vacuum inside the house dying to be filled. Within the dark recess Flora saw a pair of eyes glaring at her. Henry held the door open wide.

"Get in here!" he snarled. His voice reminded her of skin being scraped against stucco. A dog down the street yowled its song of heartbreak. Something inside Flora told her to turn and run, but something else drew her over the threshold. She walked rapidly past him, and then her steps sped up even more. She got to the service porch door and felt him close behind her. She didn't know which way to turn: down the hall to her bedroom, or into the kitchen. It was a simple labyrinth, but complicated enough for the moment. She needed to put some distance between herself and the minotaur.

She went into the kitchen. Henry flung a chair aside. He lunged at her and grabbed her hair with both fists, one at each temple, and banged her head against the kitchen wall again and again.

Flora's arms flew up and covered her face and head in an effort to protect herself, even though, strangely, she felt very little physical pain. She listened to the sound of her head resonating against the hollow wall, like the steel ball on a wrecking rig. And she heard Henry's voice.

"You think you can fool your own father. Leave this house with a twenty-five-year-old fag and think I'm not going to do something about it?"

He gave her head one last rap and then stepped back.

"How dumb do you think I am?" he snarled. None of his questions were ever really questions. Flora knew better than to respond to them as if they were. She raised herself up and hung on to the door frame.

"Think I'm going to sit here, do you, while you try to pull a fast one?" Henry jammed another chair against the kitchen table. "You little slut!"

Flora remained silent. She heard Matthew's words: "Don't be afraid of him. He can't really hurt you."

"I saw you leave the school parking lot with that Cartier creep, that mutt!" He took a swipe at her with his finger, but he was retreating.

Flora didn't flinch. She glared back at him. Now she felt more angry than frightened.

"You followed me?"

Henry wouldn't answer her.

"You followed me!" She felt her own voice trembling with hatred for this man who wouldn't even look her in the face now.

"Damn right I followed you!" He started coming toward her again. She knew it was a mistake to say anything to him, but there was a desire in her to have something that resembled a conversation, even an argument, with this person who was supposed to be her father.

He stood spluttering in the middle of the kitchen floor, like a hydrant suddenly shut off, at a loss for words. They had both heard the sound of footsteps padding down the hall.

Marleen entered the kitchen. She switched on the light and saw Flora's tearful, distorted face, and her hair all mussed up like a home perm gone astray.

"What's happened?" she cried.

Henry stepped aside with mock graciousness as Marleen raced over to Flora.

"This is your daughter," announced Henry in a tone of righteous resolve, "the slut, the liar, and the sneak."

Marleen hugged Flora.

"That's right, love her up." He sounded like a director directing a play he couldn't care less about. "Think she hasn't been loved up enough already tonight? Think that mutt down the street didn't get his fill!" His voice reared up full of spite again.

Marleen moaned and then started crying.

"It's all right," pleaded Flora. She patted Marleen on the back. "It's all right," she insisted.

"Are you sure?" Marleen looked straight into her eyes.

Flora didn't know what was going on in her mother's mind, but she said, "Yes, I'm sure," and kept nodding.

"Well," Henry butted in, "you've done yourself in this time." He righted the chair he had thrown aside earlier, and pushed it under the table. Flora and Marleen stood waiting for him to finish his statement. "You aren't leaving these premises unless it's to go to school, and you're going to school and nowhere else until"—he straightened the chair so that its back was perfectly parallel to the edge of the table—"until the end of the school year. We'll see how that grabs you." He hung back against the counter, seemingly satisfied with his pronouncement.

Flora figured wildly in her head: that was four months or more of being grounded, an impossible length of time. Marleen sucked in an irritated breath, and Flora walked right past Henry without looking at him. There was a good chance he would hit her again, but she dared to do it; it was a show of bravery.

As she left the kitchen he called after her, "And don't think for a minute you'll be staying home from school; I don't care what damn reason you've got." He tried to sound cool but his voice rattled a little and trailed off in disgust. "You little slut," he added.

As Flora came down the hall she saw Daniel and Julia standing motionless in their doorway, their eyes, like puppets', pinned on her.

"It's all right," whispered Flora. "You can go back to bed." She put her pointer finger to her lips. A crazy gesture, she thought as she was doing it, since they weren't making a sound. She must have meant it as a signal to let them know they could expect the rest of the night to proceed calmly. She started to open her bedroom door.

"You were with Matthew Cartier?" Daniel whispered. He sounded impressed. Flora looked back at him.

"Yes," she said softly, and a smile rose unexpectedly to her lips. Daniel smiled impishly and disappeared into his room with Julia tagging after.

Flora opened her door very slowly and looked at the bed. There was an elongated mound under the blankets. She clicked the door shut and went to the closet. She put her high heels back in their box, took off her coat and dress and hung them up. Then she took off her underpants. She held them in her hands for a moment. The smell was of her and Matthew mixed together. She didn't know what to do with them. She was afraid to go and wash them out, so she stuck them in a shoebox in the bottom of her closet.

She took her old flannel nightgown off its hook and slipped it down over her head. It felt cold and limp against her body. She heard her parents' door click shut. For a moment she thought of herself as an orphan child, a little girl dressing herself alone as usual in a large dark dormitory. What a pitiful creature I am! she thought with amusement, casting her eyes upward and smiling at the dark ceiling. She was filled with love for Matthew. Her head hurt and she didn't care.

A muffled voice sounded from the corner of the room. "I didn't tell Dad anything." Flora looked around and saw Janice's face peeking above the edge of the blankets.

"I know you didn't," said Flora, and she crawled over Janice and got under the covers. She lay quietly next to the wall. Henry and Marleen's door opened and closed again.

"When I came home he just grunted at me. He was sitting on the couch." Janice pulled her arms out from under the covers. "Then he paced back and forth in the living room for a long time."

"What time did you get home?" asked Flora.

"Around eleven," said Janice.

"Not much of a dance?" Flora offered this as a possible reason for Janice's early return.

"It was fine, but it was over at ten-thirty," said Janice matter-of-factly.

"Oh." Flora's voice was barely audible.

"Phil was there," said Janice lightheartedly. Flora made no response. "He was there with Tess Duban," Janice added.

"Did that make you jealous?" Flora imitated her lighthearted tone.

"Me? No. Not at all. Why should it?" Janice raised herself up and looked at the back of Flora's head.

"Me neither. They make a very agreeable-looking couple, don't you think?" Flora suddenly felt extremely tired. Her voice faded.

"You're weird," said Janice and she flopped back down.

Sometime before morning Flora dreamed that she and Matthew

were running through a maze. Her father was chasing them. He was a green monster with tusks and horns. She couldn't see him but she knew that was what he looked like. And she could hear him somewhere in the labyrinth, grunting and snarling and jarring the ground. As they were running along she sometimes glanced at Matthew and he was a girl with long, silky black hair streaming behind him. They came to some people who were bending down a tall thin tree with ropes. They said they could catapult Matthew and her out of the maze but the monster was too close behind, so they ran on even faster, taking many turns, hoping to confuse him, until they came to a big fire that blocked their path. They started to turn back, but the monster reared up over them. Green smoke poured out of his mouth and his tongue lashed out like an angry snake and blood squirted out of his horny toad eyes.

Flora jerked straight up in bed. Her heart was making her entire body throb, and she was sweating. When she realized that she was in bed with her sister sleeping soundly beside her, she slipped back down under the covers. She reached up above her head and took a rock out of the windowsill and held it on her belly. It felt good: cool and compact, heavy, like a paperweight holding something down that might blow away.

In the morning she felt sick, drained of energy. She didn't feel like facing anybody. Henry thumped loudly on the door.

"Rise and shine," he said. His voice contained no sunshine, no rising or shining.

Flora had a headache. When Janice got out of bed, the bouncing of the mattress told her that much. Her scalp burned, too. Where had her pillow gone? She rose up a little, and a hunk of galena, dark as a hearthstone, rolled off her. She put it back in the windowsill and found her pillow on the floor between the wall and the bed.

It was a cloudy day. The clouds seemed to be bumping against the kitchen windows, trying to get in. At breakfast Henry announced Flora's task for the day.

"Since you're so good at lounging around, you can sand all the rust off the lawn furniture. And then you can paint it."

It's the middle of winter, thought Flora. Leave it to him to drag out that old lawn furniture that's not even worth saving. Marleen rolled her eyes and Daniel and Julia grimaced. But Flora took consolation in thinking her father's punishments were extreme, inappropriate, wrong. It meant her love for Matthew was right. With that belief she could crack stones with a sledgehammer if she had to. She had seen cartoon characters do it. She could do it too.

Before she knew it, it was Monday morning; she would be released. But first Henry called for an inspection. He pushed his chair back from the table, tightened his lips, and narrowed his eyes. He took his pose as an authority on feminine attire. Flora stood in the doorway while he looked her up and down. She was wearing a pleated wool jumper in pale gray with eight covered buttons and eight hand-done buttonholes up the front, and a dark green crepe blouse beneath.

"Your dress isn't obscene, at least." He allowed her that much. Marleen had a pained expression on her face. It was an outfit she had sewn for Flora, a fact obviously not stitched into Henry's memory.

Flora moved aside as her sisters and brother left the kitchen. Henry regarded her face. "Take that soot off your eyes," he said. "You look like a coal miner's daughter."

Flora went to the bathroom, turned on the faucet, and rubbed around her eyes a little with a wet finger. She returned to the kitchen with her books under her arm. Marleen was at the sink working hard at washing the dishes.

"That's better," said Henry.

"I'm going to be late for school," said Flora as she spun around and out of the kitchen. She felt her earring tap lightly against her neck.

All the way to school she kept trying to think of what she would say to Matthew. She hated to tell him she was grounded again, this time until the end of the school year. It would sound ridiculous, insane. It *was* insane. Her father was insane. She didn't want to have to mention him to Matthew again. It was humiliating. It was as if she had to carry reminders of her father around with her, like photographs in a wallet, and show them to Matthew every so often —See, this is my father, and he says . . .

By the time she sat down in American history she still hadn't figured out what to say to Matthew. She spent the hour scribbling in her notebook. Crazy patterns, impossible labyrinths, webs spun by distracted spiders, feathers and wings. Last time Matthew had a solution, but what would he do this time? What would he say? "Forget it, Flora, you really are too much trouble.

I know girls who have cars. I know women who have their own apartments. I know girls whose fathers are dead." No, he wouldn't say that. But what would he say? And what could she say? What could they do? She saw him clicking the door shut to Timpanelli's washroom and coming toward her. Her feelings for him were so strong, she couldn't think straight to straighten anything out. Her brain was diluted paint swirling down a drain. She felt as though she had never really had to solve a problem before.

In Shakespeare, Mr. Langtry started in on *King Lear.* Flora didn't think she was going to like it. Right off King Lear was ordering people around, holding his daughters up to examination and ridicule.

On the way to chemistry class someone put a hand on her shoulder. She turned her head and there was Mrs. Baines's face smiling sweetly into her own. It looked like an overripe peach: past plump, shriveled into fine wrinkles, covered with fine fuzz, the fuzz dusted with a cherry tint.

"Come along with me, dear." Mrs. Baines continued to smile at nothing in particular. She sounded weary of her authority—just carrying out another one of the endless duties of her office.

Flora followed along beside her, feeling vulnerable, like a very ripe piece of fruit herself, something Mrs. Baines had picked up on her way home from the market. She didn't know what she was wanted for. When they got to the office, Mrs. Baines put her arm around her shoulders.

"We don't have any gypsies in this school," she said, smiling sadly and shaking her head slowly. Flora tried to make sense of her statement. "Gold hoop earrings are not proper school attire, dear."

Mrs. Baines was staring at her intently, as if trying to remember something.

"Flora Jackson." Mrs. Baines pronounced her name with a tone of regretful success, as when an adult plays a game with a child and accidentally wins.

So that was why she hadn't been pulled all the way to the Main Office by her earring. Flora cursed herself. If only she had realized from the start that Mrs. Baines hadn't recognized her, she could have run off. What the hell, thought Flora now. "I'm not a gypsy," she said plainly.

Mrs. Baines was already moving toward her file cabinet. By the time she found what she was looking for, her smile had begun to pucker. "You seem to have a very poor understanding of school protocol, Flora." Her voice trembled. Flora's record folder lay open in her hands.

Flora decided to remain silent.

Mrs. Baines sat down at her desk and started writing sporadically on a sheet of yellow paper that she had carefully lifted from her desk drawer. Flora felt she was observing some peculiar ritual that Mrs. Baines performed often, and with a mixture of pleasure and deadly earnest. She expected to receive her expulsion papers any moment.

Mrs. Baines finally spoke. "This . . ." She paused to write something more. "This is your detention slip. At the beginning of the lunch hour, report to the detention room and have the teacher on duty sign this every day. Bring it back to me at the end of the week." She lifted the sheet of paper gingerly off her desk, holding it up by two corners for Flora. She might have been selling panties at a lingerie counter of a department store. Flora took it from her as if she were accepting a filthy rag, pinching it between a thumb and a finger.

"Where is the detention room?" asked Flora.

"You'll find it on the other side of the student store." Mrs. Baines gave her a big V-shaped smile. Flora turned and started out of the office.

"Oh, Miss Jackson," added Mrs. Baines, "the next time there is a problem, I think we'll have to consider expulsion."

Flora looked back and saw that Mrs. Baines wasn't looking at her; she was organizing papers on her desk, a little too rigorously.

Flora turned and went out. For the second time that day, she felt her earring swinging from her ear. Mrs. Baines had forgotten to tell her to take it off.

It was too late to go to chemistry class. She wandered around the school, along all the backbones of long halls, into their protuberances, toward classrooms filled with laughing students, shouting teachers, or strange silences. Before reaching those rooms, she turned and walked out again, past storage rooms filled with who knows what, and then along pink stucco walls like rough pink skin, and along asphalt and concrete paths cutting across lawns of coarse yellow grass, not for sitting or lying on. Pink walls, yellow grass, gray paths—it was such a poor color scheme. Even Timpanelli would have made a face.

The bell rang and a multitude of students sifted through all the doors in all the buildings. Flora went to her dance class. Tess looked chipper. She was doing warmup exercises, stretching her legs up over her head while lying on her back.

"I didn't see you at the dance." She swung herself into a sitting position as Flora came near.

"I wasn't there," said Flora flatly. What else could she say? She hadn't spoken more than a dozen words since she got out of bed, not much more than that for the entire weekend. Her mouth wasn't even working.

Tess cocked her head and smiled coyly. She was sitting with her back very straight and her arms stretched back, her fingers spread out on the floor like fins. She lowered her lashes. "How was Matthew?" she asked. She sounded as if she were asking Flora for her opinion of a certain entrée on a menu. Janice must have told her, thought Flora.

"How was the fillet of Phil?" She mimicked Tess's tone, and Tess looked shocked. She seemed to have lost her backbone—she slumped down suddenly and looked away from Flora in anger.

Flora didn't want to talk like that to Tess, but she was in the mood to talk back to someone. At the moment it seemed as though nothing could be held sacred and people could say anything they pleased, say anything and then get insulted when the same sort of thing came back in their own faces. She had heard a smugness in Tess's voice, and she thought she had seen it in her gestures, and that was what she had reacted to. She went through the motions of the dance class, feeling wretched all the way. Tess was just curious, that's all, she kept thinking.

The detention room looked like a regular classroom except that the lighting was poor: there were windows along only one wall. And there was nothing on the bulletin boards. Nothing was being taught, nothing that had anything to do with the three R's, anyway.

Flora looked around the room. She saw indifferent, bitter, and sullen faces, so obvious they looked like theatrical masks. She saw girls with high-ratted hair and long black tails painted on their eyes. They looked like the kind that made it their business to fill the lunch area restrooms with cigarette smoke, gathering together two, three, and even four at a time in the same toilet stall, talking with the air of conspirators. They slouched at their desks now, some of them, toying with their lunch sacks, or twisting and untwisting their spitcurls.

Most of the boys looked like the ones who hung around the back gate and staged fights in the dusty lot beyond the soccer field. Flora hadn't entered or left school by the back gate since junior high, so she had forgotten about this side of Hazelton High—these boys with their neatly slicked hair, their shadows of mustaches, and their glossy black jackets. She was surprised to see they still existed in such numbers. It was like discovering an ant's nest. They didn't tend to move in the open anymore; they didn't walk around in packs the way they used to.

Here they were, some of them at least, hooked into this room, held in captivity for this hour, which for them, after all, probably wasn't much different from any of the other hours they spent in other rooms during the day. Their legs were stretched this way and that, way out into the aisles. A few of them eyed Flora critically when she came in.

There were also a few oddballs in the room, kids who didn't know what else to do with their lunch hour and would just as soon be in detention as anywhere. They must have made sure someone with lots of authority was watching when they broke some small school rule. Now they seemed to be tittering to themselves, enjoying some private joke.

Flora went to the teacher's desk, which was in the usual spot for a teacher's desk. Mr. Whitney looked up. She handed him the yellow piece of paper. His face looked tired and saggy, but his thick gray mustache was alive. It shifted to one side, like a little fox making room in its den for another little fox. He might have been grinning; it was hard to tell with the mustache. He signed the paper and handed it back to Flora. "What a wonderful opportunity for you to study chemistry, Miss Jackson." He sounded both bland and smug.

Flora looked up at the blackboard. *Silence is Golden* was scrawled in huge letters followed by a diagonal exclamation mark. It was the work of Mr. Whitney's insistent hand.

"Take a seat at the back," he said, as any bus driver might.

Flora walked down one of the aisles, carefully stepping over the feet of the boys. One or two of them lifted the hem of her jumper with the toes of their shoes. There were snickers here and there.

She set her books down on an empty desk at the end of a row and dropped into the seat. So here I am, she thought. She crossed her arms over her books and laid her head down. Nothing seemed to matter. She closed her eyes for a while and just rested. She could smell the varnish on the old desktop; her nose was nearly touching it. When she opened her eyes she saw, with blurred vision, a network of deep pen and pencil gouges and grooves, big as gullies from that distance.

She lifted up her head. There was a horde of initials linked by plus signs. Some of them had been crossed out and corrections made. Some of the initials were fenced in by heart-shaped corrals. Some were too big for their hearts and leapt their bounds. Some were pierced with arrows. Some were alone, included on the messy plain but alone all the same. They all seemed to be saying, Look, I was here, I'm somebody . . . Somebody loves me, even—or did, anyway, in the year indicated.

Flora started wondering about those students whose names or initials were followed by the words "was here" and an exclamation mark, a personalized variation on "Kilroy Was Here." It was as if they had voluntarily put themselves in this position, at this desk, in this room, in this school, on this earth even. Or their carvings were like tombstone markings: proof of their existence in the wake of their departure. But then, there was always some creep who would come along and scratch "So what?"—some anonymous person who couldn't resist belittling another person's existence.

Flora felt no impulse to advertise her own stint in the detention room. She was repelled by the act of marring surfaces, both natural and manmade. But the thought of having someone else come along and say "So what?" or "Who cares?" was an even bigger deterrent.

Still, she was amazed by the proliferation of graffiti on the desk before her. In the other classrooms she had been in, custodians removed desks and refinished them long before they reached this stage. Not even the desk she had in chemistry was this bad. Smack in the center there were childish drawings of genitals, both male and female. Someone with no knowledge of Latin had labeled the parts. And mixed in with the record of amorous contacts was a short history of gang wars. *West Hill Warriors vs. Scorpions. Falcons Kill the Warriors! Falcons Forever! Melinda loves the Falcons! Scorpions Sting Bad,* and a little grave with a cross stuck in it drawn next to the Falcons. Also *Surfers Suck* and *Mr. Whitney Sucks Chalk!* ("Test tubes," Flora was sorely tempted to add.) *Armadillos vs. Surfers. Surfers have Crabs* plus *I wouldn't know. Deviltones Rule!!!* and no response. Flora moved her books up farther. The longest single entry was:

> Silence is Golden. They don't care who you are.
> Open your mouth, We'll hit you with an Iron Bar!

Who was threatening to hit who? Flora wondered if the person who had written the lines would actually hit someone with an iron bar, or if this was just tough talk. She looked again at Mr. Whitney's chalked motto. The exclamation mark looked like a photo negative of the dramatic tails the girls drew at the corners of their belligerent eyes.

Mr. Whitney's head was bowed. He was reading the *Hazelton Howler,* which was spread out on his otherwise clear desktop. She saw, for the first time, a bald spot on the top of his head. It looked like a target.

The bell rang sooner than Flora expected. She bounded down the steps from the detention room. She liked the feel of the wooden steps. They bounced under her weight; they made a genuine response. She could go see Matthew now—that is, if he had come to school today. She hadn't decided what she would say to him, but she couldn't stay away from him.

When she walked into Timpanelli's room and saw him, he looked like a familiar stranger, like someone she hadn't met yet, some French waiter, or shoe salesman, a dance instructor, movie star, card shark. Her head felt like a jumble of stray photos. She kept casting these images aside until finally she saw the Matthew she thought she knew standing at his easel and staring back at her.

"Are you all right?" he asked, taking her by the arm.

"Yes," said Flora. "I'm just glad to see you again."

"You had kind of a faraway look on your face," said Matthew. "Like you didn't recognize me." He pulled back from her and looked into her eyes. She looked back at him without wavering.

"Matthew," said Flora, "my father knows we were together." She crinkled up one cheek. "But it doesn't matter," she added, shaking her head and smiling a little. "It doesn't matter," she said again. Matthew shook his head back and forth slowly, as if making an attempt to keep up with Flora's head.

"You mean"—Matthew thought for a moment, his eyes darting everywhere as he traced back over their last evening together—"your father followed us?"

"He just did, he decided to," said Flora. She felt like she was turning into cement.

From the tabletop, Tess kept her eyes bent toward Matthew and Flora. It was obvious to her they were having some trouble.

"How far did he follow us?"

Flora shrugged her shoulders. She looked down at Matthew's

suede shoes. "I don't know, maybe he didn't really follow us. But he knows we left the school together."

Matthew picked up his pencil and leaned toward his drawing. Then he just beat out an irritated rhythm on the ledge of his easel.

"He says I'm grounded again . . . to the end of the year." She tried to sound unmoved by her news, as though there were nothing to it.

"I figured as much." Matthew's voice was cool, almost icy. He started drawing again, but after several strokes he dropped his pencil onto the ledge. "I think I'm going to go, Flora. I'll see you later." Every muscle in his face was taut. His eyes looked flat black, like tarpaper. He passed by her and quickly left the classroom.

Flora felt like her soul had been yanked out of her body. A heavy stone pounded her in the chest and sank into her belly. It's all over now. Sure, why shouldn't it be? It was impossible from the start. A bad experiment. A faulty equation. She would go home and tell her father that she had made a big mistake. Unground me. It doesn't matter. I'll be good. I don't have anyplace to go. Matthew's gone. He left. The air raid sirens announcing the end of the world might as well have been sounding in her ears.

She cast a last glance at Matthew's easel. He had left his drawing behind: Two figures were expiring in fire. Blue flames were whipping up around them. Sparks of vermilion and violet were flying. It was a sacrificial offering of some kind.

No, it wasn't so! It couldn't be. They were a couple in ecstasy, gathering warmth and energy from the fire. You could see it on their faces. They were rising up out of the flames, not burning up. She took the drawing down, quickly rolled it up, and went after Matthew.

"Hang in there," said Timpanelli in an earnest whisper. Flora sent Timpanelli a frantic glance. Timpanelli rested her cheek on her fist and gazed at the acoustical tiling on the ceiling. "Why so desperate so soon? I didn't get like that until I got married—married and childless," she said to nobody but herself.

Flora ran down the hall, casting glances out of every doorway and window as she went. When she got to the end of the hall she scanned the parking lot. No movement there. Matthew was long gone, she figured. She turned around and walked back to Timpanelli's room.

At the doorway, she hesitated, wondering what she might do in there now. She looked toward Timpanelli, and Timpanelli, as if on cue, wiggled her pointer finger, beckoning to her. Tess dropped her pose with weariness, and then tried to regain it. Flora drifted over to Timpanelli's desk.

"No luck?" Timpanelli blinked at her through her cat's-eyes glasses.

"I just wanted to give this to Matthew." Flora lifted the roll of soft paper she had in her hand.

Timpanelli's hand crept across her desktop in stops and starts, like a bold yet cautious spider. Her finger leapt to her desk calendar and traced a wide wavy path down the month of February. "Valentine's Day isn't until Friday."

Flora went limp. She couldn't help but smile.

"Why don't you just take a rest for a while?" Timpanelli offered Flora a chair.

When Flora left school that day, she was still clutching Matthew's rolled-up drawing. She was beginning to think of it as a souvenir.

That evening she felt a rare emotion: she wanted to tear everything apart. She wanted to tear the curtains from the windows, rip the sheets off the bed, tear the hemp squares up from the floor, yank the drawers out of the dresser, dump the desk drawer out, jerk all her clothes off their hangers. She wanted to make chaos out of a stultifying order. Maybe by doing this she could bring Matthew back, or else obliterate him altogether, smudge out all thoughts of him.

Lying in bed in the dark she imagined all these acts of destruction that she couldn't perform. She'd like to show Henry how much she hated him by tearing the place apart. Throw the clock radio out the window, at least, but she couldn't even do that. Half of it belonged to Janice. Janice rotated from her back to her belly and mumbled something in her sleep—every other syllable was missing. It would be hard to destroy anything in the room without destroying something that was Janice's too. Anyway, she couldn't make a mess of the only place she had to go to. With that solid thought weighing upon her, she wavered in and out of sleep.

From out of nowhere she had a vision of herself floating in air, the waking sensation of rising and floating upward. It felt strangely exhilarating. Then she sank into a deep sleep, like an anchor slipping off the edge of a continental shelf. She dreamed she was lolling around in the warm surf of the Pacific Ocean. She hadn't been in the salt water for a long time, and it felt good. Suddenly the waves sucked back, dragging huge beds of seaweed with them. She looked out to the horizon and saw a monstrous wave, more horrifying than any description of the atomic bomb. And it was growing and growing and moving toward shore. All the other bathers seemed to be unaware of it. They were still splashing and swimming. She called to them and pointed in the direction of the huge wave, but they ignored her. Then she began floating up into the air. They looked up at her in fright. She pointed to the big wave on the horizon, but they were petrified by the sight of a person rising in air. "Don't be alarmed," she said, "just do as I do. Think only good thoughts, and move your arms upward slowly and steadily, like this." She lifted herself up higher and hovered over them. They only gawked at her. Finally some of them saw the wave, a gray-green wall, a hundred feet high and on the verge of collapsing, and they began to struggle toward shore, lunging and grasping at foam. But it fell on all of them. Flora watched this annihilation, feeling as high and as helpless as a newly fledged bird, and woke up sobbing with a terrific sadness.

Janice woke up, too, and started patting her on the back. "It's OK, you're just dreaming, you're only dreaming," she kept saying.

"It was awful," moaned Flora.

"You walloped me in the face with your hand, if you don't know," said Janice.

"I'm sorry," said Flora as she lay back down. She repeated Janice's words to herself: "You're just dreaming, you're only dreaming." Why do we say, It's just a dream, as if dreams weren't worth anything? I could taste the salt air and hear the screams of the other bathers. And I could float in the air as surely as I can sit down to a meal or take Matthew's face in my hands and kiss his lips. She gazed at the black wall beside her. Later in the night, she dreamed that Matthew and his father were moving out of their house on Jericho. She tried to tell him she didn't want him to, with sign language as if he or she or both of them were deaf. She was aware that she was dreaming while she was dreaming, but by dawn she had forgotten all about it.

As they were getting dressed for school in the morning, Janice said sadly, wagging her head, "That Matthew has been nothing but trouble from the start."

Flora put the gold earring through her ear, took it out again, and threw it in her jewelry box. "If you think Matthew is the source of the trouble, you have your head up a test tube!" She wanted to scream, but she only cried. Whipping her coat on, she left the bedroom and then the house. She slammed the front door, though she hadn't meant to. Henry was probably snarling in the wake of her sonic boom. He deserves everything he gets, she decided. She walked to school in a drizzle, ignoring it, and sat through her morning classes with anger smoldering inside her.

It rained on and off all morning, though not enough to make puddles anywhere. Flora walked outside on the paths between classes, avoiding the crowded halls.

In detention, someone threw a wad of bubble gum. It hit her on the forehead and then bounced off and landed on the floor, in the aisle. At the end of the hour, one of the boys stepped on it and carried it out of the room unawares.

Matthew didn't show up in Timpanelli's class. Flora pinched her pencil and drew. It seemed that drawing was the only thing she could keep on doing without having it ripped away from her or walk away from her. She kept seeing Matthew walking away from her, straight out of the room, without looking back.

A new male model was reclining on the table, looking as though he were fast asleep. Tess was kneeling beside him, peering down. They formed what could have been a tableau of Psyche gazing upon the sleeping Cupid. As the hour neared its end Flora began to feel a pain in her drawing hand. She looked at her fingers. Their tips were white. She looked at her drawing and saw herself kneeling beside Matthew.

She was starting to feel toughened by his break from her. And dull to the world. She had a gray, lusterless exterior, like a geode. No one was going to crack her open. On the inside, in among the crystalline dreams, in a place where time couldn't wear anything away, she could hold on to an unmarred image of him.

Red Tissue Paper

"Isn't it sharp yet?" Miss Corbie asked, raising her voice. Flora hadn't realized how long she'd been standing there at the pencil sharpener. It made her feel as if she'd been asleep all morning. She looked at her pencil. It had been reduced to a stub. She wished she could grind away the whole day as easily as that.

In second period, King Lear continued to rant and rave. "How sharper than a serpent's tooth it is to have a thankless child." Flora knew what her father's variation on "thankless child" was. He called his children "ungrateful pups," as if he were the one who had nursed them. And yet she could not recall a time when he had so much as stuck a spoon in her mouth or Daniel's or Julia's.

When she stepped into the dance room, it was still vacant. She did four cartwheels across the cool cement. She made several attempts at a handstand. Her toes finally maintained a position somewhat ceilingward and she took two shaky steps on her hands. Tess entered the room with some other girls. "Are you planning on joining the circus with you-know-who?" There were giggles from the group that surrounded Tess. Flora righted herself. She didn't know what to say, so she just shrugged her shoulders.

She took a place beside Tess during the class period. "Maybe I *should* join the circus with Matthew," said Flora when she caught Tess's eye. "I think I'd do anything to be with him."

"You can fall on your face for all I care," replied Tess as she bent over and placed the palms of her hands on the floor.

Matthew wasn't in Life Drawing that day either. That's not so unusual, reasoned Flora. He often stays away from school for days at a time. But the thought kept picking at her: Maybe he's staying away from you, Flora? Maybe he doesn't want to see you anymore?

That evening she took down from her closet shelf the drawing he had left behind in class on Monday. She unrolled it and studied the figures rising from the flames. She weighed their warmth against the coolness of Matthew's departure. "I'll see you later," he had said, without even looking at her. His words, the way he looked—every time she relived that scene, her entire body took the same sharp dip as if it refused to learn from experience.

He wasn't in school on Thursday either.

The next morning she almost didn't get out of bed. She pushed the curtains aside. It was so foggy she couldn't see as far as the back fence. She lay back down. Janice was already dressed. She said, "Get up, Flora," as if Flora were a dog she was tired of training.

In the kitchen, Flora was struck by the sight of Marleen in her bright pink velour robe. Janice, Daniel, and Julia had their mouths full of French toast. Marleen slipped two plump slices onto a plate in front of Flora as soon as Flora sat down, and then, flaunting a spatula, she said, "Happy Valentine's Day, Flora," in her gladdest voice.

"Oh, Mom," moaned Flora. She could hardly bear the sight of her mother trying so hard to be gleeful. "I didn't know anybody celebrated that anymore, except maybe the Hallmark Card Company."

"Maybe that's what's wrong with this world," replied Marleen, her glad front undented.

Flora started eating her French toast. Marleen said "this world" as if there were other possibilities. Flora wondered what sort of dreams her mother was having nowadays. They didn't share their dreams anymore. Marleen would be shocked by some Flora had been having lately. Still, Flora wished her mother would go ahead and ask, and she wished the asking could be as easy as snipping the ribbon on a gift.

Henry came into the kitchen. He wanted to know where the morning paper was. Daniel and Julia snickered. Flora knew they were remembering the time Daniel had gotten a roll of toilet paper for him, a one-shot joke that hadn't pleased him.

Henry leaned against the door frame and stared at the ceiling. He looked like he was studying the cracks an earthquake had made. He had a sour expression on his face. He didn't sit down until Daniel had handed him his paper. Flora got up to leave, but he stuck his elbow out and blocked her exit.

"Just a minute. Have a seat."

Flora sat back down.

"Wipe that disgusted look off your face." He unfolded the newspaper and glanced at the front page. "I'm sick of the way you've been moping around here." He looked at her. "You had better give some serious thought to rejoining this family, young lady." He whipped a page over, though he hadn't even glanced at it.

"If you haven't changed your tune by the time you get home today, you're going to find out what trouble really is." Janice put her dish in the sink and left the kitchen, and Daniel and Julia snuck out. "And I ain't just a-kiddin'."

Henry bit the air when he said "ain't," startling Flora. Then he stared at her like a baboon set on defending his territory.

She got up to go again, and he stuck his elbow out again. "Did you hear what I said?" Marleen put a plateful of French toast before him.

"Yes," replied Flora without emotion.

He let her pass.

"Thanks for the breakfast, Mom," said Flora when she was nearly out of the kitchen.

Flora walked briskly through the fog, looking only a few paces in front of her feet, and got to school way ahead of time. There were only a few other students on the paths or in the halls, and no footprints in the wet crabgrass.

She opened her locker and found a white envelope lying on top of all the books. It was bulging and business-sized. She picked it up and turned it over. "Flora" was written on the other side. It was Matthew's handwriting.

Flora's hand began to tremble. Her first impulse was to find a hiding place, a safe place where she and this package, whatever it contained, could be alone. But she glanced up and down the hall and saw no one, so she tore the end off the envelope. There was another, smaller envelope inside. She opened it very carefully. Her heart was beating with long, hard thuds. There were more envelopes placed one inside the other. Finally she came to a bundle of red tissue paper. She slowly unfolded it. In the last crease, she found a gold ring. Not an earring, but a ring for a finger. She slipped it onto her ring finger, and a black star sapphire winked up at her.

"Oh, Matthew," she moaned, clutching her hand with the ring on it with her other hand and holding them both to her chest, along with all the litter of envelopes and tissue paper. Someone stepping into the Long Hall at that moment might have thought she was trying to stanch the flow of blood from a wound. She searched through the envelopes again, hoping to find a note from him. She needed to hear his voice. She found a folded slip of paper and almost tore it in half trying to get it open.

Flora,

Please forgive me for walking away from you the way I did. I never thought there could be a time when I wouldn't know what to say to you. But that day, I couldn't think of anything. I was very angry. Not at you especially, but at everything in general, and the anger made me unable to think or talk. Also, I had the feeling that you had decided to give up on me. The way you talked, it sounded like you didn't care anymore.

Anyway, I thought I'd better leave. And do some thinking alone for a while.

It hasn't been easy, trying to get close to you. But I love you, Flora, as deeply as ever. I hope you will want to wear this ring. I hope you have not decided that I'm too much trouble.

I can stand anything but doubts about our love.

I hate the distance. I wish I was holding you right now.

Matthew

At the bottom of the paper Matthew had drawn a heart pierced by an arrow and had written "MC + FJ" safe within its bounds. Flora's tears blurred the ink. She folded Matthew's letter back up and stuck it down inside her sweater. As she cried, sadness, like a fog, seeped in and around her. It felt good to let the toughness wash away.

She picked up all the envelopes and the tissue paper and threw them in the trash can, though she hated discarding anything Matthew had touched. She saw the large envelope with "Flora" written across it and wanted to grab it up again, but she decided to let it be. Instead she took back one of the smaller ones, one she hadn't torn, and put it in her notebook.

During her first class she wrote:

Dear Matthew,

I have been so lonely without you. And I've been worried and angry and hopeless too. But now I know it was of my own doing. I don't blame you for walking out. If I seemed like a cool ember to you that day, it was because I was burning up with anger over what my father had done and yet I wanted it to sound unimportant—like it didn't matter. I dreaded telling you about it. I don't like having to mention his name to you.

But I will tell you now, my love for you burns hotter than the worst anger, and softer than candlelight.

I love you, Matthew, and I will keep on loving you beyond pain and anger, and classrooms and school hallways, and time away from you.

Yes, I will wear your ring.

Always,
Flora

She took the envelope out of her notebook, wrote "Matthew" across it, put the letter in the envelope and sealed it. Then she tucked it inside her sweater along with the one he had written to her. For the first time in a long time she felt that something had been accomplished.

In Shakespeare, as Mr. Langtry read aloud, Flora heard her own father's anger mixed in with King Lear's.

If it be you that stirs these daughters' hearts
Against their father, fool me not so much
To bear it tamely; touch me with noble anger,
And let not women's weapons, water-drops,
Stain my man's cheeks!

Mr. Langtry noticed Flora's lips forming the words along with him, and asked her to stand and read to the class. Flora began in a wobbly voice, but as Lear's emotions crept into her, she spoke out as if she meant it. Mr. Langtry beat his fist once against his chest and left it there. "A very stirring reading," he said. Flora had surprised herself. She was shaking as she lowered herself back down in her seat. Then she noticed that several students had turned around and were frowning at her. Maybe they were just puzzled.

She sat in chemistry class wishing it could be like kindergarten, with mats spread on the floor and a gentle-voiced teacher. Mr. Whitney sounded especially loud, as though he were lecturing to a hall of hundreds. He spoke about moles and liters and the constant 6.02×10^{23}, and the inability of most of the class to grasp the simplest concept. Flora thumbed through her chemistry book. How will I ever catch up? she thought. She stared at the back of the neck of the boy who sat in front of her. He had acne so bad that the red welts had crept all the way around there. If Mr. Whitney is so smart, why doesn't he come up with a chemical cure for that? she asked herself. Even when she was badly in need of some information—a page, a chapter number, or a due date—she hesitated to tap the boy on the shoulder. She knew he'd be sure to turn around completely, and politely give her the information she needed. She'd have to look at the swollen battlefield of his face. His acne had made him humble and obliging toward everyone. She could never remember his name, something Turner. He was a reminder of how cruel life could be when it got a hankering to. That was his name, Hank, Hank Turner: the boy nobody but a girl with acne would date. Flora wanted to tell him she was grounded until the end of the school year, just so he would feel better. Mr. Whitney assigned two more chapters to read over the weekend and raised his brows at the entire class, looking for an objection. No one objected.

Flora managed to get out of her street clothes and into her leotard without anyone in the locker room noticing she had two envelopes down her front. She was really in the mood for this class. She was glad it followed chemistry. But then, she had planned it that way. There were a few little things in her life she had some control over, and the order of her classes was one of them.

By the time she got to the dance room several dozen girls were already there. Tess was sitting by herself in one of the windowsills. Flora went over and sat next to her.

"I'm glad you and Phil got together." It was an honest thought. Flora had been thinking it ever since the night of the school dance, and so she decided to say it.

"I'm not seeing Phillip anymore," said Tess flatly, and she drew her feet up onto the edge of the sill.

"I'm sorry," said Flora, and she took a perching position on the sill too. If Tess couldn't tell that she was trying to talk plainly and sincerely, then Tess had to be a birdbrain. She waited for a response.

Tess looked her up and down. "*I'm* not," she said superciliously. Then she saw Flora's discouraged expression and decided to drop that tone. "Phil's a nice guy," she said with a sigh, "but I thought I'd go nuts with all his pawing."

"You're not the first person who's felt that way, I'm sure," replied Flora. They matched each other's exasperated looks and then began laughing.

When Pazetti entered the dance room her attention was drawn to two nearly hysterical girls perched precariously in a windowsill. She pictured two of her prized students cracking their heads like eggs on the concrete shuffleboard court outside and six feet down.

"Will you kindly get out of that window," she said, patting her dainty foot rapidly on the floor. Flora and Tess got out of the window and came over to her. They were trying to keep a straight face. "Neither of you look as if you're ready to dance." She bit her lip and then said, "I think you'd both better spend this period outside in the hall."

Though the privilege of dancing had been denied them for a day, they didn't look at all as if they minded. They both had their legs spread out into the hallway, their shoulders were slumping, their arms and hands, relaxed. Anyone passing by might have noted a resemblance to winos in Los Angeles using the wall of some municipal building for a headboard and exchanging fond memories before they passed out for the night. Their faces had that sort of dazed, pleasant look that inebriated males get, and females too, when they speak of exotic places and of their loves and their losses.

Flora gave Tess a few details about her evening with Matthew. She described the way Matthew's living room had looked by moon, candle, and firelight. How she loved the sight of Matthew making a fire. How embarrassed she was to take her clothes off in front of him. The velvet sofa. How good it felt to fall asleep in his arms. How she had been grounded as a result of that night with him. Tess had to guess that they had made love "all the way" because Flora was discreet, as in a PG-rated film where the camera withdraws from a room just as the lovers roll onto a bed.

In return, Tess gave Flora some glimpses of an evening she had spent in a house at the Malibu Beach Colony with someone she had met on the beach. He had lived in Hawaii for three years, surfed Diamond Head on thirty-five-foot waves. Now he "rode" for Moto, a Hawaiian surfboard company, and modeled swim trunks in *Surfer* magazine. "He has a body that won't quit." Tess was swooning almost, but she was careful not to reveal too much either.

As far as they had confided in each other, they were sworn to mutual secrecy. Secrecy was the hinge their friendship swung on. One squeak and they'd shut themselves off from one another for good. They both knew that. But for now the openness felt good.

"Flora, you've got to come out to the beach house with me some night." Then Tess groaned as if she had spilled the last bottle of booze. "But you're grounded." She laid her head back against the wall. "I swear, you're such a drag with all this grounding business . . . OK, all right, I'll take your word for it, Matthew's worth it."

She reconsidered. "He's so strange," she said, sitting up straight. "It's creepy in a way. I mean, he always looks real hard at people and then doesn't say anything. Just keeps on staring." Tess looked as if she was trying hard to figure something out. "But he's a doll. He's got beautiful eyes." Then she noticed the ring on Flora's finger.

Flora looked down at her hand. She had forgotten she was wearing it. Already it felt like a permanent part of her body, more attached to her than her fingernails, which she was forever gnawing off.

"Did Matthew give that to you?"

"Sort of. He mailed it to me."

"Mailed it to you?"

"Well, I found it in an envelope in our locker."

"So now you're engaged!" Tess was getting excited. She grabbed Flora's hand and peered at the ring.

" 'Enchanted' might be a better word for it," said Flora.

"I always thought he must've cast some kind of spell on you. You walk around like you're in a trance. Not bad," added Tess. She turned Flora's hand slightly this way and that to make the star drift back and forth across the sapphire. Then she let Flora have her hand back.

Flora noticed all the rings Tess had on her own fingers. Three on one hand and two on the other. All different styles, different colors of stones set in both gold and silver. A wiseacre might say that she was the daughter of a jewel thief. Flora knew Tess was displaying the trophies she had won from her admirers. Only one of them was a gift from her parents.

"Tess, if anyone asks about this ring," and Flora twisted Matthew's ring around on her finger, "please tell them that you gave it to me. It was one you didn't like, and so you gave it to me. All right?"

"Sure," said Tess as she regarded all of her own rings with pleasure and wiggled her long fingers. Each finger was tipped with a long, perfectly shaped and neatly polished nail. "But there's one thing I've been wondering about." Tess gave Flora a sly look.

"What?" asked Flora, perplexed.

"Where have you been during lunch this week?" Tess looked downright catty.

"In the detention room," said Flora. She put her hand over her mouth.

Tess went into a giggling fit.

"I don't know what's so funny about that. It was very educational."

Tess laughed even harder.

"Want to come with me? That's where I'm going next." Flora decided to make the most of her revelation.

Tess was bent over with laughter. From between her legs she asked Flora what she had been caught for—bony knees?

"No, for a gypsy earring," said Flora, giving Tess a bland look.

"A gypsy earring," repeated Tess as if she were making a personal record of the article. Her face was red from laughing. "You're amazing," she added.

Flora didn't know what was so amazing, or humorous, about getting accosted by Mrs. Baines. Yet she felt as flushed as if she too had been laughing hard. She looked at Tess's ears and saw a tiny gold cross dangling from each one. "There but for the grace of God go you," said Flora.

Tess gave Flora a startled look. Then she felt her earrings and broke into another fit of laughter.

The double doors of the dance room burst open and a herd of girls jumbled out, followed by Miss Pazetti.

"On Monday I'd like to see you two dancing as hard as you can laugh." Pazetti was straining to maintain a serious face.

Back in the locker room Tess saw Flora slip the envelopes down the front of her sweater. "Good grief! The things you have to resort to." She was half joking, half earnest.

"It's not so bad," replied Flora. She smiled and rolled her eyes. "Special delivery . . . for Matthew."

"Oh," said Tess with mock surprise, "I thought those were progress reports, something your father has to sign."

"Wouldn't he love to get his hands on these." Flora went along with the joke, but she gave the letters on her chest a pat of reassurance.

She didn't know how she was going to deliver her letter to Matthew. He wouldn't be in Timpanelli's today; she felt certain of that.

At the end of her hour in detention, she stood in line and waited to have her piece of yellow paper signed for the last time. Mr. Whitney pulled his mustache.

"Hope you've enjoyed your stay," he said as he scratched his initials on the appropriate line. "See you again soon."

She went to the Main Offices. The door was open to Mrs. Baines's office, so Flora walked in and put the yellow slip on the desk without saying a word. Mrs. Baines looked at it for a moment. Then she crossed her fat, rubbery hands on top of all her paperwork and smiled up at Flora.

"One moment, dear," she said, as if Flora had made a request. She got up and went to match the slip with something in her file cabinet.

The last entry in Flora Jackson's records was: "Excessive jewelry. 5 day detention, Feb. 10–14." Mrs. Baines skimmed back over Flora's history. She came back and settled down in her chair, overlapping her hands on her desk again.

"A little bit of jewelry is in good taste," she began, gracious and informative. "The ring you are wearing now, for instance, is acceptable. However, if you are not married, and I don't think you are, it is more proper to wear a ring on the ring finger of your right hand."

Flora noted that Mrs. Baines was wearing one ring on the ring finger of her left hand, a clear pinkish stone, an amethyst maybe, set in gold. She started to leave.

"Flora."

Flora stopped.

"I have one more thing to say to you. When we keep company with certain types of people, we are apt to forget our ladylike conduct." Mrs. Baines pulled her desk drawer open a little, pretended to look in it, and pushed it closed again. Her voice became suddenly hoarse and tense. "It has been drawn to my attention that you have been petting with certain boys during school hours. You ought to know that this is not permitted. A word to the wise is sufficient."

The word *petting* sounded sickening to Flora, especially coming from Mrs. Baines. But worse yet was the hurt of being informed upon. And how had "boy" gotten pluralized, and by whom? She nodded to Mrs. Baines with a lump in her throat and walked out of the office.

In Timpanelli's class she regarded Tess and Tess's male partner, and drew one female surrounded by a dozen roughly sketched masculine bodies. When Timpanelli made her rounds, she whispered in Flora's ear, "I know Matthew's been out of class for a while, but don't you think you're being a bit rash?" Then she widened her eyes and shrunk her mouth into a little *o*.

So Flora told Timpanelli everything Mrs. Baines had said, and Timpanelli gnarled her face up into all sorts of grotesque masks. Timpanelli's amusement was contagious, and Flora finally began to feel some relief.

"The world is full of rats," said Timpanelli. "Don't waste your time trying to catch them." She twitched her nose at Flora.

Nuts and Bolts

On the way home Flora passed through the corner grocery store. The color red caught her eye and she turned and saw that the card rack was filled with valentines. She rarely bought cards. She usually sent homemade ones to relatives, a habit carried over from childhood, out of construction paper, glitter, watercolors, crayons. Once she even made a valentine fringed with real lace for her sixth-grade sweetheart, which however got swiped by another boy.

Flora stood at the card display, opening and closing one card after another. She considered giving one to her mother. Then she remembered her own bitter comment at the breakfast table. Her mother would think that a bought card was some kind of joke, coming from her anyway. No, she wouldn't. She would be tickled pink. She would take it as sincere.

Flora picked out one that was "For a Mother from Her Daughter," a floral, embossed heart surrounded by a red velvet border, and when she looked on the back for the price, she saw that it wasn't even a Hallmark.

The lady at the counter beamed at the card, and then at Flora. She punched the cash register buttons without looking at them. Her lips were as red and crinkly as the corsage of carnations she wore on the shoulder of her sweater. She reached beneath the counter for the right-sized sack and then replenished her smile for Flora. Flora smiled, too. She thanked the lady for putting the card in a sack, although she didn't need it that way, and gave her the exact change.

Flora walked out of the store with the lady's smile still stuck to her own face. She took the card out of the sack and signed it "With Love from Flora," tucked it into one of her school books, and started down the last long block before her own.

As she turned the corner onto Jericho, she saw Matthew's car parked at the curb in front of his house. She felt the letters shifting lightly up and down against her skin. She glanced at every house she walked by, and in every one of their streetside windows she saw no faces. No one was out front tending a lawn or washing a car. She felt on edge, alert, like a rabbit in the open.

When she was nearly opposite Matthew's house she glanced around one more time, giving special attention to her own house. She couldn't actually see it from where she stood, but she saw no one in the front yard or in the driveway, so she dashed across the street, pulled one of the letters out of her sweater, checked to see if it was the one from her to Matthew, and pushed it through a slit in the windwing of his car. Then she dashed back to her side of the street. Her heart was racing. She walked briskly the rest of the way up the block and up her own driveway and was heading toward the side gate as usual when she saw that the garage door was open, gaping darkly like the entrance to a grotto. She walked toward it slowly until she could make out the figure of her father. He was standing perfectly still with his feet apart and his hands clasped together over his stomach. He was shaped a little like a car jack.

Flora remembered the words, "You'd better think twice about rejoining this family . . . Change your tune . . . I have full cause of weeping . . . O Fool, I shall go mad!" And so she approached him.

"Hi, Dad," she said, trying to sound as though she greeted him every afternoon, as a sort of happy habit. He broke his pose and went back to a stack of cardboard boxes at the back wall of the garage. He started jerking them around.

"See this mess. No one can find anything in here! Come over here!"

He didn't say, "Get over here!" so Flora stepped farther into the garage.

"You kids never put anything back where it belongs. Look at this!" He jerked a box onto the garage floor. Flora listened to the racket of clanking metal. Lots of nuts and bolts jingled across the cement. She couldn't think what he was after. She hadn't touched anything in the garage for years, aside from the rakes and the lawnmower and, rarely, the three-speed bike she shared with her mother and Janice. What he was getting at now was beyond her.

He hauled off and cuffed her on the side of the face. She was so taken by surprise that she flew backward and fell onto the bicycle, the very one she had been thinking of, and the pedal scraped her along the ribs. She just lay there and thought about one thing: that Matthew's letter was still hidden beneath her sweater. It hadn't been shaken loose.

"You just can't stay away from that hoodlum, can you." He reared up over her. His face looked like a thin piece of wrinkled gray leather and his mouth looked like a zipped-up zipper slit. Flora's face puckered up.

"When I say stay away," he snarled, giving her a kick in the thigh, "I mean stay away from his car, that piece of junk, too." He reached down and picked something up from the floor. It was a white envelope. Flora's heart jolted. She started to grab for it, but he already had it open. He looked at the interior of the card for a moment. Then he stuck it back in its envelope and tossed it on top of Flora.

"So you're delivering valentines today. Your mother should be flattered." He reached down and jerked her up by the arm. The bicycle, with its pedal caught in her sweater, started to rise up too before falling back down with a crash.

"Get in the house," he said. Flora picked up the card and her books and went out through the back door of the garage. She went around the house, and as she opened the service porch door she looked back. He wasn't following her. She ran down the hall and closed the door to her room. She threw her books on the bed and went and stood in the corner by the closet. Her face smarted, and her ribs and her thigh, all on the same side of her body. She could feel the blood pounding at those three points. "He can't touch me. He can't touch me!" she cried. She put her hand to her chest and Matthew's letter crinkled. Where can I hide it? she thought. She glanced all around the room. Her eyes settled on the two small bird pictures that hung on the wall beside her bed. They were actually a pair of gaudy tropical birds constructed of dyed feathers. They had been hanging there for years—exotic birds that might live in the jungles of Central America even though they had been made in Japan. Flora rather liked them. She stood on the bed and took one of them down. She wanted to read Matthew's letter again, right then, but she didn't dare. She pushed it inside the backing of the frame and rehung the picture. She jumped backward off the bed and checked to see if it was perfectly straight. It looked as though it had never been touched.

At the vanity, in its mirror, she saw a girl, wretched looking but calm. The storm had come and gone, but its marks remained: tousled hair, wet around the fringes, puffy red eyes, a swollen cheek. She lifted up her sweater and looked at her side. Nothing bad, just some scrapes running parallel to her ribs. Then she saw the ring on her finger, held it up in front of her and looked at it again. There was nothing but a gold socket gaping up at her. The stone. The black sapphire was gone.

"Oh, no," she cried. She put her face in her hands and moaned a high-pitched moan that sounded like a wounded pup. She couldn't even keep Matthew's ring in one piece for one day. The eye was missing. Now she felt as though she might as well be blinded too. She saw her own wide, wet eyes in the mirror.

"It's got to be on the garage floor somewhere." The face in the mirror spoke to her. She took the ring off and hid it in the bottom of her jewelry box. After giving a long listen at the door, she eased it open and took a few slow steps. Daniel and Julia were watching cartoons in the living room. She turned back and slipped into the bathroom, put cold water on her face, and brushed her hair with Marleen's brush. Then she went into the living room.

"Hi," she said.

"Hi," they said without taking their eyes off Felix the Cat.

"Where's Dad?" asked Flora politely, as if she needed him for something. Felix was opening his magic bag. He took out a large handsaw.

"He's out in the garage," replied Daniel, still not looking around.

Flora started to sit down on the black Naugahyde couch, then changed her mind and sat down in the coral-colored easy chair. She looked at Julia and Daniel. They were lying belly down on the floor, their chins resting on their hands. Master Cylinder was filling the screen, grinding his way toward them. The television itself, on its spindly, black iron legs, could have been staggering toward them, too. Felix let go of his saw and it floated through the air, sawing off one of Master Cylinder's appendages. Master Cylinder rebuilt his severed limb, hardly breaking stride . . . A Wonder of the Tool Age, a Miracle of Nuts and Bolts. Flora had seen this one years ago. She felt like screaming now. Julia and Daniel were as quiet as pillows.

She got up and went back to her bedroom. When would she get a chance to search the garage floor?

Janice entered with her drill team uniform draped over one arm and a stack of books in the other. "What happened to you?" was the first thing she asked. With Janice it always seemed simply to be a matter of curiosity.

"You-know-who and I had a misunderstanding." Flora gave Janice a discouraged smile.

"Matthew hit you?" said Janice, alarmed. She smacked her books down on the table in protest.

Flora took a deep breath and sighed. "If Matthew ever hit me, I wouldn't be here right now. I'd go hang myself."

"Oh," said Janice. She curled up one side of her lip. "Where's Dad now?" she asked.

"Scrounging around in the garage," said Flora. She grabbed her chemistry book and flipped through it as though she had a grudge against it. She figured she had at least six chapters to study over the weekend in order to catch up. She looked at Janice.

"Would you explain moles to me? I have no idea what they are."

"Sure," said Janice. "It's simple . . ."

"Not now," said Flora, just barely touching her sore cheek, "but sometime this weekend." She watched Janice hang her uniform in the closet. "Drill practice?" she asked.

"No," said Janice, "tryouts. I'm on the committee to choose next year's team. Didn't you see the notice?"

At the dinner table that night, Henry wouldn't look at Flora. He wasn't looking at anyone else either, or telling them anything. He seemed to be pouting. Flora saw her mother taking glances at her swollen cheek.

Marleen's eyes started getting red around the rims. It was obvious to her that some sort of scene had taken place in her absence.

"The dinner tastes good, Mom," said Flora with enthusiasm. Marleen smiled and nodded and started eating too fast. Flora reached for the bowl of mashed potatoes. She couldn't stop thinking about the black sapphire.

The Fallen Chair

Saturday morning Marleen scurried around the table serving up equal portions of scrambled eggs to her children and a double portion to Henry. Henry dished out the chores for the day. Daniel was to accompany him out to The Ranch, as he still called it. There were fruit trees to water and some brush to clear. Julia was told to stay out of the house and help Janice with the yardwork, both front and back. The flowerbeds were, as he put it, a disgrace.

"You can forget about the yardwork this week," he said, turning his attention to Flora. He had determined that she actually enjoyed raking and weeding. "I want you to clean out the garage. And I don't want you to stop until it's finished." He looked her in the eye and smiled a hateful smile. Then he took a careful bite of scrambled eggs.

Flora couldn't stand to watch him eat. He didn't seem to care what the food tasted like, or what it was. His only concern seemed to be a mechanical one: whether or not he could get it into his mouth neatly. If she focused on the bit of egg that clung to his lower lip, perhaps the disgust she felt would cloud the gladness that was rising up too quickly inside her.

An hour later she stood in the garage with a broom in her hand and waited while Henry backed the family car out of the driveway with Daniel sitting motionless beside him. She knew what he meant by "clean out the garage." He meant put every item back in the box he thought it should go in, move all the boxes around, and sweep under them. Don't throw anything away. Just sweep up the dirt and debris and any sycamore leaves that might have blown in.

She dropped the broom and went over to where the bicycles stood tilted on their kickstands. She scanned the floor. She got down on her hands and knees and swept the floor with her hand, whisking aside a few leaves and some scraps of old newspaper. She got up and moved the bikes out onto the driveway. Then she got down on her hands and knees and looked again, running her finger, with her nose right over it, down the grooves and cracks in the concrete. No black stone, not even a pebble or a piece of asphalt.

The day would not last forever. She glanced around at all the junk and fought off a feeling of despair. It has to be here somewhere, she told herself. It must be. She squeezed her eyes shut, and when she opened them again something winked at her. She slowly retraced the path of her sight, and it winked at her again. She crawled over to a waist-high stack of *Sunset* magazines and laid her cheek against the floor. There, nudged between the bottom magazine and the concrete, was a small chrome bolt, and beside it, not more than a half inch away, was Matthew's black sapphire, a shining oval no bigger than a small pea.

Flora held it pinched in her fingers, hardly able to believe it was in her possession again. With her eyes fixed on it, she ran with it around to the back door of the house. Marleen was vacuuming the living room, humming a song in the same key as the vacuum cleaner. Flora fetched a tube of cement from the catchall drawer in the kitchen and headed for her bedroom. Marleen was sucking ashes off the hearth, still singing, and had her back to her.

Flora felt around in her jewelry box until she found the gold ring. She set the sapphire down on the vanity and twisted the top off the crumbled tube of glue. Her hands were shaking. Just one drop in the right place, she whispered as she tried to hold the ring steady. She got what she asked for, picked up the stone, and set it in place. She looked around the room for a safe spot to hide it while it was drying, and decided to put it up in the high window, behind a rock.

By the time she looked back to the tube of glue, a big drop had seeped out onto the vanity top. She ran to the bathroom for some toilet paper. She wiped at the glycerin-like puddle, but it had already begun to dry. The toilet paper stuck to the glue and to the vanity. Flora huffed with annoyance and ran back into the bathroom. She found a razor blade in the medicine cabinet and returned to her room. She scraped carefully at the smear of fuzzy glue until it gave way. But so did some of the white enamel paint, and the top of the vanity was scarred.

"How could I be so dumb!" groaned Flora. She recalled the time when she and Janice, having been sent to bed too early as usual, had turned their restlessness into a game of balancing on the high windowsill, perched like fledglings, steadying themselves with their hands on the ceiling, and then springing, bottom first, onto the bed. The thrill of it had been worth the risk of having Henry walk in on them. He yelled his customary warning from the living room couch: "Another sound out of either of you and you'll find yourselves sitting on the service porch floor!" Many nights they had become humble, cold, and sleepy while sitting on that floor, but not this particular night. Henry must have been too absorbed with a TV program. In the morning, however, they found they had trapped themselves. There on the ceiling was an awful sight: a crazy patch where a herd of wild fingertips had scuffed up the dust. In a panic, they took turns running frantically back and forth between the bathroom and the bedroom with a clean and a dirty sponge while their parents slept. Finally they gave up in despair. All they had succeeded in doing was to create a large charcoal-lined cumulus cloud.

When the blotch was discovered, they admitted to the bed bouncing and were sentenced to a whipping—first Janice and then Flora, according to age. As with all organized punishings, they were told to go to the bathroom, take their pants down, and bend over the bathtub. They were supposed to wait like that until Henry, taking his sweet time, got the knotted clothesline cord from its hook in the utility closet and decided to apply it.

If Henry ever said anything while he was flailing her, Flora never heard a word of it. She was always wrapped up in a private rage that blinded and deafened her. At the time, not even the sting seemed to belong to her. But now the thought of those neatly arranged whippings made her furious. She felt like a hornet inside.

"The hell with it," she said out loud. She tossed the glue in the kitchen drawer and went back out to the garage. "I was repairing something, I spilled some glue. It was an accident. I'll fix the vanity top when I get a chance," she repeated to herself as she swept and shuffled boxes. "What are you going to do about it?" She wanted to add that challenge but decided to drop it. He found reason enough to hit her as it was.

Even though the garage and all the junk it contained wasn't anything she cared about, she worked with satisfaction. She was setting things in order. And Matthew's ring was all in one piece again.

Julia peeked in the garage twice. Both times she said, "Wow, it sure is dusty in here."

At about three o'clock Daniel and Henry returned from The

 Ranch. They both looked scruffy and exhausted. Flora wondered how a dozen scrawny fruit trees could do that to them. Henry stepped into the garage.

"That all has to be done over there." He waved at the west wall. More junk, partially contained in cardboard boxes and army surplus crates, mounted to the rafters.

"I know," said Flora. She stopped sweeping for a moment.

He glared at her and walked away. He came back with a shovel, a garden hose, and a scythe and dropped them on the garage floor. "Put these where they belong," he said and went into the house.

Flora hummed the tunes of "That's How Strong My Love Is" and "Under My Thumb." She tried to imagine what Matthew's bedroom looked like. She saw herself cleaning his room as he continued to work at his easel. Just in case he ever worked in a mussed-up place, she would know how to clean around him without disturbing him.

She climbed up on a big crate, braced herself between the studs of the garage wall, and pushed against the crate with both feet. She felt little curiosity toward it even though its lid was nailed shut. Most likely it was filled with the miscellaneous metal parts Henry had bought at a war auction years before. That was what he had bought, something called a box of miscellaneous parts, and through the years that was what it had remained. When the crate budged she landed on a box of roller skates—old rusty, tangled-up ones, probably close to six pairs in all. It was the box that the Goodwill, a long time ago, had supposedly carried off by mistake. Marleen had suggested this as a plausible answer to the mystery of the missing skates. The Goodwill people had come by while Henry was off on a flight, and, unsupervised, they had taken a box they were not entitled to. How were they supposed to distinguish between give-aways and precious possessions? Marleen had been admonished for not keeping an eye on the Goodwill people, and Janice had made an indignant show of discarding her skate key in the trash can. Flora could still see her chugging across the back yard toward the alley, tearful and mad.

Flora held a matching pair in her hands now. Endless trips around the block came rolling back to her; she recalled the hypnotic clicking of metal wheels over the seams in the sidewalks. Alone or in packs, the kids on the block had done it all summer long for hours at a time, even during the heat of the day. After supper they'd clamp their skates on again and roll around until well after dark. Flora had been an excellent skater, both backward and forward; she could change the direction she was facing at full speed, and do spins and leaps and fly off curbs while holding on to the rear fenders of bikes. It seemed to her now that Henry had hidden the skates back here in the corner of the garage where no one, not his own children or the children of people who shopped at Goodwill, could find them or use them.

She dropped the skates back in the box, took a few swipes with the broom, and pushed the crate back to where it had been. Finally she was big enough to budge Henry's heavy crates, now, when no one on their street roller-skated any more, not even Julia. Girls Julia's age went ice-skating for two-fifty an hour at a local rink. Only one girl, a retarded girl Flora's age, named Angie, who lived around the block, still roller-skated—all year round with a smile on her face and a transistor radio pressed to her ear.

The box of lost skates was really no more disturbing to her than the boxes of broken toys Henry still kept in the garage. As a child, Flora moaned over these toys that Henry had refused to repair. She and Janice, and later on Daniel and Julia, got to view the contents of these boxes about once a year—when Henry was moving other boxes around to get at something else he wanted. It always seemed to them that they had come across the broken toys quite by accident. They fondled the pull-toy duck with its disengaged train of ducklings, the dolls with their severed arms and pushed-in eyes, the wingless airplanes, the metal merry-go-round that would never go round again. He claimed to have always bought them the highest-quality toys, and Santa Claus too was acclaimed for having delivered only the very best. In effect, the Jackson children were always being presented with toys that would not break unless they had been abused by bad children, children who were bent on destruction. To Henry's mind, it was the children, not the toys, that needed to be straightened out.

Flora regarded the boxes of roller skates and broken toys with the same sad smirk she gave the box that contained the letters, postcards, and valentines that Marleen and Henry had exchanged during their courtship. The box was taped shut now, and Henry had written PERSONAL in block letters on the lid. Why her parents had married she no longer wanted to know, and she didn't like musing about why Henry had taken the roller skates out of circulation. He did so many indecipherable things that it was impossible to be bothered with them all, especially things that had happened years before.

She didn't open any boxes that were taped, tied, nailed, or

screwed shut. She knew he would be checking later to see if she had tampered with anything. She didn't even peek in the shoebox that he had purposely left unsealed. She knew what it contained: a collection of marbles, a wooden top, a small tin airplane, and a smashed-looking felt Santa. These, he said, were "all" the toys he had ever received as a child, and they were "well cared for." She dusted and straightened his collection of old flight manuals, and shifted his old suitcases around, which were probably still packed with his charcoal-gray, cigarette-scented flight uniforms. She was feeling dirty and tired and wished the job was done.

After sundown Marleen came out on the front porch and told her that dinner was almost ready. Flora remembered the valentine she had forgotten to give her mother. "All right," she said, wiping the hair out of her face.

"Don't you need some light out there?" asked Marleen and stepped back into the house. Flora flicked on the light switch. As far as she was concerned she had cleaned the garage beyond dispute —well, just about. She gave the center of the floor one more sweeping, put the broom in its proper place, turned off the light, and started to lower the garage door from the inside. It almost crashed down and might have snapped its heavy-duty springs, but she slid backward, pushing up against the door with all her might to slow its descent.

"How many times do I have to make that mistake?" she said aloud. She stood with her hands on her hips in the solid blackness of the garage and caught her breath. Henry had remodeled the garage door with an eye to modernizing the front of the house. That meant covering some perfectly good tongue-and-groove with a ton of plywood. The door was too heavy even for him to open or close from the inside. It was a major effort for any of them to raise or lower it from the outside. Henry said it was a deterrent to burglars, or anyone, thought Flora, wishing to get anything out of the garage. She felt her way to the side door. She locked it as she went out—another one of Henry's rules.

At dinner Henry didn't say anything directly to her, or look at her, but he was talking again. He complained about how deer had chewed the bark off his fruit trees. One peach and two apricots were obviously dead and a couple of others probably wouldn't survive.

Flora took a sideways glance at Daniel. He was just barely eating. He looked dazed. Flora knew that look. On TV it was the look of someone who had just been through electroshock therapy. At the dinner table it was the look of someone who had been badgered too long. She wanted to take her plate and fling it in Henry's face. He wouldn't know what hit him, she thought, using one of his own favorite phrases.

Henry was going on and on in a drone about how Daniel kept running off and he couldn't get any work out of him. "All he wants to do is throw rocks or climb all over them. When I finally got him to do a little work, he moped and sulked like a baby. He's lazy. He's just lazy. You'd think you could get at least an ounce of work out of a twelve-year-old boy. He doesn't know the meaning of the word *work.* He's just lazy."

Henry gave his head a weary shake and looked at Daniel, who was looking at his food. Then Henry looked around at everyone else. He was waiting for a sign of agreement, but they all just looked down at their own plates. Henry scraped his chair back from the table and stood up. "I'm living with a goddamned bunch of mutes!" he said and slung the chair back at the table. It teetered and fell over as he left the kitchen. Everyone looked at the fallen chair. "A fuzzy-headed bunch of mutes," he called out as he passed through the living room.

They looked around at one another. Flora figured they were all thinking pretty much the same thing: Henry rarely cursed. More than that, he never cursed the entire family at the same time. His way was to pick on one person, two at most, and try to make allies out of the rest of the family, as he had started out trying to do tonight. Did he think anyone was going to agree with him about Daniel being lazy? Daniel was always scraping and scurrying according to his father's commands. He probably cut an acre of brush today. He did everything his father told him to. He even got his hair cut according to his father's wishes, and his head always looked like a patch of freshly mown grass. His head was bowed now; he was trying to hide his face.

They all heard the master bedroom door close. "Good riddance," mumbled Flora. She got up and righted Henry's chair. Marleen gave her an apprehensive look, as if to correct anything Henry had done might be a big mistake.

In the morning Marleen found Flora's valentine sitting on the stove, and when Flora came into the kitchen Marleen gave her a big hug. "You're a good girl," said Marleen, and there were tears in her eyes.

Together they started preparing everyone's favorite breakfast, cinnamon toast. Everyone's favorite breakfast but Henry's. Janice came in and stirred the powdered sugar and milk for the frosting. Daniel and Julia entered with a big slab of newspaper, the Sunday edition. With his teeth Daniel cut the string that bound it, and he and Julia, like two coyote cubs pouncing on a piece of meat, took the paper apart until they found the choicest section. Then, quite like civilized creatures, they gave each other fair shares of the comics.

Henry lay in his bed staring at the pale blue ceiling. He couldn't bear the sound of their voices, and yet he strained to hear precisely what they were saying. The congenial atmosphere they were creating among themselves in the kitchen, in the kitchen of his house, without his help or his permission, forced him out of bed.

"Candy for breakfast," he said, eyeing their plates.

"Good morning," said Marleen.

"I'll just have tea." He sat down. Marleen had already put his teacup with its green teabag in it on the table. She reached around him now with the kettle, and the only sound in the kitchen was the spluttering of boiling water as she filled his cup.

Somewhere in the middle of breakfast she told him, "We're going to the shopping mall today." Her voice crunched into the silence like a set of teeth into the broiled frosting of cinnamon toast. Flora and the rest of them looked up with surprise. "You can come if you want." Marleen had a set look on her face. Marleen never made any plans for the family, especially not on Sunday. She had stopped trying to take the children to church years ago.

"Sure, take off," he said. "I've got work to do." He was slumped in his chair, stirring his cup of tea as if he could keep on stirring it forever without any intention of drinking it. His voice sounded faraway and furry.

Actually Janice had plans to spend the day with some friends and left at noon. Marleen said good-bye to Henry, who was again resting on his bed. He said nothing. As though she'd just tucked him in for a nap, Marleen gently closed the bedroom door and tiptoed down the hall.

Flora liked going on these rare shopping trips with her mother. She knew Henry would refuse to come along. Window shopping irritated him. Flora could think of better things to do herself, but except for doing the dishes or sometimes washing her face or brushing her teeth, it was the only thing she and her mother did side by side.

Daniel stopped off at the music store to look at the guitars and listen to records in a soundproof booth. Marleen, Flora, and Julia continued to stroll around the mall. Flora could have chosen a dozen record albums. She saw lots of clothes she would like to have, too. Marleen kept wanting to buy her this or that blouse, sweater, or skirt, but Flora kept saying no and giving excuses that the color or the cut was wrong. Marleen gave up in exasperation, but Flora couldn't help it. She didn't want Marleen to buy her anything. She'd rather not bring anything new home.

Four boys Flora recognized from the beach strode by in a tight bunch and grinned at Flora without saying a word, since Flora was flanked by family. Otherwise, like other girls in the mall, who were alone or in groups, she might have found herself surrounded by them, maybe even going around with them for a while, watching them goof off in front of a display window, try to buy beer at a café. And maybe they'd succeed, since Victor, who was a fast talker and almost had a mustache, was one of the four. They'd ask her why she wasn't at Malibu anymore, and she would want to tell them that it was because of Matthew. Matthew didn't go and so she didn't go. Besides, she was grounded, not that that mattered. And anyway they would have said, "Matthew who? . . . Oh that guy, I know who." Then they'd give her a quizzical look and go on around the mall without her.

Marleen broke the daydream. "Why can't boys keep themselves looking decent any more? It's such a shame," she said, puzzled and a little angry.

Flora glanced back. Victor and the other guys had their heads screwed around too, and they were still grinning, their hands stuck in their pockets, their shirts hanging out beneath their short jackets, flapping like napkins on a line. A whole row of them, all the same.

"Do you know those guys?" asked Julia, with a squinty face.

"Sort of," admitted Flora. They were good guys, but they did look a little ragged. But that was the way guys tended to look these days. Even Matthew wore his shirt hanging out sometimes, though usually, without looking like a mama's boy, he was much neater. He wore wool flannel or corduroy tailored jackets over collared shirts, and corduroy slacks, never jeans. She'd never seen him wear a T-shirt. But then, she'd only seen him through one season. If she was lucky maybe she'd see him through the spring. His ring was resting safely in the windowsill.

Marleen had stopped at a jeweler's window and was bending forward to peer at the rows of rings and bracelets and necklaces, all cushioned in velvet. Flora looked too. She wished she had put Matthew's ring in the bottom of her jewelry box. When Marleen looked up and saw the reflection of herself and her daughter side by side in the window, she gave Flora a hug around the waist. "What a beautiful daughter I've got." She beamed.

Julia nudged up beside her.

"What two beautiful daughters I have!" She hugged them both and beamed again.

Flora was glad that the guys she knew were somewhere else. Her mother's mushiness, when it came on in public, was embarrassing. Marleen let go and pointed to a rack of earrings.

"Oh, look at those," she exclaimed. She always got excited about jewelry wrought in modern shapes, either free form or geometric designs. She lifted up the side of Flora's hair. "Where is that earring you've been wearing?"

"I don't wear it anymore," said Flora.

"Well, let's pick you out a nicer one, a pair," said Marleen.

"That's all right, Mom, I don't need any." Flora tried not to sound offensive.

"Why can't I have my ears pierced?" asked Julia. "There's a place right over there that'll do it." She pulled at Marleen's coat sleeve. Marleen looked around at the beauty salon and then at Julia.

"You know what we've decided. Sixteen is soon enough."

"I didn't agree to that." Julia shrunk several inches and pouted.

"Besides, if you get your ears pierced now, what will you have to look forward to?" Marleen tried to soothe her.

Flora thought back to the day she found the gold hoop earring tucked under the grass at the edge of a sidewalk. She felt it was a good omen. She put it in her pocket and walked on home, feeling a private joy. She kept the earring hidden in the little wooden box where she put her allowance money. On the day after her sixteenth birthday, Marleen took her to get her ears pierced, at the family doctor's, just to be safe. Even after that, she kept the gold hoop hidden and wore the amethyst studs Marleen had bought her. She was afraid that in the time it took her to turn sixteen, it might have switched to bad luck. After meeting Matthew, she dared to wear it, and look what it got her: a week in detention. But, she reasoned, if it hadn't been for the earring, Mrs. Baines would've gotten her for something else.

"I sure hope your father's in a good mood," Marleen wished out loud as they pulled into the driveway. Daniel blew several more notes on the harmonica he had bought and then hid it in his pocket. He jumped out of the car and heaved the garage door up. It teetered near the top of its arc and came down fast. Marleen cringed as Daniel tried to catch it with the tips of all his upturned fingers. There was a racket of springs sounding discordant groaning notes, like a hundred harps falling over. He hoisted the door up again with a bigger show of strength, but it floated up no higher than the first time and started to come down again. Flora leapt out of the car, and together they got it to stay up.

When they unlocked the door to the house, they saw Henry sitting on the black couch with his real estate papers spread all around him. "What's in the bags?" he asked. Julia and Marleen held up the sweaters they had bought, and he scoffed at them.

"They were on sale," said Marleen. Julia held her sweater against her front and looked at her reflection in the picture window. She had been begging Marleen for a lavender sweater all winter.

"I've never seen a female under eighty who looked good in that color." Henry folded up one of his maps and stared at Julia. Two tears crawled down Julia's cheeks. She looked back to the picture window and slowly lowered the sweater. Flora thought she'd just as soon never bring anything home if it had to be inspected by him. She left the living room.

When she opened the door to her bedroom the first thing she saw was scraps of paper littering the bed. "What in the world?" she said. She went over and took a closer look. She saw a finger here, some hair there, an eye, lots of blue lines. It was Matthew's blue-flame drawing, all in pieces and scattered like an unworkable puzzle. She opened her mouth to cry out, but Henry had followed her down the hall and was standing in the doorway.

"We don't allow pornography in this house. If you want to do trash like that, you can get out."

Flora felt a breath escape from her that was somewhere between a cry and a laugh. She put her hand over her mouth and looked back down at the bed. He doesn't even know who drew it, she told herself. Tears fell on the satin bedspread as she tried to gather up the debris. The tears will leave stains, she thought. She tried to hold them in. He doesn't even know who drew it. That's really funny, she cried. She didn't know what to do with the pieces.

"Leave that trash alone and come over here," he commanded. Flora looked up. He was standing by the vanity.

"I suppose you know how that happened?" He insisted that she get down close and look at the scarred surface, so close that her vision blurred.

"Yes," she said, righting herself. "I was repairing something and some glue leaked out of the tube. I intend to fix the vanity." She backed up against the closet doors and stood stiffly.

"Repairing what?" he demanded.

Flora stepped over and searched her jewelry box. She didn't know what she'd come up with until she spotted a little clown pin —a little silver clown holding a cluster of balloons set with dots of garnets, something he had actually picked out for her for Christmas a long time ago. She showed it to him.

"No respect for anything," he said with an air of disappointment. He looked around the room as if examples of his daughter's worthlessness were displayed everywhere. He pulled the door shut as he left.

Flora picked up all the scraps of paper and let them fall in the wastepaper basket. Then she cried again. Nothing's safe. You get one thing back together and something else falls apart. Falls apart? Gets *torn* apart! She thought of Matthew's ring, still lying in the windowsill, and reached for it. She pushed aside some rocks. She crawled up on the desk and looked behind all the rocks. It wasn't there. "Ohhh," she groaned. She felt as if she had received a blow to the head. She sank down in the desk chair and buried her face in her arms. There was a loud buzzing in her head, which she tried to think beyond. If I ask Mom if she's seen it, she'll want to know where I got it. I could tell her that Tess gave it to me. But then she'll want to know why I left it in the windowsill and why I didn't show it to her before. I can't say I had to repair it. I already told *him* I was repairing that clown pin. Fat chance he won't be talking Mom's ear off in bed tonight, telling her about the vanity. Then she'll go and mention the missing ring, just trying to be helpful. He probably has it anyway. I'm sure to be trapped any way you look at it. Hell, a simple lie can grow like mold without any help at all! I won't say anything to Mom. She rubbed her forehead back and forth on her arm. Why would she know what has happened to it anyway? All she ever does in here is vacuum, and dust. Dust with the brush attachment all over everything. She doesn't pry, she just vacuums. The vacuum—that might be it. Flora clutched her head with her hands. That *has* to be it.

Her fingertips felt so cool on her cheeks. I shouldn't get crazy like this, she reminded herself. Even if a jackhammer had smashed the ring to smithereens, that couldn't keep her and Matthew apart. Matthew would understand if the ring was gone. He could laugh about it. His drawing was gone too, for sure. He might even laugh about that. That was the way he was. He hadn't given her the drawing, though. He had left it and she had taken it. Taken it as if she had a right to it. No, she had tried to find him and give it back to him. And he hadn't even mentioned it in his letter. But the ring, if the ring was lost . . . that might be a bad sign.

The vacuum cleaner couldn't be checked until everyone was asleep. She picked up her chemistry book. She tried to read it, but she was just seeing words that wouldn't link together. They were wiggling away from her. Janice was still gone, although it was nearly dark outside. The tree branches were as black as wrought iron and the sky was gray and sooty. She drew the drapes shut, just in case Henry was wandering around in the back yard inspecting his plants or cloudgazing. She switched on the desk lamp and got a piece of drawing paper out. Just a small piece. Henry probably wouldn't enter the room again so soon. She held a soft-lead pencil over the paper and made lots of sketching motions without ever touching it. She pictured Matthew's drawing of them rising together from the fire. There was no way she could replace it. She just wanted to get over an empty feeling. She drew for a long time but finally had to admit, the figures looked awkward—like they didn't know quite what they were doing.

She tore the paper up into little pieces and let it fall into the wastepaper basket on top of Matthew's drawing. She was filled with a feeling of waste—wasted time, wasted effort, wasted material.

Janice had come home jolly, excited almost, and Flora had to wait a long time for everyone to bed down. She even went to the trouble of breathing deeply and evenly for Janice's sake, hoping it would lull her to sleep. Janice tossed and turned for a long time, as though she were practicing for drill team. When she finally dropped off, Flora eased out of bed, trying not to jiggle her or make the mattress springs creak. She stood by the door and waited. Not a sound, except for Henry's occasional snore, more like a snarl, and farther off, the grumble of an overloaded refrigerator. She opened the door so slowly that her arms got tired, and then moved down the hall like someone stepping over thin ice, barely lifting her feet. She inched open the door to the service porch closet. It squeaked like a poorly blown note on a clarinet. She listened for any responsive sound from down the hall. Nothing. She stared at the vacuum cleaner, which looked a lot like bombs she had seen in war movies. The metal canister gleamed up at her. The sounds of the refrigerator and, vaguely, Henry's snarl were now joined by the gurgle of the hot water heater. She eyed the blue flame that flickered beneath it. In the darkness it was a frightening sight. If the flame got blown out somehow and gas fumes went everywhere, the house could blow up with the smallest spark. Didn't anyone care about that? The vacuum cleaner looked harmless in comparison, with its long hose, its chrome pipes bending upward and hanging on a hook in the closet wall (Henry's idea, so that no one would get beaned by the sweeper attachments every time the door was opened). It took on the shape of a narwhal with a bent tusk. She carefully unhinged the latches on its head. Clumps of debris fell on the floor. She reached inside the bag and clawed around in slow motion, trying not to raise too much dust. She could smell the mustiness of it. It was like reaching into soupy clouds, an old nest, or ostrich down. She came upon something hard and brought it out and peered at it in the darkness. It was a marble. She put it back in the sweeper bag and searched some more. She came up with several safety pins and put them back in, too. A paper clip, several hairpins, a couple of buttons—Marleen must be getting tired of bending over for these little things. Something hard and metallic went onto her pointer finger. She pinched it between that finger and her thumb and pulled it out. She didn't have to see it in the light; she knew it was Matthew's ring. Good ol' Mom, she said to herself and blew the dust off the ring. She put it in her mouth, where she knew she wouldn't lose it, and with her hands blindly swept the floor in front of the vacuum cleaner. She dumped what she could back into the bag and relatched the head on the vacuum as smoothly as if she had often practiced doing such things, like a member of a bomb squad —only now the pressure was off. If there was any dust on the floor in the morning, Marleen would be the first to see it, and Flora could say, if it was necessary, that maybe someone had emptied their pockets out right there, and offer to clean it up. She tiptoed into the bathroom and washed her hands.

“Is anything wrong?” called out Marleen in a strained whisper.
Flora took the ring out of her mouth.

“I just needed a drink of water,” Flora hissed softly. She rinsed out her mouth.

“Sweet dreams,” said Marleen.

“Sweet dreams,” said Flora, closing her bedroom door. She kissed Matthew’s ring and tucked it beneath the velvet lining of her jewelry box.

When she crawled back in bed, she realized she was chilled. It took her a long while to warm up. She lay there wide awake, staring at nothing, thinking nothing in particular. Just awake. Mentally too tired to get up and study for any class. Too tense to sleep. She turned toward the wall even though she’d heard somewhere that you dream more on your back.

Just before dawn Matthew was trying to open a door for her. It seemed to be stuck, or the doorknob didn’t work right. The dream was vague, a mere insinuation of a dream that vanished when Janice punched the alarm off.

She got up thinking that maybe today she would see Matthew. After breakfast she went back to the bathroom and searched around in Marleen’s cosmetic drawer. She found a nearly-used-up compact of pale powder and smoothed some over the bruise on her cheek. Then she went into her bedroom and slipped Matthew’s ring on her ring finger. She left the house with that hand in her coat pocket, clutching the compact, and her other hand cradling a load of books.

The morning classes went by rapidly, like flipping through the pages of a textbook. King Lear was whisked away and Mr. Langtry promised a month of sonnets. Mr. Whitney got out his Bunsen burner and his asbestos tiles and put on a hocus-pocus show. He added a drop of liquid to a spot of white phosphorus in a test tube. There was a loud pop and then a puff of dense bluish smoke. With his hands in the pockets of his lab coat, he surveyed his students with a satisfied grin. Half of them hooted like baboons. An acrid smell floated through the room.

In dance, Miss Pazetti announced that the entire class, in groups of four, five, or six, would do interpretations of the same piece of music. She put Vaughan Williams’ *Antarctica* on the phonograph and watched her girls mill around the room, grouping and regrouping like beetles on a crowded pond. Tess hooked arms with a girl who for her limberness was known as Wiggles, and they swept up to Flora.

"Now all we need is one more," said Tess, looking about the room.

Flora watched Tess's friends from the Hills, all good dancers, gather into a group of six at the far side of the room. She wanted to put together a good dance, an amazing dance, but had no idea who else they could get. Wiggles wasn't concerned. She was stretching and swaying her long arms over her head. A plump, spongy-looking girl came over to them.

"Do you mind if I join your group?" she asked in a voice as quiet as the shifting of sand under water.

"No," said Flora. Tess gave Flora a quick nose twitch and lowered her eyes. Tess held plump, quiet girls in disdain.

Vaughan Williams' music grew like an unhindered crystal, and most of the groups around the room had begun to take shape. Still, they looked so ungainly.

"Let's just sit down and close our eyes," suggested Flora. "Maybe we'll get a clearer idea of what to do." Tess and the other two girls agreed. They all plopped down.

Before long, Flora saw the wind ripping up the vertical walls of icebergs and blowing powdery snow into arching drifts across plains of ice, and a blushing aurora borealis, black water filled with whale calls, seals howling on blocks of ice, and lonely moaning polar bears wandering away. She opened her eyes reluctantly and saw that Tess was staring at her, waiting for her. So were the other two girls.

They wanted to know what she had gotten out of it, and she told them in brief. Tess cleared her throat a little and said it was better than the mess of snowflakes she had seen. Wiggles suggested they be a series of waves with seals or fish or something like that weaving through them.

"We could build on that," she said. She arched herself into a backbend. "Like this," she said, talking upside-down. "And our hands could be the foam," she said, still in a backbend, but raising herself slightly and undulating, her hands churning the air. Then she flipped over and with more hand gestures explained how three of them at a time would be waves and one would be a creature going under them, and they would be constantly changing from waves to creatures and back to waves, and so on. Cassie, the plump girl, slumped down like a dejected walrus. Being a wave was nowhere within her means. Even Tess let her tongue hang out, her indication that she thought the idea was too much. Wiggles was discouraged. Flora said that at least it wasn't too hard to imagine the slick concrete floor as a field of ice. They all agreed. But beyond that, should they be seals or séracs, whales or the northern wind, water or polar bears? Some combination of these, or something else? Flora gave a demonstration of how they might be whitecaps. She scooted herself along the floor, raising her bottom abruptly according to the music. Wiggles watched another group of girls without much interest in anything. Tess said, "That sounds better than it looks."

They finally decided on seals, both in and out of choppy water, and by then the class period was over.

Flora headed toward Timpanelli's room, hoping that Matthew would finally be there drawing his lunch hour away. It had been exactly seven days, one muddled week, since she'd seen him standing in front of his easel. She was trying to picture him standing there when he came up behind her in the hall and grabbed her around the waist. She sucked in her breath like a dying frog and then allowed herself to be pulled along by him.

"Run away with me, Flora!" he whispered in her ear. His voice sounded urgent. She pulled away from him. His face looked tense, his eyes as serious as black beetles.

"I can't," she said. Suddenly she felt afraid. A spark of anger flicked inside her head. "I can't," she repeated. She stamped her foot at him. "Don't you understand! You are forbidden, you are forbidden to me by crazy . . . by crazy and stupid people!" She felt her father slugging at her and was afraid that Mrs. Baines was watching them at that very moment. She saw icebergs clanking together. She started backing away from Matthew, but he caught her by the hand.

"No, Flora," he pleaded, half laughing, trying not to laugh at all. "Listen, there's something I want to show you." Flora held on to his hand. It felt warm and strong. She couldn't let go of it. "It's on the other side of school," he said, and they went out of the Long Hall together.

If holding hands is forbidden, thought Flora, then Mrs. Baines's office would be crammed with irate cheerleaders shaking their crepe-paper-stained fists in protest. Flora wanted nothing more than to be able to walk next to Matthew with her hand fused to his and no one around to say otherwise.

They walked in the direction of their Spanish class and turned into one hall, then into another side hall. It was rather dark, lit only by the daylight coming in through two windows. Matthew led her over the oblongs of light that crossed the linoleum. Flora didn't use this hall unless it was raining. Like everyone else, she usually entered and left Spanish class by its outside doors.

Matthew stopped in front of a door with the words OFF LIMITS stenciled in black paint at eye level. It looked like all the other storage room doors: painted gray-green, with a bulky padlock hung in the loop of a heavy metal latch. He glanced around, then pulled at the latch. The door opened soundlessly. The screws were missing from the latch on the side of the door frame. Before Flora could figure out how that could be, Matthew pulled her inside the room and drew another latch on the inside of the door. He started to embrace her.

"Are we safe?" whispered Flora. She could hardly see his face in the darkness of the small room.

"And sound," said Matthew, and he pressed himself against her so that she could feel his bones and a tremor deep inside him. She didn't think they could get away with this, but when Matthew kissed her, all of her misgivings dropped away from her like needless clothing.

"I got your letter," he said. "You said you would love me beyond school hallways . . ." He took her hand and held it close to his face. He saw what he hoped he would see. He touched the stone with his thumb. "So, here we are."

Flora could see his glistening eyes now. He kissed her hand and then opened up her coat and unbuttoned her blouse. He unbuttoned his own shirt. Flora couldn't get over the idea that someone was behaving this way toward her—the very person she wanted to act this way toward her. When she felt his hot chest against her, she felt like she must have been freezing ever since they had separated.

"Let's lie down," said Matthew and he drew her down onto an opened sleeping bag. Flora saw a flash of dark red flannel and flying green mallards, and then Matthew was pushing up her skirt and pulling down her pants, and his. To her he felt like a cat, a panther prowling paw-soft over the dim terrain of her body. He raised himself up.

"It's been so long, I don't think I can wait any longer," he said. She didn't want him to. She wanted him to leap into her. For an instant she glimpsed those crystal-clear geyser pools she had seen as a child in Yellowstone Park. Her father had told her that they were as deep as the center of the earth, and she still believed, even now, that they were. Sure, why shouldn't they be? Wouldn't it be easy to step off those narrow plank paths and fall into the scalding holes? And sink down past the crusty aqua and orange earth? Just as if it were an accidental tripping, or a crazy impulse. Her father had taken her to a lot of dangerous places: beyond the safety chains on the top of Morro Rock, to the ends of piers during high surf, during tidal wave warnings, along sandstone ledges at nightfall, up in a small aircraft into the fog.

But she felt safe with Matthew now. She looked up over her head and saw the afternoon sun like a galaxy of stars through all the tiny holes where the black paint had flecked off the windowpanes. For several moments she felt that she was pushing herself up inside Matthew and that he was receiving her. His eyes looked like black star sapphires, like dark wells with the water glinting far below. She could have been very high or very low. She felt like she was being emptied and filled, emptied and filled. She wanted to squeeze all the liquid out of him and pump it back into him again. She wanted to take all he gave her and spew it back into him like a fountain. She wanted to be Matthew.

"My serpent," said Matthew after they had settled down. Flora felt the abrupt breath he took and let out. Embarrassment found a little hole in her head and rushed in. She saw vaguely the rows and rows of empty shelves that rose up on either side of them.

"How did you think of this?" She wanted to change the subject to something less personal and yet still personal. She waved her hand at the walls and the ceiling and then held him around the waist. She wished she had said something that sounded more appreciative.

"You said you would keep on loving me beyond pain and anger, and classrooms and hallways, and beyond time. After that, it was easy to jump a fence in the dark and loosen a few screws." He pressed himself against her side.

"I will, Matthew, I'll love you no matter what." She felt secure and soft all over.

Matthew felt the rough marks on her ribs. "What happened here?" he asked, rising up and trying to peer at her side.

Flora ran her fingertips along her ribs. "An accident; I ran into something."

"Your father?" Matthew kept his voice from lashing out.

"Scrapes go away," said Flora.

"You can mention him to me if you want to," said Matthew. He wasn't challenging her. He was just telling her. Flora moaned. The vision of Matthew's drawing, whole and then in shreds, floated into her mind, caught in a slow eddy where images never sink out of sight.

"What is it?" asked Matthew, hovering over her, concerned, anxious.

"I took your drawing home with me and my father found it and tore it up." Flora felt herself shriveling.

"It doesn't matter," said Matthew. "There are a lot more where that one came from." And then he was inside her again and they stroked together as smoothly as rowers on a glassy sea. The lunch bell rang and they were flung ashore.

PART THREE

Stretching the Canvas

Tubes of Paint

Timpanelli stood at her desk with her fingers hooked under its overlapping edge as a way of steadying herself. "I want everyone to work in color today." She paused until she had caught the eye of her two deaf students. "Color today, no pencils. I want everyone to get a box of oil pastels, except for those of you who want to work in oil paints." Flora and Matthew looked at each other and then at Timpanelli. She lifted her pencil and made a little loop in the air as if she were highlighting a grace note. She lost her grip on the pencil and disappeared behind her desk to retrieve it.

"Those of you who want to paint," she said, standing up again, "come with me." She laid her pencil neatly on her desk and waited. There was a shifting, a somewhat sluggish movement of her class in the direction of the supply cabinets. Only Matthew and Flora were headed for her. She knew she would snag them.

She led the way to a door that was directly across from the washroom. She pulled a long chain of keys from her sweater pocket, and pinching one key in her fingers, she let all the rest dangle at the end of the chain; it swayed before Matthew and Flora like a burnished censer. They stood silently as she turned her back on them and unlocked the door.

"Come on in," she said, and the three of them squeezed into the narrow room. It was another supply room, similar to the washroom or the OFF LIMITS room, with shelves mounting to the ceiling. Only the tools and supplies in this room were neatly arranged. Timpanelli started pulling down all the things they would need for stretching and gessoing canvases, and as she did so she gave them instructions, so clearly and precisely delivered that Flora was struck by the sensation of being initiated. She felt like one in a continuous line of students who filed in and out of Timpanelli's influence, receiving encouragement and approval in the form of this briefing and all these tools and supplies—hammer, nails, saw, staple gun, pliers, glue, rulers, canvas, wood for stretchers—which Timpanelli was handing over to them one by one. Standing there with her arms laden, Flora was filled with a sense of belonging, a sense of being accepted into something grand and lasting. She let her arm brush against Matthew's side, not to distract him, just to make contact. She wanted to embrace him and Timpanelli at the same time.

"I want to see sketches before you squirt any paint out of these tubes," Timpanelli said, lifting a handful of oil paints—some new tubes, some crumpled—out of a shoebox. "Any good painting begins with good drawings. Lots of drawings." She dropped the paints back in the box and left.

Flora and Matthew looked at each other. The small room, so full of things to create with, so strong with a sense of itself, breathed a warm and wispy breath upon them, as if it had lots of secrets to tell. Flora felt folded in, wrapped up in some scheme she could never escape, and yet at the same time totally free to express herself as far as her imagination would stretch. It was a hot, tense feeling, one that she wanted to act upon at once and not think too much about.

When she and Matthew returned to the classroom, it seemed to be humming. They chose a vacant corner and laid everything down. Flora arranged and rearranged the strips of wood. She concluded she wanted her frame to be twenty-nine by thirty-six, and Matthew helped her measure off the inches and cut the wood. Then he sat on the floor with his legs crossed and rocked back with his hands on his knees. "If it's good enough for you, it's good enough for me," he said. Flora had never seen him looking so downright happy. She saw Matthew *the child* for the first time. He must have been a beautiful baby. Look at him now.

"Matthew," she said, "I'm so happy I could sing."

He gave her a look like, Why don't you? She opened her mouth, but she didn't sing. Instead, she hummed, "She's got everything she needs, She's an artist, She don't look back," and helped Matthew put his frame together.

To Tess it looked as though they were being punished: down on their hands and knees, sawing, nailing, gluing, clamping, struggling for square corners.

Matthew showed up in Spanish class, and when he was called on to speak he responded promptly and in Spanish. Flora was surprised. After class she told him she wanted to learn Spanish; she was going to work at it. Matthew spun the combination on her locker and opened it. "¿Por qué, Señorita, you tired of gringo already?" He gave her a sly smile and started moving away from her.

Flora clutched him around the waist. "No tan aprisa," she said. "I just want to learn another language." She thought of the prostitute who had sat down beside Phil in Tijuana. She wished she could've understood all that the woman had said, so many rolled *r*'s, so sultry. She kept her arm around Matthew. One of the members of the Girls' Dress Board passed by, frowning.

"What's wrong with *her?*" asked Matthew, looking sideways at the girl.

Flora shrugged. "Maybe she has heartburn." She was feeling giddy. She tightened her hold and they both watched the girl waddle on down the hall as if her legs were bound together at the knees.

"I'd like to walk home with you," said Matthew, "but your father probably has a private investigator stationed at the front gate." He gave her a long kiss on the mouth and said, "Hasta mañana."

"Hasta mañana," repeated Flora. She watched him walk away. He's probably right, she thought: a private investigator, or Janice, or Henry himself.

She walked home slowly. She had no urge to get there. When she turned the last corner, she saw Matthew standing on his porch leaning against a post. And when she passed by, he smiled out of the corner of his mouth. Flora barely allowed herself a smile. A ripple of pleasure traveled up through her like a stream of bubbles. She wanted to laugh.

Once she stepped into her own house, there was no chance of anything inspiring happening. It was a house of closed doors—everyone shut off in cubicles. She thought of it as time spent away from Matthew, a quiet torture that left no visible marks.

She looked at her face in the vanity mirror. The bruise looked like no more than a pencil smudge. No wonder no one had asked her about it.

She lay back on the bed and tried to think about what she wanted to paint on her canvas once it was ready. She wanted to do some drawings, but Janice was there in the room with her, unimposing, but still there. And there was no guarantee that Henry wouldn't barge in at any moment. She opened her Spanish book and copied a few sentences. She read something in each of her other courses, too, even chemistry, and worked several algebra problems.

Somewhere in the middle of the night she woke up with a strange weight on her chest. She felt it and knew it was her Shakespeare book, spread open face-down. She got out of bed with the book still clutched to her chest and switched on the small desk lamp. She had gone through nearly a dozen sonnets that evening before dropping off, tracing and retracing lines as if she were searching for something precious she had lost, something she needed. She wanted to hear Shakespeare, with the help of Mr. Langtry's voice, say something about the way she felt about Matthew, something about her secret love. Mr. Langtry had said, "These sonnets are the songs that are singing in the dark corners of our own hearts." Then he took a handkerchief out of his pants pocket and wiped his face with it. The sonnets were a chore to understand—grasp one phrase and try to hold it, try for another phrase and the first one would slip away. Yet here and there she had found something that stayed with her long enough to sink in and touch her own feelings. She looked down at some lines she had underlined:

> When most I wink, then do mine eyes best see . . .
> All days are nights to see till I see thee,
> And nights bright days when dreams do show thee me.

When most I wink . . . In the dream she had just had, she and Matthew were in a boat. Matthew was rowing, taking big sweeps and twisting his head around to keep his bearings on a small pier. She wanted to say that she could row too. She wanted to help, but she was afraid that if she stood up, she'd capsize the boat. She looked around and saw the expanse of choppy, olive-green water behind them and the dark clouds lowering over the lake. He nodded and smiled at her. He kept stroking with all his might, lunging slightly toward the pier, drifting away from it whenever the oars came out of the water. We can make it, she told him, but she felt panicky.

"Not exactly a bright day," said Flora out loud, sighing. Then she looked around, thinking she might have awakened Janice. But Janice showed no signs of life. The sheets were pulled up over her face.

On the Slate of a Gray Dawn

At the beginning of lunch hour on the following day, Flora threw all her books into her locker. She turned around. Matthew was supposed to magically appear as soon as she got rid of her books, but the trick had misfired.

It was a cold windy day. Silvery eucalyptus leaves were spinning to the ground, racing around over the lawns and patches of asphalt. They looked like schools of sardines being chased by invisible predators.

Flora stood at a hall window and watched the frantic leaves. She turned to another window. Students were filling up the lunch area, moving around in tight groups, trying to create windshields for each other. She saw Tess cross the gully by way of a bridge, close to the spot where Matthew had leapt down to retrieve her lunch sack so long ago, the day he was being born in her mind.

Tess was walking alone, going to the cafeteria or maybe to their old eating spot, the table under the mimosa tree, which was probably naked now. Stan and Victor and Phil, too, might be there. Tess's skirt was being whipped every which way by the wind. She wasn't even wearing a sweater, just a short-sleeved blouse. That was like Tess: suffering and showing off her tanned, goosebumped arms, and maybe a little thigh, to all the boys when it was a cold February day.

Flora got the sudden urge to follow her to *their* table. Matthew's absence on this dreary day made him seem like something that could be too easily erased on the slate of any gray dawn. It was as if she had only dreamed him or drawn him, and accidentally he had gotten erased and there was nothing she could do to bring him back. She didn't want to think about all the ways he could disappear, about *any* possibility of losing him.

She sat down at the table next to Tess. Stan was there and several of the other girls and boys she used to see at parties. She had sat or stood at their parents' bars, sat on their sofas with Phil, while the parents were off visiting other bars, trying out other sofas. She couldn't think of anything to say to these people, but they didn't seem to care.

Tess said, "So, you've developed an appetite?" and grinned, shaking off the cold. Flora produced the lunch sack Marleen had prepared for her that morning, as on every schoolday morning. She held it up for all to see. Only Stan acknowledged it, with a doubtful roll of his eyes.

"I'm surprised you're not in the cafeteria," she said to Tess. Tess was shivering by now, still trying to ignore the cold.

"I can't stand the meatloaf," Tess said, gazing off across the lunch area.

The boys talked about last weekend's surfing expedition. They had driven all the way to Santa Barbara hoping to find some surf worth surfing on. Victor had broken the nose off his board. As Stan put it, there was one rock on the whole beach and Victor couldn't miss it. Victor stroked his mustache and blushed.

Flora laughed along with everyone else, although the thought of all that fog made her feel sad and vacant. She could remember only one thing she really enjoyed about the several drizzly trips she had taken with Phil up the coast: the hot little corn and cheese burritos they had eaten by the dozens while waiting for someone else to show up. Only a group of boys all going out together made braving the chilly waves worthwhile. She had tried surfing on a board a couple of times but it had seemed just about as crazy as trying to cling to a sofa being hurled out of an upper-story window. She preferred to sit on the beach, watch those who made it look easy, and eat burritos. She rarely felt hungry, but on those days she had been ravenous. She couldn't remember what the snack stand where they had bought those things looked like—a stucco box, or a wooden shack with splintering white paint? The Mexican woman who handed the burritos over was just a warm brown blur against the gray day. She and Phil had sat on the beach, wordless. Phil, cross-legged, sitting on a towel. Herself with a towel over her shoulders. Both of them crunching on the burritos, driving the mist back a little and watching the gray-green waves collapse and collapse like the refrain of a sad lullaby. Oil from the melted cheese would run down their chins, through their fingers.

Today the boys had something to boast about, some good rides on some head-high waves, and the girls were listening and agreeing, their hands clasped together and thrust down between their legs in an effort to keep warm. "My little honey," said Stan, slinging his arm around a girl Flora didn't recognize, "ran the battery down in my car while I was out."

"It was god-awful cold," she said, flinging her mouth open, "and you were out there forever!"

Flora couldn't forget the long vigils: watching the rising and dipping of the black specks, trying to pick Phil out in his black wetsuit, one among many. She had watched them all being driven to shore by every dinky wave that came along, and she remembered being hopeful and then dismayed every time Phil scooted onto the beach and then jumped back into the foam with his board and paddled out again. But even back then, she was in no rush to get home. She felt lucky to have gotten out of the house at all.

It was impossible to think about those trips up north without recalling one awful thing. Once, on a typically dreary day on a beach below some oil piers in Ventura, a dead sea lion had been washed up on the wet sand. It was very bloated. From where Flora sat, a hundred or so feet back up on the dry sand, it looked like a shiny black dirigible. The incoming surf spanked up against its broad, inert side, and spray shot into the air. She watched a group of kids, boys and girls about her own age, walk up to it. They walked around it several times. One of the boys gave it a kick. They stood looking at it. Just when she thought they'd continue on down the beach, another boy put his foot on the upper side of the sea lion's body and pushed off it so that he sprung into the air. Before long, three or four boys were running in circles, leaping onto its body and bouncing into the foaming surf. She watched with amazement. When the gray bubble burst, one of the boys found himself standing knee-deep in rotting flesh. He let out a bloodcurdling groan of anguish that might have been heard all the way down to Los Angeles. He leapt out, scrambled, fell, and hurled himself into the water. Everyone who had witnessed this at close range was moaning and groaning and laughing in a medley of disgust and hilarity. Flora still wondered why they hadn't foreseen the consequence of their game. Maybe, she thought now, that was it. Maybe it was another version of Russian roulette: they really did know that one of them would get it eventually.

Flora couldn't eat her lunch. She stuck her sandwich back in its sack. Phil sat down at the table, not near her or Tess, but a few people down. He glanced at her and their eyes met for a moment. She thought his eyes looked as splendidly blue as the summer ocean, as innocent as a baby seal's, a seal of a species destined for extinction that hadn't the faintest idea of its predicament. She knew it was ridiculous to feel that way about Phil. There wasn't anything wrong with him. He wasn't any more or less inept than anyone else she knew, including herself. Still, she felt sad about him.

She stared down at the asphalt, into a corner where two walls met and a whirlwind was whipping mimosa leaves and plastic bags and candy wrappers all together in a mad swirl. Then it just dropped them flat. She felt she had to leave. She needed to find Matthew.

She nudged Tess in the elbow. "I'll see you in Life Drawing," she said. Tess nodded her head. Her teeth were chattering.

Flora went back to her locker and got the hall pass Timpanelli had filled out for her several weeks ago. She stuck it in her coat pocket and traveled down a couple of halls until she got to the art room. She peeked in. Matthew wasn't there and Timpanelli didn't see her. She took off across campus. When she started up a ramp, the hall monitor there, a pale boy with glasses and mousy-brown hair, the same color as her own but sheared off at the sides and top, suddenly stepped in front of her and demanded to see her hall pass. He waited with both hands in his jacket pockets while she felt around in her own for the pass. When she held it out to him, he reluctantly took one hand out of his pocket and took the pass from her. The way she was speeding along, he must have figured she wouldn't really have one. He looked at it.

"The art classes are on the other side of campus." He gave her an accusing look.

"I know," said Flora, "but I'm getting art supplies." She took the pass out of his hand and put it back in her pocket.

"Oh," he said, and she went on down the hall. She didn't know where that answer had come from; she hadn't premeditated it. She looked all around her and turned into the little hall to the Spanish class.

She half tiptoed, half flew down the dark glossy linoleum until she got to the door marked OFF LIMITS. She looked both ways, pulled the door open and stepped inside.

Matthew was standing at the opposite side of the storage room, leaning against the window. There was a circle of white winter light in one of the panes. He must have scratched some of the black paint away. She slid the latch closed on the door and approached him timidly. He seemed so still, like a mannequin. And so distant, five paces away, but distant. She touched his arm and he took hold of her and pulled her against him.

"Matthew!" she gasped. Maybe she would never get used to his surprises. She hoped not. They frightened her, but she loved them.

"I thought maybe you had forgotten your new address—but you fiend, you . . . Do you want me every day?" He kissed her on the neck.

Flora thought she might mention that he had been waiting there first. But who had gotten there first or last didn't matter. She was anxious to show him how much she wanted him, not just every day, but every night as well. She slipped her arms inside his shirt.

In Life Drawing that day they helped each other stretch their canvases and got the first coat of gesso on.

Beneath a Dark Netting

When Flora was a little girl she used to wonder at the fashion models in the Sears catalogue, especially the ones who wore the broad-brimmed hats with black nets. The nets were speckled with tiny rhinestones and came down in front to obscure the top half of the models' faces. She felt she was wearing something like that now, obscuring her own face, hiding her fascination for Matthew. People might be able to tell that she was in love, but they couldn't tell with who, or how much.

There was no M.C. calligraphied all over her book covers. There was nothing at all upon them, nothing added to the plain brown paper of the grocery bags they had been cut from. After being with Matthew and before leaving school, she went to the restroom and checked herself. She made sure there was not the slightest hint of Matthew upon her, not anything that could be traced back to him: no red flannel lint from the sleeping bag clinging to her clothes, no smudged mascara, no dark hair woven in with her own light brown. She brushed her hair vigorously, and a rare length of Matthew's went floating down the sink like a fine ink line on perfectly white paper.

As she walked home from school, the glow she felt for Matthew was guarded as beneath a dark netting. As soon as she turned the corner onto her own block, she took the sapphire ring off her finger and put it in her pocket. When she walked in the back door, or even before, she felt Henry's eyes upon her. His eyes, picking at the corners of her eyes. Wavering along her hemline. Looking for a loose stitch, a speck of lint, something, anything. Scanning her collarbone, her neck, looking for some sign. Studying her mouth.

 She felt him looking at her back as she went on down the hall to her room.

She didn't think anyone on Jericho could link her with Matthew. They couldn't truthfully say much about Matthew, except that he drove a T-bird, a blue one, and sometimes ate a bowl of cereal while sitting on his porch steps, and left the lights on in his house late into the night. And yet an ever-changing body of *facts* about the Cartiers was dragged up and down the block like a carcass being claimed and reclaimed, snatched and resnatched, by a pack of tireless hyenas. Henry was always bringing home some scrap of information and tossing it out at the dinner table. Once he said that Cartier was mixed up in some kind of racket. He said there'd been a black Cadillac parked in front of the Cartiers' house with phony license plates on it. A kid with frizzy hair drove away in it. Clinton, thought Flora: chauffeur, bartender, and now thief of his own car.

That night at dinner Henry said that Cartier was bringing home women, undesirable types, and more than one at a time, at all hours of the night and day. "Floozies," he said, "and engaging in orgies with his son." And the Zelenoviches were still smelling marijuana, he added.

While Julia was asking what floozies were, Henry was staring at Flora, trying to distill a tincture of emotion from her bland face.

"It's none of your business," he growled at Julia and recommenced eating.

Julia shut up for the rest of the meal, but Henry continued to talk. With food in his mouth, he commented on conditions around the house. To him everything was going downhill slowly but surely. Things were getting goopier, shabbier, dirtier, grimier, more scratched up, more worn out, wilder, cheaper looking, more expensive, less predictable, more dangerous. And he always came back to Cartier, Cartier's son, and the house they were renting. If he said something about how the lawns looked up and down Jericho, he ended up on Matthew's front lawn, which was the worst lawn on the block and was bringing property values down. The paint was peeling off their shutters, too. But what could you expect from a couple of drifters? They had no respect for property. And then he was sure to look at Flora.

Everyone else at the table was beginning to look a little fed up. But Flora didn't look like anything. She didn't look like anything Henry could point his finger at.

Though she didn't know its source, Marleen was secretly thankful for Flora's newfound composure. Flora's face seemed to mimic

—no, to reflect—her own efforts at domestic tranquillity. For weeks there had been no yelling or crying to speak of. No new bruises, knots, or welts. No unfinished meals or slammed doors. Marleen found herself spelling the word *mimic* in her head: *m, i, m, i, c.* She didn't know why she was doing that, since there was no doubt in her mind that she knew perfectly well how to spell that word.

Henry wadded up his paper napkin and dropped it onto his plate. "I told you we should have sold this house and moved out to The Ranch when the time was right." Marleen knew that he was addressing himself to her alone, but she pretended she didn't hear him.

Flora's even temperament baffled Henry. After a while it began to irritate him. The one sure way to hatch her out of her shell, he believed, was to pile on the chores. April was a good month to start fixing up the outside of the house, so he told her to scrape and sand the sashes and trim on all the front windows—one hour every day after school, and three hours on Saturday and Sunday. "And don't try to make a quick job of it, 'cause it won't get you anywhere," he told her. "The sooner you finish, the sooner you'll start painting."

It seemed to Flora that he was constantly searching for a cleavage point, the perfect spot to whack her and make her split cleanly in two. He badgered her about her midterm grades in "math" and "science," as he called them. He held her B and C-minus up alongside Janice's double A's. He said her grades were evidence of a sloppy, careless mind, and he warned her about her lazy study habits, although she knew he couldn't have a very clear picture of how many hours she spent studying, musing, or sleeping. He rarely opened the door to her and Janice's room while they were in there together. He didn't want to disturb Janice, Flora supposed, Janice in her critical year of high school. That was one advantage of rooming with Janice. Maybe the only one.

One morning about a week after April Fool's Day, Henry came into the kitchen just long enough to announce that he had real estate business to take care of. "Now that spring's here, I've got my hands full. I won't be home for dinner." Marleen wanted to ask him when he thought he would be home, but decided against it. He showered, shaved, put on a suit, and left the house.

When Flora returned home from school, right on time, she found him there, as she had thought she might. His behavior that morning had seemed just a little too stiff. And now there he was, sitting at the kitchen table with all his papers spread around like placemats for a Mad Hatter tea party, only he was the only one present.

Flora said, "Good afternoon," and he said, "Good afternoon," very politely, but his face looked sour.

Flora thought she'd better add something to make herself look gullible, and so she said, "I hope your business went well today?"

"Yes it did, thank you," said Henry. He was looking down at his papers again. Flora had caught sight of his snare and had avoided it.

A few days later, while she was sanding away at the sash around the picture window, he came out and stood on the porch.

"You've been at that window for a week now. Don't you think it's time you moved on to the next one?"

Flora stopped sanding. "I'm just about finished."

He seemed agitated. He teetered on the edge of the steps, looking up and down the street. "There's only a few of us original home owners left on this block." There was a strange grittiness to his voice. He paused. "A For Sale sign just went up in front of the Andrewes' house." He swung around and pinned his eyes on Flora. "Looks like the Cartiers will be moving out."

Flora didn't blink. She felt like laughing, partly to let go of some tension, and partly because his efforts to upset her were so obvious. She had been given plenty of warning. This one was like a reflecting sign on a dark highway saying SLOW, BUMP AHEAD. But she was tired of having to be on guard so much of the time. Every moment she had to spend with her father's eyes upon her sucked energy out of her. Only recalling things Matthew had said to her could bring her relief: "I hope you have not decided that I am too much trouble —I can stand anything but doubts about our love."

Henry finally reached the conclusion that he had squelched something in Flora, some vital drive in her, something essential, something he didn't want to name precisely, not even to himself. He began to worry that he had gone too far. She was looking and acting like a limp dishrag. He thought he'd better ease up a bit.

That Friday at dinnertime he said, after clearing his throat twice, that he had reconsidered the conditions of her grounding. "You haven't been anywhere for almost a month. If you want to," he took time out to serve himself more peas, "you can go with Janice to the dance tomorrow night."

"What?" cried Janice. Several peas rolled out of her mouth and she caught them in her hand. "That's not fair!" She nearly threw her fork on the floor but stopped herself at the last second and only clanked it down on the table.

Janice's protest didn't seem to register in Henry's mind. He kept his attention focused on Flora.

"You think I have a car of my own? I'm not a chauffeur, a chaperon!" Janice was red and huffing, ready to burst into tears.

"Don't get excited, Janice," said Flora. She looked at Henry. "Thank you for the offer, but I don't want to go to the dance." She was saying more than she wanted to, but it looked as if he was trying to pit Janice against her. Rile Janice up and toss them together in some guy's car. What an offer!

Henry narrowed his eyes at Flora. She was afraid he might go into one of his black rages. But he didn't rise up. He sat steady and gripped his silverware.

"So you think you're too good for school dances, do you." He had hoped she'd accept his offer. He was almost sure she would grab at it. He was thrown off stride. "You spoiled brat," he blurted out. He knew that didn't sound right the moment it left his mouth. The ulcer in his stomach burned all the way up to his teeth. "You slut," he muttered, "you'd rather make out in the back seat of a heap with the first hoodlum that comes along."

That cut Flora to the bone. Matthew was no hoodlum.

"I'm just not in the mood to go to the dance," she said as slowly and as plainly and as calmly as she could.

Henry didn't seem to hear her response. He steamed like an overheated engine for a while and then stalled. He sat for a few more minutes, morose and silent. Very quietly he said, "Excuse me," got up, and left the table. Everyone else stayed put. Daniel and Julia looked scared. Janice, with her jaw clenched, looked furious, and Marleen, pinching her nose, was trying to keep from crying. There was still food on Henry's plate.

What do I have to do, Flora thought, in order not to cause anybody any trouble? She pictured herself with her mouth taped shut and her body in a body cast. I'd go to the dance with Janice and her date, John Tucker, or anyone, if I thought that would relieve any tension around here. She ate a pea with her fingers. But there's no way Janice would forgive me for that one, no matter how inconspicuous I could make myself. He must want to see us at each other's throats. She glanced at Janice, and Janice scowled at her. If he could get Janice mad at me, thought Flora, Janice would be much more likely to tell him anything she knew. Maybe that was his ploy?

Actually Janice couldn't know much, Flora figured. Janice never saw the sapphire ring slip on and off her finger. And Janice never set foot in Timpanelli's room; she looked on it as some kind of opium den that *she* would never be tempted by. Janice should never know anything about Matthew and me, thought Flora. That way she won't ever have to lie for me, or to me.

They could still talk to each other about such things as the price of pencils in the student store, whose night it was to do dishes, when last they had washed their hair, and who would use the bathroom first. But Janice would never know who had been running his fingers through Flora's hair, and what's more, it seemed as if Janice didn't care to know. Flora smiled sadly at Janice, and Janice got up and stomped out of the kitchen. A moment later the house was rumbling with the sound of the bathtub faucets going full blast. Then remote splashing could be heard. And after that, quiet, like the doldrums.

Marleen served Daniel and Julia ice cream. Flora washed the dishes even though it was Janice's turn to do them.

When she closed the door to their room and switched on the light, everything—bed, dresser, vanity, desk—seemed to sink and shrivel before her eyes. Stuck in here again tonight, she thought. She sat down on the corner of the bed and stared at her hands. They seemed to be swollen and pulsating visibly. How have I ever been able to draw in this place? She might have been asking her hands. She hadn't attempted anything at home since the day Henry made rat's litter of Matthew's drawing. And then, as she just sat there staring through her hands at nothing at all, the high-pitched whine started up. It seemed always to come on in the evening with the yellow lighting and the close flat walls, and it kept up as long as anyone was milling around in the house. It wasn't the sound of electricity in the appliances or of any insect whirring. She claimed it as a sound coming from within her own head, the high whine she got from knowing that she and her family were doing the same thing night after night, preparing themselves for another day like the day before—curling hair, beating out doormats, changing light bulbs, ironing blouses, polishing shoes, putting out milk bottles, brushing teeth, stacking schoolbooks in the same order. But tonight these things weren't going on. It was as if each member of her family had been frozen in place. Marleen and the kids stuck at the kitchen table. Janice maybe frozen in the bathtub. Who knew where Henry was? Perhaps his breath was frozen in the crack of her bedroom door. Everything was dangerously still, and yet the high whirring was insistent. Flora pulled on the same old nightgown and crawled under the covers. She refused to listen to it.

After all the lights in the house were switched off and everyone else was asleep, or so it seemed, she drew and redrew in her mind the drawing that might become her first oil painting. Timpanelli said, "Drawings, I want to see lots of drawings." Drawings on top of drawings. Heaps of drawings.

The Gentleman Caller

When all the lights in all the houses on Jericho were out, a light was still on in Matthew's room. Anyone peeking in his window would see that the light came from a lamp aimed at a drawing board, a drawing board leaning against Matthew's unmade bed and resting on Matthew's crossed legs.

A person could get cold and stiff waiting for him to do something besides hunch over his drawing. He worked for hours without a break. Like an autistic child, he concentrated on one thing as if it were the only thing in the universe. He nearly drooled as he traced an invisible path that took him everywhere late into the night, early into the morning, his pencil leaving a silvery, sinuous trail, the sort that snails make during the night.

Then suddenly, as if something had pricked him somewhere, he jumped up and set his drawing board down against his bed. He moved around his room in a seemingly aimless manner, gesturing both abruptly and gracefully, talking mutely to himself, himself and maybe someone else. Just as suddenly, he sat down again and rejoined his drawing.

His room was in disarray. Like autumn leaves, some clinging, but mostly fallen, his litter was all of a kind. Sketch paper lay in clusters on the floor, gathered into corners as if a wind had put them there. Some of the drawings were tacked to the wall, among them the green-eyed portrait of Flora.

A faint veil of smoke hung from the ceiling. It was rising in a thin, undulating ribbon from a brass incense burner. The scent was as sweet as a bonfire of dried leaves.

Sometime shortly before dawn he looked at his unmade bed and then lunged into it. He slept so deeply and awoke so abruptly that any memory of his dreams was brushed away as easily as the matter cobwebs are made of. He wouldn't have minded seeing them, but they were whisked away as if by some extremely efficient maid inside his head.

What had awakened him was the sound of his father making coffee and shutting cabinet doors in the kitchen. There was the voice of a woman, a sleepy laughter, more like a song on a radio wavering in and out of tune. That was Stella, the slow-moving, sensuous, auburn-haired woman his father had been seeing for at least a year. This morning she was cooing, but more often the first sound of the morning was the front door slamming. The whole house would shudder, even Matthew's bed. When he got home from school on those days, he'd see two cups full of cold coffee sitting on the kitchen counter and find his father passed out on the living room sofa, an unshaven, hoary-faced mess. Stella was starting to complain about his father's drinking, or rather the results of it. She'd threatened to leave him, but Matthew, even from his own room, could tell that she wished she didn't have to.

Once in a while Matthew heard the sound of another woman, one he had seen only once so far. She laughed in high, gay spurts, a little like Woody Woodpecker. When his father introduced Vivian to him, she had done a little shimmy. Matthew didn't know what to make of her.

His thoughts were broken by Stella's voice, which switched to a loud, static treble. "Oh sure, that'll solve it. Trade me in for a newer model." Then she was sobbing. Matthew heard his father's apologetic voice, that familiar warm mumble. He waited for Stella to slam the front door. All he heard was the sound of the door between the kitchen and the hall being carefully clicked shut. He wished his father could hold on to one woman. Actually, he wished one woman could hold on to his father long enough to ease him up out of his drinking.

He rolled over in bed and looked at the drawing board lying on the floor. He and Flora were embracing there. They seemed heedless of time. He imagined their bodies being made out of marble. He wanted them to be that firm and steady, that resistant to bruises and cuts, and yet, like a Rodin sculpture, still filled with a tender passion. He considered doing his oil painting from this drawing. To sculpt their forms with brush and paint so that they looked like everlasting stone—that would be the challenge. Tones of gray set against a background that would be as full of color as the walls of

Timpanelli's washroom. He carried these thoughts with him into the bathroom. After dousing his face, he looked at himself in the mirror. He felt the skin on his jaw. He didn't need to shave. He never needed to shave. That didn't bother him anymore. Flora had said, "How smooth your skin is," not as if she thought it was funny but as if she liked it that way.

On the way out of the house, he called out to his father and Stella, "Don't let your coffee get cold."

He got into his car and drove down Jericho, and the next thing he knew he was waiting behind a big blue bombshell of a car. It was taking an extra long stop at the corner. He almost honked his horn but decided to forget it. Maybe the guy had heard a siren or something.

As the car, a station wagon, turned the corner, Matthew saw who was driving it. Flora's father. Matthew wished he could fade into reverse, just back up and go another way, but then an inkling of curiosity and maybe even defiant pride kept him rolling in the same direction as Mr. Jackson.

Long before it was necessary to begin braking for the next stop sign, Mr. Jackson's car halted with a jerk, as if its brakes had malfunctioned. Matthew slammed on his own brakes and skidded to a stop, his front bumper only a breath away from Mr. Jackson's rear fender. The red taillights were reflecting off the hood of his T-bird. He backed up a little and then pulled slowly around Mr. Jackson. He wanted to see the expression on his face. Mr. Jackson glared bitterly at him. Matthew sped on down the street, quickly putting as much room between himself and Flora's father as he could.

"I'm sorry, Flora," he said as he stopped at the first red light, "your father is a real polished madman." Maybe he wanted to be sent through his windshield and I disappointed him? The thought of that kind of behavior cooled Matthew to the bone.

He pulled into the school parking lot and sat in his car for a moment. He still felt unnerved and not ready to expose himself to the April wind that was swooping leaves and lunch sacks across the asphalt.

He tried to use me somehow and I almost fell for it! thought Matthew. He watched hundreds of students moving among each other and cars and trees and metal posts, without getting bumped unless they wanted to get bumped.

I guess he uses, or tries to use, Flora all the time. What in the hell is she doing in that house? Matthew grabbed several books and his rolled-up drawing from the seat beside him, jumped out of his car, and slammed the door shut.

Despite his anger he decided not to mention the incident to Flora. He passed between the posts at the edge of the parking lot and onto the campus proper, toward his first class. He was late. He looked back as he mounted the stairs to his class: his last chance to see Flora that morning. All he saw was yellow trampled crabgrass and a few tardy students running up other steps.

All through the morning the thought stuck with him: He uses her. He abuses her. He tries to abuse her. He remembered the trail of scabs he had felt on her ribs. He heard his own voice saying, "Don't be frightened; he can't really hurt you." Maybe he *could* really hurt her, badly, if he got enough chances to.

By the third class of the day he felt numb. He saw himself sitting there at a desk, doodling in his notebook, and he shook his head at himself. He had a feeling of dread that he couldn't clearly grasp. Neither could he shake it off. Whatever it was kept sailing in and out of his head like a carrier pigeon. And each time he tried to grasp its message, it fluttered off again.

When Flora came down the hall at lunchtime, from a long way off she saw Matthew leaning against her locker. "Matthew!" She was surprised and glad to see him there. She pressed her head against his shoulder as she twisted the dial on her locker and dumped her books inside. He shut the locker door. His eyes searched her all over as if he were looking for something amiss.

"What is it?" asked Flora. She looked down at herself: maybe she had a hole in her sweater, or her blouse was hanging out. Everything was all right, as far as she could tell.

Matthew slowly bit his lower lip. "I'd like to take you to lunch." The idea had just that instant occurred to him.

Flora saw the interior of the storage room in her mind: rows of dusty, empty shelves, a wrinkled sleeping bag on the floor, and a black window with one bright light. It felt as if the door had been slammed shut. She saw Matthew's cream-colored, cable-knit sweater and then his black, both-here-and-elsewhere eyes looking at her.

"Lunch? Is something wrong?" She searched his face.

"Lots of things are wrong," replied Matthew coolly, "but not you and me." He took hold of her hand and they went to the cafeteria.

A warm whiff of body heat and cooked food met them at the door. They stood in the cafeteria line for what seemed like a long time.

Flora felt as if she was wavering between two extemporaneous roles as she stood there, next to and slightly behind Matthew. Either she was a stranger standing by chance rather close to another stranger, or she was Matthew Cartier's secret lover chancing a public appearance. In either case she didn't feel free to touch him. She slid her eyes over the crowd of bobbing heads and talking faces beneath the bright yellow lights, and kept everything a blur. She wished she could stare at each and every face and have their eyes turn aside first.

Matthew carried his tray down a narrow aisle between two long tables, and she followed him. They went to the far end of one table and sat down facing each other. Flora longed to feel at ease and blend her voice in with the steady rumble and hum of the large room. But she couldn't speak to Matthew. Everything she thought of saying didn't seem like the sort of thing a person should say over a plate of food in a loud place. She felt as if she had only the freedom to look at him, occasionally. He must be feeling the same way, she thought. They both ate in silence for a while. When she looked up, a dozen pairs of eyes were aimed at her and Matthew.

Matthew laid his fork down in a pile of chicken hash and looked at Flora. "Let's go to Timpanelli's," he said. "I thought this might be a good idea, but it isn't."

Flora nodded.

When they got to Timpanelli's room, Matthew clapped his hand against the doorjamb. "I forgot something. I'll be back in a minute." He spun around and ran down the hall.

Flora was glad to be back in Timpanelli's domain, smelling its blend of powdered paint, newsprint paper, ink, and white paste. The room was so out of the ordinary, there was something 'off limits' about it. It was a wonder how anyone could just walk right in, freely, without having to fiddle with a padlock, slip in on the sly. She looked over to the canvases she and Matthew had prepared. They were really there, still leaning against the wall. She got a sheet of sketch paper and started drawing the vision she had while falling asleep the night before:

A door is ajar and a female form, ornately dressed, as if she were wearing the plumage of a tropical bird, stands half-hidden behind the door.

A male form, also elaborately dressed, stands before her, one foot on the threshold. He holds a bouquet of wildflowers behind his back—poppies, lupines, loosestrife.

In a window off to the side, a dimly lit face is peeking through a curtain, eyeing the "gentleman caller."

It is after dark on a moonless night. The shapes of evergreens on either side of the porch steps can barely be discerned.

The only light in the vision comes from the two figures. They glow in the dark.

But the sketch wasn't going well. Her pencil marks on newsprint were a far cry from her vision of luminous colors floating in inky velvet space. She stood back, exasperated. The figures looked raw and shaggy, like bark on the trunks of shedding eucalyptus trees.

When Matthew entered the room clutching his rolled-up drawing, Timpanelli's eyes followed it like a searchlight that had found what it was after. She watched him unroll the drawing for Flora, and she watched Flora's face change shape, her mouth slowly open with awe and then turn up into a smile. Matthew looked cocky. He gestured languidly as if he were telling an easy story. His eyes looked like the points of charcoal pencils. Timpanelli imagined she could see fine black lines extending from his eyes to Flora's.

"You don't sleep at night, do you?" Flora ventured forth on the tight wire Matthew had drawn between them.

"No, I go to sleep around dawn and then I get up and go to sleep again during my morning classes." Matthew rolled his drawing back up and looked at Flora through it as if it were a telescope.

"What do you do at night if you don't sleep?" Flora knew that must sound like nonsense. "I mean, besides draw." It was hard for her to imagine anyone being able to draw all night.

Matthew unrolled his drawing again, looked at it, and stuck it up on his easel.

"What do you think I do?" He looked sweet and sly, but inside he felt a swell of nausea as the depressing incident of the morning came back to him.

"Take walks—go out?" Flora liked to picture him free to go out after dark.

"Yes," said Matthew as if he were conspiring with her, "I walk over to your house and I stand outside your window. I do dove calls, but you never open up."

"You don't even know where my window is!" Flora laughed but she also felt a twinge of fright at the thought of Matthew standing outside her window.

"I know exactly where your window is," whispered Matthew. "But I'm not that big a fool." He found a pencil lying on his easel ledge and began drawing straight lines back and forth across the bottom edge of his drawing. He wished he could cross out everything he knew about her father.

"I draw," he said after a while, "and I talk to you." His straight lines switched to curled and linked designs.

"At times I thought I was hearing you," said Flora.

Matthew picked up on her mystical tone. "Oh yeah? What did I say?"

Flora couldn't remember any exact words at the moment so she decided to make something up. "You said, 'Flora, go empty the trash. I'll meet you in the alley.' " She waited with wide eyes for his reaction to that.

"Yeah?" Matthew smiled. Her fabrication amused him. He squinted at her. "Do I always give you orders?"

She didn't expect a response like that. She had never heard Matthew giving her orders. "No, I think you speak my mind," she said decisively.

"I do?" Matthew tilted his head. "Did I tell you you wanted to run away?" His mouth made a you-would-if-you-could smile, sort of mischievous and one-sided.

"Run away?" Flora looked baffled.

"Yes, you know, meet me in the alley?" Matthew was making zigzags down the edge of his drawing.

"Oh," said Flora, wondering. "But I didn't say run away, did I?"

"Then what did you want to do in the alley?" He tried to lure her on anyway, see what she would say.

"How should I know? It was your thought I was hearing, not mine." Flora was feeling pleasantly harassed.

"Yes, but I thought I was supposed to be speaking your mind?" Matthew went on.

"All right," admitted Flora. She had forgotten her own words. "I confess, I just made that up, or dreamed it or something." She picked up her own pencil. "But I do think I hear your voice sometimes."

Matthew wanted to tell her that he had talked to her about running away as he drew at night. He made plans with her. But the time wasn't right to talk about them. "Did you make that up in your sleep?"

Timpanelli saw Matthew tip his head toward the drawing on Flora's easel. And then she saw Flora put her hands over the drawing as if to shade it from the light of day. Timpanelli frowned and shook her head.

"It's just my first attempt. I don't like it," explained Flora.

Matthew leaned back on his stool and crossed his arms. "Can't I have another look at it, in that light?"

Flora slowly lowered her hands. She felt foolish hiding it from him. Either destroy it or show it off. Matthew was always eager to show his work to her. But then, his drawings never looked like a clutter of stiff and ragged lines. She dared look at what she had done and was surprised. It didn't look so bad after all. There was some feeling poking through here and there, like tough blades of grass in hard-packed earth.

Matthew stepped up closer. "You just did this?" His mind took a wide sweep around all the obstacles that came between them. He liked the way the figure at the door was inclining her head.

"Yes," said Flora. She moved back so that she stood halfway behind her easel.

"It's amazing the way you can get desire to show through all those crisscrossing lines."

Flora felt both offended and pleased by his words, somewhere in between.

Matthew looked back and forth from his drawing to hers. "Sometimes when I draw I feel like I'm wandering, like I don't know where I'm going."

This was a revelation to Flora. She had always imagined he was carefully following a course that was clearly mapped out in his mind. Moving with deliberation. Now was he saying that he didn't know where he was going to end up?

Matthew went on. "But you, it looks like you leap right into the center and start spinning away madly, like you're making a web, or a cocoon . . . like you're not afraid of work, or a struggle." The image of her father's bitter face flashed in his head. It struck him like a sharp pain over one brow.

"I guess I'm just impatient for the results," said Flora. She didn't know what else to say. She had the sensation that they were talking in riddles, that something important wasn't being said. Matthew didn't say anything. He was just standing there frowning at his own drawing—those two people embracing.

Timpanelli couldn't stand it any longer. She thought she'd go blind or deaf with the strain. She got up and went over to them.

"That's a good start," she said, looking at Flora's drawing. "Especially this here." She pointed to the face, off to the side, of the voyeur.

Then she looked at Matthew's drawing.

"Do you intend to do this on canvas?" She knitted her brow at him.

"I thought I might." Matthew knew she was testing his sense of confidence.

"You'd be a fool if you didn't." Timpanelli went back to her desk.

The end-of-lunch bell rang. Flora felt as if a seam ripper had torn its way down the middle of her drawing. She wadded it up, got a new sheet, and started drawing immediately. Matthew went to get one of the canvases. More students entered the room, jocular and jumpy, fresh from the lunch area, and a few left reluctantly and headed for their legitimate classes.

There was a racket of metal jangling against metal. Jill, The Cat, was yanking on the alarm system and looking around the room with blazing eyes. "Mrs. Baines!" she hissed as she rushed back to her easel. She settled herself on a stool and held a pencil poised in her hand. She looked like the eager student she wasn't.

Timpanelli closed her magazine and was setting her vase on the floor beneath her desk when Mrs. Baines appeared in the doorway. Mrs. Baines rested there for a moment with one hand on the doorjamb. She gave the room a critical once-over and then traveled briskly over to Timpanelli.

Tess was about to enter the room when she saw Mrs. Baines leaning over Timpanelli's desk, her hindside facing the class. Tess's mouth shaped the word *Whoa* and she stepped backward, in a cartoonish, slinky manner, out the door. Flora instinctively reached for her drawing, to get rid of it somehow, but stopped herself. It would be better just to sit perfectly still. Even Matthew was fixed in place, midstride, with his canvas in his hand.

Mrs. Baines whispered something to Timpanelli.

"No," said Timpanelli, shrugging her shoulders. "Chris Dalavantes? No, I don't know anybody by that name. Is that a he or a she?" Flora wondered if Chris was still making bets and sitting in on other people's classes. The Cat made a silent shriek and hid her mouth in her hand as Mrs. Baines withdrew from the room.

For the next hour Flora erased and redrew lines on her new drawing and Matthew sat perfectly still. He stared back and forth at his drawing and the blank canvas. He hadn't been able to put one line on it.

Flora slipped into the storage room, and Matthew wasn't there. She looked at the bright patch cast on the floor by a dusty shaft of light and followed the shaft to one small pane of glass, the pane Matthew had scratched clear of black paint while waiting for her one afternoon. And beneath the window, on the floor, she saw the sleeping bag, all rolled up. The sleeping bag and the clear pane of glass were the only two things about the room that could convince her that she and Matthew had ever been there before.

She went over and sat down on the sleeping bag. She didn't like being in there without Matthew. In fact, she started feeling that something bad might happen. She wondered if Matthew, the times he had been there before her, had felt the same way. She got the sensation that all the empty shelves were about to fold in on top of her. She stood up at once. Then she saw the shadow of her own head in the light patch on the floor and quickly moved aside. What if someone were passing by outside and had seen her? She braced herself at the side of the window and listened for sounds, any sound. There were no footsteps, nothing. But in the black paint of the pane nearest her eyes she saw where Matthew had etched "So & So + So & So." She found his writing tool, a little bent nail, lying on the sill. There were smudges in the dust where his fingers had picked it up and laid it down again. Her stomach gave a knock of fear. Maybe those aren't Matthew's fingerprints? And maybe that's not his writing? She looked at it again. Yes, it is his handwriting, a small and stilted form of it, but his.

What a funny home they had made for themselves, she thought, smiling. What an odd address: So & So + So & So, OFF LIMITS, Hazelton High, San Fernando Valley. No hearth, no running water. Black paint instead of curtains, no bed but a sleeping bag. She wished she could at least bring a candle for them to burn, especially on a chilly day like this one, but they couldn't chance the glow, or the smell of burning wax . . .

There was a tap at the door and Flora startled. Then she heard Matthew whisper her name. She leapt to the door and let him in. Matthew drew the bolt in the latch, tossed his rolled drawing onto one of the shelves, and hugged her, rubbing himself up against her so hard that Flora thought they'd both ignite. His face felt icy, but his body gave off waves of damp heat. He drew back slightly.

"God, I'm glad you're here," he said, heaving a breath. "I looked for you in Timpanelli's first." He looked a little wild, as if he'd been running against the wind.

"I hoped you would come here today." She pushed back his jacket and kissed him on the neck, unbuckled his belt and undid his pants. He lifted up her skirt and they stood pressed together, kissing for a long time. Flora felt as though a torch had been set against her and she would be fused to Matthew. He pulled away from her and spread out the sleeping bag. When he lay down she flung herself on him as if she were protecting him from the hazards of an earthquake.

"Slow, slow, let's go slow," he whispered in her ear. She tried to get her underpants down and ripped a side seam. He took hold of them and tore the thin strip of lace that remained. He ripped the other side, too. She watched him with astonishment as he slowly slipped them away. They both wanted to laugh out loud.

"How would you like it if that happened to yours?" whispered Flora. Matthew made a move to tear his own underwear off. "That's all right," said Flora. She lowered herself down onto him. She liked to feel the contrast between his cool, dry pants and the damp heat of his loins rubbing on the insides of her legs. She wondered how it felt to be him, sticking up inside of her. She wanted it to feel like the best thing he had ever felt. She felt like crying.

Crying was part of the way she released herself. Matthew knew she didn't need consoling. After a while he asked, "What do you do at night besides listen to me, and cry?" He meant to tease her a little.

Flora slid around beside him and laid her head on his chest.

"Well . . ." She mused for a moment. "I don't just cry *all* the time. I think of you." She stroked the few dark hairs that formed a V on his chest. "When the lights are off I lie in bed and think of you."

"What do you *think* of me?" asked Matthew. He put his hand on top of hers and she stopped stroking him.

"I think you're wonderful." She sighed. Matthew wanted to hear something less vague than that, but she went on. "I also see ideas for paintings. And when I fall asleep I usually dream about you, and if I wake up before the alarm goes off, I think about my dreams. Do you remember your dreams?" She glanced up at him.

"Only my dreams remember my dreams," replied Matthew. He wondered if she could tell that this was an old line, one he had played with before in his head.

"I guess you think that's a funny thing to say?" Flora whispered. She thought about how oblivious Henry was to dreams and quickly erased the comparison. "Would you like to hear the dream I had last night?"

"Yes, if it's not too noisy," Matthew whispered and kissed her on the forehead. Flora gave him a puzzled look.

"Well, I don't know what it might mean," she apologized.

"That's all right," Matthew said encouragingly.

"Well, it was summertime and I was walking out of a village, a village made of shacks and tents. Half of them were collapsing and the rest of them were ready to collapse. I kept walking up into some hills, across dry foxtails and wildflowers and then under some of those huge oak trees, where the shade is almost black." Matthew nodded in agreement, and Flora went on, "And then farther up a hill I saw you under one of the oaks, leaning against its trunk. You didn't seem to recognize me. I called your name, but you didn't answer. So I ran up close to you and asked you if you wanted to climb the tree. You laughed at me and said, 'Sure, why not.' Then we climbed as high as we could and looked out over all the yellow hills and all the other oak trees that looked like dark green cushions scattered everywhere." She made a scalloping gesture with her hand.

"Is that all?" asked Matthew.

Flora felt at a loss. Matthew breathed deeply so that her head, still resting on his chest, rose and fell. She felt as though she were on a raft, and with Matthew's arms wrapped around her, she couldn't slip off. Just as she thought that, he let go of her and folded his arms up under his head. He seemed to be gazing right through the ceiling, to someplace far away. Flora raised herself up on one elbow and looked hard at him, at his bare chest, his quiet face. In the gray light he looked as smooth and cool, as remote, as a statue. "Matthew," she whispered, "I feel like I'm dreaming you. I feel like I'm dreaming *us.*"

Matthew looked at her with mock surprise.

"I mean," she continued, "it's like looking into a three-way mirror. I see image after image of us holding each other, and I forget which one is real." She reached out and touched his forehead, lightly, as if her fingers might pass easily through his flesh.

Matthew took hold of her hand and clasped it tightly. "If you can't tell, what difference does it make?"

When they got up and Matthew was buckling his belt, he eyed Flora's underpants on the sleeping bag. They looked like tattered clouds obscuring some of the green ducks that flew across the red sky. He bent over and picked them up.

"I hope your bottom doesn't get cold," he said, half jesting.

Flora straightened her wool skirt, smoothing down the pleats all the way around, one by one. "When I was a kid I used to dream I had gone to school without my underpants on. I guess this is it."

Matthew put them in his jacket pocket.

"What are you doing?" asked Flora.

"Helping you get rid of the evidence, what do you think?" He looked at Flora with a wrinkled brow.

"Oh," said Flora. She didn't know what she had been thinking exactly. Matthew wouldn't be saving her underwear. She started folding up the sleeping bag.

When they were in the Long Hall, Matthew told her he wished she could draw at home. He said he wished she could come over and draw at his house. Then he tacked on a short regretful laugh.

Flora saw the rolled drawing under his arm. She said she wished she could, too, but that she tried not to let it bother her. She was feeling strange walking down the hall without any underpants on. She was on the alert for a gust of wind that might whip her skirt up. It would have to be a windy day, she thought. Every time they passed by an open door, she held on to a few pleats as a precautionary measure.

The end-of-lunch bell rang and other students started seeping into the porous hall until Flora and Matthew were mingled with the crowd. Flora caught pieces of conversations: "She didn't even say she'd go out with you." "What's playing at the Sepulveda Drive-In?" "That place is a bust." "Then meet me at . . ." "No one's going to be there tonight." "I wouldn't go out with that creep if he paid me!" Then it struck Flora. It was already Friday. She glanced at Matthew's face. He looked as relaxed as if all the commotion were as wholesome as an ocean breeze—something sent along to soothe him. All Flora could think was that soon she'd have to wait all the way until the middle of Monday to see him again. And the crowd of excited students was an irritation to her. Her eyes were burning and ready to water.

She entered Timpanelli's room several minutes after Matthew, opened up the storage cabinet and reached for her unfinished drawing. It wasn't where she had left it, so she got a stool and felt around at the back of the shelf. She found it way in the back, where it had gotten pushed in the shift and shuffle of communal space. She was on the brink of anger and caught herself. We're all just a bunch of molecules bumping around in a container, she thought, seeing Mr. Whitney swirling a beaker full of cloudy liquid and jeering, and some force keeps shaking us up. She was glad to have her drawing, small beginning that it was, back in her hands again.

She got down from the stool and looked toward Timpanelli. Timpanelli's desk and the entire school seemed more crowded, more lively, on Friday afternoons. It was as if everybody was clustering together, practicing, getting in the mood for Friday night, Saturday night. They used Timpanelli as a sounding board, trying out their schemes on her:

"My ol' man will probably send me out for a six-pack. I'll use his ID and take off."

"Jill dared me to show up at the Body Shop. I bet you anything *she* doesn't show up!"

"We're going to smuggle back a case of tequila from TJ."

"If they go to Tahoe, like they said they would, we'll have a party."

Timpanelli nodded, rocked on her chair, smiled, screwed up her face, rolled her eyes, stared out the window.

Flora saw that Matthew, regardless of the agitated atmosphere, had begun to work on his canvas. She hesitated to go over to him, but he looked up and seemed to be waiting for her.

It was plain to see, even from the first few strokes, that this drawing was going to be even better than the drawing he was working from. His inspiration seemed to be growing. Flora felt that her own efforts amounted to little more than exasperated huffs. She felt she could be easily distracted, easily disturbed. Her rolled-up drawing was sticking to her hand, and for a moment she wanted to throttle it as if it were her own fragile windpipe.

"I think I should move my easel so that it's away from yours a bit." She had just been struck by the need for this move. She had to have some privacy.

Matthew leaned back on his stool and watched her turn her easel so that it faced away from him and more toward the wall.

"Whatever feels better," he said, smiling to himself.

Flora moved her chair around in front of her easel and sat down.

She tacked up her drawing and looked over to Matthew. What she had succeeded in doing was positioning herself so that she could still see him but not what he was drawing, and vice versa.

Matthew put his hand in his jacket pocket and showed her the slightest fringe of white lace. He continued to draw.

There was no escaping Matthew.

The Black Sofa

Tiny flecks of white paint kept popping Flora in the cheeks and the eyes as she scraped away at the frame around her parents' bedroom window. This was the fourth weekend she had been removing old paint from the windows on the front side of the house.

Late in the afternoon Henry came up and felt the sill with his fingertips. "You've still got plenty of work to do here, but I think you ought to go in and get cleaned up. I want you to offer your babysitting services, free, to your neighbors." He nodded across the street. Flora gave him a quizzical look. "You use their pool in the summertime, don't you?" He walked off, wiping his hands on his pants.

Flora groaned. They had gone over there twice for a swim, the whole family, and no more, because Henry said they didn't want to wear out a welcome. But that wasn't what made her groan. She didn't like to babysit. It frightened her. Caring for plastic dolls as a child was one thing, but being expected to step in as a *real* mother to real, live, fragile little people in a strange house was another. So many things could go wrong. It was an unfair request. But she couldn't explain this to her father; he would call her ungrateful and selfish. And so she phoned Beth, the mother across the street, and arrangements were made.

At dusk she went over and knocked on their door. She always got a feeling of dread when knocking on a stranger's door. The door was jerked open by a small boy no higher than the doorknob. Up rushed his little sister. She hid behind him and fixed her wondering eyes upon Flora. Then Beth appeared, wearing a sheath dress of a shiny black fabric and diamond or rhinestone earrings that sparkled at the sides of her face.

"Oh, Flora, you're a doll!" she said, sweetly and sadly. "I'm so glad you've come." She reached out for Flora and took her by the hand. "I want you to meet my mother."

Flora felt as if she were being ushered into a plush party. She got whiffs of Beth's gardenia perfume as she followed her down the hall. The warm summer scent was mingled with a sickly, medicinal smell. In one of the back bedrooms Flora was shown a small, overweight woman who was lying in a queen-sized bed with her head propped up against a pillow at nearly a ninety-degree angle. Her face looked as gray as uneaten oatmeal, but her hair was neatly curled and her dark eyes gleamed.

"Mom, this is Flora Jackson, from across the street. She's going to be sitting with the babies for a couple of hours."

Beth's mother's mouth lifted into a half smirk and then was pulled down again by pain.

"We won't be gone long," said Beth. She gave her mother a peck on the cheek and retreated from the bedroom. Flora nodded and smiled to the grandmother and followed Beth back down the hall. She thought she heard the sick woman say, "I know how long a couple of hours is."

They passed the nursery room. Against each wall there was a piece of white enameled furniture—one dresser, one small bed, and a massive crib, all sitting pertly on an unseamed spread of slick linoleum patterned with cows jumping over moons, happy eggs tottering on walls, dangling spiders, and alarmed maidens tumbling off cushions. Jack and Jill looked like they would spill out onto the hallway carpet.

"My mother isn't well. She has terminal cancer," said Beth without turning to look at Flora. She might have been saying, My mother has a cold, she won't be going to the dance tonight. Flora didn't know what to do with all this personal information.

"She's in a lot of pain," added Beth as they entered the kitchen. Her son opened a lower cabinet door and slammed it as if to announce their entry. The baby girl covered her ears with her hands and squealed.

From down the hall, Flora thought she heard a groan, the sound a wounded animal might make.

"Mother can't tolerate a lot of noise," admitted Beth. One of Beth's hands rose up and pressed against her mouth. She held it there as if she were holding down a little burp as an act of politeness.

"I'm sorry," said Flora. She'd never been in the same house as someone who was dying. She stooped and lifted the baby girl into her arms.

"My name is Flora, what is your name?" Flora tried to give a lilt to her voice. The little girl stared at her as if she had a large mole on her nose.

"That's Karen," said Beth's son with a burst of authority. He was pushing a matchbox truck between the legs of the dining room table.

Beth smiled bashfully. "Russell has an answer for everything."

Tom appeared at the kitchen door. A cigarette teetered in the corner of his mouth. He smiled and squinted through the smoke.

"Hi, Flora, how are you?"

"Fine," said Flora and she gave Karen a gentle bounce in her arms.

"Are you ready?" Tom shifted his attention to Beth. Beth felt for her earrings, first one side and then the other.

"Yes," she said. She crawled under the dining room table and gave Russell the hug and kiss he had been waiting for. She gave Karen a sorrowful look, kissed her on the lips, and said, "I'll be back very very soon." She looked at Flora. "We'll be home no later than eleven." Tom helped Beth into her coat, then winked at Flora and pulled the door shut.

Karen started crying, so Flora sat her down on the carpet next to Russell and handed her a seemingly harmless miniature car.

"She can't have that truck, it's mine," said Russell and he grabbed for it.

Flora shielded the car from Russell's thrusting hand. "Yes, it's your car," she said, trying to sound sympathetic, "and Karen knows it's your car. She just needs to use it for a little while."

Russell grabbed for it again but stopped when he saw that Karen had already let it fall to the floor in favor of a rubber dog. "I want to play in my room," he said and jetted out of the kitchen. Flora picked Karen up and followed him. By the time she got to the nursery he was flat on his back beneath Karen's crib.

"I'm dead," he said, as if there was no doubt about it.

Flora stood in the doorway and frowned. Karen imitated her frown and then struggled to get down.

"Let me down!" she said in a clear demanding voice.

Flora lowered her onto the nursery rhymes. She was wondering how big Karen's vocabulary was when a voice grumbled like distant thunder. Flora closed the nursery door behind her. Russell scrambled out from under the crib, saying he was a wild gorilla and gurring so that Karen went into a fit of scared laughter and clambered up Flora.

"Be quiet," the voice groaned, sounding like the wounded animal again. Flora set Karen down. There was silence.

All three of them were absolutely still for a few moments. Then Karen said, very matter-of-factly, "Dat's Grandma. She's died." She saw Russell eyeing a xylophone on wheels and they both went for it.

Flora might have enjoyed their toy-banging exuberance if it wasn't for the painful protests that kept coming from beyond the nursery door. The last and loudest time Beth's mother demanded quiet, Karen stomped over and yelled an order to the closed door. "Go to sleep, Grandma, go to sleep!" She rapped her tiny fist against the door once and then she stomped back to Flora and Russell and sat down on a pile of plastic toys and Little Golden Books.

"Let's see if we can play very quietly so your grandmother *can* go to sleep." Flora tried to make it sound like a new game.

"Okay," said Karen. She tore back over to the door, opened it with wonderful dexterity, and was already in her grandmother's room before Flora could get to her feet.

"I'm going to be quiet, Grandma. Grandma, I'm going to be quiet, Grandma," Karen was insisting, tugging at her grandmother's leg.

Flora gathered Karen up from the side of the bed. "That's a good girl, Karen, but we won't come into your grandmother's room again. That way she *can* go to sleep." She carried Karen out of the room and started to close the door. "I'm sorry," she said, glancing back at the sick woman.

"Leave the door open," she demanded in an irritated gasp.

Flora carefully pushed the door all the way open again and left on tiptoes. Karen gave her a *What fun!* look. "Be a horsy," she said.

"I don't think we can play that game," said Flora.

"Be a horsy!" repeated Karen, jogging in her arms.

"No, be a Tyrannosaurus Rex!" said Russell. He pointed a Tinkertoy stick at her.

"I don't think we can play that game either," said Flora. She set Karen down and picked up a book, *Rootie Kazootie—Detective.* "I'll read you a story?" she offered. They ignored her. Karen tried to see if she could reach the light switch, and Russell ran his Tinkertoy stick along the bars of the crib. There was a moan from the other room.

"Where are the rest of your Tinkertoys?" asked Flora, whispering. "Let's see if we can build something."

Russell looked around the room once and said, "I don't know."

Flora wished Russell and Karen would give up and say they wanted to go to bed. The clown clock on the dresser said a quarter to ten. At a quarter past ten, she started encouraging them to go to bed, but they seemed determined to stay up. They kept exchanging moods. For a while one was giggling and tumbling around and the other one was yawning and sitting as inertly as a stuffed animal in Flora's lap as she sat crosslegged on the floor. Then they'd switch parts, and one would drift off as the other one came back to life again.

When Tom and Beth came home they were greeted by their two pajamaed children, who beat Flora to the door and jerked it open. Tom and Beth looked tired. Flora wanted to apologize for not already having Karen and Russell bedded down, but in the next moment she felt like the only nonrelative at a happy family reunion.

Tom pulled out his wallet and flicked through his money as he counted up the hours. "I'm sure you've more than earned it," he said, taking Flora's hand and placing the money in it.

Flora gave it back to him. "Thank you, but I didn't expect to get paid. I did it for nothing."

Tom looked blankly at her.

"I mean," she stammered, "I was glad to be able to help out." Russell and Karen looked as if the evening had been a thrill a minute.

Tom stuck the money back in her hand and she stuck it back in his again. "I don't feel right about not paying you," he said.

"Have a good night," Flora said. She moved quickly onto the porch and sidestepped down the steps.

"Good night, Flora. Thank you . . . Don't spend it all in one place," Tom joked. Beth had already disappeared with Karen and Russell.

Flora was relieved to be out of their house. She looked back. The light was still on in the den, where the grandmother lay dying. She ran across the street. It was like flitting over a quiet, silvery river. As a child, when she stayed out on summer nights playing hide-and-seek with Janice and a group of neighborhood kids, she had dared to hide in the darkest hedge, or in the bushes beneath lighted windows. She had darted back and forth across the street many times, traveling with the other kids like a flock of fairies. Now she seemed to be the only one out, and she was anxious to get her feet firmly placed on the opposite curb. She scampered across her lawn and onto the front porch.

The light was on in the living room. The picture window drapes glowed with a pale lime-colored light. The bird-of-paradise pattern, from the back and robbed of its color, looked less like flowers and more like the flaring fingers on witches' hands. Flora got her key out of her jeans pocket and unlocked the door. Henry was sitting alone on that sticky black couch. Ever since the sea lion incident, she couldn't sit on it at all and she didn't want to see anyone else sitting on it either. But there he was. His skin looked gummy and drab yellow, the texture and tone of mild Cheddar cheese. Maybe it was just the lamplight. The eleven o'clock news was announcing itself, and he was refolding what looked like a brochure. She could see lush foliage on the glossy rectangle of paper he held in his hand.

"Hi, Dad," she said. She felt a sympathetic tone sneaking up the dark alley of her throat. He looked as if he were ailing, not just from his usual conviction that nothing was going right, but from some physical pain as well. "Do you feel all right?" It was the first question she had asked him in months.

He narrowed one eye at her. His other eye seemed to be off dreaming somewhere.

"I'm fine," he finally said in a tone that said, What do you want to know for?

Flora caught the tone, but she was afraid to answer a question he hadn't actually asked her. He might accuse her of being a smart aleck if she said anything that sounded as though she were trying to see into him.

"Where's Mom?" She switched to what she thought was a simple question.

"She's gone to bed. She doesn't want to know what's going on in the world anymore. Office gossip is all she's interested in." He clucked his tongue and gave his head a little jerk.

Flora started down the hall.

"Did they pay you?"

"No."

He tipped his head forward like a bull and glared at her suspiciously.

"I didn't let them," she said. She stared back at him for a moment and then left the living room.

She found Marleen standing in the bathroom, fairly well camouflaged in her layered nylon nightgown that matched the pale aqua walls and the shower curtain. Only her head, which was covered with dark, bristly hair rollers, stood out starkly. She looked as if she were being attacked by sea urchins. But her face rose into a creamy smile when she saw Flora.

"Flora!" she said, turning toward the hallway with both arms raised, her fingertips patting at the rollers. She sounded glad it was Flora and not someone else.

"Hi," sighed Flora, coming to lean against the door frame.

"How did it go tonight?" Marleen deftly spun up a last strand of hair at the base of her skull.

"All right. They're very spunky children. Pretty noisy." Flora watched her mother raise a large can of hairspray above her strangely enlarged head. "Did you know that Beth's mother is dying of cancer?"

"Well, she's getting cobalt treatment, Flora." Marleen was slightly annoyed at her daughter for speaking so bluntly. She gave her head three quick blasts from the spray can from three different angles, and a corrosive-smelling mist filled the bathroom.

Flora took a step back from the door.

"I feel tired tonight. I think I'll just go to bed and read a while," said Marleen. She clapped the oversized plastic lid on the spray can and padded across the hall. She stopped at her bedroom door to give Flora a goodnight peck. "Sleep tight," she said.

"I think I'll read for a while too," said Flora.

"Well, don't stay up too late."

Flora wondered, Why not? Her mother's advice, when it came, sounded so useless. She watched Marleen turn down the flowered satin bedspread on her bed. The fabric, as it moved over itself, made an icy wheezing sound. Marleen switched the light beneath the frilly lampshade beside her bed from high to low, propped up her pillow, and climbed into bed with her paperback copy of *The Carpetbaggers.*

Henry's perfectly made bed, covered with a matching spread, was pressed tightly up alongside Marleen's. It was as if their beds were two boulders forced together by glacial action, or one large boulder cracked in two by the force of frost. Flora remembered the pistol that Henry kept under his mattress, and she cringed.

Daniel and Julia's door was shut. They were sound asleep, it seemed. Flora drifted into her own room. Janice was still out somewhere. Three pairs of nearly matching nylon stockings were strung out on the dresser top. Several more singles, obvious rejects with wide tracks running down them, were sprawled on the hemp floor. They looked as though they had been trampled on. Janice had a stocking trauma, thought Flora. She went over to her own underwear drawer and looked for the two perfect pairs of stockings she knew she had left there unused for months. One pair was gone. Janice had helped herself. Flora smiled.

She put on her threadbare flannel nightgown, the one she liked so well, and crawled into bed with her volume of Shakespeare. She turned to the section of sonnets. But instead of reading, she pictured the grandmother with her neatly curled hair surrounding a pained face, her father sitting on that bloated black sofa, scowling at the news, Marleen propped up in her narrow bed, down in the sweaty South somewhere, turning the pages of her paperback. She saw the icecube-blue walls of her mother's room flatten out. She and Tess and the other two girls were trying to work out their dance to *Antarctica,* and kept slipping on the ice and sliding away from each other. And then she spotted Matthew. He was sitting far away on the edge of a cliff of ice, dangling his feet, waving her lacy white underpants in the air. She wanted to warn him to stop doing that. Someone would notice. Don't do that. She wanted to tell him that she was trying to get over to him.

Alligator Pears

Janice was sitting in bed flipping the pages of a book. It was morning. Sunday morning. Her elbow kept grazing the edge of Flora's pillowcase at regular intervals, and the rasping sound was magnifying itself inside Flora's head until she thought she would have to scream. But instead she turned over and moved her pillow and her head closer to the wall. Finally she gave up trying to sleep and sat up.

"Do you want a chemistry lesson now?" asked Janice gaily.

Flora yawned enormously and accidentally knocked the back of her head against the windowsill, hard enough to make some rocks rattle.

"I guess it's worth some stockings," she said, yawning a smaller yawn. She found her Shakespeare book between the bed and the wall and tossed it to the foot of the bed.

"I only borrowed *one* pair," said Janice, flipping the pages of the chemistry book more briskly. Flora recognized the book as her own plainly covered one.

"That's the right chapter," she said and stuck her fingers into the flying pages as if she were a child testing the blades of a rotary fan.

"This won't be so painful," said Janice cheerfully, and she began a long episode of alternately skimming and then explaining the text to Flora. She allowed Flora one quick break to go pee and wash the sleep out of her eyes.

Henry gave their door three rapid thumps.

"I'm tutoring Flora," Janice called out proudly.

He opened the door and looked in. He saw Flora sitting on the bed with her back against the wall, chewing on a thumbnail. A sheet of paper covered with scribbling lay like a napkin in her lap. Janice was sitting cross-legged on the bed with a book open and balanced in one hand. There was a clutter of papers all over the bed. He leaned in and flopped a glossy brochure down on top of it all. "I think you'd better read this." He nodded at Flora and gave her a grim look. Then he backed out of the room and pulled the door shut.

Janice grabbed the brochure and Flora inspected her thumb, which was throbbing because she had ripped the nail down too far.

"Avocados?" said Janice, puzzled. "This thing's about growing avocados!" She tossed it to Flora.

Flora looked at the pictures, read all the bold type, refolded the brochure, and tossed it back on the bed. Henry was always telling her that she would end up a prune picker if she didn't straighten up. This was the first indication that maybe avocados were in store for her too. She had read *The Grapes of Wrath.* A family came to California to pick oranges, peaches, grapes, whatever was in season, and they had gotten packed into little wooden, cratelike houses themselves. Picked on, bruised, and left to spoil. It was a frightening thought, a life like that.

Henry is so full of it, she told herself. She pictured him carefully eating slices of salted avocados. Slices Marleen had carefully cut from an avocado that she, Flora, had carefully picked from a tree. Have any more of those alligator pears? he'd keep saying, chuckling every time.

He thumped on the door again. "Your mother could use some help in the kitchen," he said.

Janice was already getting dressed. She pulled a sweater down over her head. "I hope you understand what a mole is now."

"I think I do. Thanks for the help." Flora gathered up all the paper from the bed and stuffed everything but the brochure into the wastepaper basket. She had the sudden sensation that Matthew was embracing her. The feeling was so strong that she remained bent over the wastebasket as if she had been cast in that position.

"Is something wrong with you?" asked Janice.

"I'm just a little stiff from sitting so long." Flora slowly straightened herself up. She wished she could be alone with Matthew for a few minutes before having to join the family in the kitchen. When Janice left the room, she stood perfectly still and waited, but he was gone.

She dressed quickly, scratching and scraping her way into a sweater and a pair of jeans. She entered the kitchen holding the brochure.

"How did you sleep?" asked Marleen. She diced several slabs of Cheddar cheese and dumped them into a bowl of beaten eggs.

"All right. I dreamed I was dancing on ice. How was your night?"

"My book sent me into a deep sleep." With Marleen it was always "my book" until she had reached the last word. And she would never give up on a book, even if she thought it had turned too risqué, or boring, or violent, or depressing. She followed the dictum, Finish whatever you start. "I feel well rested," she added. "What's that?" She pursed her lips and raised her brows at the brochure in Flora's hand.

"I don't know," said Flora. "Something Dad gave me." She laid it down on the counter. There was never an easy way to get rid of the magazine articles, newspaper clippings, government pamphlets, and advertising brochures Henry was always handing out. If she threw it away, she'd probably get hit. If she handed it back to him, she'd be lectured, tested, retested, and finally failed. But if she laid it down somewhere, there was a chance he'd forget about it—for a while, anyway. Janice was the only one who chose to return his information to him directly. She always read what he gave her and seemed to enjoy competing with him for total recall of the articles and arguing with him over points where his own memory had failed. He called her Professor Jackson when she was getting too far ahead. He never hit her but fumed for hours when he felt she had won the competition.

Shortly after everyone sat down to breakfast, Janice asked Henry what the brochure was about. Henry looked over at Flora with one eye straining as if he wore a monocle. That meant he expected a complete summary from her. Flora finished chewing and swallowing a mouthful of scrambled eggs.

"Avocados," she said and took another bite. She saw his eyes narrow, as she knew they would. Being able to predict the ignition point of his temper and the circuit it would take made her feel weary. She got up and squeezed past his chair. He twisted around and pointed his finger at her.

"You're heading for a big fall," he said, and gave her a poke in the solar plexus with every word.

She went back to her room and curled up on the bed.

An hour or so later, Janice came into the room. "Dad wants to plant several hundred avocado trees out at The Ranch."

Flora rolled over onto her back. "The Ranch?"

"Yes, The Ranch," repeated Janice.

"That rattlesnake bed, gopher hole, slab of sandstone? You've got to be kidding me. What's he going to use for water? Spit? Sweat? Piss?"

"You don't have to get so foul-mouthed! City water will be out there by this summer," said Janice matter-of-factly.

"Wonderful," replied Flora. "I'll ask Mom to take me to the mall so I can buy a pair of overalls. I wonder if avocado picking is hard to learn?"

"Stop exaggerating. He just wants us to come out to The Ranch today to mark some rows for the trees."

"Who's us?" Flora wanted to know.

"The whole family!" Janice was getting irked now.

"Well, according to him I'm not part of the family, so I'm not going." Flora rolled back over onto her stomach. She didn't have to ask Janice to deliver her message. Janice would anyway.

Henry had let her get past the breakfast table. Maybe he had given up on her for the day? If so, now he was probably thinking that leaving her behind while the rest of the family went on a Sunday outing would be a kind of punishment. Let her know what it feels like to be alone.

Flora heard the front door slam for the last time, and Julia and Daniel's excitement. Henry had promised they could do whatever they liked as long as they didn't break their necks. No scything weeds or hauling water. They could spend the day swinging from scrub oaks, building shelters, throwing yucca stalks like javelins, warding off invisible mountain lions with showers of stones, picking wild pea and morning glory vines and festooning their shelters with them. Galloping down the graded roads, kicking up the ruddy earth like deer outrunning a brush fire. Prodding snake holes. Catching lizards. She and Janice had done all that, too, once. She couldn't understand why in the world Janice would willingly go out there now.

She listened to the family car coast out of the driveway and accelerate down the street. She didn't know anything about growing avocados. Maybe the earth out there was good enough for them? She only knew that they were pear-shaped like the uterus, leathery tough-skinned, and swamp-green like an alligator. Inside they were creamy and nutty. Mostly seed.

She wondered what would become of her or any of them if they took Henry up on any of his schemes. Would they really end up tending avocado trees? Or would they be managing a trailer park in the Sequoias now, living in a deluxe mobile home, waiting for the tourist season to begin? Would they be living out at The Ranch in a hacienda-style house, cooling themselves beneath the grape arbor in the courtyard, taking dips in their own swimming pool, riding the promised horses? But that was just it: they *did* take Henry up on his plan to build a house out there, wholeheartedly, and he hadn't made a move. He hadn't made a move. He was the kind of person who just went ahead and let his dreams pile up, one on top of the other, without ever making anything of them.

Flora couldn't remember the last time the house had been emptied, leaving her the only living creature in it—her and any other organism that might have survived Bon Ami, Lysol, Spic and Span, and the vacuum cleaner. An afternoon of guaranteed solitude stretched out before her. She looked at the clock radio on the desk. Its minute hand clucked forward just as she focused on it. What an irritating thing it was, snapping off minutes, making the sound of cracking plastic. She wanted to make special use of this time alone, but she couldn't lift herself off the bed. She felt heavy all over, as heavy as a mattress. She closed her eyes.

When she woke she felt as if she had been embedded sideways in the bed by some tremendous force. She sat up and saw the impression of her body in the satin spread and a wet spot where she had drooled. The side of her mouth was wet, too. She hadn't felt that sensation since she was a little girl waking up from a long car ride.

She pushed the curtains aside and was surprised to see that it was still bright outside. She listened but couldn't hear anything more than a couple of crows in the sycamore trees out front. Then she remembered: they had all gone to The Ranch, to the Avocado Plantation. She glanced at the clock again. She'd been asleep for only fifteen minutes. A line of sunlight was stretching across the wall, crossing over the bird collages. It made their tailfeathers blaze. She liked thinking of herself and Matthew as this pair of birds in flight, migrating to some exotic place. She let go of the curtain and the shaft of light vanished. How easily things can change. By Sunday afternoon she always had the feeling that Matthew had been reduced to a memory. No more Matthew. Just the sensation that she was wandering around in a cloud of love, touching nothing.

She got the urge to draw and jumped to her feet as if she had been jabbed. She took a large piece of paper down from the closet shelf and pulled her drawing board out from between the mattresses. She sat down on the floor with her pencil in one hand and an eraser in the other, sucked in a deep breath, and once again began the scene of Matthew standing on her porch holding a bunch of wildflowers hidden behind his back—herself half-hidden behind a half-open door. She felt the pressure of her own palm against the edge of the door frame, and the tension in Matthew's arched spine, his bold gaze—faunish, enticing, drawing her out. Off to the side, she swiggled a few faint lines to indicate the face of someone peeking through the curtains. Until now, the effort she had put into this drawing was like a long night spent struggling with an uncooperative dream. At times she had been on the verge of letting the whole conception dissolve into the chaotic nightmare it seemed bent on becoming.

But now all the lines were running along smoothly, doing exactly what she wanted them to do. It was as if she had spun a shawl of silvery thread around herself as effortlessly as a creature that had an instinct for spinning such things. Her sense of anything beyond her work was muffled. The crows and the clock were silenced. She didn't feel the numbness in her legs or the braids of hemp rug making ridges and grooves on the sides of her feet and calves. Matthew had actually appeared at her door and he was about to hand her a bouquet of flowers, and no one was going to faze them.

A couple of car doors slammed. At first she thought her ears were popping. Then she realized that her family was already home. She unbent her back and a burning sensation raced up her spine. It felt as if some nerves had been stretched too far. She shoved the drawing board under the bed, jumped up, and almost fell over again with the prickly sensation in her legs, but the sound of the front door opening made her regain her balance.

Janice burst open the bedroom door and let in the wild, dry aroma of sage and sandstone. She looked as though she had been through a survival test. Her hair lay like mats of fine, pale plant roots on her shoulders. Dust had gathered and darkened around her eyes, and the bristly ends of foxtails showed through her socks and at the cuffs of her rolled-up jeans. She flung herself on the bed.

"I'm so exhausted I could die!" she groaned.

Flora picked her pencils and her erasers up off the floor without Janice noticing.

"First we marked off some rows for the trees. Then he wanted us to hike up along some ridge, and then on up this fire trail, and down a new way to the main road."

"And that's what you did?" Flora laid her pencils and erasers in her drawer and closed the drawer quietly.

"Well, he'd already gotten us all the way out there!" Janice wiped her fingers under her eyes and inspected her fingertips. Then she flipped onto her side and propped her head up in her hand. She appeared to have revived. "Dad says he knows you're still seeing Matthew."

"How does he know that!" Flora felt a jolt of fear and protested without thinking.

"How does he know what?" Janice raised her brows and smiled. She had just witnessed Flora unravel a little for the first time in weeks, maybe months.

"What he *thinks* he knows," said Flora. She couldn't hide her agitation. Her secret had a hole in it and Janice was doing her darnedest to peep in.

"So, you're still seeing Matthew. I can't believe it." She wagged her head and gave Flora a little *tsk-tsk.*

"Well, don't then!" Flora was getting madder and madder at Janice for being an accomplice in Henry's trick. And she was incensed at herself for having fallen for it. She made an attempt to patch things up. "Matthew and I have a Life Drawing class together; you damn well know that."

Janice shrugged as if that piece of information meant nothing to her. "Oh, I didn't know that," she said and smiled with her mouth hanging open.

"Stop smirking at me!" Flora was trembling with anger. She gripped her Shakespeare book and was about to throw it at Janice, but then used it only to shove several other books off the desk and onto the floor.

She hated herself for that show of violence.

Janice just lay there in the same position, with her head balancing on her fist. Just like Henry, thought Flora, staying cool while others were sad and angry. Sadness and anger he had provoked on purpose.

"He hasn't seen or heard a single thing, and you know it." She picked the books up from the floor and came up close to Janice's face and whispered into her eyes. "And if you let on to him," she hesitated, "that you have any idea, even the vaguest one, about Matthew and me, so help me, I'll never speak to you again." Flora didn't know how else to threaten her sister. She slumped down at the side of the bed and wept.

Janice got up with a bounce and left the room.

Despite herself, Flora reached under the bed and pulled out her drawing. It was nearly finished. She carefully untaped it from the board. Someone knocked on the door.

"Your mother could use some help in the kitchen," said Henry.

"I'll be right there." She quickly rolled up the drawing and then realized she'd never get it out of the house like that, so she folded it into six sections and stuck it in her Shakespeare book. She tucked the board back between the mattresses, went to the bathroom and doused her face in cool water. She decided she'd enter the kitchen looking as though she'd been studying inorganic chemistry all afternoon and had just had a pleasant chat with Janice. She knew Marleen didn't want any help before dinner except for setting the table. Mostly she wanted someone to clean up the mess afterward and put out the milk bottles and the garbage without quarreling about it.

By the time Flora got to the kitchen, everyone was already seated. Daniel and Julia were in their pajamas, about to fall asleep in their plates. She hoped her face didn't look as chapped, as dismal, as theirs.

"I'm sorry I'm late," she said.

"That's all right," said Marleen. "We're just having a little snack tonight. There's chicken soup on the stove, and a cheese sandwich in the broiler for you."

"Always letting her off the hook," complained Henry as Flora rose up on her toes and eased around him into her own seat.

"Don't you think you could at least manage to make it to the table on time? Pretend you're really with us?"

"I try to," said Flora with a nod. She thought of the many nights Marleen had tried to keep the dinner warm on the stove while they all waited for Henry to return from who-knows-where, two or even three hours later than the time he had said he'd be home.

"You haven't tried very hard at anything except sneaking around." He chomped a perfect semicircle out of his sandwich and added, with his mouth full, "Ever since that Cartier creep moved in down the street."

He doesn't know a thing, thought Flora. Matthew is still just that creep down the street. Little ripples of fear came and went, and she felt calm again. She took the two triangles of her sandwich and lined them up neatly along their hypotenuses, pulled them apart and watched the strands of melted cheese stretch thin and let go.

"You come and go like you think this place is a motel. Can't even help your mother with the meals. Whimpering around here, lovesick for that creep."

Marleen let a little sigh escape, which was her sign to Henry that she wished he would ease up.

"Why don't you just move in with him! Then you'll find out what's tough! Pack your bags and get out?" He shifted his milk glass from one side of his plate to the other. "What do we need you around here for anyway!"

Flora felt that tonight she couldn't possibly be goaded into revealing anything, no matter how close he accidentally came to stating the truth. She would act on the belief that he didn't know anything. She felt tough already, and untouchable. And yet a tear came out of nowhere and trickled down her cheek, and then another and another. Where did they all come from? She thought she had drained them all away earlier, and had been on the verge of silently thanking Janice for her unintended good deed, when the first tear appeared. Well, anyway, Janice had managed to forewarn her about Henry's mood, and even though he had gotten tears out of her, he would get no words. Words were weapons to him, to turn around and use upon all the people he swore were against him, trying to trick him. She kept thinking, He's not my father. I have no father. He's Henry, Marleen's husband, Henry.

"Why don't you just get out!" He was bracing both his hands on the edge of the table and leaning toward her.

Is he asking me, or daring me? wondered Flora. Does he really want me to leave? Doesn't he remember what he told me?

"I'm grounded," she said, frowning at him.

He hauled off and cuffed her. Daniel ducked instinctively and

Julia let out a kitten cry. Flora twisted her face away and he got her in the side of the head, above the temple. As he was clasping one hand in the other, obviously stinging from the hardness of her skull, she got up and excused herself.

"I've got a better idea," he said, pivoting around in his seat. "Why don't you tell me what you do during lunch hour at school?"

Flora's eyes almost leapt all the way to Janice, who was taking something off the relish dish. But she stopped herself and remained staring at the curved chrome legs of the kitchen table.

"Dad wants to know why you eat your lunch on the way home from school every day," said Janice, crunching a carrot.

Henry shot Janice a look full of sparks.

There was silence while Flora felt her insides flip over in slow motion and then settle down again. He doesn't know anything about what's going on inside the gates of school. He must be spying on the way home from school. That's all there is to it. Flora looked straight at her father.

"I'm not hungry until then." She told him the truth. The last thing she saw as she left the kitchen was the hunched form of her mother and the marble-round eyes of her little brother and sister.

She went to the bathroom and held a cold washcloth against her forehead. She looked at her face in the dark mirror. What's with Janice? It was hard to figure.

Janice opened the door and flipped on the light. "How long are you going to be in here? I have to take a shower."

"It's all yours," said Flora, slipping past her.

"Don't forget, it's your turn to do dishes," said Janice as she pushed the door closed.

Flora crawled into bed that night with a deep, indefinable sorrow that could be soothed away only by imagining that Matthew was holding her in his arms, himself asleep and breathing deeply and evenly. Through two closed doors she heard the sound of her mother's alto voice singing Brahms's lullaby to Julia, the same improvised verse over and over again. Daniel had outgrown the lullaby and being tucked into bed, but he still shared a room with Julia, so he still got the lullaby. Flora could remember when Daniel was a baby and Marleen could put him to sleep by tracing her finger lightly around the thin pink rim of his ear and humming to him.

Flora was wrapped in a deep sleep before Janice came to bed. She dreamed that Henry beat her up and forced her across the street by grabbing a wad of her hair at the temple and kicking her repeatedly on the tendons in the back of her ankles. "You're going to see how tough it really is," he said. He got her over to Matthew's house and rapped on the door. A henna-headed woman with lots of gold bracelets on her arms immediately opened the door as if she had been standing just inside it waiting for them. She batted her lashes and some flecks of glitter fell from her eyelids. "Yes?" she asked. Henry demanded to know where Matthew Cartier was. "He's unavailable now," said the woman and closed the door. "There!" said Henry, and he flung Flora toward the closed door. "Your new home!" He took off down the sidewalk and she started to come down off the porch after him, but she missed the first step, or rather, the first step was missing. And the fall jolted her awake. Below her there had been no more sidewalk, only a vapor-filled chasm of terrifying depth, something only an earthquake could make.

For once she didn't mind the sensation of Janice's body, like a firm bolster, pressed up alongside her own.

When Flora got up in the morning, she couldn't use the bathroom because he was in it, so she washed her face in the service porch sink and sat down to breakfast with a full bladder.

Four tall cereal boxes made the center of the table look like a miniature downtown L.A. Advertisements with cannons, elves, baseball players encouraging the consumption of cold cereal covered the sides of the skyscrapers. Flora flipped the roof open on one box and poured herself a bowlful of puffed-up wheat. She dumped some milk on top and taxied the sugar bowl up alongside.

"Dad's up," she announced in a low voice. She scattered a spoonful of sugar on her cereal. Daniel and Julia sped up their eating. Marleen, who had been standing at the kitchen sink gazing out the window at the budding apricot trees, started scouring faster.

"What's he up to now?" she wondered out loud.

"Why don't you ask him sometime?" asked Janice. She clanked her empty bowl in the sink. The spoon was still jingling in it when she had disappeared from the kitchen.

Daniel and Julia grabbed their lunch sacks from the line of them that Marleen always arranged on the countertop in the order of her children's ages. After a couple of *Bye, Mom*s and some punch-clock kisses, they got their coats down from the hooks in the service porch and hurried out the back door.

“Do you want yours?” Marleen held up a lunch sack. She sounded discouraged, doubtful.

“Yes,” said Flora, getting up, “I just don’t like to eat it all at once.” She took it from Marleen.

“I thought maybe you don’t like what I fix you.”

“I do,” insisted Flora. “I’m just not very hungry at noon.”

Marleen vaguely remembered one of Flora’s grammar school teachers sending a note home by way of Flora. It said something like, “Flora seems to have difficulty finishing her lunch in time to join the other children on the playground. Could you please . . .” Please do something. What was it they had wanted her to do?

“I’ll fix the lunches if you want,” said Flora. She didn’t especially want to; she was just trying to prove to Marleen that she really did believe in lunches.

“No, that’s all right, I know what everyone wants. I mean, I know what Daniel and Julia want. I don’t mind making them. I . . .” Marleen looked distracted. She saw another sack on the counter. “Somebody’s forgotten to take their lunch.” She was puzzled. She peered at the name on the sack and looked inside it. It was Janice’s.

“I’ll be late,” said Flora. She put her hand on Marleen’s shoulder and gave her a kiss on the cheek. It felt odd kissing a woman, even though it was her mother, someone she had been kissing all along.

She was on her way out of the kitchen as Henry came in. He looked pink, almost raw with scrubbing. He had a scowl on his face. Flora looked at him. He was standing in her way. I’ll just try to get through this as quickly and as easily as I can, she told herself.

Henry puffed himself up. “You still haven’t answered my question.”

“What question?” asked Flora. She couldn’t remember it.

Henry’s scowl gave way to an expression of insult. His mouth formed a tight oval, like a challenged monkey, and his brows came together.

Marleen said she thought she’d better go take the curlers out of her hair. She’d be late for work. And she left the kitchen.

“I want to know what you do during your lunch hour!” He said each word slowly and with mounting force, as if he were dictating the same line for the fourth time to an incredibly dumb secretary.

“The same thing Janice does,” replied Flora, backing away from him.

Henry clenched his teeth.

"Socialize," added Flora, in a zestful tone.

Henry glared at her for a moment. "I don't think you have any friends," he snarled. "Not any worth mentioning." Instead of hitting her, he put his hands in his pockets and rocked back on his heels, looking rather smug. Flora saw the tiny alligator on his shirt. This is his hang-around-the-house attire, she thought. He's got all day. She stood there wondering how she was going to get around him. She heard Marleen open the front door and click it shut.

Henry took his hands out of his pockets and started straightening some little glass jars on the countertop. He put the one filled with safety pins next to the one filled with paper clips and buttons, and then apparently decided against that arrangement and moved it back to where it had been in the first place, beside the jar of rubber bands and chalk butts.

"I'm going to be late for school," Flora said, pleading ever so slightly.

"Whatever happened to Patricia?" He always called Tess by that name. "And what's-his-name, Phil Rudley?"

"I still see them." Once again she had the urge to remind him that he had grounded her, grounded her until the end of the school year, but she just added, "In class, between classes." She acted as if that were an adequate, an agreeable, arrangement. "And during lunch," she added.

"You've got so much socializing to do that you can't find time to eat your lunch." He was trying to trip her up, pretending he hadn't already heard her say that she wasn't hungry until after school.

"I manage," said Flora. She decided to try to get past him.

"I just bet you do!" Henry swung around and blocked her way with a stiff arm braced against the doorjamb.

Flora backed off. "Just what exactly are you trying to get at?" She looked him directly in the eyes.

He gave her his all-knowing smirk and moved his arm away so she could pass. He had given up on her for the time being. He was just taking stabs in the dark. All she had to do was keep cool and not panic whenever he came close. She pictured him as a blindfolded knife thrower. She didn't like to picture herself at the other end of that act, but the scene was inescapable. She had been born into it. And she had to learn to keep control of her emotions, like a performer in a circus.

She went to the bathroom and grabbed her coat and books from the bedroom. She dashed back into the kitchen and picked up her lunch sack again. She said good-bye to Henry's back and left.

He was sitting in his chair stirring his tea slowly. His other hand was held across his belly as if he had a bellyache. He grunted in return.

"You'd better straighten up and fly right," he said. "Straighten up and fly right." But she was gone.

After a while he got up from the table. He saw a lunch sack on the counter. He saw Marleen's perfectly penciled script on the side of the sack.

"Janice?" he muttered, and then he stared out the window at the scribble of apricot twigs against the overcast morning.

Fractures in the Cement Floor

When Flora slipped into class several minutes late, Miss Corbie called her up to her desk. She had her finger fixed on a line in her rollbook, and her lower lip quivered. "I need to remind you, the rule is five tardies and a student must be failed from a course." She showed Flora the three neat black X's lined up after her name.

"Failed?" Flora saw her face reflected in the lenses of Miss Corbie's glasses.

"That's the rule." Miss Corbie opened her history book as a sign she wanted to begin class.

"I won't be late again. I'm sorry," said Flora. She went to her seat, thinking how hard it was to obey all the rules, how hard it was not to offend anyone.

Tardies never seemed to bother Mr. Langtry. With a wave of his large hands, he'd welcome stragglers into his room. Then he'd return to the sonnets—exquisite mazes, he called them. On this particular warm May morning, he sat on the windowsill and read aloud, tracing and retracing lines.

On her way to the storage room, without moving her lips, Flora chanted a couplet she could almost remember. She liked the way the words tripped along:

Lo, thus, by day my limbs, by night my mind,
For thee and for myself do quiet find.

She took a new route, a more roundabout one, and when she opened the door, Matthew was already there waiting for her. He was sitting on the rolled-up sleeping bag, his back against the wall. She sat down beside him and he put his arm around her. He kissed her on the cheekbone, so lightly. It was as if Matthew's spirit, not Matthew, had touched her with his lips. He seemed so contemplative, so quiet. He pulled back her coat and her blouse and kissed her on the breasts. He undid his own shirt, wrapped his arms around her, and held her against his bare chest without saying a word. He acted as if they had all the time in the world to be alone. And when he made love to her it was as if he were carefully unfolding the petals of a flower that wasn't quite ready to open.

His tenderness filled Flora with a sorrowful passion. He seemed to be saying good-bye. She kissed him everywhere she could reach, silently asking him to please not go. She laid her face against his chest and breathed in the smell of his body. It was like warm salty bread. He combed her hair with his fingers and traced the rim of her ear. And then, so gradually, as if it had been there all along, she heard a heavy rumbling sound. It seemed to be vibrating up through the floor. She lifted herself up and listened.

"What's that sound, Matthew?"

"They're excavating the field."

"Oh," said Flora. She took in his calm voice and then heard the undercurrent of discontent.

"What for?"

"The new school," said Matthew. "The one that'll take the place of this one." His chest rose and sank deeply.

"When?" asked Flora.

"I don't know," said Matthew.

Flora put her head back down. They lay there silently for a while, listening to the bulldozers straining against the earth. Shoving, scraping, grumbling. The dump trucks hauling it away.

"Let's go," whispered Matthew.

When they got to Timpanelli's room, Flora unfolded her drawing, the one she had nearly finished on Sunday. She showed it to Matthew. He ran his fingers along the fold lines as if to smooth away the creases.

"I wouldn't mind being able to come to your door like that," he said. "Maybe if I wore a mask?" he added in jest.

Timpanelli came up to them and Matthew handed her Flora's drawing. She looked at it, stretching it taut in an attempt to get rid of the annoying fold lines. She was spiritless and cranky.

"Are you going to get started painting this?" She seemed to be reprimanding Flora.

"Yes," said Flora, "I'd like to."

"You'd better," said Timpanelli. "Time is running out." She looked at the drawing again. "It's a good drawing," she said, nodding slowly at it. She handed it back to Flora and started to walk away. Then she turned back again. "I put the paints, and anything else you two'll need, in the washroom." She gave them a drawn-on smile and walked off.

"Thank you," said Matthew and Flora, almost in unison.

Timpanelli turned back again and looked at Flora. "Your sister came in a while ago. She said she wanted to know if you had her lunch."

Flora pinned her drawing onto her easel and came over to Timpanelli's desk. "What did you tell her?" she asked timidly. She rested her fingertips, as lightly as feathers, on the edge of Timpanelli's desk.

Timpanelli considered for a moment. "I said something like, 'What would Flora be doing with your lunch? She doesn't even eat her own.' " She rested her cheek in her hand and looked sideways at Flora. Flora waited for something more.

"And she couldn't say," added Timpanelli. She erased some pencil marks on her desk in an absent-minded way. "I'm sorry I said that to her."

"Why?" asked Flora. She hated to see Timpanelli looking so droopy.

"Because," said Timpanelli, "she looked destroyed." She started fussing around in her desk drawer.

Flora went back to her easel. Matthew had put her canvas on it and repinned her drawing up alongside it. He was drawing on his own canvas, adding the final touches.

The end-of-lunch bell rang. Flora drew right on through it, very gently, for she was afraid of denting the canvas. She thought about Janice and smelled her sage-scented hair. She saw her trying on stockings, trying on Tess's black lace push-up. Flipping through the pages of a chemistry book. Filing her fingernails as a deterrent to biting them. And scribbling mathematical calculations in her notebook as if they were maddening and vital. The smell of linseed oil, turpentine, and oil paint drifted over to Flora. Matthew had begun painting.

For the rest of the week, Matthew and Flora worked in Timpanelli's room for two straight hours every day. Flora wished he would have suggested they go to the OFF LIMITS room one of those days, but he never did. He seemed completely absorbed in his painting. It looked wonderful to her, his lines delicately wrapped in color, his figures becoming solid in tones of gray tinged with color.

Toward the end of the class period on Friday, Timpanelli made an announcement. "There's not going to be any class on Monday. A general assembly has been called during this period. You're supposed to go to the main gym after lunch." She crumpled up the bulletin and tossed it in the wastebasket. There was a short spell of moaning and groaning, which was drowned out by the sound of the bell.

At breakfast on Saturday Henry told Flora he wanted her to start sanding the garage door.

"Can't I wait until the sun gets around to the front of the house?" asked Flora. "So I can see what I'm doing better."

"So you can get a suntan, you mean." Henry punched his newspaper.

That afternoon Flora stood before the garage door wearing a pair of shorts and an old pink T-shirt. She had her hair tied up in a faded scarf. "It hardly even needs repainting," she muttered. But she pretended she was preparing a large canvas. By dusk she was ready to quit. Her arms ached from the weight of the sander, and she was covered all over with white paint dust.

Matthew drove by with the top off his T-bird. It looked like he was wearing his blue suit jacket, dressed to go out someplace fancy. He glanced in her direction, just a quick twist of his head. Maybe he thought she was Janice. She hoped so; she didn't want him to see her looking such a mess. I should be in that car, riding along with him, she told herself. There was a lump in her throat and the dry, bitter taste of paint in her mouth.

She sensed someone watching her, and looked around. Henry was standing on the porch with a strange smile on his face.

"I'll work on it more tomorrow," she told him and heaved the garage door up.

On Sunday she spackled and sanded for nearly four hours straight. What else did she have to do, after all? From the driveway, she couldn't even see Matthew's house. She was cut off from him entirely. She half expected to see him driving down the street again, this time in the opposite direction. But she was glad she didn't. Henry was out there the whole time, arranging and planting an assortment of cactuses in the flowerbed that bordered the front porch. That night Flora soaked in the bathtub for almost an hour, and everyone but Marleen complained about it.

On Monday morning she was halfway to school when Matthew passed by, going in the wrong direction. At least, she thought it was Matthew. The top was back on his car, so she couldn't really tell if it was him or not. She waved, just in case. All through her morning classes she kept seeing him driving past, driving past, not waving, not seeing her.

By the time she got to the dance room, it was already filled with limbering and lounging figures. At the far end of the room Tess was kicking her legs high enough to disturb the Northern Lights. Flora walked over there and Tess slipped down into the splits and folded herself over until her cheek rested on her thigh.

"I saw Matthew at a party Saturday night," she said from that position.

Flora felt her insides ripping in all directions, but on the surface she remained unruffled. She stood against the back wall of the room, her palms and spine pressed against the enameled stucco.

"I don't need to know that." Her voice was steady.

"If I were you I'd want to know," said Tess nonchalantly. She rose into an inverted T and stood up.

Flora didn't want to hear why she, Flora, would want to know. It couldn't really have anything to do with her and Matthew.

Tess was waiting to be questioned.

"We've got a few minutes to practice our routine," said Flora. She avoided looking at Tess.

The ice cracked beneath her feet as they went through the movements of their dance. She stretched and slid over jagged fissures in black ice, feeling like a very pliant seal. No one seemed to notice her rubberyness or the fractures in the cement floor. Matthew can be out on the weekends. He can be out any night of the week if he wants to, she told herself. He has a right to be. And he has a right not to be snitched on. No, it wasn't a snitch exactly. She didn't want to exaggerate what Tess had said. It was only a useless piece of information.

So Matthew had gone to a party. So what. Maybe a girl had sat down next to him even, like that woman had sat down next to Phil in Tijuana. Wouldn't a girl, lots of girls, feel like sitting down close to Matthew? How could they know he was already taken? What was Matthew supposed to do, get up and sit somewhere else? Was he supposed to ask them to sit somewhere else? What did Tess want, anyway?

Pazetti clapped her hands loudly. "Today we'll see what you've put together for Antarctica." Everyone drifted back to the sides of the room and waited to see which group Pazetti would call on first.

Flora snuck out of the dance room several minutes early, while the last group was performing, and was leaving the locker room as the other gym classes were rushing in. She traveled recklessly across school, in a hurry to get to the storage room. At the entrance to the side hall, she stopped in her tracks.

A custodian was mopping the floor. She watched him for a moment. He had his back to her and moved backward down the hall, taking wide languid swoops with his mop. Like an elephant he swayed from foot to foot rhythmically. He was in no rush to finish. It was a big school. A heavy old man like that could give himself a heart attack if he went about it like he thought he could mop all the halls in one day.

Flora backed away and headed for Timpanelli's. It was a warm, windless day. No one else was wearing a coat. Matthew would be wearing a short-sleeved shirt. Not even his corduroy jacket. Suddenly it occurred to her that he might have gone to the storage room before her, before the custodian had appeared. He'd still be in there, motionless as a cat, listening to the sound of the swishing mop, the squeaking floor. But he hadn't said he would meet her there. They hadn't gone there for a whole week. Maybe he didn't even come to school today? His car was going in the other direction. No, he would want to work on his painting. She was almost running by the time she reached the door to Timpanelli's room.

A couple of students were gathered together in one corner, talking amidst a scramble of chairs. Several more were working alone at easels. One person was sitting with Timpanelli, gazing out the window, pulling up and down on the cords of the Venetian blinds.

Flora walked in slowly. She heard a little of what Timpanelli was saying: ". . . becoming a father isn't the worst thing in the world. Some people would even be envious." The boy had a tattoo on his arm of a ship sinking in a heart. He got up and left.

"Chris," Timpanelli called after him.

"Dalavantes," said the boy, with a jerk of his head. Flora finally recognized him.

"Dalavantes," repeated Timpanelli. "It'll all work out."

"Sure," said Dalavantes. As he went out the door, he said hi to Flora, hardly looking at her, almost too low to hear. Flora smiled and nodded. How easy, she thought with a pang, it was to lose contact with someone.

Matthew's unfinished painting was hanging behind Timpanelli. At the end of class Friday, Timpanelli had banged a nail in the wall. Matthew had protested having it hung there, but Timpanelli insisted it was the safest place for it.

"Matthew hasn't been in yet," said Timpanelli, before Flora had a chance to say anything.

Flora felt like leaving but didn't know where else to go. She sat down in a chair that faced Timpanelli, the chair Chris had just been sitting in, and looked down at her own hands. She was clutching them together so tightly that they were mottled pink and white.

"What would happen if you had to do without Matthew?" Timpanelli gave her a long look.

Flora noticed for the first time that Timpanelli's eyes, beneath her cat-shaped glasses, were bloodshot and tired. She looked beyond Timpanelli to Matthew's painting—his "painted sculpture," as he called it. The figures looked as if they would embrace forever. They'd never get tired. Never get separated.

"I don't know, I don't think about it," said Flora. Her face went hot with the lie.

Timpanelli shook her head as if that wasn't satisfactory. She leaned over and pinched Flora gently on the ear lobe.

"Listen." She stared Flora straight in the eye. "I want to see paint on *your* canvas. Your work is too good to let fall by the wayside." She let go of Flora's ear and gave her a surprised face, which she held in suspended animation. She couldn't resist making faces that anticipated the responses of others.

Flora sat up straight, surprised at herself for having come into the room without giving one thought to her own drawing. She went over to her canvas and picked it up. Almost every line looked correct, even the difficult profile of Matthew's nose. She sat on the floor and pulled a pencil and an eraser out of her coat pocket. A few lines here and there needed to be improved, but she felt ready. She looked over her shoulder at Timpanelli. Timpanelli had her head bent over a magazine.

Flora went to the washroom. The first thing she saw was Matthew's palette lying on one of the shelves, inert beneath a sheet of oilcloth. The washroom felt warm and humid, undisturbed. It was as if no one had entered it since the January day she and Matthew had been in there together. She took several brushes out of a jar and felt the tips of them. She chose two and put the rest back. *What would happen if you had to do without Matthew?* She heard Timpanelli say it again. Impossible, she whispered back. She found two little metal cups and filled them with turpentine and linseed oil the way she had seen Matthew do. From a box she took a square of rag that looked like a piece of someone's napless faded nightgown. Impossible, she repeated to herself. Matthew is everywhere.

She stacked everything on a palette and carried it to her easel, went back for her canvas, and there he was, waiting to be painted. She was staring down at the box of paints and all the other things she had arranged on her stool when Timpanelli stepped up to her with what looked like another rag. "You might need this," she said.

"Thank you," said Flora. She unfolded the cloth and saw that it was a man's long-sleeved shirt decorated down its front with a few paint stains. She took off her coat, hung it over the crossbars on the backside of her easel, and put on the shirt.

She unscrewed the cap on the tube of crimson red light and placed a small blotch of it on the palette. She made a small blotch of thalo green, too. She didn't know what she was going to do with them. Dab by dab, she mixed the two colors together. She was amazed by how easily two brilliant colors could turn to brown, a red brown, like dried blood. When she looked very closely, she could see red reflected onto green and green reflected onto red. And when she looked on the surface she could see the ceiling lights shining off the wet paint. It reminded her of mopped and waxed linoleum. But all in all, the red and green had turned to brown. A little ivory black could easily switch the brown into a deep shadow. A little zinc white wouldn't even make a noticeable change. A lot of zinc white made a ruddy beige. She put a dab of purple down on the palette. It was nice to see a vibrant color again. "MAUVE (True Purple)," the label said, and in tiny print, "laque violette."

All the while, as she experimented with the colors, she kept a portion of her senses on the alert for Matthew's entrance. Crazy thoughts raced along in the back of her mind. He hasn't been home since Saturday night. He's far away now, still driving. He's in the storage room losing his temper. He's in the V.P.'s office being interrogated—Is this or is this not your sleeping bag? She tried to shut it off, but one ridiculous conclusion followed another. And Matthew never showed up. She hadn't put one speck of paint on her canvas, but her palette was a smeary mess. She went to the washroom and meticulously cleaned everything she had used. She hoped Mrs. Timpanelli wouldn't be mad at her for wasting paint, but she hadn't seemed to notice. She gave Flora a glazed-over smile and a nod good-bye. Flora rushed off to the assembly.

When she entered the main gym she felt as though she were inside a huge seashell. The building drummed and roared with the distant rush of a thousand liquid voices. And the floors, the walls, and the ceiling glowed with a pearly golden varnish. She hadn't stepped foot in the gym since some sock-hops, some shoeless dances back at the beginning of tenth grade. She hadn't liked that kind of dance—a romantic function confused with an athletic event, couples bouncing around on the hardwood floor as if they were competing in a Ping-Pong tournament. And now, as then, she couldn't seem to see anyone she knew. Finally she spotted a group of girls she had gone around with in junior high. They were standing at the perimeter of the crowd, which had almost completely filled the gym room floor. They looked as timid as ever. The bleachers were full. She saw Stan and some other guys; Victor was there. Farther up she saw Tess sitting straight and expectant, looking toward the plywood stage that had been set up at the far end of the gym. She was surrounded by a clutch of Hill girls.

Just an hour ago she and Tess had performed their Antarctica dance. Beforehand, Tess had apologized coolly for telling her that Matthew was at a party. Flora wanted to say something to smooth things out, but she only felt her mouth gaping, letting in dry air. Their dance hadn't gone very well. The two other girls in the group were plainly disappointed and puzzled as to why the performance had gone so poorly compared to the last practice. It seemed to Flora that Tess was dancing too aggressively, throwing the rest of them off balance, out of step. Tess cast a glance down from the bleachers that said, You're the one who did it.

The student body president, a wiry little guy wearing tight jeans and a tweed jacket, jumped onto the stage. After he had spent several minutes fiddling with the microphone and calling again and again for the attention of the assembly and not getting it, Mrs. Baines waddled up to the microphone and cried, "Silence!" Almost everyone looked up to see where the harsh sound had come from.

"If you don't quiet down this minute, the assembly will be canceled and you will be sent back to your classes!" By the time she had finished her statement she was screaming to a pool of silent faces. She huffed off the stage.

The student body president returned to the microphone, adjusted his striped tie, and announced with much enthusiasm that they were all here to celebrate the beginning of the construction of their new school. A cheer went up all around as other student officers unrolled a large tinted drawing of the new structure. They taped it to the wall behind the stage. The president stepped aside so that everyone could get a full view of what looked like the upper decks of a battleship: an apparently windowless mass of cubes and rectangles painted in shades of bluish gray. Drab green trees, non-specific ones, billowed up around the proposed buildings.

Flora looked over the crowd, searching for Matthew. She would've liked to have been standing beside him, but she couldn't even see him. So it was true. She took a deep breath. The old school was going to be taken away from them, and they were going to be given this in return. She looked toward the stage and her eyes got bleary. The president was back at the mike again, holding a sheet of paper in one hand, reading off a list of the new school's virtues, thrusting his fist in the air after each entry and waiting for the crowd to cheer. Air-conditioned classrooms, he said, and an air-conditioned cafeteria, up-to-date science labs and shop classes, new basketball and tennis courts. Before long most of the students were thrusting their fists in the air, too. And the cheering got more insistent.

Finally a group of boys with instruments got up on stage. They milled around, arranging and rearranging the extra mikes, plugging in their guitars, untangling cords. The drummer tucked in his shirt and accidently knocked a cymbal. He looked out on the crowd and blushed. One of the guitar players put his mouth to a mike. He started to say something and the mike let out a sound like a hundred screeching truck brakes. He gave it a disgusted look and tried again, this time with his lips a little farther away.

"We're just up here to help celebrate the rise of our new school." The screeching sound started up again. He gnarled up his face and turned around to his group for succor. With no further introduction they played "I'm Looking Through You" too fast and sometimes out of beat. Then they started in on "What a Day for a Daydream."

Flora wanted to get out of the gym. She was looking for an exit when she caught sight of Matthew's profile. He was standing near one of the side doors, still as a statue, while other students danced in place around him. His hair, in the bright light of the gym, looked blue-black, and his face, from the side, looked translucent and smooth, like milky marble. He was wearing a short-sleeved shirt, as she knew he would be. And he had his hands in the pockets of his pants, as if he had just stepped in for a moment—just an observer at the edge of the commotion.

Flora felt a queasy longing for him, like mild seasickness. He was so near and yet so unreachable. She didn't dare take her eyes off him. Then a few people shifted and he was hidden from her. She saw a silky blond head instead, and then Phil's face turned toward her. Phil looked startled. He jerked away, out of her sight, and she could see Matthew again. He looked in her direction, but he didn't seem to see her. Flora repeated his name to herself several times in a futile attempt to get his attention.

A dozen cheerleaders hopped up on stage, and the gym resounded with "Hazelton High, High, High," yelled by nearly three thousand voices. It sounded to Flora's ears like the roar and thrash of mad waves. She watched Matthew step behind a teacher acting as sentry and slip out the side door. She tried to weave her way politely over to the same exit.

The student president was announcing a candybar drive, a way to raise money for the new football stadium with lights, so that Hazelton's Staghorns could win some of their night games at home, instead of winning them *all* on foreign fields. The gym throbbed with laughter. Then there was another cheer: "S-T-A-G-H-O-R-N-S, Staghorns, Staghorns, Staghorns forever!" Boxes of candybars could be picked up in first-period classes the next day. The student president called it the senior class's gift to the remaining student body. Bright lights and pimples, thought Flora, hardly amused. She was still trying to ease her way through the crowd when the assembly was officially dismissed. She was still far from the door. Now she had to yield to the slow exodus.

Outside, the warm May air was scented with the bitter oil of eucalyptus. It floated down from the huge old trees and rose up from the well-packed dirt of the lane. No one seemed eager to return to class. They lagged along the lane as if they were half etherized. Flora felt her books slipping away from her.

"Why don't you skip your math class?" Matthew swung her books at his side.

"Matthew!" cried Flora. She was startled to have him so close to her again. "I saw you in the gym. I tried to come over to you, but . . ."

Matthew smiled his smile. "I know."

* * *

He leaned close to her as she worked the combination on her locker. "Can you imagine what it's like to hear the sound of mopping instead of your voice at the door?"

Flora went with him to their hall. They had to wait around at the entrance until a couple of students who had taken the indoor route to class finally closed the door at the far end.

The old linoleum was slippery now. Flora held tight to Matthew's hand. Once they were inside, she stood there trembling. The last time she had lost sight of him, she felt he was gone for good. Everything seemed to be telling her that—saying she would lose him. Now she could touch him again. He drew the latch and turned toward her.

"Oh, my cold Flora, wearing a coat on a warm day. Let me warm you up." He put his arms around her, and she squeezed her face against his neck and tried with all her might not to cry. Timpanelli asked her again what she'd do without him. Matthew was pulling her down onto the sleeping bag, undoing his pants, and pushing up her skirt. I'm not going to listen to anyone else, she swore to herself. She stared into his eyes as he moved in and out of her.

"We should always be together," he whispered.

"Yes." A sigh rippled up through her and fluttered off. She saw herself as a child sitting in the grass, taking the lid off a jar of butterflies and letting them all go free.

"Let's leave," urged Matthew. Flora felt the first spurt speeding out of him. The bell wouldn't ring for quite a while. She couldn't understand his haste to go. "Let's go to Mexico," he said, still pressing her. She saw tropical plants swell up beyond him and exotic birds fly back and forth across the ceiling. Matthew raised himself up and waited for an answer. He had a wild look in his eyes.

Flora felt herself traveling away, cushioned in his arms, hugged by his confidence, his determination. She saw his pale skin turn slowly to creamy copper. She saw him emerging from the sea, naked, shedding warm salt water . . . the Gulf of Mexico. She saw him standing at his easel, drawing, painting. She never wanted to lose sight of him.

"Yes, let's go," she replied.

From the excavation site, men's voices could be heard yelling back and forth to one another over the racket of grinding and groaning machinery. Teeth taking bites out of the earth.

"We could stay and work on our paintings until school's out. And leave after that." Matthew leaned down and kissed her. A drop of his sweat fell on her cheek as he rose back up. Salty, wet, and warm; he already felt like Mexico, what she could imagine of it. She took hold of his hips. "Do you think we'll be able to lie together on a beach down there?"

"One after another," was his answer. She felt him swell up inside of her again with one strong pulse. She saw a shimmering two-lane highway stretching out before them. An ebony-black road. A zinc-white stripe down the center of it. Pale ochre sand. Turquoise sky. Turquoise-tinted water, bathtub warm.

"Will we be able to paint outdoors, do you think?"

"With the cicadas and iguanas." He was daring her.

"I'll paint them," said Flora wistfully.

"Will you let me paint you in the nude?" asked Matthew.

"Yes," said Flora. She lifted up her hips and pressed against him.

"¿En qué puedo servirle?" Matthew slid his hands under her shoulders and held on to her at the base of the neck. His voice sounded secretive and foreign.

Flora thought for a moment and then said, "Usted sabe lo quiero." She held on to his hips. "I want you," she added, to make sure she had been understood.

The bell rang as if it could go on ringing forever. Matthew and Flora ignored it. It sounded remote and puny from where they were. Nevertheless, out in the halls, it could still make the cardboard walls shudder. The shuffle of students filled the void where the bell left off.

The Motel

Flora went to turn the brassy doorknob on the back door and saw her own hand. It didn't look like it belonged to her. Finally she was feeling like the thing her father so many times had said she was: a stranger using this house as a motel.

She held her hand on the knob, not wanting to go in. She thought of all the doors she could see on her way to school. Lots of houses had screen doors, on the street side yet. Little children stood just inside them, calling, or banged them open with a flick of their small hands and came running out, as if to demonstrate how easily they could leave their own houses. Her own front door was always locked. What a front door: not even a small window, just a plain brass mail slot and a doorknob—a gladless mouth and a large mole. No doorknocker either. And the doorbell sounded like a rattlesnake, ever since Henry had fooled with it. She'd just as soon enter the house by the back door. At least, with its weatherworn paint and its flyspecked and fingerprinted window, it looked more approachable.

She opened the door and stepped onto the dull service porch floor. What was once a glossy marbleized sea-green was now a chalky mint. The washing machine had stained the linoleum with streaks of rusty orange, and there were clusters of dents where the machine had jumped around with its heavy loads. It didn't work anymore, but it still sat there, holding a weekly accumulation of newspapers and a pair of shoes Henry wanted polished.

The flame under the water heater flared up and the water heater gurgled. It sounded to Flora like an upset stomach. Phil had gone to Mexico once, as far south as Mazatlán. He and Victor and Stan had gone without taking any girls along. He sent a postcard featuring an unknown couple posing beside the mosaic crest of Mazatlán, an anchor flanked by two mermaids. He had written, "Montezuma's Revenge makes you feel like your insides have turned to scalding water and have to get out. Miss you, but glad you're not here . . . Love, Phil." The heater gurgled again as she passed by it.

The television was on in the front room. She peeked in. Daniel and Julia were sitting on the shiny black sofa, their feet tucked up under their haunches. Each of them was clutching a bunch of raw spaghetti. They gnawed away at the brittle sticks and watched Betty Boop get kidnapped by a mob of white cowled characters and carried down a long winding staircase.

"Are you hungry?" asked Flora. This was the first time she had even thought to ask them that.

After a moment Daniel said, "Yeah," and then Julia said, "Yeah," without taking their eyes off Betty Boop's dilemma.

"Where's Dad?" asked Flora when a commercial came on.

"Don't know," said Daniel, still without removing his eyes from the TV. "He wasn't here when I got home."

"Me neither," said Julia. She snapped off several sticks of spaghetti.

"Would you like me to cook some spaghetti and tomato sauce?" said Flora impulsively. She wasn't even sure she could.

Their heads twisted around to her. "Yes," they said together.

Their heads sprang back to the TV and Betty Boop let out a melodious squeal. She was being tickled with torch flames.

Flora walked down the hallway. The master bedroom door was closed. She'd never dare open it to see if he was in there or not. She could feel when he was. She held her breath and stepped by, and she could tell he was lying on his back, holding his breath and waiting for her to pass.

Janice was sitting at the desk in her slip. Her hair was pulled back into a ponytail with a thick rubber band. She would wear her hair like that only if the weather was very hot (which it wasn't) or if she was very seriously trying to study. Two textbooks were propped up against the wall in front of her and she was reading from a third in her lap. Papers were spread out all over the desktop. Her lunch sack sat open on the floor by her chair. She was holding a wedge of sandwich in one hand and a ballpoint pen in the other.

"So you're home early today," said Flora in an encouraging tone.

"Yeah," said Janice with a mouthful of peanut butter and bread.

The sight of Janice eating her lunch reminded Flora of Janice's maneuver. "Mrs. Timpanelli said you came in last week."

"Who's Mrs. Timpanelli?" asked Janice. She scratched out a few words in her notebook.

"My art teacher," said Flora.

"Oh yeah," said Janice. She had apparently forgotten about the incident. "Where were you?" she suddenly demanded. She straightened up like an alarmed horse, her ponytail whipping around. "I wanted to know if you had brought my lunch to school with you."

"I figured if you left it on the counter, that's where you wanted it. It didn't occur to me to bring it to school." Flora watched Janice chew her sandwich. "I guess you forgot it again today?"

Janice shook her head. "Uh-uh." She swallowed. "There're student government meetings all week during lunch. I don't have time to eat."

"What made you think I'd be in Timpanelli's room?"

Janice's face sagged as she thought back for a few seconds. "I went to that table of yours in the lunch area and Tess Duban said you'd be in your art room."

"Oh," said Flora.

Janice cleared her throat. "I like your painting, by the way."

"What painting?" Flora glanced around the room, fearing that something was exposed.

"The one behind your art teacher's desk," chided Janice.

"That's not mine. I haven't started painting yet."

"Oh!" said Janice, slightly taken aback. She chewed on the plastic top of her ballpoint pen for a minute.

Flora was confused. Something felt out of place. Or something was missing from what Janice had said. Then she hit upon it: Timpanelli had hung Matthew's painting up on Friday, several days after Janice was supposed to have come in. Janice must have come in, or at least peeked in, again since then.

"The girl in the painting looks a lot like you. Whose painting is it?" said Janice.

"Why don't you take a wild guess?" Flora felt that she had already said far too much. She really couldn't tell whether Janice was being sly or stupid.

Janice started scribbling on one of her papers. It didn't look to Flora as if Janice was going to give an answer. "Who do you think the guy in the painting looks like?" She was going to force the obvious answer out of her.

"Matthew?" asked Janice. She looked up at Flora with unusual timidity, then switched her tone. "How would I know!" She sounded bothered. "I've never seen him in the nude." She made the word *nude* sound cruel.

Now Flora felt like the slink, the one who was thinking sly thoughts. Janice might be innocent, this time anyway. She bit her lower lip and kept quiet. Janice gave her a half-smile and made some more indecipherable marks on her paper. "It must be nice having someone so devoted to you. Putting you in his paintings like that?"

Flora wanted to change the subject. She was sitting on the edge of the bed, gripping the bedspread in both fists.

"What are you working on?"

Janice dropped her pen and sighed. "My graduation speech. I have to submit it to Mrs. Baines tomorrow."

Flora was about to ask her why Mrs. Baines had to approve her speech and then realized. "You're valedictorian! Congratulations!" She rushed over and attempted to hug Janice, clutching her by both shoulders and pressing her cheek against Janice's cheek.

Janice accepted this with a "Thanks" and a halfhearted hug of her own. Flora's Spanish book fell off the bed, so she went over and tossed it back on. Janice turned back to her notes.

"I don't think I'll be going to the prom." Janice made a discouraged confession.

"That's still a week or so off, isn't it?" offered Flora as she pulled on her afterschool jeans.

"That doesn't make any difference," said Janice very slowly, with special emphasis on the word *any.* She flipped over a chunk of pages in one of the books on the desk. "John's going out with that Jill Buckley now," she said with resolve.

Jill Buckley was a cheerleader. Flora knew that much. She had seen her performing on stage only this afternoon: bouncy, breasty, with a smile like an orange wedge, only gleaming white, and a pleated skirt that didn't want to stay down. With feigned modesty, she kept pushing it down with her pompons.

"Things can change." Flora tried to speak with an upbeat.

"Oh, get off it, Flora." Janice flung her pen down on the desk and let her head hang to one side.

Flora was going to ask her why she wanted to spend prom night with a tackle anyway, but decided not to. "It'll work out."

Janice didn't say anything.

"Good luck on your speech," said Flora, after waiting for a moment in the doorway. "I'm going to fix dinner tonight."

Janice looked up, but Flora was already out of the room.

Flora tiptoed through the hall. She tried not to rattle the pots or bang any cabinet doors in the kitchen. She didn't want to rouse Henry and have him standing around interrogating her while she was trying to cook. She cranked open a can of tomato sauce and wondered what Matthew was used to eating. They had tried to eat chicken hash together once in the cafeteria. That was the only thing she'd ever seen him eating. Maybe, like herself, he didn't have a big appetite.

When Marleen got home from work, Julia told her that Henry was still gone somewhere. Marleen went to her bedroom to change her clothes. Indeed, Henry was not lying on his bed. Only then did she smell something unusual in the house. Something, some sort of synthetic fabric being ironed under too hot a setting. Something cooking on the stove, already?

When she came into the kitchen, the table was set and Flora was tossing a salad. There were scrapings from burnt garlic bread in the sink.

"Well, this is a real treat," she said. "Is there something I can do to help?" She picked up a piece of raw spaghetti from the floor and dropped it in the sink.

"No, just sit down," said Flora, adding more dressing to the salad.

"I think we should wait for your father," said Marleen.

"Well, why don't you go wake him up?" Flora pulled open the broiler door. "Oh gosh, I almost burned them again."

"He's not in the bedroom," said Marleen.

"He's not?" Flora wheeled around.

"No, he's out somewhere." Marleen took a sponge and started wiping some tomato sauce off the countertop.

"Well, everything's ready. Let's go ahead and eat."

"I really don't think we should, Flora." Marleen was nearly pleading. It wasn't as if he was gone on a flight. Since he'd stopped flying, if he was just out somewhere, she always set the serving dishes in a warm oven and waited for him to come home.

Janice rushed into the kitchen. "For crying out loud, Mom, he didn't even tell you he was going to be gone at all!" She served herself from the stove and sat down. "You can't count on men," she said. She twisted her fork in the center of her spaghetti.

"We're starving," cried Daniel and Julia, scrambling into their seats. Flora dished up platefuls for them.

"Come on, Mom, sit down," said Janice, reaching for a piece of garlic bread.

Marleen slowly lowered herself into her chair. She lifted some strands, rolled them around on her fork, and looked around. All of her children were eating.

They left the pot on the stove to keep warm for Henry and put a large portion of salad in a plastic container in the refrigerator.

Flora studied Spanish for a while and then went to bed. With the lights on in the room and Janice still working hard on her speech, she turned toward the wall and closed her eyes. What followed was a silent stream of brightly colored, ridiculous cartoon images: Tinkertoy children flying off a Tinkertoy ferris wheel, Porky Pig eating a plateful of spaghetti, the spaghetti turning into ropes that chased after Betty Boop, a moron joke ("The big moron falls off the cliff. Why doesn't the little moron?"), a big wire cage filled with flitting birds. Then her father's voice started warning her never to go to Tijuana. He was holding Phil's postcard from Mazatlán, pinching it at one corner as if it were contaminated. They'll bust you for nothing, he was saying. Confiscate your car and your wallet. Take all the money you were dumb enough to bring down there. Throw you in a jail cell full of cockroaches and rats. Then there was a switch. Flora was standing on a stage, trying to do a striptease in front of a sequined curtain with a real palm tree as a prop, but all the lights flashed on. They'll do anything they please with you, he said, and it won't be no picnic. If I ever find out you've been down there, even one foot across that border, I'll blister your hide.

Flora opened her eyes. She was wide awake. I've got no money, she thought, blinking at the dark ceiling. I don't have a job, that's a fact. "Keep painting those pretty pictures, you'll wind up a ditch digger, a fruit picker." No high school diploma, no college education, no skills, no money, no nothing. "You're cutting your own throat." Henry ripped his pointer finger across his own neck.

Flora was still awake when the blackness gave way to a wash of cool gray. It was a slow dawn, a very slow dawn. Doves were cooing, probably a pair of them sitting on the wire that went from the house to a pole in the alley.

Shafts of Crimson Light

Dance class was now a matter of preparing for a final solo. The room looked like the dayroom in an insane asylum, each girl moving oddly to her own private tune, sometimes coming close to another girl but veering away before touching. The cool static air of Antarctica had been replaced by the breath and odor of some sixty bending, writhing, springing, humid bodies. It was as if all the warmth of the morning had been drawn into this room.

Flora occupied a small space. She did a few limbering exercises while sitting on the floor. She didn't know what music she would do her solo to. She wondered where Matthew would be today. He had missed working on his painting yesterday. He probably wouldn't go to the storage room.

"Are you dancing inside your head?" asked Pazetti. When Flora looked up and saw Pazetti standing over her, she realized she must have been sitting there, with her legs crossed and her spine bent, for some time.

She gave Pazetti a wry smile. "I'm trying to, I guess." She considered for a moment. "Do you have any Mexican music in your record collection?"

"No, I am sorry, no. The collection is very small," said Pazetti with a pout. "However, a number of the other girls who cannot practice at home have chosen a piece from Carlos Montoya. And if that does not suit you, some others have chosen a song from *West Side Story.* And also, there are a few who want to dance to the *Pink Panther* theme song." She made a skeptical face as she moved away from Flora.

The sound of *The Pink Panther* came from a phonograph in one corner of the room. Three, maybe even four or five girls were slinking around not too far from the source of the music. They gave the impression of cats closing in on a desirable trash can. When the song was over, one of them pounced toward the phonograph and put it on again. Flora looked out the nearest window and did some deep knee bends, some forward bends. She stood on one foot, with the other one pointed up and out behind her. She changed feet and heard the thrumming of a guitar. When she looked around she saw two girls standing over the phonograph, looking down at it as if they couldn't figure out what it was. Flora liked the sound of the music. It sounded far away, but it was coming through clearly, every beat. Then the bell rang, and rankled on and on as if everyone couldn't hear it easily enough.

In the locker room, Tess stuffed her leotard in their locker and turned to Flora. "I'm not going to be modeling anymore. I already told Mrs. T."

"But why not?" asked Flora. She picked up Tess's leotard, which had fallen out of the locker, and stuffed it back in again along with her own. "I thought you liked to model."

"I'm tired of it. All you do is stand there being gawked at." Tess whipped on her blouse. "Sometimes I feel like everyone's looking right through me, or right into me. And most of the guys are such leches. It doesn't take much imagination to tell what they're thinking. That's the only reason they take Life Drawing. It really makes me sick." She was holding her belly.

"Maybe you're coming down with the flu?" It seemed likely enough to Flora.

"Whether I am or not, I have no intention of standing up there anymore like a centerpiece. You know as well as I do there's only a handful of people in that class who even *like* to draw. So why should I waste my time." She sucked in her breath and buttoned her skirt.

"It's going to be strange having someone else up there." Flora stepped into her dress.

"Why don't you try it sometime?" Tess gave her a playful sneer. "Come on, I dare you. It would really throw Matthew for a loop."

Flora pictured herself surprising Matthew like that. She wished she had enough nerve to do it. "You know me, Tess. I'd sooner crawl under the table."

"You're hopeless," Tess said with a sigh. She suddenly looked wan, and as though she couldn't care less where Flora climbed or crawled. She slung her purse over her shoulder and left Flora bent over tying the laces of her sneakers.

When Flora got to Timpanelli's room, she saw Matthew working at his easel. He had his palette in his hand and he was tilting it this way and that so he could see the colors from different angles.

Timpanelli was watching Matthew from behind her desk. Someone had put a bunch of ragged spring flowers in her little ceramic vase. Her mouth looked as if it had been sealed shut with superglue, her lips straining and turned down at the corners. Flora had never seen Timpanelli looking so small, so sucked in. Her desk seemed too big for her. When her eyes moved in Flora's direction, Flora dipped her head a little and smiled. Timpanelli only turned her mouth up and then quickly down again, as a person who was adjusting her dentures might do.

There was only one other person in the room. A boy with a very narrow head and a pointed nose, someone Flora had never seen before, was drawing from a plastic model of a jet bomber. He peered at it through long greasy bangs of dark hair, his tongue protruding from his mouth with the effort. Bits of foil and chocolate bar wrappers were strewn around his chair.

Flora got her canvas, and with her palette balancing on top of a box of oil paints, she went over to her easel. Someone had moved it back alongside Matthew's.

Matthew turned toward her. In the space between them, he held out his wet brush and pretended to trace her shape.

Flora backed up a little, half in jest and half for fear that Matthew might actually dab her with paint. He was impulsive enough to do such a thing. Maybe he thought her cotton dress looked too summery for the day. That morning Marleen, seeing the dress, had given her a glad spurt of a laugh and told her to wear a sweater, but she hadn't bothered to. All morning, except during dance class, she had felt a chill. Only now, near noon, was she beginning to warm up, and Matthew smiled as he stared at her pale bare arms.

She tried to remove the cap from a crumpled and gummed-up tube of alizarin crimson. How can Matthew and I go to Mexico? The aggravating thoughts of the previous night crept back. No, it was rather as if they had swaggered up next to her and were standing there like arrogant policemen, waiting to arrest her.

Matthew, how can I go to Mexico with you? I don't have any money. I don't think I'd be able to find a job. We know how to speak only a few words of Spanish. She didn't want to have to say these thoughts out loud to him. She hoped, somehow, the feeling of hopelessness would pass. She kept twisting at the cap. She considered wrenching it off with her teeth.

"We'll sell our paintings, even if we have to travel back up to San Diego or L.A. once in a while to do it," said Matthew as he continued to stroke paint onto his canvas. It sounded as though he was talking out loud to himself, or to his painting.

The cap suddenly came off the tube of paint. It seemed to have popped off, and a long worm of deep glistening red hung down and touched Flora's palette. She wound it into a coiled mound and glanced at Matthew. He hadn't seen what happened. She looked over to Timpanelli. Timpanelli was lifting the flowers out of her vase. She let them fall back in again.

"Do you really think we'll be able to sell our paintings?" asked Flora.

Matthew gave her an indignant look and smiled. "Besides, my father is giving us a thousand dollars in traveler's checks. He calls it a head start."

"Your father knows we're planning to leave?" asked Flora. "You've told him, and he's going to help us? Your father doesn't even know me."

"He thinks he does," replied Matthew, continuing to paint. "He wanted me to invite you to his wedding. I had to tell him you'd never be able to come." He paused. "And why."

"He and Vivian are getting married?" asked Flora, not knowing what to expect next.

"No, he and Stella," Matthew lifted some of the crimson off Flora's palette with a diamond-shaped palette knife and wiped it onto his own palette. "And you and I will go to Mexico. Unless, that is, you want to stay here and watch this place get smashed to bits," he whispered. He leaned toward his painting and began giving Flora's marble shoulder an aura of crimson light. "Don't worry," he added.

Flora felt dazed and ready to fly. She wanted to leave instantly, drop everything and go. She glanced over at Timpanelli; Timpanelli had lifted her glasses off and was rubbing her closed eyes with her thumb and forefinger.

How does a person just go, without a schedule, without a ritual —how does a person say good-bye? Flora didn't know. Maybe you just take off and explain it later, when you can figure out how, how to say it, to say what you've done, and why you've done what you've done.

She put several more colors on her palette, smaller portions. Matthew made her feel hot on the inside and chilled with goose bumps on the outside. She started painting the gown of the girl who stood behind the half-opened door. The paint slipped onto the canvas with surprising ease. A weightless touch, without force, was what was needed. She felt herself relaxing and slowing down. Beside her, Matthew moved as leisurely as a koala filled with eucalyptus leaves.

Flora was sorry to see that, true to her word, Tess did not show up. A girl from class had taken her place on top of the table. She looked boneless, like a beanbag doll of creamy muslin. A black bikini, just two tight bands without straps, wound around her breasts and hips. She had what looked like charcoal smudges on her thighs; she probably had the kind of skin that bruises easily. She sat back in one chair with her feet resting on another and snapped her gum rhythmically. It must have been bubble gum. She blew a few large bubbles. No one seemed to mind. Mrs. Baines would have, but she hadn't poked her head into the class for a long time. The dangling alarm system was covered with a thick layer of dust.

Timpanelli gazed out the open window beside her desk. Jill, The Cat, was ratting another girl's hair. The boy with the pointed face was cooing to his bomber. The deaf couple were comparing drawings. Some boys were conferring over by the supply cabinets. Half of the people in class were leaning toward whoever was at the easel nearest to them. Flora took it all in, everything in the amber cast of this room. And the room hummed with a sound like bees gathering nectar from a lawn of blooming clover. She knew she would miss that sound.

When Flora came home from school, there was a flatbed truck loaded with cedar shingles parked at the curb in front of the house, a large stack of shingles at the base of the driveway, a couple of ladders leaning against the front eaves, and more small stacks of shingles on the roof.

Henry was standing in the driveway talking to three men. Whenever he got the chance he liked to talk to people—mechanics, plumbers, surveyors, doctors—in the jargon of their trade. Now he was talking to the roofers as if he were a member of the Roofers' Guild, tossing out words like *flashing, shakes, courses, hips,* and *valleys* as if they were part of his everyday vocabulary. He seemed to be addressing himself to some spot on the asphalt just in front of the roofers' feet. The roofers were giving him puzzled, slightly amused glances, apparently wondering why he didn't reshingle his own roof since he knew so much about it.

Flora went through the side gate and round to the back door, undetected by Henry. No one else was home. She dropped her books on the desk and fell backward onto the bed. She had often seen Henry talking to people that way, trying to impress them, let them know he couldn't be easily fooled. She wondered what it felt like, being him. His head seemed to be filled with the names of things. He wouldn't tell her to rake under a bush, he'd tell her to rake under an oleander or the acanthus mollis. He'd never just bump a bone, he'd bruise a mandible or a tibia. And the Cartiers weren't just undesirable neighbors, they were *personae non gratae.*

Flora looked at the pair of birdfeather collages. Isn't it too bad, she thought, the only professions he doesn't have any jargon for are the arts. He wouldn't know the difference between limelight and chiaroscuro. Or an arabesque and a burlesque. He'd fail that quiz for sure. He doesn't even know the difference between vermilion and viridian. It wouldn't matter so much, but he always wanted to argue with Marleen about the color of a piece of fabric she had just bought and taken out of the sack for him to see. He called magenta "hot pink" and indigo blue "funeral black." Marleen stopped buying greens because he called them all khaki, made a prune face, and told her to take them back. The clothes she did, but the cut lengths of fabric she couldn't, so she just folded them neatly and stored them in a big cardboard box in the hall closet.

Janice came into the room. Papers were sticking every which way out of her armload of books. Usually she looked as neat at the end of the day as she did at the beginning, but today she looked frazzled, as if she had fallen into a hedge on the way home.

"Still working on your speech?" asked Flora.

"I'm so sick of this I could die. I can't wait until it's all over." Janice sniffled loudly. A couple of books, a lunch sack, and a box of chocolate bars slipped out from under her arm and fell on the floor. A bunch of papers came loose.

"Oh, damn it!" she said, slamming the rest of her books down on the desk and stooping to pick up what had fallen. "Don't ever become valedictorian." She whipped her hair back over one shoulder.

Flora could see red pen marks all over the writing on her papers. "I don't think I'll ever have to worry about that." Janice didn't seem to hear her.

"And Mister Know-It-All is having the roof reshingled. That's all I need, a racket like that while I'm trying to write this thing." She slapped the desktop with her papers and then let them fall out of her hand. She yanked the chair out from under the desk and dropped into it, clamping her hands over her ears.

Flora sat on the edge of the bed and listened to the muffled sound of hammers tapping, the wheezing of nails as older shingles were pried up, the clapping down of new shingles, the soft crunching as the workers walked around on the roof. It reminded her of Janice eating crackers in bed, turning the pages of a book, and clicking her ballpoint pen in and out.

Janice was still sitting motionless at the desk.

"Do you want me to make you a cup of tea?" asked Flora.

Janice looked around, astonished. Her brow was wrinkled like wide-wale corduroy.

"Or do you want a bottle of aspirin?"

"Get out of here!" snapped Janice.

"No, really, I'll fix you a cup of tea if you want."

Janice looked down at her papers and nibbled at her lip. "All right, thanks," she said, and then she mumbled, "I'd just like to cram it all."

"Why don't you write a speech for Mrs. Baines and the rest of them, and then say whatever you want to say on graduation day?"

"Are you out of your gourd?" Janice looked terrified.

Flora didn't really know. "Hasta luego," she said and left Janice with a perplexed look on her face.

As Flora put the kettle on the stove she tried to imagine herself doing what she had just suggested to Janice, but she couldn't. All she could see was a lot of scribbling with red marks all over it, and a microphone that was too tall, and then too short. It whined loudly when she tried to speak. She was staring out the kitchen window at the new leaves on the fruit trees when the whistle on the kettle blew.

That night when Henry came to the dinner table, he brought a crummy mood along with him. He complained that the workers were doing a sloppy, slipshod job. He was really going to have to straighten them out the next day. Marleen tried to be sympathetic. She figured maybe he had banged his head on one of their ladders, or something like that. Janice figured the workers had walked away while he was still talking to them.

"What have you got to be so happy about?"

Flora looked up and saw that he was addressing her. She had been thinking back to the sight of Matthew working on his painting, lifting the excess red paint off her palette. She hadn't realized that she was looking so pleased. She thought of an answer as quick as she could. "I guess it's because school is nearly over."

"Planning on having a wild summer, are you?"

Flora started to make a response, something vague, such as "Not especially," but didn't say anything when she saw he had returned to stabbing his food.

He looked at Janice, who was stabbing her food, too.

"What's eating you?"

Everyone else stopped eating and waited to see what Janice would say. Janice continued to fork lettuce with a cruel deftness.

"Cat got your tongue? I asked you a question." Henry narrowed his eyes at her.

"Just lay off." Janice narrowed her eyes at him. They looked like two cats on the verge of a scuffle. "Do you think you're the only one who has the right to be in a bad mood around here?"

Janice had not told Henry she was the one who had been given the honor of writing and delivering the graduation speech. That's all she needed: his assistance on top of her senior civics teacher's, her class counselor's, and that "prig of a V.P.," as she had come to call Mrs. Baines during the past week. She got up, and with an air of having been terribly insulted, she left the kitchen. There was still food on her plate. Flora knew Janice couldn't bear to be away from her speech for very long: she hadn't opened her lunch sack today or even touched her cup of tea.

To everyone's amazement, Henry merely focused his attention on his own plate and started eating again, in a more subdued manner.

Flora opened the front door and set out the empty milk bottles. When they stopped jangling in their metal carrier, she could hear the sounds of the neighborhood at dusk: voices floating out of open windows, families talking loudly in their kitchens, dishes being clanked in sinks, laughter coming from TV sets, children squalling, two cats singing in the alley, penned dogs complaining about it, someone emptying a load of glass into an empty trash can. And then there was the otherworldly wail of a siren.

It blurped on somewhere out on the nearest main street. Flora listened to it swerve its way around several corners. She wasn't too surprised to see its blinking red light. Somehow she knew it was going to turn onto Jericho.

The ambulance flashed past her, stopped, and backed up. By this time Marleen, Julia, and Daniel were standing at the door beside her. It swung into their driveway, backed out of it and up into Tom and Beth's driveway. Two men jumped out. In the fading light their white outfits nearly glowed. They carried a stretcher up the porch steps. Tom held his front door open by pressing his back up against it. It looked as though the door was attached to heavy-duty springs and would slam shut if he didn't use all his strength to hold it open. Flora was too far away to see the expression on his face, but she thought maybe she could see the whites of his eyes.

Henry pushed everyone else aside and rushed forward to a sudden stop at the edge of the porch steps.

"I knew it was going to happen, I knew it," he insisted. "Tom told me just the other day, he said, 'She's stopped complaining, clammed up,' and I said, 'Thomas, that's a sign—she's on her way out, she'll be gone before you know it.' " Henry turned around and gave his family a serious nod and a wink.

"But you don't know that she's dead," protested Marleen. She was still drying her already-dry hands on her dishtowel.

"I'll bet on it," said Henry, and he glared back at her.

"Who died?" asked Daniel.

"Nobody, according to your mother," said Henry.

They all stood there waiting for something to happen while the beacon on the top of the ambulance swung around and around, flashing the shrubs and the tree trunks and the houses with shafts of crimson light. As the dusk shifted into night, people had banded together into several groups on both sides of the street, up and down from Tom and Beth's house, and they were getting flashed by the red light, too.

After a long while, the ambulance drivers came out of the house, wheeling the stretcher. They lifted it down the porch steps and rolled it across the dark driveway to the rear of the ambulance. Beth's mother was just a bulge beneath a white sheet. Tom and Beth stepped out of the house and stood motionless on their porch.

"Flora, get over there and tell them you'll take care of the children," commanded Henry.

Flora stepped backward onto the doorsill. There was no sign of the children. She wondered if she was needed. She didn't want to be an intruder.

"Hurry up and get over there. What are you waiting for?" Henry raised his hand as if he might cuff her.

Flora leapt down the steps past him and dashed across the front lawn like a put-out cat.

Tom backed his car out of the driveway and followed the ambulance. Flora went toward Beth, but Beth turned and went into her house, leaving the door ajar. Flora stood at the threshold and knocked on the door frame. She called Beth's name three times, first quaveringly, then with a note of doubt, and then with undeniable urgency. But there was no answer. She held herself perfectly still and listened—no sound from anyone. "Beth," she called again, in a slightly lilting voice, "are you there?" Maybe the children were asleep? She didn't want to wake them. She waited on the porch, wondering what to do. She took one step into their house and peeked into the kitchen. The lights were off. She stepped back out and looked over to her own house. Her father was the only one standing there now, backlit by the living room lamp, with his hands in his pockets, watching her. He'd say she was a failure. She dreaded hearing that. She walked slowly back across the street. When she was halfway up the driveway, he said, "Really made yourself useful, didn't you," and he turned his back on her.

Late that night when all the Jackson children were asleep, Henry was still awake. He insisted that Marleen stay awake too and listen to what he had to say.

Marleen couldn't believe it—he still wanted to go over this thing about Flora and that boy down the street. She wanted to sigh real big and say, Henry, don't you think you're making the whole thing up?

Instead she yawned and said, "Henry, I really don't believe that Flora would still be seeing him. She's too sensible for that. And even if she weren't a sensible girl, how could she still be seeing him? She hasn't even been out of the house, except to go to school." She yawned a huge yawn and shut her eyes, hoping for silence.

"You've got your head stuck in the sand as usual," Henry hissed through his teeth. "Where there's a will there's a way, and I'm telling you, your daughter is a sneak."

Marleen opened her eyes to the dark ceiling, but she refused to respond.

“If you don’t get to the bottom of this, I will,” Henry growled.
He flopped over in his bed, shaking the headboard and rattling all the miniature marble vases. The top-heavy ivory bust of Nefertiti teetered over.

“I refuse to spy on my children,” whispered Marleen, and then she braced herself. Henry rolled back over onto his back and slowly raised himself up on his elbows.

“What did you just say?” he dared her.

“I’ve got more important things to do, like be at work at eight in the morning.” Marleen trembled as she said this.

Henry reared up over her with his hand drawn back, ready to strike her. “Are you saying I don’t take care of my family? Say it. Just say it!” he insisted.

Marleen bit her lip with fright and cowered down in the blankets. Finally she shook her head no, and Henry sank back down into his own bed.

“Just make one more insinuation like that and you’ll wish you’d never opened your mouth.”

Henry had threatened to thrash her many times during their marriage, but he had never once carried out his threat. Even so, Marleen was afraid that someday he might, and then she’d get a beating that would make up for all the years he had held himself back. She couldn’t figure out why he hit the children and not her. All he had ever said when she asked him not to hit them was, “Children have to be knocked into shape.” She saw the welts on the backs of her children’s legs, their swollen faces. She saw Flora getting her head banged against the kitchen wall, Daniel getting whacked in the back with a rake handle. Marleen felt like one of those little fish that hide, unharmed, among the tentacles of a sea anemone, watching other creatures get stung and devoured. She curled over on her side, with her back to Henry.

Please be a good girl, Flora, please, she prayed silently.

When Henry was sure everyone was asleep, he snuck out of bed and went to Janice and Flora’s door. He listened there for a moment. Then he carefully turned the knob and looked in. Janice was lying on her back in the center of the bed. Flora was curled up facing the wall. He carefully reclosed the door and went back to bed. His heart was pounding hard; his stomach burned with a searing pain. He lay still for a few minutes, and then he remembered his gun. He felt down between the beds and under his mattress.

Timpanelli couldn't knock herself out of the low mood she'd been in for days. She sat at her desk and plucked wool balls off the sleeve of her cardigan. Someone had stuck flowers in her vase again, but that wasn't the source of her foul mood.

"You teach for nearly thirteen years in a place, a room," she muttered to herself. "You see a bunch of seventh-grade squirts come in here scribbling, scrubbing with their brushes, scared or complaining. And you see a handful of seniors walking out of here with brushes stuck behind their ears, ready to paint the world." She continued to pluck fuzzballs off her sleeve. "And then some big-shots, some crumbums from downtown and over there"—she wagged her thumb over her shoulder toward the administration buildings—"want to bulldoze it all down."

Matthew, Flora, and several other students came into the room. They saw Timpanelli sitting there doing nothing but flicking bits of lint off her desk. Matthew and Flora came over and asked her how she was. They took their wet paintings down off the wall behind her.

"Swell," she said, sounding hollow. "Keep up the good work," she added without looking at them. What did they need her encouragement for, anyway?

Those two, she mused, as they set to work at their easels, carry on like they've found the perfect niche and nothing's ever going to change. She watched Flora place her hand lightly on Matthew's hip and whisper something to him, and Matthew lean over and whisper something back to her. He poured turpentine into their palette cups as if he were making an offering of cognac. What will they do when this place is nothing but a pile of rubble? She lifted the wilting flowers out of her vase, and took a sip, made a sour face, and stuck the flowers back in it.

As she walked through the halls in the morning she couldn't help noticing an increase in smashed-in wallboards and broken windows. The hall floors were lined with rubbish: bits of plaster and broken glass, and lots of chocolate bar wrappers mixed in with the usual litter. The custodians couldn't keep up with it. Most of the students, as far as she could tell, were eager for the sight of wreckage.

In the last couple of weeks she let the rowdiness of the class rise a notch. She wasn't going to struggle too much against the general mood of gleeful abandon. She did put an immediate stop to several paint fights, boys flicking wet brushes at each other in the washroom. It was an imbecilic waste of precious paint and an abuse of good brushes, and she had told them so. And she had dared anyone to see what would happen if just one more spitwad were flicked, one more eraser were tossed, at the new model.

And there stood Matthew and Flora, working away as if bedlam hadn't been let loose. She could remember a time when Flora would flinch at anything—a dropped eraser, a rise in her voice. Now, thought Timpanelli, she doesn't even seem to hear me. She's nearly as cool as Matthew. I hope to heaven they get away with whatever it is they think they're getting away with.

Just then she heard the rhythmic jingling of hardware. She took a peek out her window and saw a heavyset custodian lumbering alongside Mrs. Baines. They seemed determined to get somewhere. Mrs. Baines was frowning terribly, lurching forward on her too-high high heels. With every step, all the keys and small tools attached to the custodian's utility belt announced their progress. He was as round in his belly as Mrs. Baines was in her bosom. The two of them could fit together perfectly, like interlocking pieces of a jigsaw puzzle, thought Timpanelli with only a glimmer of amusement. She turned back to her desk and started leafing through the issue of *American Artist* that had been left in her mailbox that morning. She glanced at her vase. The poppies were hanging down, limp. Some blue spires looked all right, but something else looked like wads of pink chewing gum. "Doesn't someone know you're not supposed to pick wildflowers?" she grumbled.

PART FOUR

Turpentine Fumes

Apricot Silk

Flora flung her bedsheets off. It was hot. The sun was shining in through the window, hitting her on the head and heating up the sheets. It must be late. She could hear the rest of the family in the kitchen, the almost musical clinking of silverware. A dish clanked in the sink, and the faucet jerked on. The plumbing throughout the house rumbled. She wondered why no one had awakened her. She searched back, and all she could remember was painting: the sight of her canvas, brushstroke following brushstroke, wet glistening colors blending together. She had gone to sleep with that, and nothing more. She had done nothing to send Henry into a rage these past few days. If he was mad now, it was probably because Janice had refused to share her graduation speech with him, or because the roofers were "lamebrains." They were supposed to be here again today, to finish up the job, but there were no sounds on the roof. Just someone washing dishes in the kitchen.

The sheets felt warm and soft, worn smooth from the tossing and turning of sleep, and laundered down to the softness of baby skin. They might have been the same sheets she slept on when she was just a grammar school girl, a young girl teasing and being teased by the boys, bringing home nothing but good reports. Now she was alone. She didn't share anything with anyone at home anymore. She just came here sometimes. It was as if she had dropped in sometime during the night. Just a motel guest that mustn't be disturbed. In between staying and leaving. A part of nothing. Her heart throbbed in her throat with a panicky feeling. What if, when she left this house for the last time to join Matthew, he wouldn't be there? She'd open the door and be sucked into the breathless and weightless expanse of nothing.

Henry said, "Not there. There!"

Flora rolled onto her stomach and pulled the curtains aside. Henry was holding onto the handle of the push mower. Daniel was crouching over the blades with an oil can in his hands. Flora whipped the curtains back together, but it was too late. Henry had already seen her, and in a flash, the look on his face had gone from surprise to scorn. He made her feel as though she had been trying to spy on him. She swayed back and forth on the edge of the bed with her hands on her cheeks and her bare feet planted on the cool hemp squares. She wished Matthew were holding her. She did not regret, not in the least, all the time they had given to their paintings. And yet she wished they had taken a little more time to be alone together. He felt so ungraspable now. His father was getting married today, and she couldn't go to the wedding. She had to pretend it wasn't happening. She planned to be nowhere in sight when the reception guests arrived at Matthew's house. She would have nothing to say if Henry asked her about it.

She went into the kitchen and ate some leftover scrambled eggs out of the skillet.

"You slept long enough, didn't you," said Janice as she removed the vacuum cleaner from the closet.

"Where's Mom?" asked Flora.

"She's at the laundromat. I'm surprised you didn't get wrapped up in the dirty sheets." Janice went down the hall, tugging the vacuum cleaner after her.

Flora went out to the back yard. Half the lawn was mowed. Daniel stopped to clean dichondra off the mower blades. Julia was holding on to the redwood fence, bouncing up and down in a trash can full of yard clippings. Flora heard the grating sound of a rake against asphalt. She looked over the fence. Henry was in the alley making large piles of leaves and trash, evenly spaced piles all along the back side of the fence. He always said, "The sanitation department doesn't seem to be aware of the fact that we have an alley."

He didn't see her. She went around to the front and looked at the garage door. It looked raw and mottled. Henry still hadn't bought the paint. She looked at the lawn. In the dappled shade healthy patches of flowering spurge and slick runners of crabgrass were taking over the dichondra. He would approve of a weeding job. She got a fork and a cardboard box and sat down at the edge of a lush patch of weeds. Before long she had the sensation that someone was watching her. She looked around. Beth was standing at the curb on the other side of the street, waving her hand over her head, beckoning to her. Flora dropped her forkful of weeds and got up. Beth started walking back up her own driveway. Flora followed her. At the front porch, Beth turned around and stood still.

"I want to apologize for the other night," she said. "I really appreciated the way you came over here. I . . ." Beth took a big breath and looked back at her front door. "I just couldn't talk then." She was silent for a moment.

"I understand," said Flora. She didn't know whether to join Beth on her steps or remain standing in the driveway. She stared down at the shining mica in the asphalt.

"Things got so out of hand. I sent Russell and Karen to my sister in Altadena for a while." Beth sank down on her porch steps.

"Maybe I could've taken care of them at my house." Flora had a hard time imagining anybody's mother dying. *Mommy.* She tried the word out in her head. Her own mother was close by, at the laundromat operated by the man with the bubble-gum face. Beth was staring down at the driveway too. Flora realized the ridiculousness of her offer. "Well, after school, anyway."

Beth laughed a little. "I don't think your father would've appreciated that."

Flora looked up, startled by the certainty in Beth's voice. How did Beth know about her father? What did Beth know about her father?

"He told Tom last week that he had his hands full with problems of his own."

Flora felt her mouth dropping open. She tried to picture her father saying anything personal, however vague, to any of their neighbors.

"Flora, I just want to tell you, and I hope you don't feel we are intruding, but Tom saw your father knock you down in your garage not too long ago, and we just want you to know that if you need any help, well . . . Tom knows a lawyer that deals with abuse cases. So if you need any help, just let us know." Beth nodded sympathetically to her.

Flora felt like she was being stretched inside out. Her thoughts came to a standstill; there was no space in her head for the words she was hearing. *Abuse* . . . a name for something between her and her father? She snapped back to her normal shape. "That was ages ago," she said. "Thank you, but everything is all right now." She glanced over to her house, but couldn't see any activity there, not even a disturbed curtain. "Everything's all right. Thanks anyway," repeated Flora.

Beth was peering at her.

Flora didn't know what else to say, but she wanted to say something nice for Beth's sake. "I hope everything is all right with you, too?"

Beth sighed and stood up. She crossed her arms at her waist. "We had to do a lot of waiting. I mean, she really wasn't enjoying being alive. It's better that she passed away." She took a swipe with her fingers under her eyes, and then brushed her hair away from her forehead. "I really do mean it," she said. "If you decide you need any help, don't be afraid to ask us." Beth's eyes were sparkling with tears. She turned toward her door.

"Thank you, I won't forget," said Flora. She walked briskly across the street and got back to her job of weeding.

Flora went into her house at the first sign of wedding guests arriving at the Cartiers'. Soon cars were parked all up and down the curb, on both sides of the street.

Mr. Zelenovich had pulled his own car out of his garage and parked it at the curb, and was standing guard over his wife's row of camellias, the one that bordered the Cartiers' lawn.

Other neighbors stopped tending their yards to watch gay clusters of people emerge from the cars and turn up the walk to the Cartiers' house. Mr. Cartier and Stella got out of a white Cadillac. Mr. Cartier caught Stella at the waist and twirled her around so that her pale blue gown furled out, making transparent blue shadows on the sidewalk and sending plum petals scurrying before them. Matthew stood on the porch, one hand in the pocket of his midnight-blue tuxedo, the other hand extended to welcome guests. Stella said, "You won't be wearing that for long." As she floated past him, she gave the sky-blue bachelor button in his lapel a little flick with the tip of her finger.

Flora had shut herself up in her bedroom. Janice was in there too, studying for her exams. Every so often she switched to her speech notes. She sucked on a strand of hair and nibbled at her nails. Flora tried to study, too. When her mind wandered, she took up a fresh sheet of paper and tried to write farewell letters to her family. Most of her attempts she scribbled over darkly with a pen and tossed in the wastebasket beside the bed. Several sheets she hid among the pages of her textbooks. Once Janice left the room. She came back shortly with a crazy gleam in her eyes. "Looks like Matthew's getting married without you." Flora could feel her face wadding itself up into a puckery mess. It was as if she actually believed what her sister had said. "Oh, come on, Flora, I'm just fooling." Janice giggled. "But there are a bunch of people going into his house. Looks like a big party." She slid into the desk chair, wagging her head and humming a little.

"Thanks for telling me," said Flora. Her heart was beating irregularly, as if it had just been whacked.

Henry stood in his driveway and watched more people turning single file up the Cartiers' walk. A guitarist, two violinists, a bass player, and an accordion player. "A family on this block is in mourning for the death of a family member, and the Cartiers decide to have a bash." Henry bowed his head as if he had just finished delivering a sermon. He saw the toes of his own shoes and realized he couldn't just be standing there doing nothing. He turned and went into the garage and came out again with the edger. He inspected the tufts of grass that were lapping over onto the sidewalk, kicking them with the side of his shoe.

As he pulled and shoved the edger along, he kept an eye on the proceedings up the street. Nothing much to see. A white Mustang double-parked, and that fag, David Beauchamp, got out and swaggered up the path. A van arrived and some kid rolled a dolly stacked with cardboard boxes up the Cartiers' walk. A little later, a man and a woman came out of the house. The woman was trying to steady the man. They got in the white Cadillac and disappeared below the seats. After five or ten minutes, they drove away.

At dusk, when Henry was raking decaying leaves into piles in the gutter, a police car with its light twirling, but no siren, double-parked behind Beauchamp's white Mustang. Two policemen strode up to the Cartiers' door. The door swung open, emitting sudden music, like a jukebox. The policemen went inside, and the music shut down abruptly. What seemed like an hour later, when it was almost too dark to see, the policemen came back out of the house, empty-handed. Henry could see the lights on all over the Cartiers' rented house, and hear the rise and fall of dance tunes and the unsteady clamor of gaiety. The Cartiers were clearly violating the peace and quiet of the twilight hour. He gathered up his lawn tools and went inside the garage.

By dinnertime, he was in pain, it was plain to see. He sat at the table hunched over. Now and again he gave himself a squeeze at the back of the neck, obviously wanting someone to ask him if he was all right so that he could say that he wasn't. Everyone was afraid to ask, but Marleen felt an obligation to do so.

"No, I'm not," he said. He squeezed the back of his neck again. "I had to stay out until after dark doing yardwork that should have been done by someone else in this house." He shot a pained and bitter look at Flora.

"I'm sorry you have a sore neck," she said, staring straight back into his eyes. She wished he would get up and go to bed, for his own sake.

He looked down. "This dinner tastes like warmed-over death." He made an awful face at his plate. Marleen looked as if she would faint from the shock of hearing him say that, whatever it meant.

Henry got up from the table and stalked out of the kitchen. As he went down the hall, he shouted, "Do you think electricity grows on trees? I'm living with a bunch of lamebrains." They could hear him slapping light switches off. He slammed his bedroom door shut.

It was prom night at Hazelton High. Janice obviously wasn't going or else she would have appeared at the dinner table with curlers in her hair. She'd be in the bedroom by now, flinging stockings around, or she'd be steaming up the bathroom. As she ate, she looked pale and sullen, like someone who has received very bad news and can't talk about it. Marleen pretended she didn't know this was the night of the prom. She and Janice had picked out a pattern and fabric for a prom gown—empire waistline, apricot silk. And then a week later Janice told her not to bother to sew it up. What could she say to her daughter now—"There'll be other dances"? She got up and started washing dishes before her children were finished eating.

"What's for dessert?" asked Julia.

"Isn't Disneyland on, or something?" said Marleen.

Blue Cake

Henry sat down to the Sunday meal and served himself a hill of mashed potatoes, a third of a serving bowl of string beans, and two pieces of fried chicken, and started eating as the others were taking their places at the table.

Julia was eager for everyone to finish eating so she could clear away the used dishes. "Don't rush me," Henry said twice, but finally he let her take his plate away. She placed the little dessert plates in front of everyone. Marleen looked giddy sitting there as Julia scurried about.

Flora knew that the inevitable was about to happen. She had wished that just this one time her mother had felt too tired to bake, either from scratch or from a mix, the traditional angel food cake. Given her detachment from the family this past year, she didn't deserve this kind of attention. The ritual would be embarrassing. She braced herself as Julia turned toward her with a white frosted cake ablaze with candles. She wished she could banish herself from the table as they all broke into "Happy Birthday." Even Henry, looking at his plate, sang in a contained baritone.

"All seventeen candles," demanded Julia, with impish glee.

Flora gazed up at the white enamel ceiling and performed the only part of the ceremony that could be regarded by her conscience as being unhypocritical. I wish, she thought, after a moment's consideration, for no one to be hurt by what I plan to do. Then she extinguished all seventeen flames with one gusty breath. Henry made a big show of leaning to one side to avoid the draft. Everyone else cheered.

Flora busied herself with the cutting of the cake. The inside was tinted with blue food coloring. That was a first.

"My Blue Angel," announced Marleen, as Flora looked up with surprise. Flora handed a slice to Marleen.

"Really, Mom, you shouldn't have."

"Maybe one of these years she'll wise up and bake you a devil's food cake," said Henry as he accepted his piece.

"I think it's so beautiful," said Julia.

"So do I," said Flora. "I just didn't want you to go to all the trouble."

"It's really no trouble," said Marleen, trying to put Henry's comment out of her mind. "I made it from a box mix."

"Well, it tastes very good," said Flora. She didn't feel like eating cake of any kind.

"Can I get them now?" pleaded Julia, leaning against Marleen.

"Yes, you may," said Marleen, and Julia disappeared for a few minutes. She reappeared with a stack of gifts, which she balanced carefully against her chest.

"You won't believe what we got you," she said, beaming like a cherub, delighted by the act of making an offering. She squeezed past Henry and deposited the gifts on the table before Flora.

"All these for me?" Flora stuck to the standard lines, hoping the ceremony would move along smoothly and be over soon.

"We didn't get them for ourselves," said Daniel, and he gave her a blank look. That wasn't a standard line. Flora couldn't decide whether he was depressed, or developing a sarcastic style of humor, or both. He didn't nudge her in the arm as he sometimes did when they were supposed to be sharing a joke. She opened the small package on the top of the stack. The tag said, "From Daniel and Julia, Your Loving Brother and Sister," in Julia's round and curly script.

"Orange Blossom perfume," sighed Flora. She pictured Julia and Daniel counting out and combining their allowance money. "Thank you," she said. She was going to cry. She carefully removed the plastic blooms that were wound around the cap, and unscrewed the cap and held the bottle under her nose: grammar school field trips to the San Fernando Mission, fond memories of the neighborhood five-and-dime, the store that had everything a child could want, and sometimes afford. "Mmmm." She dabbed a little behind each ear and offered some to Marleen and Janice.

Marleen rubbed some on her wrist, and whiffed it. "Oooh, nice," she said.

Janice said, "No, thank you."

Julia eagerly accepted, and leaned way across the table, dragging her blouse through the frosting. Flora gave her a dab behind both ears, and another one for her wrist.

Henry sank back in his chair.

"Can I borrow it from you sometime?" asked Julia. "I just love it." She rubbed her wrists together vigorously.

"Sure," said Flora.

Then she opened a small soft package from Janice. It was a satin brocade coin purse, a Chinese import with a cerulean blue bird of some kind, a crane or a heron, unfurling on a wine-red background. "It's beautiful," she said, pressing the purse gently in her hands, as if it were a wounded sparrow. "Thanks, Janice." She could already imagine stuffing it with her savings. Privately this birthday celebration was turning into a farewell party.

She looked down and saw a white envelope. Inside was a flowery birthday card: a glossy photograph of a bouquet in a vase. She opened the card and her eyes skipped to the signature. "From Henry," it read in Henry's careful, jagged style. Then she glanced at the words printed on the card.

"Thanks, Dad," she said, trying to keep her voice from wobbling. He blushed and rested one elbow on the table and leaned his back against the wall in a pose of indifference.

Flora quickly unwrapped Marleen's gift. Marleen usually gave her art supplies of some kind, and an apology for the kind of gift and its quality. Flora opened up a neat wooden box containing a small set of oil paints. She regarded the array of colors through a prismatic mist. There was another box from Marleen, too: a set of twenty-four Very Fine colored pencils. Her face started puckering up, and so she bowed her head and took a closer look.

"Thank you, Mom," she said, in a tight little voice.

"I didn't know what you were using now. Janice said she thought you were using oil paints, but she wasn't sure." Marleen looked to Janice for help, but Janice looked either bored or tired. Her hands were supporting her head and stretching her face out of shape.

"Anyway," offered Marleen, "maybe you can use the paints next year."

Henry rolled his eyes to the ceiling.

"I'm sure I'll use them all," insisted Flora, looking up gaily and drying her eyes with her napkin.

"How many art classes you get to take next year depends on how well you do in summer school." Henry gave her a wink and pushed himself away from the table.

Flora didn't make a response. She knew he was excusing himself for his favorite wildlife program. He went into the living room and turned on the TV set.

"I've got to get back to my studies," said Janice, heaving a breath. She got up, too.

"Of course," said Flora. "Thank you for all the gifts. This has been a wonderful birthday for me." She hugged Daniel, the person nearest to her, and gave him a kiss on the cheek.

"Don't stand next to a fan with that stuff on," he warned, leaning away from her.

"Thanks for the advice." Flora laughed. She got up and gave Julia a hug and kiss, too.

"How about me?" Julia smiled over at Daniel.

"The more *you* put on, the better." He cowered with pretended fright as Julia raised her fist at him.

"You creep!" she cried.

"Thank you, Mom, for the oil paints and the pencils." Flora put her hand on Marleen's shoulder and gave her a kiss on the cheek. "They're just what I needed."

Marleen smiled. She looked pleased but doubtful.

"And thanks for the blue cake, too. I really am happy, you know."

"I hope so." Marleen drew away from Flora a little and looked at her with her wavering eyes that reminded Flora of riverstones rippling beneath water. Maybe her mother couldn't see clearly at close range anymore?

"I really am," she repeated. She started gathering dessert dishes from the table. "I'll clean up," she added. That would be going against protocol: in the Jackson household a person having a birthday wasn't supposed to lift a finger.

"Oh no you don't," protested Marleen when she realized what was happening.

"Really, Mom, it's all right. I want to," insisted Flora.

Daniel left the kitchen, and Marleen and Flora started cleaning up. Julia stayed at the table and inspected the gifts Flora had received. She rearranged all the oil paint tubes and the colored pencils. Then she took the cap off the perfume and took a long whiff. With her tongue protruding, she concentrated on screwing the cap back on. She found the little plastic blossoms among the wrapping paper and held them over her ear. She tipped her head and batted her eyes at her reflection in the kitchen window.

Marleen made billows of suds in the sink and then cranked the window open wider, until Julia could no longer see herself from where she sat. "It's such a beautiful night." Marleen leaned over the sink to get closer to the night air. She inhaled deeply. "I can smell the flowers." She handed Flora a steaming clean dish to dry.

"Maybe it's my new perfume," said Flora. She flounced her hair like a glamour girl, hoping to amuse her mother. She had no intention of reminding her that no one had planted any fragrant flowers, or tended any—no roses or carnations or amaryllis—around the house for ten years or more. And Henry's fruit trees had already dropped their blossoms. But then, maybe her mother was smelling something that was blooming somewhere beyond their own back yard? Unlikely, concluded Flora, especially with all the orange blossom perfume at such close range.

"There are so many stars out." Marleen had missed Flora's gesture. "And look, there's the moon." Flora looked and saw a lopsided wedge of it in the top branches of the apricot trees. Marleen thought that the sight of the moon, regardless of what phase it was in, was a good omen on her children's birthdays.

"Yes," said Flora, feigning enthusiasm, "there it is."

"Oh, Flora." Marleen dried her hands on the dish towel Flora was holding. "I really do hope this will be a lucky year for you."

"I hope this will be a lucky year for all of us," said Flora.

"Oh," said Marleen suddenly, "we almost forgot to read your forecast." She got the newspaper from the top of the stack on the washing machine and shuffled through it until she found the right section. "Here it is, June tenth. Let's see, Geminis: Stop your dreaming! This month you can really make things happen for yourself. Be careful what you say and all will go smoothly."

"That could apply to anyone," said Flora. "I could find out just as much by reading the comics."

"Be careful what you say," chided Marleen with a clownish smile.

Flora sat her stack of gifts down on the vanity and picked up Henry's card. A slip of paper fluttered to the floor and she bent over and picked it up. It was a fresh twenty-dollar bill. How had she missed seeing it before? She looked over at Janice, who was in a typical posture, bent over her books, oblivious to anything else happening in the room.

Flora unfolded the four quarters of the card and found something written on one of the inside squares: "I didn't know what to get you for your birthday. So here is a little something you might use to buy yourself something with." And wedged in the corner: "With Love, Your Dad."

She folded the card back up. She was almost angry at him for doing that. What was he trying to prove? He hadn't given her any gifts, not even of money, for many years. The last thing he had given her was a quartz-crystal necklace. He presented it to her personally just before her junior high school graduation ceremony. She didn't have much occasion to wear it, but she liked to lay it on the white windowsill when the sun was shining there, and watch the spikes of color lengthen and contract as she slowly rolled the string of quartz from side to side. He usually let Marleen do the buying, wrapping, and presenting of gifts. She wrote all his personal correspondence, even the monthly letter to his own mother. And she signed his name before her own at the bottom of every card or letter, making no attempt to forge his signature.

Now this. Flora unfolded the card again. She reread the two sentences several times. She turned it over and read the Hallmark message, hoping to find a hidden meaning in it, but it was so vague it could have passed for a sample of calligraphy and nothing more: "Wishing You a Happy Birthday, And the Best in the Coming Year." It looked like windblown grass on cream-colored sand. And then, "From Henry," way down at the bottom. The *H* and the *r* had been retraced several times so that they were much bolder than the rest of the letters. On the whole, it looked as if he had been trying to write on a jet plane during turbulence. But Flora knew better; his writing on survey maps, which he so often left spread out on the dining room table, looked the same way—séracs of ink, hooked staffs, and harpoons at the heads of words, and long straight tails that faded off at the ends. And she had watched him in the labor of signing report cards and checks: pinching the pen too tightly in his left hand, lurching forward, halting in the middle of a stroke, and then jerking forward again. He drove the same way, with the entire family rocking back and forth in unison, wondering what he was going to do next, glancing at each other and not daring to say a word.

She folded the card up again and looked at the front: a bright cluster of flowers—chrysanthemums, roses, and violets. No black-eyed Susans, or thistles, or cactus blossoms. No cracks in the vase. She folded up the twenty-dollar bill and put it in the satin coin purse Janice had given her. She put the purse in the bottom of her jewelry box, along with Matthew's ring. She avoided looking at herself in the mirror. She knew she'd only see an ashamed and confused girl.

Janice looked over to her. She had heard the annoying jangle of rhinestone bracelets, pot-metal necklaces, junk left over from childhood.

"Don't you have anything better to do? Don't you have any tests to study for?"

"Yes," said Flora. She sat the bottle of orange blossom perfume in among the other little bottles on the vanity. She smiled when she saw that Julia had wrapped the plastic flowers back around the cap. "As a matter of fact, I do." She got up and put her new art supplies in her drawer. Then she picked up her textbooks from the dresser and tossed them on the bed.

Blue-Bellied Lizards

Miss Corbie walked slowly up and down the aisles, slapping exam papers face down on each desktop. She looked like an exhausted waitress in an all-night diner distributing menus. She had probably been up way after midnight trying to compose a just and thorough exam. Too tired to set her hair, she had let it hang limp like black yarn about her face. Her glasses were slightly askew, and she left them that way. Miss Corbie laid down exam papers in advance for those students she knew would be tardy, even on this day.

Flora felt sorrow mixed with pride for this woman walking alone up and down the aisles, who had all year long kept struggling to teach, with not much, if any, encouragement, and no thanks. It didn't seem as though anybody but Miss Corbie cared about American history. Flora was glad she had stayed awake last night long enough to read several chapters, skim a few more; she wanted to do well for her own and Miss Corbie's sake.

"All right, now you may turn your exam papers over. Don't forget to put your John Hancock in the upper right-hand corner."

Flora wondered what Miss Corbie would do over the summer: teach summer school, take a Greyhound Bus to Sacramento, or Washington, D.C., or Philadelphia? She tried to picture Miss Corbie with a traveling companion.

Mr. Langtry wanted each one of his pupils to select and recite a short passage from Shakespeare, something they had especially liked from one of the plays or sonnets they had read during the semester. He thought this would be something that would be enjoyable for everyone. Most of the class moaned and complained.

Mr. Langtry held on to his podium and looked back to the blackboard for help. He hadn't written anything there.

"Well, yes," he said, turning back to his class and pretending he hadn't heard the ill response. "Is there anyone who is eager to deliver his favorite lines?" He scanned the room with his wide, tired eyes. No one made an offer. "Well then," said Mr. Langtry, bowing his head, "let's take five minutes for reflection. Then we'll begin by hearing from you, Mr. Everhart." He nodded to the boy seated in the front row in the aisle farthest to the left.

Flora thumbed through her textbook. She gazed above the blackboard at the framed etching of Shakespeare, then to another one of King Lear wandering in the wilderness, lightning striking all around him. She turned through the pages of *Lear.* She was sitting on the opposite side of the room and had nearly an hour to make a choice. *King Lear* looked so confusing. Every passage she skimmed from *Othello* sounded vicious, or desperate, or sly. She didn't know the number of the sonnet she had liked the best, so she turned to *Romeo and Juliet.*

"No, 'tis not so deep as a well . . ." The first student had begun to recite.

All but one of the next six students chose the same play. The one oddball refused to read anything at all. Flora glanced again at *Othello* but ended up turning back to a place she had marked with her finger. When her turn rolled around, she stood up beside her desk. "Farewell! God knows when we shall meet again. I have a faint cold fear thrills through my veins." She could hear herself. The words were coming out too fast. "My dismal scene I needs must act alone." She tried to stretch that out, make it sound like she meant it. "Come, vial." She felt she should make some sort of gesture.

She paused, uncertain as to whether to go on. Mr. Langtry read the next few lines, leading her, and she echoed a few phrases until she could pick up the pace again by herself. Now she was reading about suffocating in the bad air of a tomb, strangling before Romeo showed up. She swallowed several times and looked around. Most of her classmates were grimacing.

"Continue," said Mr. Langtry, and he waved his hand forward, sweeping the air. She lost her place and jumped several lines. She remembered this part. It was about waking up too soon and seeing rotting bodies and hearing shrieking spirits. It was about going crazy. She stopped reading.

"Go on!" insisted Mr. Langtry. He had a wild look on his face.

"O, if I wake, shall I not be distraught, Environed with all these hideous fears." Now she was considering the possibility of dashing out her brains with a bone. The book shook in her hand. She tried to steady it by pressing her pointer finger down harder beneath the line where she read. "Romeo, I come! This do I drink to thee." Surely that was enough. She sank back down in her seat and stared back at the mass of words she had just read. She hadn't intended to choose such a gruesome passage—all she had really fixed her eyes upon was "Farewell! God knows when we shall meet again."

"Truly a difficult decision for Juliet to make. A very nice reading, Flora. Next, please."

Matthew and Flora went to the storage room that afternoon and found a shiny new padlock on the door and bright new screws in the old latch.

"We've been coming here long enough anyway," said Matthew. He touched the new screw heads lightly with his fingertips.

"Let's get out of here," whispered Flora as she looked both ways. Matthew clasped her hand and they walked briskly out of the hall.

Flora's heart thumped twice for every step they took. She kept glancing around. The distance they put between themselves and the storage room didn't calm her. The rows of rouge-colored buildings, with their frequent windows, looked bright and content, not capable of harboring any harmful forces, yet Flora felt she and Matthew would be ambushed at any moment. Matthew turned to her outside Timpanelli's room and saw her pale face.

"You look like you've seen a ghost." He ran his fingertips in circles on her cheeks in an effort to bring the color back. Flora couldn't smile.

"I just wonder if anyone knows it was us?"

"So, you want to be famous?" Matthew made a wry smile.

"Matthew," she said, twisting her head away, "I don't want to be famous at all. I just want everything to go smoothly. I mean, I don't want us to get caught."

"I know," said Matthew, gripping her by the wrist, "don't worry. I can assure you, my mother didn't embroider my name on the sleeping bag. My father didn't either. We're as good as free, so don't worry."

Flora fastened her eyes on his face and concentrated on his words. "All right," she said, taking a deep breath, "I feel all right now." She turned to go into Timpanelli's room. Somehow, it looked safer in there.

Matthew tugged at her. "Wait, I have something for you, something to help everything go smoothly." He put his free hand in his jacket pocket and pulled out a long thin paper sack.

Flora stopped pulling away from him. She opened the sack and unrolled some tissue paper. Inside there were four thin, round sable brushes. "Oh, Matthew, thank you." She twirled one of them slowly between her fingers and regarded the point. "They're so fine." She gave him a puzzled look. "How did you know it was my birthday?"

Matthew wadded up the wrapping paper. "I didn't know it was your birthday." He stared at the brushes in Flora's hands. "I just wanted you to have a little going-away present, something you could use right away. The brushes around here aren't too good."

Flora put her arms around his neck and kissed him. "Thank you, Matthew."

"Happy Birthday anyway," he said.

Flora used one of the brushes that day. She worked on the profile of Matthew's face: thread-fine lines of light against a dark background. She held her breath every time she thought of how they hadn't been caught and could have been.

Timpanelli sat with her fists on her cheeks and her elbows on her open roll book and regarded the newest model. The girl in the black bikini had finally stepped down in disgust, saying, "This is humanly impossible." In her place, looking as if he thought he was the guy every girl dreamed about, stood last year's all-star front crawler. A few pounds of extra weight had made him lag behind this year, so he was quick to volunteer when Timpanelli sent someone to the pool for another model. Now he was enjoying the attention he was getting, even the kissing sounds The Cat was making at him.

Timpanelli liked his nonchalance. She had the feeling he was calming the choppy waves in the room, soaking up the end-of-school agitation. She went over to the supply cabinets and pulled out a long length of sheer curtain material.

"Sit down," she said, pointing to the chair that was on the table with him. He sat down. "Put this over your shoulder." She tossed him the curtain. He flung it over his shoulder so that he looked like a slave hauling a load by a rope.

"Not quite like that," said Timpanelli, bunching up her face. She pulled up another chair and used it to step up onto the table. "More like this." She took both his hands and placed them on his knees.

He didn't resist or object. She carefully draped the curtain across his chest and around his hips so that his swim trunks were hidden. She went back to her desk and regarded his neatly delineated pectoral muscles, his partially exposed chest. She thought he looked like a young Neptune. She wished she had a trident for him to hold.

Flora knew him. He was one of Phil's friends, one of his surfing companions. She had watched them enough times bucking the riptide, knee-paddling out, riding in. She had sat at the lunch table when he was there, too. But now, when their eyes crossed paths, he acted as if he didn't recognize her. If he meant to look aloof, he was doing a good job. His one bare shoulder looked chiseled and cold. She was glad she wasn't trying to draw him.

After Spanish class, Matthew mounted the chain-link fence with one leap, swung over the top and jumped to the ground beyond. From the steps of the classroom, Flora watched him stride over the soft brown earth and bound over the tire ruts. He looked around and waved to her. She thought he might have been grinning. He went behind a dump truck filled with dirt and then reappeared, stepping gingerly along the sheer edge of an excavation, tipping pebbles in here and there with the toe of his shoe. Taking a chance.

Flora opened her locker and found a white envelope lying on top of the pile of books.

"Oh-oh," she said, "I don't think I need this." Her heart started fluttering like a butterfly in a jar.

She picked up the envelope and turned it over. "Flora" was written in a tiny script with a ballpoint pen that had moved through spells of droughts and clogs. Following her name, in the same gunky blue ink, someone had drawn a mouse with a long crooked tail. She took a closer look: no, it was a rosebud with a thorny stem.

This was not Matthew's work, she was sure, nor Henry's, and it certainly wasn't anything official. She opened the envelope. Maybe Tess had left her a message? No, Tess had an elegant scrawl.

Dear Flora,

I think of you as a rosebud that I tried to pry open again and again. I thought that you had pricked me with your sharp thorns, but then I looked at my hands, and finally realized that I had wounded myself by my abruptness, my eagerness to be with you.

 Flora selected her books and closed her locker. She continued to read the letter as she walked down the hall.

> I am glad you held me off, Flora, for now I can say to myself that I really didn't hurt you.

She glanced out a hall window and saw only some stragglers like herself.

> I am stronger now for what I have learned. I know now that it was not right to try and unfold your perfect petals before you were ready. It was an insult to you.

Flora couldn't believe the words she was reading. Who is this? She skipped to the end:

> I love you,
> Phil

"Oh, no." She frowned and cast a glance out another window. Is this what he has been thinking ever since the last time we went out together—that night at that party when I didn't want to touch or be touched by him? Refused to kiss him, even.

> You don't ever have to be afraid of me. I will never again try to force you to do anything. I would only like to invite you to come to a graduation party on Friday night. I could pick you up at eight o'clock, if you like.
>
> Please leave your answer in my locker, #1581, Long Hall. But if you don't feel like answering, I will understand.
>
> I love you,
> Phil

Flora folded the letter and put it in her notebook. She wished she could just wad it up and throw it away: pretend he had never written it. But she had to answer him.

All the way home from school she thought about him: the shy new guy standing by the cafeteria wall, looking at the asphalt as if it were interesting. His fluorescent hair in the lavender light of the movie screen. The way he paddled frantically to catch a head-high wave. She watched him walking up a beach, coming toward her with his hip jutting out, balancing his board there on a tanned bone. He was beaming and chattering from the cold, in a pose, a sexy confident one, that surfers tried to perfect. Only a goon would carry a surfboard, like a jug, on his head. I can't waste time on thoughts like this, thought Flora as she passed the corner store. She pictured Phil zipping around in his sports car, with her in it, and without her. She usually didn't know where they were going: to a movie, a party somewhere, a hilltop. She saw the headlights go out and the lights of the valley below. Phil was always persistent. Persistent but gentle, and kind. Always kind. His letter was persistent, and kind too. It showed a desire to be cooperative and understanding. But it's a crazy letter, thought Flora. He doesn't understand me at all.

She tried to walk without stepping on the cracks, an annoying game she could never resist once the thought of it occurred. I'm anything but a rosebud. I'm more like a succulent of some kind. Break me apart and stick me in the ground in lots of different places and I'd manage to take root. She walked by a border of cactus, singular-looking creatures set in a bed of gravel, covered with spiteful thorns. I'm not like *that;* I just didn't want him to touch me. She felt him clutching her neck, her waist, reaching beneath her dress. She wanted to break free.

She crossed the street and walked faster in response to the anxiety she was feeling. Phil had sometimes stopped there beneath those glossy, cherryless cherry trees at night. And she had always said no, she didn't think they should. Once he had taken off his sweater. He draped it on the rearview mirror to shield them from the lights of approaching cars. She had told him that she'd rather not. He had groaned. Then he had popped his clutch, and they jerked forward and on around the corner of Jericho. That was the only time he had ever seemed angry.

She turned the corner and remembered the new lock on the storage room door. She stopped in midstep, altered her pace so that she would step on every crack the rest of the way home. She didn't dare glance at Matthew's house.

From the service porch she saw Henry sitting at the dining room table. He had a ruler in one hand and a pen in the other. Two marble candlesticks from Rome were holding down the corners of a survey map. "Hi, Dad," she said from the doorway. He looked over and nodded to her in an official way. If he can't be bothered, that's a good sign, she thought, and walked on down the hall. She sat very quietly on the bed, waiting for any afterthought he might have. But nothing happened.

Later he came to the dinner table in a dither over the boundaries of some land somewhere. He talked on and on about some project he had the upper hand in, and minced his pork chops and beets with the competence of a dedicated surgeon. He apparently hadn't received any news from school. Matthew must be right—no one could link them to the storage room.

Henry sensed Flora's eyes upon him. "You might as well apply for summer school, because if I don't like the looks of your grades, that's exactly where you're going." He waited for her to respond.

Flora nodded.

"She does enough studying," said Janice. "Why don't you lay off her?"

Henry held his breath until his face looked hard, like concrete. Finally his mouth moved.

"That's the last time I'd better hear anything like that out of you, Professor Jackson. I'll cut your college tuition off." He reached for the wall switch and blinked the overhead light off and on again. "Just like that."

Julia and Daniel looked alarmed. Marleen was annoyed. She couldn't resist saying it: "I think you ought to know, Janice is valedictorian."

Henry calmed down in an instant. His head bobbed slightly and his gaze settled on Daniel.

Daniel, bewildered, looked over to Janice, who was pursing her lips and giving Marleen an accusing glare.

"Well, I figured as much," said Henry. He looked away from his son and back to Janice. "Will you be giving the graduation speech?"

"Yes," admitted Janice, dolefully, and then added, "but I'm not supposed to have any assistance."

Henry straightened his napkin, and looked at his plate. The beet juice and the grease from the pork chops had formed a puddle of magenta globules.

"Oh . . . I see," he said.

After dinner Flora sat on the bed with her back against the wall. With her notebook open on her lap and books at her sides, she looked as if she were studying. Actually she had intended to study, but when she opened her notebook, there was Phil's letter. The rosebud looked like a little paw, held up, asking for a word with her, a word from her. All those idle hours they had spent sitting in his car, on the beach, at the lunch bench, and almost nothing had been said between them. Now she needed to say it all in one letter. She wrote in her notebook:

Dear Phil,

I think you ought to know, I am in love with someone else. I love him more than anyone else on earth.

No, he doesn't want to hear that. She scribbled over those words and began again.

Dear Phil,

Please don't blame yourself for anything that happened or didn't happen between us. Believe me, I'm no rosebud! I'm not an orchid, or a Venus's-flytrap either. If anything, I'm more like a straggly weed in someone's well-kept lawn, soon to be eradicated.

I believe that when you do find a rosebud, you will treat her very well, and you'll be thankful that I didn't stay around and get in your way. I'll be leaving California on Friday.

I hated the way we acted like we were ghosts when we passed each other in the halls. I wish we could've just been good friends, and go on being friends for many years to come.

I'd like to be able to go to the graduation party with you, but I've got to be going. It's hard to have everything go the way we want it to.

He probably doesn't need to hear any of this either.

The bedroom door swung open slowly and Henry leaned his hip against the door frame. Flora turned to a page filled with chemistry notes. Henry glanced at her and then he looked at Janice.

"So, you don't feel like you have to tell your ol' dad about what's going on." He waited for an answer, but Janice didn't say anything. She didn't even turn around. Flora tried to look busy.

"I'm talking to you," he said, raising his voice.

Janice looked over her shoulder.

"Oh," she said, "I thought you were talking to Flora."

Flora picked up her chemistry book, turned a few pages, and pretended to be reading.

"How's the speech coming?" demanded Henry.

"I told you before, I'm not supposed to have any assistance."

"As your father, I think I have the right to see it." Henry took his weight off the door frame and stood firmly on both feet.

Janice swung completely around in her chair.

"If I give it to you to read now I won't be able to work on it, and I might not get it done in time." She used her most reasonable tone and gestured to him with her palms up, beseechingly. Henry narrowed his eyes at her. He didn't like being outreasoned.

"Okay," he said slowly. He thought for a moment and then

 raised one brow at her. "But when you have to stand up in front of those bleachers full of people, just remember, I offered to help." He gave her a solemn nod and pulled the door closed.

Janice waited a moment, and then made a sound like air escaping from a balloon. She turned back to her speech notes.

Flora turned back to her letter to Phil. She read it again and then scribbled it all out. She started over:

Dear Phil,

Most of what I try to say to you is nonsense.

She crossed out several words and wrote, "must sound like nonsense." She crossed those words out, too, and wrote, "will probably sound like nonsense to you."

I'd like you to know that even though, as it turned out, I wasn't in love with you, I am very grateful that we met and spent some time with each other. I have no regrets, and I don't want you to have any either. I enjoyed watching you surf. We saw some good movies together. You never got drunk, like some of the guys, and you always got me home on time. I liked your sense of humor, and your cheerfulness. I'll remember you as being gentle, and caring. I guess I wasn't quite ready for what you had, *have* to offer. Maybe we just weren't made for each other. I'm sure you'll meet a bud on the verge of blooming someday soon, and she will love you . . .

Flora bumped her head back against the wall. "This is just getting worse," she mumbled.

Janice looked around. "Do you need any help?" she asked.

"No, no, thanks anyway." Flora straightened up and began again on a clean page.

Dear Phil,

Thank you for writing to me and inviting me to go to a graduation party with you.

I don't want you to have any regrets about what happened or didn't happen between us. I don't have any myself, except for the way I didn't speak to you when I should have, and the way we became invisible to each other whenever we crossed paths. Other than that, I have only good memories.

I'd like to accept your invitation, from one friend to another, but I have other plans for the evening, which I feel I cannot break.

I wish only the best for you in the future.

Sincerely,

Flora

She thought about drawing a bird-of-paradise flower, or a weed of some sort, after her name, and decided not to. She tore the page slowly out of her notebook, folded it up, and put it back in her notebook.

She felt exhausted and unsatisfied with her effort. The textbooks lying around her were an irritating clutter. She discovered she was half sitting on her algebra book. It had given her a sore hip. She piled all the books on top of her notebook and carried them over to the dresser and set them down.

"Do you want to use the desk?" asked Janice. She looked up, dazed. "I think I'm going to bed."

"Oh, I don't know . . . Yes, I guess I will." Flora waited while Janice gathered up all her papers and books. "How's your speech going?"

"Excruciatingly." Janice let her tongue hang out the side of her mouth.

Flora plopped down in her place. "Well, I'm sure it'll come out great."

"If it comes out at all," said Janice, turning away.

Flora reached for her chemistry book, opened it, and stared at the print. Oh Matthew, where did you come from? Why did I ever have to lay eyes on you? Why did you have to touch me? You make me feel like a lizard that has to feel warmth or die. She thought of lizards, blue-bellied lizards warming themselves on rocks in the desert. She pictured Matthew and herself lying together in warm sand. I love you so much. What are we doing? I can't even study this stupid chemistry book. You're such a heartache, Matthew. I love you, my poison . . . Flora could feel her head slumping down, heavy as a chunk of lead. I can't even stay awake, she told herself.

Janice said, "Good night," and switched off the overhead light. She crawled into bed. Now only the little desk light was on.

"Good night," said Flora, straightening up a little. She eyed the drawings of test tubes in her chemistry book, small vials filled to different levels with different colors of ink. She listened to the squeaking of the mattress as Janice searched for a comfortable position. She closed her chemistry book and let her head rest on her folded arms.

Sometime later Janice called over to her, "Hey, what's wrong with you? Do you want to get curvature of the spine!"

"Oh," said Flora, waking up. "Sorry." She got up and dressed for bed.

As Flora entered the front gate of school, Mr. Langtry zipped past her in his little English sports car. He walked up beside her as she headed up the lane to her history class.

"Good morning, Miss Jackson," he said with a hint of a bow.

Flora said, "Good morning." Then there was silence between them. She felt she should be quoting a line or two from Shakespeare for him, but she couldn't. What if I wake, Won't I be distraught . . . ? These words came to her, but they had nothing to do with greeting Mr. Langtry.

"You have such a flair for Shakespeare, Flora. Are you planning on majoring in English literature at the university?" He peered around at her as they walked along.

Flora gave him a distressed look. A flair for Shakespeare? She imagined herself bursting into flame. She didn't know what to say. She didn't want to say, What university? That would sound impolite. Out of the corner of her eye she saw Matthew walking along another path and coming in her direction. He looked as though he were out for a morning stroll and had just happened to end up on school grounds.

"Well," she replied, "I haven't decided yet. I won't be graduating this year."

Mr. Langtry blushed. "Excuse me," he said. He threw his head back dramatically, pursed his lips, and then lowered his gaze on her. "I mistakenly assumed you were in this year's graduating class."

Flora took a quick glance back, and Matthew gave her an impish smile. Was he following her? "No, I'm not," she confessed, stark-faced. "I'm a junior." She had never called herself that before. It sounded so silly.

"Well then, I hope to have the pleasure of your presence in one of my classes next year. Maybe Twentieth-Century American Literature?" He tipped his head toward her.

"I'm sure I would enjoy it," said Flora. She looked back again, but Matthew had disappeared. Mr. Langtry was looking up at the mature eucalyptus they were walking beneath. He seemed to be regarding them with admiration. Then he gave her a broad smile and extended his hand to her.

To shake, thought Flora. She held out her left hand. He chuckled softly, holding her hand in his right hand and pressing it gently with his left hand.

"So you're sinister-handed, too?" he said, sustaining his smile.

Flora withdrew her hand and blushed.

Mr. Langtry gave her another slight nod of a bow. Then he drifted off in another direction.

The tardy bell rang. Flora was halfway up the steps to her history class when she remembered she had a letter to deliver. She stepped down the stairs backward and hurried toward the Long Hall. As she pulled the letter out of her notebook, it dawned on her that she didn't know the exact number of Phil's locker. One-eight-something. He had given it to her in his letter, but she had destroyed the letter. She didn't need to hear her father calling Phil a fag poet because Phil had called her a rosebud. And she didn't want to hear him ask her what it was that Phil had been trying to pry open. It was one-eight-something, with another *one* at the end. She knew the approximate location of his locker. She kept going in that direction. It faced a window, not a wall. She had stood there once with him, and when she had looked out the window, she could see the student store and the steps to the detention room. She had to deliver the letter now. She didn't want to wait and ask Stan or Tess what Phil's locker number was. They probably wouldn't know anyway. And since she wasn't Phil's rosebud, and never would be, she wasn't going to give him the letter in person. It would be too embarrassing to face him again. One-eight-five-one looked and sounded right, so she dropped the letter through the vent in the locker and raced back to her history class.

The room was empty. A notice was scrawled on the blackboard: "No Class Today. Please Report to Study Hall."

Study hall was a dreary room, no better than detention, connected to the library, a low-lying building in a remote corner of the campus. More like a storage room for books, way beyond the boys' shop classes and the Big Gym. Flora had been there two or three times in five years.

She didn't bother to go there now. She wasn't in the mood to read desk graffiti or cram for a chemistry final. She felt she needed to keep moving, so she walked the halls. With Timpanelli's pass in her pocket, she didn't care if a monitor saw her. The school looked vacant anyway. Everyone was taking an exam or waiting to take an exam. She saw the broken windowpanes, the smashed-in walls, the stretches of worn linoleum, so worn that at every entryway, patches of the underlayer of black felt paper showed through like dark bruises. The school was truly run-down, but she didn't want to see it thrown away. Like an old shoebox, it might still be good for something.

Every time she turned the corner of a hall, she hoped she would see Matthew walking toward her, and it would be as if she were seeing him for the first time all over again. She leapt over a gully in her mind, and there he was, just barely. She had to squint because the sun was in her eyes, but she could tell he was smiling at her. Why are we staying around here anyway? Why didn't we leave last week, or weeks ago?

She came to the end of a long hall and looked both ways down its side halls. At the far end of one, two deaf students, a boy and a girl, were standing close together and talking to each other in sign language. Silhouetted and backlit by a window, they reminded Flora of black ants communicating with their feelers.

She thought she'd walk on out through the end of the long hall, but when she got to the doorway, she stopped abruptly. There were no steps or ramp below, just a four- or five-foot drop to a bed of dirt. She turned around and went back the way she had come.

When the bell rang she headed for her Shakespeare class. Mr. Langtry's face looked hot pink. It made his wavy hair look especially silvery. He had the kind of transparent complexion that could change from pale peach to pink to red, like rows of bulbs in a neon sign. A moment later it had switched back to pale peach again, and he was handing out the exam papers with his usual formal flair: lifting each one carefully from the stack in his arm with two fingers, laying it face up on a desk, and making sure it was perfectly positioned before each of his pupils. Phil had taken her to a restaurant on the top of a building on Sunset Boulevard once, and the waiter had put their napkins down like that, nodding to them politely as he moved along. Mr. Langtry smiled at her. She looked down and saw that she was gripping her pen in her left hand, and she blushed.

Flora made it through her chemistry exam, and the next thing she knew, it was nearly her turn to perform a solo dance for Miss Pazetti. She stood at the sidelines, in a perimeter of fidgety girls, and watched another girl move frantically toward the end of her performance. She must have been moving too fast, or else forgot a few steps, because when she made her final collapse on the floor, the music was still going. And it was still going when she sprang up and ran to camouflage herself among her classmates, just one black leotard among all the others.

Miss Pazetti smiled, made a note in her roll book, and then called for Flora Jackson.

While Flora was watching the last performance, it had dawned on her that she might not be prepared for what was supposed to follow. She hadn't practiced it much. Now Miss Pazetti was tipping her head at her, waiting for her. Tess was standing at the phonograph waiting to lower the needle. From Pazetti's record collection, she had chosen something called "Tanguillo-Zambrilla" played by Montoya.

Her mind felt as bare as the cement floor that spread before her, but she had no choice. She walked to the center of the vacant area and gave Tess a nod.

Tess dropped the needle down on top of the first guitar note, and Flora was jolted into a response. Now she knew she would have only the outline of her scheme to direct her; for the most part, her dance would be spontaneous.

She followed the music, or rather let it pull her through, and somewhere, well into her dance, something snapped, and she felt like her head was detached from her body. Her body moved on without her help, and she was free to look around. She saw Tess still standing by the phonograph, waiting to pick up the needle. She saw her ring of classmates: each girl one by one, the color of their hair, their eyes, the shapes of their faces, the shapes of their bodies. One was trying to fix a bra strap. Another one was scratching her knee. One was braiding her hair. She saw Miss Pazetti, with her clever smile and her compact body. And next to her, standing with her arms folded over her chest and the usual painfully tight smile tugging at her face, was Mrs. Baines.

It was only by chance that Mrs. Baines had appeared in dance class today, for her end-of-term inspection, at that very moment, in time for Flora's performance. Flora felt no surprise when she saw her standing there, no anxiety for being entirely skirtless. I'll never be in her clutches again, was all she thought. I'll never be in her sight again.

Flora felt an elation and a defiance spreading throughout her body. It stretched to the tips of her extremities. She saw herself being watched. She knew she was a spectacle, but that was all right: a person couldn't hide away all the time. She felt herself flinging sprays of energy from her fingertips.

When her dance was over she felt faint, and her vision was blurred. She couldn't focus on anyone. The other girls looked like a string of paper dolls that stretched and tore apart in one place as she came toward them.

Tess stepped up to her. "That's not the dance you practiced," she said in a slightly accusing tone.

"I couldn't remember what I was supposed to do." Flora took a deep breath and let it rush out again.

Tess stared at her in silence for a moment. "Since I doubt we'll be seeing each other again until who knows when, I'm saying good-bye to you now." She put her arm around Flora's shoulders and hugged her.

Flora had never heard Tess sound so discouraged. Did Tess guess that she and Matthew were leaving? She hugged Tess, too, and patted her on the back.

"I'm going to the Bahamas with my mother," said Tess, pulling away.

"That's wonderful!" cried Flora. She still felt flushed and dazed.

"Not so wonderful," added Tess. She folded her arms across her midriff.

Flora thought that her hands, her slender, heavily ringed fingers, looked especially frail; flaring out beyond her elbows, they reminded her of the pin feathers on a nestling's wings.

"I'm pregnant," said Tess, as if she had been forced to answer a question.

Flora felt her vital organs squeeze close together.

"My mother insists that I go through with it, but she wants me out of the sight of her friends."

"You mean you're going to have the baby?" asked Flora. Tess nodded. She looked as if she might cry, so Flora broke into tears. "Oh Tess, I'm so sorry."

"Listen, Flora." Tess brushed her bangs to the sides of her brow with her fingertips and recrossed her arms. The bangs immediately bounced back to where they had been. "If you're not already pregnant, I'd do something to prevent it if I were you."

Flora took a quick glance into her past. Impossible, there wasn't a chance, she figured. "All right, I will . . . Oh I'm so sorry, Tess." She didn't know what else to say. She tried not to look at Tess's belly, which she imagined was swelling up like an inflatable ball at this very moment, stretching her leotard out of shape. She was afraid to ask who the father was, or might be.

"I'll be all right," said Tess. "At least I made it through high school, for whatever good a diploma will do me. I really don't give a darn about the graduation ceremony." She heaved a big sigh and let her eyes rove all around the dance room and back to Flora. She looked like someone who had tried a lot of things and was tired of trying. "You're the only person besides my parents that knows." She sighed again and changed the subject. "Now that school's over, what are you going to do about Matthew?"

Flora considered saying something like, "Put him out of my mind, I guess," but she couldn't. "Matthew and I are leaving for Mexico tomorrow evening." She beamed at Tess through her tears.

"You're running away? You're actually running away. You and Matthew, to Mexico?"

"Yes," affirmed Flora, nodding her head repeatedly.

"I can't believe it!" cried Tess. Flora thought Tess was happily surprised, but then Tess shook her head and her face got small and crumpled up. "You can't do that, Flora. You can't leave like that! What if he dumps you down there?"

Flora acted as if she hadn't heard Tess's burst of doubt. "You're the only person who knows we're leaving."

Tess was silent. Her face had smoothed out again, except for one deep wrinkle between her brows. She stared down at the floor. The theme song from *The Pink Panther* dinked away in the background.

"I'm sorry we had so many fights . . . misunderstandings, anyway." Flora spoke to the top of Tess's head. "I'll write you." All their bad words, the intentionally cruel ones, the ill-chosen and poorly placed ones, and all the painful blanks where words should have been, were gathering together now into one hard clump at the base of Flora's throat.

"I'm sorry, too," said Tess. A dime-sized splotch of wetness hit the floor like a big raindrop. She quickly rubbed it into the cement with the sole of her dance slipper. "Use my home address. And if you stay in any one place long enough, send me your address." She pointed her toe and traced a small invisible figure eight on the floor in front of her.

"I will," said Flora with solemnity.

"I wouldn't like to get a letter from anyone I couldn't write back to," warned Tess. Flora got a stern look from Tess's dark cat eyes, and then Tess dropped her head again.

The bell rang and they both jerked their heads up, startled like deer in a glade. All they saw—*for the very last time,* thought Flora—was the sight of dozens of black figures in a rush to get out of the dance room.

"Well," said Tess, softening, "I'm glad you decided to tell me your plan." She started to say something else, but added instead, "Are you sure you know what you're doing?"

"Yes, I'm sure. I'm taking a chance. I know that. But then"—Flora felt the ache in her throat again, and she pulled at one shoulder and then the other of her leotard, which felt sticky and constricting all of a sudden—"I'm taking a chance if I don't leave, too." She thought for a moment. "I don't expect anyone to guarantee my happiness."

Tess gave her a skeptical smile.

"No, not even Matthew! I just want a chance to live with him."

"Well, good luck," said Tess.

"Good luck to you, too," said Flora and she felt like hugging Tess. When she put her arms around Tess's shoulders she knew she had never felt so close to another female before—never so close to her mother or her sisters. And she hadn't been very close to Tess.

She had a vision of Tess swinging a baby in her arms, dangling its little feet in the warm foam of some Caribbean surf, and laughing. She let go of Tess.

"Tess, are you going to keep your baby?"

"Time to lock the doors, girls," Miss Pazetti called to them from the doorway.

"Yes," said Tess with surety. "He belongs to me."

Timpanelli was giving no final exam. The day before, a few people had suggested she get up on the table so they could draw her as a final exam. She told them to drop the idea or she'd give them all an anatomy test and grade it. Today, the classroom was nearly deserted. Flora and Matthew were bent close to their easels, and five former students of Timpanelli's were gathered around her desk for a last visit with her in the old room. They passed her vase around. Timpanelli looked in good spirits. She was laughing at their jokes. One of them held up her vase and scrutinized it as if he were a museum curator.

"It's not exactly a masterpiece. It might not even be a work of art." He swiveled it in his hand.

"Give me my vase," demanded Timpanelli. She reached for it. Her face was screwed into wrinkles. He handed the lumpy thing back to her.

She cupped it tenderly in her hands. "One of my retarded students made this for me." They all laughed. They thought she was fooling. "It's shaped like a classic ampulla, can't you see." She took a sip out of it and put it down on her desk instead of passing it around again.

"Hey, Mrs. T., look at this."

She slowly twisted her head around and snickered when she saw the caricature of herself that one of them had just drawn in oil pastels on the window behind her. It was her, gritting her teeth and wagging her fingers with her thumbs stuck in her ears—something intended for the Main Office or the world at large.

"Still majoring in graffiti, I see." Timpanelli rolled her eyes.

"How's ol' Mrs. Baines?" asked one of them. "Is she still slinging her weight around? I have the most vivid image of her barreling down the halls."

"Yeah, and everyone scattering out the side doors," someone else added.

"Ol' Charlotte Baines may look like a block of cement teetering on a pair of high heels, but she's a lot more than that." Timpanelli put her fingers in the little lopsided handles of her vase. "Aside from being a holy terror and organizing a bunch of perfectly decent girls into a band of ferrets"—Timpanelli waited while the group around her busted up with laughter—"it was her idea to bring handicapped kids to the school and blend them in with the regular students. That's how this room became one of the mixing bowls." They all quieted down and looked as though they were reconsidering their own pasts. Timpanelli gazed at her vase.

One of the boys reached up and took hold of the rope to the alarm. "You ought to have this thing bronzed, Mrs. T." He pulled lightly on it so that the disjointed arms and legs of the baby doll did an odd dance and the cans and palette knives made a lame clanking sound.

Flora and Matthew turned their heads around. Timpanelli snapped out of her reverie. She got up from her desk and went over to them. "These are my new star pupils," she announced, looking back to her guests. "Star-crossed star pupils," she corrected herself. Her guests' smiles changed to polite laughter. "These *were* my star star-crossed pupils, that is," Timpanelli corrected herself again, "because, of course, school is over." Everyone around her desk laughed louder.

Flora felt Matthew draw back from his painting. He had a set look on his face. Flora stopped painting, too. She'd never seen him become self-conscious before. It was enough to keep her from having awkward feelings of her own.

Timpanelli leaned over unsteadily and peered down at Flora's unruly palette. "Your palette reminds me of a chameleon," she said. "Every time I look at it, it's changed colors. The same goes for your painting." Timpanelli was examining her painting now, her nose dangerously close to the wet paint.

"One color seems to lead to another," said Flora in a small voice. "I guess I feel like I need to use them all." She rolled her brush slowly in her fingers.

"It's not the last painting you'll ever do, I hope," said Timpanelli, and then hiccuped. She patted Flora on the back.

Flora opened her mouth to tell Timpanelli something, but Timpanelli had already turned around and was heading back to her waiting guests. Flora looked to Matthew. He raised his eyebrows and shrugged his shoulders.

"We can tell her tomorrow maybe," he said in a whisper and started painting again. Flora hated to postpone the announcement.

She went back to her painting. A month ago, less than a month ago, she would've been choked up and petrified by what Timpanelli had said about her work. But she had too much to think about now, and besides, she knew she had to paint her painting her own way. That's what Timpanelli always insisted on: Decide for yourself what has to be done, and do it. She added some ultramarine blue to a spot of carmine on her canvas. She heard Timpanelli say, "Matthew likes grays." As Flora painted the girl's gown, she thought of Janice's gown—six yards of uncut apricot silk lying on the closet shelf. She wondered if her father would rather see Janice as valedictorian or prom queen.

"Oh gosh, Matthew, I forgot to ask you about your father's wedding."

"The ceremony went on forever," said Matthew without taking his eyes from his painting. "Everyone was really ready for a party." He glanced over at her. "My father tried to play the violin, and Stella was so happy drunk, when some cops came to the door she invited them in and tried to show them how to tango."

"Didn't your father get jealous?" asked Flora.

"He thought it was hilarious," said Matthew, and he made a long steady stroke on his painting, then swished his brush in the turpentine cup.

Gray Lather

"Why don't we go visit them?" asked Julia. She and Marleen were sitting on the front porch hearing more than seeing Beth and her children out in front of their own house, enjoying the warm evening, too.

"I guess that would be the neighborly thing to do," said Marleen.

So while Marleen visited with Beth, Julia tried to play tree tag with Russell and Karen. They hung about her knees and squealed whenever she let them catch her. Then they begged to be swung, and so she swung them, first Karen, hands locked in hands, and then Russell, but because of his size he and Julia both toppled over on the grass. After a while they all went inside Beth's house. Julia wanted to see Karen and Russell's Mother Goose floor.

Henry was in his bedroom, peeking out the window, trying to figure out what Marleen and Beth were up to. Marleen never went out of the house after dark, not without him.

Since Julia was out, Daniel was in the room they shared, enjoying his privacy. He stood at the dresser and arranged his collection of model airplanes and took them for flights around the room. He toned the sound effects way down so they were barely audible. Some had safe round-trip journeys. One collided with a lampshade and spun to the floor. Another had landing-gear trouble and slid down the runway on its belly. Two, with full loads of passengers, had a midair collision. They fell in slow motion into the dark lake of the canyon between the beds. The planes seemed to be self-destructing. Propellers twirled off. Wings were ripped from bodies and scattered over foothills of pillows.

"These are my planes. I can destroy them if I want to." He spoke under his breath. "Look at that sloppy job—glue everywhere. And look at that crooked seam." He imitated the tone of his father's voice. He lay back on his bed with a plane poised in each hand and aimed them at one another. In a week he'd be graduating from La Creuse Elementary School. As he brought the two planes together, nose to nose, he recollected how he had talked tough to boys bigger than himself: especially that big fat kid with the fake alligator belt he liked to take off and snap at the younger kids. He'd fought with those bigger guys, and he had won sometimes. He'd been inside the girls' restroom on a dare. He'd made out with three of the girls in his class, once in a hedge on the way home from school. He knew how to spend his money. He bought doughnuts and Cokes from the takeout stand where the motorcycle gangs hung out. He hadn't used up any money on things like bubble gum or pistol caps since the fifth grade. From his allowance and lawnmowing earnings he had seventy-five cents left, and that was in his pants pocket. He set down his airplanes, got out his money, and counted it. Well, sixty-eight cents. His father had told him, "Next year you'll have to straighten up and act like a man." Henry had opened the bathroom door and said that while Daniel was peeing. "You'll have to start being responsible for your actions," Henry warned him with an all-knowing wink and a nod. He had missed the toilet.

Daniel put the money back in his pocket and got a sock from his sock drawer. He shook it by the toe, and a harmonica fell out on the bed. He never played it out loud at home. He took it out of its case now, put it to his lips, and pretended to play.

He had decided to buy the harmonica only after staring for a long time at a glass display case full of them. He had looked back and forth from one shape to another while fingering the seven dollar bills and stirring the change in his pocket. Finally he chose the best one he could afford, and after the sales tax, when Julia asked him if he was going to help pay for the perfume she wanted to get for Flora, he had been able to hand over only fifty cents. Julia had thrown herself on her bed in a fit, changed her mind, jumped up, and left the bedroom.

Daniel took the harmonica out of his mouth and polished it on the front of his shirt. He checked it for scratches. He put it back to his lips and walked around in circles, playing silent music.

Janice had skipped dinner. Ever since she got home from school she had been working frantically on her speech. At eight o'clock she let out a whoop and started wadding up sheets of used paper and batting them with the palms of her hands, hard enough so that they bounced off the walls and ceiling like shuttlecocks and landed everywhere. She went hopping around the room as if she were a wounded shorebird, flapping her arms, and crying in the rash, hushed scream that she reserved for ecstatic moments.

"It's finished! It's finished! I'm done! I don't care what anybody says!"

Flora laughed, but remained lying on the bed. When Janice had gathered up all the wads of paper and was again sitting at the desk, shuffling through the pages of her speech, Flora went back to gazing at the ceiling. It had been an exhausting day of examinations. Her eyes were jumpy. Words and numbers and symbols banged into one another, bounced apart, spun and raced around, like protozoa in a drop of magnified pond water. Some sort of demolition derby projected on the bedroom ceiling. She had given the tests her best effort. One thing at a time, she had told herself. She would have something to leave her father when she left: an official report card filled with honorable grades.

Mr. Whitney had done one of his laboratory experiments before handing out the exams. Everyone watched the clock and squirmed. After cleaning himself up, and the counter, he unlocked his desk drawer and withdrew the stack of papers they'd all been waiting for. "Two students among you are possible college material." He stood at the head of the first row and counted the students, front to back. He gave the first student the correct number of exams and moved on to the next row. "The rest of you would do well to consider returning to grammar school." Some students had already begun while others were still grabbing, and the ones in the rear corner were frantic with waiting. Flora had read it over so many times, she could almost see the test paper now: two long wordy problems that had nothing to do with Mr. Whitney's lab demonstration. And yet, as she scratched and scribbled her way into the test, the sight of him juggling his test tubes and grinning beneath his mustache kept popping into her head. When she turned in her paper, he gave her the same look he had given her when she had left the detention room, that you'll-be-back-again look.

Mr. Langtry had given an easy exam: matching characters and quotes with the titles of the plays they had appeared in. He wrote one of his favorite quotes on the blackboard. Decoration for your examination, he called it. It was something like:

> With Love's light wings did I o'erperch these walls;
> Stone limits cannot hold love out,
> Whatever love can do, that's what it will try;
> And so thy kinsmen cannot stop me.

Flora could see Mr. Langtry's blushing face as if it had been painted there on her bedroom ceiling. She didn't think she would ever forget his face, or his quaking voice, and his wild gray billowy hair. Depleted by the day, she closed her eyes. The fingers of her left hand remained squeezed together as if they had something more to write.

Do I still have something to write? She tried to think. The bedroom walls seemed to be pulsing. She could hear Janice softly mouthing the words to her speech. "We have learned, in our few short years here, to be each other's servants, to share the joys of learning. We have come a long way toward becoming responsible adults. Now we must go . . ." Then there was a rushing in Flora's ears and the walls spread outward and dissolved into the night beyond. At the last moment Matthew appeared, looking like a luminous line drawing of a spirit in flight. He took her hand in his and they rose away together.

She was awakened by Henry's angry voice. She sat up and looked around. Janice was sitting at the vanity, rehearsing her speech with the aid of the mirror. She had her hand held out as if she were offering herself something. Henry yelled, "Get back here!" and feet were thumping fast down the hall. Flora sprang to the door and opened it. A shot was fired: a loud smacking sound that hurt her ears. She screamed.

This is what happened: Henry was sitting at the foot of his bed cleaning his pistol when Daniel came out of his own room.

"Come in here," said Henry. "You're old enough to learn how to use this." He waved the pistol in the air.

"I don't want to learn. I don't like guns," mumbled Daniel.

"What did you say?"

"I don't like guns," repeated Daniel, more clearly.

"Why you sniveling little brat." Henry jumped up, and Daniel took off down the hall. Henry lunged out the door after him. "Get back here!" he yelled, and he slipped on the hall rug.

The pistol went off, and a second later the back door slammed shut.

Flora stood at her bedroom door with Janice behind her. They watched Henry get up and go back into his room. He sat down at the foot of his bed and started polishing his gun as if nothing unusual had happened. Then he looked across the hall.

"What are you looking at?" he said in a calm but challenging voice.

"Nothing," said Flora. She pulled the door shut with a shaking hand and turned around to face Janice's astonished face. They both heard Daniel scrambling over the back fence.

When Marleen and Julia came home, Henry told them that Daniel had run away.

"What?" cried Marleen. "Why?" She was horrified.

"Because he can't follow some simple instructions." Henry walked past her and started washing his hands in the service porch sink. "I want all the doors locked, and left locked." He scrubbed his hands all over with a stiff brush. Gray lather ran down his arms. He banged his elbow on the door to make sure it was really shut. "He can stay out all night."

"But where will he sleep? It's cold out," cried Marleen.

"That's his problem," said Henry.

Flora peered through the bedroom window into the darkness and listened for a sound from Daniel. She took a chunk of rosy quartz out of the windowsill and rolled it around in her hands.

"We heard him go over the fence," repeated Janice.

"But what if he's wounded and lying in the alley somewhere? I'm going to go look for him." Flora sprung off the bed, tossed her rock on it, and went quietly down the hall. Henry and Marleen were in the living room. Henry was staring at the television, and Marleen was fretting silently. Flora tried the latch on the back door. It was tight. She was twisting the doorknob when Henry came into the service porch.

"Where do you think you're going?" he hissed.

"He might be hurt," said Flora. The words barely came out.

"Hurt, my foot," said Henry through his teeth. He came closer, and Flora backed up against the door. "The bullet went through the rug. Now you get back in your room before I put your head through that door." He jabbed his finger toward the door.

"What's going on?" said Marleen. She stood behind Henry, clenching her hands.

"Your daughter wants to take an evening stroll."

Marleen gave Flora a look that said, Don't do it, don't upset him.

Flora took a peek under her arm at the locked latch. She walked past Marleen and Henry. "Good night," she said.

Janice had turned the lights off and was in bed. When Flora crawled in alongside her, Janice whispered, "You heard what he said, the bullet went into the rug. That's all. Anyway, Daniel was already halfway out the back door. Don't worry, he's all right. He'll be back soon."

Flora didn't respond. She lay on her back and waited for Henry to go to sleep. He watched television for several hours and then tossed and turned in his bed. Somewhere near dawn Daniel tapped on the window above Flora's head. Flora went to the back door and let him in. He trotted lightly, like a fox, back to his bedroom. Flora tiptoed back to hers.

A little while later, when it was light enough to see, she got up, went into the hall and pulled back the throw rug. She got down on her hands and knees and looked at the hardwood. She ran her hands up and down the smooth boards until she got tired of looking. It seemed futile, anyway; she didn't know what a bullet hole would look or feel like. She started to go back to bed and then felt an impulse to go to the living room. It was lighter in there. She searched the wall opposite the hallway door and finally found the hole.

The bullet had gone through the water jug that was balanced on the head of the Egyptian woman in the painting over the mantel. Flora nearly expected to see water spurting out of the jug. But it was as if nothing had happened. The veiled woman continued to walk along, oblivious to the hole in her jug. The jug must be empty after all, thought Flora. The woman was on her way to the well.

Flora snuck back to bed.

In the morning Henry left the house while the rest of them were seated at the breakfast table. He slammed the front door, and then the garage door, too.

Everyone listened to the sound of the car backing out of the driveway. When they were sure he was really gone, Janice, Julia, and Daniel got up from the table and prepared to leave for school.

Flora remained seated.

Marleen looked at her. "You'll be late for school."

"That's all right," said Flora. "I just want to ask you something, and I don't want you to get upset."

"What?" asked Marleen, already upset.

"Well, I don't know how you can sleep when you know Dad keeps a gun between your beds." Flora waited for an answer.

"What can I do?" said Marleen. There was a sad, panicky look in her eyes. Flora shook her head. She didn't know what to do either.

"Just in case you don't already know, I'm going to tell you: Dad chased Daniel down the hall last night with the gun in his hand, and it went off. A bullet came out of it."

Marleen's mouth dropped open. She just stared at Flora as if she were struck dumb.

"He might've killed Daniel, or wounded him at least."

Marleen continued to stare at Flora. Finally she got up and started picking dishes up off the table. She put an empty milk bottle in the refrigerator and came back for the butter dish.

"I'll be late for work," she said. Two tears raced down her cheek and splattered on the table. "Do you think you can help me with this mess?" She gave Flora an angry look.

A Cat Face

School would be over by midday. Each class session was cut in half. Flora was bothered by this condensed schedule. The bells rang too soon. The only requirement of the morning was to carry around a report card and present it to each teacher. She felt as if she were being shoved along.

In art class, Matthew and Flora worked on their paintings and waited for their names to be called. Matthew didn't offer to show his report card to Flora, and he didn't ask to see hers either.

Timpanelli's students, some reluctantly and some with a swagger, approached her desk in alphabetical order. Most of them left the room after having done what Timpanelli called "cleaning up any messes you've made and taking away whatever's left over."

The first, The Cat, listed in Timpanelli's roll book as Jill Abbot, accepted her grade of C and then pulled up a chair and sat close to Timpanelli, close enough to read off the names. Timpanelli didn't ask for her help, but Jill wasn't going to miss this last chance to call out the nicknames she had for other students. She approved of her own and signed her drawings with a cat face.

Flora had always kept away from Jill. She remembered seeing her fight another girl at the back gate a long time ago. Jill fought with all ten fingernails, and with a ferocious delight that was scary. She tore clumps of hair from the other girl's head, and as the girl retreated, ripped her blouse down the back. In class Jill spent more time using her penknife than her pencil. She whittled with it, tossed it at her drawing board, used it to carve initials in desks and clean her nails. This evening she would be graduating. Flora wondered what she would do after that. It was hard to imagine such a creature abandoning the territory she had held, in her own way, for so many years. Today, Jill's smirk had a little bit of a sour twist to it.

She called out, "Cartier, the Slick Lick," something suggested to her by his satin-black hair. She hated the way he wasn't afraid to get caught looking at her. He would keep on looking until she was the one who felt like turning away.

Matthew winked at Jill and opened his portfolio for Timpanelli to flip through one last time. It was a polite gesture performed by both of them, Timpanelli and Matthew, that is. Jill glared at him as if she wished she could scratch his eyes out, until it was time for her to start thinking about calling the next name. Timpanelli scribbled an A and her signature on Matthew's card. "For what it's worth," she said.

"Crowley, the Lizard," Jill called out, and a thin boy with a thin face and dark greasy hair came forward. He stood at the opposite side of the desk from Jill and stuck his tongue out at her as he handed his portfolio and his report card to Timpanelli.

Timpanelli riffled through his drawings: no human forms, just pictures of his model jets, and a few futuristic cars, and at the very end a flying saucer. She handed his folder back to him. "I suppose there are human beings inside some of your machines," she said. He gave her a blank look, and she gave him an A for his nonstop effort.

Matthew had gone back to his easel and was painting again. He saw that Flora was fidgeting with her paintbrush. She let out a sigh when Jill finally called for "Jackson, Flora the Wilt." She laid her brush on her palette and picked up her report card. When she came up to Timpanelli's desk, Jill gave her the lip-quivering grimace of someone who is sickened by the sight of something. Flora's sunless complexion reminded her of a discarded mattress. *Wilt* was both an impression and a command. Her own skin, which she took pride in, was like red adobe soaked in linseed oil—a quality she had been born with and had enhanced by lying in the sun on Malibu Point.

Timpanelli took Flora's report card and regarded the stack of A's broken by one C. "I don't guess you have a collection of drawings?" Flora saw drawings sliding into wastepaper baskets, a small stack on her shelf at home, rather personal ones, and a few in the supply cabinet.

"No, not really," she replied. "Well, I have a few in the supply cabinet. I'll go get them." She started to turn away.

"That's all right," said Timpanelli. She puffed up her cheeks as if she were going to blow out a big gust of air, and looked cross-eyed at her desktop. She added another A to Flora's report card. "Good luck," she said, handing the card back to Flora.

"Thank you," said Flora, and returned to her easel as Jill was protesting her grade to Timpanelli.

"She doesn't even have a lousy portfolio."

Timpanelli beckoned to the next student on her list, a lanky girl with curly blonde hair and slightly crossed eyes. Jill crossed her arms and pouted out the window while Timpanelli nodded her way through a thick collection of sketches, most of which were studies of faces (a few had the likeness of Tess) and hands in different positions. When Timpanelli gave the deaf girl an A, the deaf girl made a gesture as if her heart were palpitating wildly, and Jill reached for the roll book again.

Finally the last name was read off. Jill gave up her post and left the room. She waved to Timpanelli in parting. "See you in detention," she called back. That was her standard joke. Timpanelli closed her book. The room was deserted now but for Matthew, Flora, and herself.

"Here come my strays," mumbled Timpanelli. Flora glided over and stood before her desk. Matthew slipped into a chair next to her. He seemed to be concentrating on his outstretched legs as if maybe they were his landing props. Feels like an invasion, thought Timpanelli. "I sure hope this is good news," she said.

"Matthew and I want to tell you good-bye. We're leaving," said Flora, and she started fiddling with Timpanelli's desk calendar. "I mean, we're going away."

Timpanelli didn't look surprised. "Me too," she said, quite frankly. And then she got up and walked out of the room.

Flora stared after her in disbelief. Just like that. Without cleaning out her desk, without taking her stack of art journals, her roll book, her pencils, without even saying good-bye? Matthew got up, and he and Flora followed her.

Timpanelli stopped a little ways outside the classroom and took her chain of keys from her skirt pocket. Flora and Matthew waited silently behind her while she fingered every key with the care of a child who's been given a string of buttons or beads for the first time. She stopped at one key in particular, and turned to the door opposite the washroom. Matthew and Flora stepped back and watched as she pulled out what looked like a bunch of old paint-splattered canvas frames.

"This is a drying frame. You'll need it for carrying your paintings around, wet or dry." She held out the contraption, and Matthew took hold of it. He and Flora looked it over. It was made of hardwood sticks, four layers of sticks held together into squares by long bolts and wingnuts.

"Thank you." Their voices coincided.

"Stick your paintings in here, face to face, tighten the nuts, and wrap a sheet around the whole thing," said Timpanelli all in one breath. And then she walked back into her classroom.

Matthew took their paintings off their easels and tried them out in the frame. Timpanelli stood by them, a silent supervisor with her lips pressed tightly together and her eyes pinned on the canvases. Flora tightened one of the wingnuts. She wanted to cry because everything was changing too fast.

"That's perfect," said Matthew. He had told Flora he would figure out a way to fit their paintings safely in the back of his car. His design hadn't been as simple as this. There was another stretch of silence. Finally Timpanelli broke it.

"You might as well take the palettes with you," she said. "Take any good brushes you can find, too." She watched Flora scrape gummy paint off her palette with an old palette knife and thought of large-scale earth-moving operations. "If they can afford to build new schools, they can afford to buy new brushes and palettes and palette knives," she grumbled as she turned and went back to her desk. She pulled the wide, shallow drawer open and pushed it shut again. She called over to them, "Take any paints you need, too."

Matthew and Flora knew better than to keep thanking her for her offers. She'd be irritated if they refused to do some pillaging before they left. They went to the washroom with everything that needed cleaning. The room was as hot as a sauna. Molten color seemed to be sweating from its walls. The Cat had just painted a cat face on the window: whiskers were lashed across every pane, and some of them were still dripping. They might have tried to open the window, which probably hadn't been opened for years, but both of them seemed content with the humidity and even the dense turpentine fumes that swam around them as they scraped their palettes in the sink.

Matthew found an empty shoebox. He sorted through some other messy boxes of oil paints until he had selected all the colors that he and Flora had been using, and a few more tubes as well. He stopped when the shoebox was half full. Flora cleaned the brushes they had used that day. She wrapped them in a paper towel and laid them in the box.

Matthew leaned back against the sink and wrapped his arms around her. He gave her a long, liquid kiss.

"The last time we'll ever see each other in this place." He sighed and rolled his eyes around at the walls.

"Please speak in full sentences," said Flora, mocking herself.

"This is the last time we'll ever see each other."

Flora gasped. She tried to hold on to him as he pulled away from her. He picked up the brushes she had packed, slipped one of them from the rolled paper towel, and walked over to the paint-thickened back of the door. He looked at all the names and initials that were painted, drawn, scraped, scratched, and cut there. He looked back at Flora. She looked like a cigar-store Indian, except she was much paler and instead of a box of cigars she was holding a shoebox of crinkled paint tubes. She had a grim expression on her face.

"You didn't really believe me, did you?" He frowned and smiled. "Do you think I'd ever leave you, here, or anywhere?" He turned back to the door and with the nub of the brush he etched "Flora and Matthew Forever" in a careful script.

"I've had the urge to do that for a long time," he said, and he rolled the brush back up with the others and dropped them in the box that Flora was still cradling in her arms.

"Don't be upset, Flora. I'm sorry. I thought you'd know I was only joking." He put his arms around her again. "Are we still leaving together?"

"Yes," said Flora. She still felt stunned, but she managed to smile. Matthew got the palettes and opened the door to the washroom. When they went out, Flora closed it behind them. She didn't like doors left ajar.

She set the shoebox down on Timpanelli's desk and tipped it slightly in Timpanelli's direction. "This is what we took from the supply shelves." Her voice was steady, but her hand shook.

Timpanelli frowned at the box. "That's nothing. Take more." She waved her hand as if she were shooing a fly. The bell rang and she stuck her fingers in her ears and squeezed her eyes shut. Flora and Matthew grimaced too. "That damn bell," said Timpanelli.

Matthew picked up the drying frame. With one hand he weighed it up and down. With their paintings in it, it still felt light. Flora put the lid on the shoebox, stuck it under her arm with the palettes, and looked at Timpanelli. She figured what she was going to say would sound dry and tasteless, but she didn't want to say nothing.

"Thank you for everything, all your help," she said, and started backing away.

Timpanelli spread both her hands palms down on her desktop. She looked as if she was going to stand up, but she just sat there stiff-armed.

Flora stood still for a moment, and then lunged back to Timpanelli. She threw her free arm around Timpanelli's neck and kissed her on the cheek. "I'll never forget you, Mrs. T."

The box slid out from under her arm and paint tubes rolled all over Timpanelli's desk. Flora started gathering them up hastily, as if she were a sparrow swiping crumbs near the feet of a stranger.

"We'll see about that." Timpanelli helped Flora pick up the paints. "Send me an invitation to your first showing," she said as she dropped the last tube in the box.

"I will," swore Flora, and then flushed. "That is if . . ."

"Geez, of course there will be showings," interrupted Timpanelli.

Matthew came over and took Flora by the hand.

"Where are you headed?" asked Timpanelli.

"Mexico," said Matthew. He tilted his head at Timpanelli.

"Keep your eyes open," said Timpanelli, and she gave them a wink.

Alone, Timpanelli pulled her desk drawer open and stared at the confusion of pens and pencils, thumbtacks and paper clips, bits of erasers, the thin pad of hall passes, the nearly unused pad of detention room slips. A small velvety black spider stared back at her, spun around and raced for the rear of the drawer. It occurred to her that Flora hadn't asked her for her home address. "Not that I'll always be sitting around in the same place." She pouted as she rummaged through her drawer. Underneath the official forms she found a sketch she had done not too long ago, at the end of one of those days she had felt too tired to get up and go home. It was a sketch of her vase, a feathery-stroked still life with wildflowers arching up and out of it like sprays from a fountain. The vase itself had disappeared from her desk yesterday afternoon sometime. She wondered why anyone but her would want it. She passed it off as another part of the process of being stripped. She stuck the sketch in her roll book and walked out of the classroom with the roll book in one hand and her purse dangling from the other. She didn't bother to close the door.

Sparkling Quartz

Flora walked home very slowly. Matthew had relieved her of all their art supplies. She had only her notebook to carry, and so she let the fingers on her free hand run along the chain-link fence. By the time she had gone the entire length of the school, her fingertips were dry and gray and tingling. At a field of chewed-up earth, she waited while a dump truck full of gravel crossed the sidewalk. "Watch out, little lady," said the driver and grinned. Flora stepped back one step. On the far side of the field they had already started to lay concrete foundations. A half-dozen orange-and-black-striped cement trucks crept around like potato beetle larvae.

Next to the rising dust stood a row of run-down apartment buildings: pale fleshy pink stucco, the same color as the old school, with a foot-wide strip of crabgrass between their front sides and the sidewalk. Between the buildings there were side yards, sparsely grassed corridors of almost constant shade. And white painted wooden stairways and landings where women sat or stood and kept an eye on their children below. As Flora passed by she saw a young woman, no older than herself, holding on to the railing of a landing and looking out in her direction. Flora thought of Juliet in the balcony scene, and then the girl screamed, "Raymond, if you step one foot nearer that road I'll beat the livin' daylights out of you." A pretty child with a dirty face looked up at Flora. Flora said "Hi" under her breath and took a close look at his face. There was food on his cheeks. It looked like mustard. And black dirt around his mouth and in the corners of his green eyes. He didn't say anything. He just stared. The girl screamed, "Raymond, get your butt back here," and he spun around and ran back into the shade.

Flora gave up on the idea of touching everything within arm's length of the sidewalk. She passed by a picket fence that no longer appealed to her, and then by the new aluminum siding on the corner store. Just the sight of it brought a tart taste to her mouth. Her fingers curled into her palms for protection. She stepped into the store. All the red and pink of valentines had been swapped for the silver and white of wedding and graduation cards. She wandered up and down the aisles looking at the cans and jars and boxes of food, acting as though she had something to buy. She tried to leave by the turnstile and got knocked in the stomach by its chrome bars. When she passed by the checkout counter empty-handed, the lady at the cash register returned her smile and then watched her exit with a skeptical glare.

Daniel and Julia had gotten out of school early too. They were seated at the kitchen table with Henry, waiting for lunch to be served. Marleen was turning over cheese-filled hot dogs. She closed the broiler when Janice appeared in her blue graduation gown.

"You look beautiful," Marleen exclaimed.

Janice sat down at the table. "I'll be glad when this thing is all over," she said.

Henry spread mustard on his bread, and said, "Ha!"

Marleen served up a plate of hot dogs and then got an apron from the service porch closet. She was tying it around Janice's neck when Flora came in the back door.

"I'm not going to drip anything," said Janice.

"Well, just in case," said Marleen.

"Do what your mother says," said Henry. "Well, look who's wandered in. Get lost on the way home?"

Flora didn't answer him. She washed the metallic dust off her hands in the service porch sink and sat down at the table. Marleen had already put mustard on her bread.

"I really do wish you'd change your mind and go out to dinner with the rest of us," said Marleen.

Henry took a hot dog out of his mouth. "It's her decision whether or not she wants to be part of this family." He gave Flora a haughty look.

"I told you I'm coming to Janice's graduation," said Flora. Janice craned her neck and gave Flora an astonished look over the top of Daniel's crew cut. "And we're all eating together now, aren't we?" Flora took a big bite out of her hot dog as if to prove it. She took a gulp of milk. Janice gave her a quick smirk.

"Can I have another one?" begged Julia. Marleen jumped up to check the broiler.

"Which reminds me, I have to change clothes." Flora jumped up. She was so nervous, she was afraid she was going to say too much.

"If you've got any ideas about having visitors here while we're out, you'd better think twice," Henry called after her.

Henry chose a place midway up the bleachers and ushered his family in before him: first Daniel, then Julia, Flora, Marleen. He looked at the boards beneath him and then sat down.

"You're wearing the orange blossom perfume," said Julia, inhaling and smiling.

"Yes," said Flora, smiling and tucking in her lower lip. She could have worn some, for Julia's sake, but she had forgotten to. She had trouble enough deciding what clothes to wear. She ended up in a sleeveless flowery dress, maybe a little too bright for the occasion. But the sun felt good on the back of her shoulders, and the smell of the dry grass on the athletic field made her feel as if everything lay before her, everything was going well. It was a sweet smell, the smell of traveling down a road that cut through fields and fields of hay.

"I'm so excited," said Marleen. She put her hand on Flora's arm.

"So am I," said Flora.

The graduating class appeared on the opposite side of the field and paraded slowly along the track path from two directions: a blue thread from the left, and a white thread from the right.

Henry told Daniel to take his feet off the vacant seat in front of him.

A siren blared down the boulevard, and most of the people in the audience turned their heads to see what they could see. In the meantime, the graduating students had begun to weave their way into their own bleachers. Flora didn't spot Tess among them. She really didn't expect to. Janice was already seated in the bottom row, squinting into the sun.

"There she is," said Julia. "I'm so glad she got a blue gown."

Henry told her to lower her voice. He aimed his camera toward Janice, then lowered it and made an adjustment, raised it again, lowered it again without snapping.

"How many pictures do you have left?" asked Marleen. Henry thought about that for a minute.

"I got four of her standing on the porch: two with her cap on and two with her cap off," he informed himself and checked his camera.

Everyone was asked to stand for the national anthem and to remain standing for the school anthem. At least several dozen members of the graduating class started to sit down after the first song and then popped back up again. There was laughter in the audience.

After several short speeches from people like the principal and the student president, the band played "Blue, Blue, My Love Is Blue." And then Janice swept up to the microphone with unexpected speed and started delivering her speech.

Marleen clasped her hands together and took a deep breath. Flora pictured Janice practicing in front of the vanity mirror and was pulling for her, too. But from the start, her voice was an unpleasant surprise: blurred and echoing, blaring and high-pitched, and, like an air raid siren, seeming to come from no particular source.

Janice, for the entire graduating class, thanked those teachers who made learning an interesting, a pleasurable, even an exciting, experience. Flora saw Timpanelli sitting forlornly behind her desk, and started to cry. She saw Mr. Langtry clutching his podium and glaring happily, and that made her feel like crying and laughing.

Janice said, ". . . open minds and humanitarian dreams." Flora half saw, half felt Matthew. She knew he had seated himself somewhere about five or six rows above and behind her, and a few yards over.

Janice was saying that microscopic organisms live in our bodies and count on us for their survival. We count on them for ours. They evolved along with us. "They spin around on the surface of our eyes, for instance, and like the earth revolves around the sun, they . . ." Henry made a sucking sound and shook his head. He gave Marleen a disappointed, I-warned-you look.

"And for this reason . . ." continued Janice. A jet passed over Hazelton High's athletic field and blotted out a minute or more of her speech.

"Scholastic aptitude is not the only measure of a worthwhile life," she was saying. "Learning to share our . . ." Henry wiped his hand down over his face.

Daniel had his head bent over. He let some drool drop from his mouth and watched it fall through the bleachers all the way to the ground. Flora glanced at Henry and then back over her shoulder. She linked eyes with Matthew.

He cocked his head and waited. She gave him a very slow nod. Their plans were sealed. Matthew blew her a kiss. Then he jumped up and left the bleachers, up over the top and down the back side somehow.

There was another song from the band, "The Impossible Dream."

After that, Mrs. Baines came to the mike. She was wearing a navy blue dress with a huge pointy white collar, and looked a lot like the duchess from *Alice in Wonderland.* She smiled magnificently. "Out of respect for each and every member of the graduating class of 1965, we request that everyone in the audience refrain from applauding and remain seated until the last name has been called." Then she began the long list of names, first, last, and usually middle. There were even a few with numbers. Janice, as the top grade winner, was called nearly at once, just after the student president and other student officers. As she reached for her diploma a small cheer went up for her—not from Marleen or Henry, but from her own classmates. Marleen clasped her hands together again and took another deep breath, and Henry actually took a picture.

Then followed a short list of other honor students. Flora had

forgotten that Phil would be graduating until she heard his name.
"Phillip Henry Ridley the Fourth," called out Mrs. Baines.

Henry, said Flora to herself. Her eyes got big.

"Doesn't he look handsome?" whispered Marleen, nudging her. Phil looked stiff and serious, like a Gothic statue.

"Yes," said Flora, but Marleen could see the sparkless look in her eyes. She turned to her other side and whispered to Henry.

"Phil Ridley's an honor student."

"That's what they say," said Henry.

The senior class, like a rectangle of blue and white fabric unraveling from a loom, continued to come down from its bleachers for a long time, its two colors gradually parting and trailing away—a seemingly endless reeling off of names. Mrs. Baines tripped more and more over pronunciations and her voice got raspier as the list went on.

When it was all finally over, Henry and Marleen stepped down from the bleachers, with Julia and Daniel following after them. Daniel looked around. "Aren't you going to come with us?"

"No," said Flora, "I think I'll go on home. Good-bye."

Daniel gave her a worried look. "Bye," he said.

"Bye, Daniel."

He puffed out his cheeks as if he wanted to say something more or else blow a bubble for her, but instead he twisted around and bounded down the bleachers.

Marleen was telling Henry that she had made reservations at Fu Li's because the Mandarin Inn was all full up. Henry was pinching Julia on the shoulder for some reason, making her squirm. Flora watched them all head over to the Big Gym, Daniel lagging behind a little. Janice would have to wait in a long line, turn in her cap and gown, and trade in her fake diploma for a real one. Then they would all be going out for a dinner of Chinese food. That's what Henry had said they would do.

Flora hurried home. Without running, she went as fast as she could go. She jaywalked a couple of times, and when she entered the house, she tried not to look around at it. She rushed into her bedroom and closed the door. She pulled an old leather suitcase out of the closet. There was a finely tooled dove on the lid, all scuffed up. She tried to undo the latches but her hands were shaking out of control. Then she remembered the pistol and left the suitcase lying on the bed.

She went into Marleen and Henry's room and carefully wedged

the beds apart with her knees. She flipped up Henry's bedspread and his blankets, and lifted up his mattress. There it was, like a scorpion under a rock.

She lifted it up by the handle with two fingers and took it into the service porch and set it down on the washing machine. She pulled the garbage bin out of the closet and scrounged around in it until she found a good can. Pork 'n' beans. She placed the gun in it and then found another can, a large V-8 juice, and put it over the smaller can. She put the cans in a grocery bag and folded it up.

She went out the back door and over the back fence. She walked casually, like any schoolgirl coming home from school. After eyeing several trash cans that were either full or overflowing, she finally came upon one that wasn't close to full. She dropped the bag in it and pressed it down in the other garbage without looking at what she was doing. She rejumped the fence and washed her hands in the service porch sink. Her hands were still shaking.

This is it, she told herself. I'm really going through with it. I've got to stay calm. You've got to stay calm, she told her hands, and she dried them on the towel.

For days she had been making and remaking lists in her mind. Matthew had taken the paintings and the palettes and the shoebox of paints home with him. He told her not to worry about any camping gear, he'd see to that. And he'd bring towels and bedding. He had bought two new sleeping bags the day they found the new latch on the storage room door.

He hadn't left her much to do, and yet she was scurrying around the room, moving things from here to there, or merely touching things and leaving them be. Opening and closing drawers. She felt like she was going through one of her father's air raid drills and had forgotten her assignment; she had almost no time at all to grab a few belongings and flee the house.

But Matthew wouldn't be pulling up behind the house, idling in the alley, until eight o'clock, dusk. It was only six-thirty. She reminded herself again to slow down.

She opened a dresser drawer and removed a wooden slide-top pencil box. Her grandfather, her father's father, had given it to her when she started grammar school. She had always kept crayons in it. She opened it up. It was still filled with crayons, all broken and stripped of their labels. She looked around for another container to put the crayons in and couldn't find anything better than an old white sock, the kind she used to wear when the family went hiking.

She poured the crayons into the sock, knotted it, and put it in a drawer.

From her art drawer she took the colored pencils Marleen had given her for her birthday, and the brushes from Matthew, and some more drawing pencils and erasers, and put them all in the pencil box. She also got out the box of oil paints, Marleen's other gift to her, opened it and glanced at the beautiful little undented tubes, little cocoons of color.

She opened up the suitcase and found it half full of faded and limp doll clothes. "Heavens to Betsy Wetsy," she said aloud. She clutched them all up, wadded them into a ball, and stuck them in the back of her underwear drawer. Then she put her art supply boxes in the suitcase, took them out again, and went to the closet. She brought down the stack of drawings. The ones she had done alongside Matthew she pulled out and laid in the bottom of the suitcase. She put the pencil and paint boxes back in.

She dragged a large handbag from the bottom of the closet, a many-compartmented leather thing, a hand-me-down from Marleen. From the bathroom she took two washcloths, her toothbrush, a bar of Ivory soap (just in case there wasn't any in Mexico), a half-filled bottle of Halo shampoo, and a metal nailfile (she planned to stop biting her nails). She stuck all these things in the various compartments of the purse, then glanced at the pocket-sized Spanish-English dictionary on the desk and put that in the purse, too.

She didn't want to think about how little Spanish she knew. Instead she searched through the bottles of perfume on the vanity and found the orange blossom essence and also the bottle of Heaven Scent Marleen had given her one Christmas. She'd bring these along for the memories, not to wear.

She dug around in her jewelry box and came up with Matthew's ring. She put it on and tipped her hand from side to side, regarding the black stone. She switched on the overhead light and looked at it again; the star didn't shine much in the artificial light.

She went back to the jewelry box, and from the bottom, beneath all the junk jewelry she had collected as a child, she brought out the silk coin purse Janice had given her. It was plump with her life savings: ninety-two dollars from allowances and gift money, and in addition to that the crisp twenty-dollar bill from her father. Something bright shone out; she untangled her quartz-crystal necklace from several other strings of beads and held it up to the light by one end, as if it were a dead garter snake. Every facet glistened. She carried the necklace into Daniel and Julia's room and placed it inside Julia's jewelry box, which was full of dyed macaroni necklaces, strings of cowrie shells, and polished stones. Flora wondered how she was going to leave her own collection of rocks.

She went back to her room and the curtains whipped back against the screen. She gasped and jumped back. Only a puff of wind, but enough to set her heart pounding. She sat down on the bed for a moment and forgot what she had been after. From the corner of her eye she saw the bird in the feather collage peering down at her. She hadn't thought about Matthew's letter being inside that picture for quite a while. She wondered if she should remove it, destroy it maybe. No, she would leave it hidden there: leave something of Matthew there on the wall. Let somebody find it a hundred years from now.

She got up and put the coin purse in the small inner compartment of the leather purse. She heard Henry inside her head saying, "They'll take all your money and throw you in a jail cell full of cockroaches." She heaved an irritated sigh and turned around to see what had to be done. There were no clothes in the suitcase.

The clock on the desk said a quarter after seven. Time had been lunging forward behind her back. She recalled the childish game "Mother-May-I?" and started taking her flowered dress off.

What am I supposed to wear? she asked herself. She didn't want to say "to run away in." It wasn't running away: it was running to, running to something. She pulled open more dresser drawers. She threw her five best pairs of underpants in the suitcase, along with her blue flowered bikini. She gazed down at the contents of the suitcase: art supplies and underwear.

What will the weather be like tomorrow? she wondered. Where will we be in the morning? Is it always hot in Mexico? She wished she had bothered to learn something about the country. Maybe they would end up dressing like the Mexicans—wearing ponchos and things like that. She pulled on her most comfortable pair of jeans and laid two more pairs in the suitcase.

It occurred to her that she had no suitable nightgown, nothing to wear at night with Matthew. She looked at her threadbare flannel one and stuffed it back in the drawer. Henry was always wanting cleaning and polishing rags. "Go get me a rag," he'd say, as if the females of the house had an endless supply, a mysterious source of rags. She pulled something else out of the same drawer: the tops and bottoms of the cotton Chinese pajamas she hadn't been able to get into since she was nine or ten. They were even too small for Julia now. She loved the appliquéd children juggling pins on the front of the top, and so she had hoarded the pajamas in the back of her drawer. Now Henry could use them for polishing the car.

She stood in front of the open closet and ran her hands back and forth through the rack of clothes. Some of them she had outgrown years ago, too. And there was a whole group of skirts that had been hanging idly on account of Mrs. Baines and her dress code. She came across the dark Prussian blue dress she had worn on her one evening with Matthew. She pulled it off its hanger and folded it into the suitcase. The clock said seven twenty-five.

She chose four blouses from the closet: a white one with short sleeves and lace trim on the collar, a long-sleeved lavender muslin with a sash, a striped one with a drawstring collar, and a rather plain sky-blue blouse with short sleeves and pockets on the chest. The fourth one she put on. She tried to button it and put the other blouses in the suitcase at the same time. Her fingers were trembling. Her entire body was trembling. She let go of the buttons and concentrated on getting the blouses folded neatly into the suitcase. Then she buttoned her blouse and crawled across the bed. She pushed the curtains aside and put her face close to the screen. It was warm out. Almost balmy, despite a breeze. It was nearly dusk and very quiet, as if the entire neighborhood had gone out for a Chinese dinner.

She went back to her closet, brought out a mohair cream-colored sweater, put it on top of everything else, and closed the suitcase. The lid went down easily, with a hollow plopping sound. What a surprise. All the years she had spent in this room, and the suitcase wasn't even full.

Neither was her purse. She hadn't forgotten anything. She didn't think she'd need anything else. She got down on her belly and pulled her favorite, well-worn sandals out from under the bed, sat on the floor, and buckled them on.

Then she sat down at the vanity, just to be sitting there for a last time, looking into that little three-way mirror. Her face looked bewildered and plain, even in triplicate. She felt her earlobe, even though it was obvious that the gold loop wasn't there. But there it was, in plain sight in the top of her jewelry box. She put it on and pulled open one of the vanity drawers. It was filled with scarves. She searched for a particular one, lavender and lilac orchids with a striped border, and tied it around her neck. She gave herself another look in the mirror. She still looked scared but not so dull. A little more dashing, she thought, and she laughed nervously. She took a handful of scarves out of the drawer, reopened the suitcase, and dropped them in. She re-latched the latches and stood still. The sky outside the window was wavering between blue and aqua. She glanced at the clock: twenty till eight. Her heart pounded. And then, as if to echo it, there was a hard knocking at the front door. She froze, and her eyes got as big as doorknobs. "Who in the world can that be?" she whispered. Had Henry forgotten his wallet, and maybe his house key, too? Was Matthew changing the plans, as a sort of joke, coming to the front door, early? The doorbell rattled madly once, and then again. She flew on tiptoe down the hall, made a tiny break in the picture window curtains, and peeked out.

An overweight man with wrinkled trousers and mussed-up gray hair was wiping his face with a handkerchief. At his feet rested two display baskets filled with brushes of all kinds and sizes, every kind except paintbrushes—scrub brushes, whisk-broom brushes, grooming brushes . . . Flora crept back to her room, picked her brush up off the vanity, gave her hair several stokes all the way around, and tossed the brush in her purse.

She looked around the room, went over to the bed, lifted up the blankets, and took several pieces of paper from between the mattresses. The first one she unfolded was the letter she had written to Janice. She read it over rapidly:

> Dear Janice,
>
> You were always better at talking with Dad than I ever was. If you get this note before he does, will you please tell him that I finally took his advice and got out of the house.

That sounded a little harsh, but if she took time to rewrite it, she wouldn't be getting out of the house.

> Maybe things will be less tense around here now? I'll write you soon and tell you what I'm doing. In the meantime, know that I am on my way to make a life for myself—for better or worse, but I really believe for the better. I hope everything goes well for you at college.
>
> Thank you for helping me with chemistry.
>
> You can have, or use, anything I left of my own in the room. I will miss you.
>
> Take care, with Love,
>
> Flora

She rushed over to the desk, got a pen from the drawer and added a P.S.:

> Dad forgot to ask me for my report card. Maybe he will want it as a souvenir now.

She stuck her report card inside the letter, and laid the letter on top of the desk. Then she unfolded her letter to Marleen:

> Dear Mom,
>
> I truly hope this doesn't cause any trouble between you and Dad. I think you know that I left because I really had to. It was time for me to try to create a life for myself. So please don't worry about me. I think everything will be better for *all* of us now.
>
> I'll write you soon and tell you how I am. I know I will miss you very much. Of course, I cannot say when I will be coming home for a visit. Probably not for quite a while. Please say good-bye to Daniel and Julia for me, and to Dad.
>
> I took with me all the art supplies you gave me, and I will try to put them to good use. Thank you for everything else too.
>
> Your loving daughter,
>
> Flora

That would have to do, thought Flora. She folded the letter into a small rectangle and went into her parents' room. Henry's bed was still pushed aside, and his blankets were still flipped up. She cringed to think of his rage when he discovered his gun was missing. But at least *then* he wouldn't have it in his hand. She straightened his bed and put the letter inside Marleen's novel, on the same page with her pressed-flower book marker, and laid the book back down on the nightstand.

She peeked into Daniel and Julia's room, half hoping to see them there so that she could give them a reasonable explanation of why she was leaving. Even if they didn't understand her, they wouldn't lose their tempers. She had tried to write letters to them both, but the truth was, she felt as if she hardly knew them. Even though they were a boy and a girl, and very different in their looks and their ways, she kept seeing them as identical twins jumbled together in the same box, this room across the hall. Her immediate pain was caused by the realization that she never would get to know them. When and if she ever got home again, they'd be complete strangers and she'd be a strange visitor. Or else they'd be gone too. Who knows? She stood at the threshold of their room and looked around; it held a blend of boyish and girlish things. A pile of plastic planes, some broken, clusters of figurines and tiny perfume bottles, all on the same dresser top. And over the dresser, that same set of velour and cardboard cutouts, faded since her own childhood: Snow White surrounded by the seven dwarfs. No, Happy and Sleepy were missing. And the twin beds looked funny: one was loaded with stuffed animals, and the other one was bare. It was as if the animals had chosen one bed and scorned the other. She looked at the windows. The aqua sky had yielded to a glowing green. She rushed back into her own room.

The clock said three minutes to eight. She looked around. Her flowered dress was lying on the floor. She hung it in the closet. She picked up her suitcase and purse and looked around once more. The room looked neat, unruffled. It would do fine without her. So would Janice; Janice could have her own private room now, until she left for college. She closed the door.

Then she reached back inside and clicked the overhead light switch off. Matthew and she had agreed: when the bedroom light was off, that was a sign that everything was going smoothly. Everything had been well planned, she thought as she went down the hall. But she had a tingling in her spine, as if someone was in close pursuit of her, almost breathing on her. And then a crazy little voice, a voice inside her head, was chanting, "I'm late, I'm late, for a very important date." She used to say that to herself when she was in danger of being tardy for grammar school. But she wasn't late now. She was right on time.

When she got out the back door, Matthew was already there. She could hear his car purring in the alley. She dashed across the yard and tripped on the garden hose, but it only sent her flying forward faster.

She slung her bags over the redwood fence and sat them down on a trash-can lid. Then she put her hand on the fence post and swung herself onto the top slat of the fence. She had done this once already today. She had done this many times as a child playing chase with other children. Only now, as she teetered there, the entire length of the fence wobbled with her weight. The posts were rotting off at ground level. Henry was always complaining that the fence needed to be replaced. The slat she was perched on was about to break loose.

Matthew jumped out of his car when he saw her. He steadied her as she came down on the alley side, and he held her for a moment.

"How do you feel?" he asked.

She looked at him. He was wearing blue, too, and smiling anxiously. She laughed. "I feel like . . ." She gulped air. "Like I've been breathing turpentine fumes. I'm so excited."

Matthew opened the trunk of his T-bird, laid Flora's suitcase beside his, and slowly lowered the trunk lid. Flora got in the car and looked back. Their paintings were occupying the back seat. They were neatly swaddled in a pale blue bedsheet—a comforting sight. They'd make good traveling companions.

Matthew slipped silently into the driver's seat, and he and Flora started rolling down the alley. Clusters of trash cans glowed, leaves glowed, and fence posts, and telephone poles. It was that wonderful time in a summer day when the sun has just set and everything seems to be holding on to a bit of sunpower and giving off a faint fluorescent light. And overhead, above the web of power lines, the sky was pale mint-green, and yet dim enough to show some large stars or planets and a slim crescent moon like a neat nail trimming.

Flora unbuckled her sandals and crossed her legs on the seat. We're going far away, south of the border, south of the border, she breathed to herself. For hours and hours, whenever she pleased, she would be able to look to her side and see the beautiful profile of Matthew's face. He looked determined and calm. She rubbed her damp palms together and discovered a long redwood splinter sticking out of the center of one of them. She picked at it.

At the end of the alley Matthew brought the car to an easy stop. He looked both ways up and down the cross street. Then he let his hands slip off the steering wheel and the gearshift knob. His entire body went limp and he laid his head back against the seat and closed his eyes.

"Flora," he said, "I just can't go through with this."

Flora felt as though she had been hurled against the windshield. Everything in front of her shattered into little fragments of sparkling quartz. She thought she saw a blue station wagon ripple by. She wouldn't have enough time to get back into the house and collect the letters, much less hide the suitcase. Henry would probably be waiting for her at the back fence.

Matthew opened his eyes and looked at her.

"I was just kidding," he said. He leaned over and kissed her as he shifted gears. They turned out into the street.

EPILOGUE

Finishing Touches

The Shell

It is sweltering hot. The sky is too bright to look at. Flora sits up and squints up and down the beach. There are no trees, just some clusters of jagged maroon-colored rocks. Pumice, she thinks. Poking up through the sand, they look like miniature volcanoes. She pushes her feet into the sand. The sand is as fine as chalk powder. It does not rise in dust. The weight of the heat holds it down. Holds everything still, except the cicadas that shrill in a grove of willow brush beyond the beach. They shrill with a rhythm that rises and recedes like waves of heat. It's as if the heat is what makes them sing.

Matthew lies beside her, beneath a canopy made of sticks, twine, and a silky blue fabric. She looks at him. He has drifted off to sleep. His mouth has fallen open, as if he too is singing the heat. But his skin looks cool because it is tinged with blue from the shade of the canopy, and translucent, like mother-of-pearl. He looks perfect, she thinks. She imagines she has just come upon a flawless shell lying slightly embedded in the sand, and it is Matthew. She wishes sometimes he were small enough to hold cupped in her hands. She could care for him, polish him as if he were a priceless art object. She loves him so much, she wants to cry—shed tears in this dry place, so dry it seems a shame to lose one drop of moisture. She looks away from him. The gulf is a glinting mirror that makes her eyes water anyway.

She gets up and leaves him to rest. After wading out a long way, she is finally waist deep in the warm water. Back on shore Matthew is a tiny motionless form with a patch of cerulean hovering low over him. The water is too warm. She moves back in to where it is shallower. Her foot touches something hard in the silt. She digs it out with her toes and reaches down for it. It is a shell, not a smooth, polishable one, but a complex spiral of wings, sawtooth sharp. The top ends in a tiny nipple, and the other end in a delicate spurlike spout. The wings ruffle back to show a pearly interior as purple-pink as a baby's mouth. It is empty. She holds it to her ear and hears nothing. She puts her mouth close to it and calls Matthew's name in a singing voice. He is so near and yet so far away. He can't hear her.

He is so far away and yet so near. She turns the shell over and over in her hands. An empty shell is like a memory, she thinks—a record of the past, an unmoving, nonliving skeleton of the past. "You must draw a figure from the inside out," Timpanelli used to say. "You must start with the bones, and learn how they move in their joints . . ." But what if the bones *are* the outward form, and there are no movable parts, and there is nothing on the inside, nothing left but air? She carefully sets the shell back down on the glossy white windowsill. She longs to be with Matthew.

She swings the casement window open wider. The sun shines in on her and makes her tingle, a warm salty tingle. A slight breeze riffles the hair on her arms like grass on a hillside. Blue curtains wave in about her, like ribbons of sky drawn in through the window. Shredded sky. She lets the edges of the curtains run through her fingers. All she can see of the Pacific Ocean is a sparkling wedge framed by a chimney and a steeply pitched roof. She moves away from the window. Blue shadows, like flames, stretch across the floorboards.

She goes back to her easel, pushes her stool back, and paints standing up. With a small brush held close up at the ferrule and her face only inches away from the canvas, she traces the lines of her drawing. Without her looking, her brush finds the turpentine cup and the folded rag covered with tadpole-shaped paint stains. She holds her palette out to the side. It's like a flipper, helping her to keep her balance. She rests one foot on the base of the easel, and whenever she shifts her weight, the bulky old wooden structure pivots slightly and creaks like an old ship. She has just begun this painting. It is hard to tell what it is going to be. The pencil lines are very faint.

Next to the easel, running along one wall of the room, there is a narrow table of varnished wood. On the table, lined up neatly, as if for exhibit and not for use, are cans and jars holding pencils, pens, paintbrushes with shining ferrules, clean palette knives, sticks of incense. There are also wooden boxes concealing small tools such as screwdrivers and files, and old biscuit tins filled with tubes of oil paint.

Above the table, tacked on the white enamel woodwork, there is a litho of the phases of the moon, and next to that a pen drawing of the cross-section of a nautilus shell inscribed in a golden section. Just below that, several strands of violet-blue seed beads strung with shells—augers, turrets, and murex—hang on the wall so that they swag with different curves. Off to the side there is a lizard stuck to the wall with a long brass pin—just its crisp outer form, in perfect condition. It apparently died without violence, of cold or starvation. Curled up, and with its tail pointing downward, it looks like a question mark.

On the other side of the room, there is a wavering line of paintings and drawings. Most of them are framed in antique frames, and some of them are just matted. None of them are askew. More paintings are stacked on the floor against the wall. A black portfolio case with a handle repaired with copper wire is also leaning against the wall. Beside it is a pair of dusty low-heeled sandals that look as if they've been kicked off.

There's a large oil painting over Flora's bed, of a winged or caped figure dancing, on the verge of flight. Her bed is carefully made, covered with a striped madras spread in muted tones of lavender, gray, and pink. Next to it, there's a fruit crate covered with a piece of black fringed velvet. A gilded lamp, designed to look like a flower stalk and topped with a satin bloom-shaped shade, sits on this nightstand. Beneath the lamp is a color print of Cupid fleeing from the bed of Psyche, pasted on the front of a spiral notebook; beside that, a brass incense burner with a thin purple stick sticking out of it and a neat pile of ashes on the black velvet.

All in all there's very little furniture in the room. Guests would have to lounge on the bed or on the floor on a faded Oriental carpet, or sink into the one overstuffed armchair. A small hexagonal table on the rug must serve as the dining table. The only other piece of furniture is a low chest at the opposite end of the room from the bed. A white candle in a marble candleholder is sitting there on top of a doily, a lavender swirl of scallop patterns—something Flora's mother might have crocheted while waiting for Flora to be born. There is also a little alabaster vase holding magenta carnations. Silk and ricepaper fans are arranged almost symmetrically around a large oval mirror, a mirror large enough to give the impression of being a porthole into another room.

Actually, beyond this main room there's a tight, galleylike kitchen, and past that, coming as a sort of surprise, a spacious, tiled bathroom big enough to dance in. Flora's addition to this room is a collection of semitropical plants. Ferns and orchids line the sink counter, fuchsias and velvet plants hang from the ceiling.

Her entire apartment must have been merely the master bedroom in the original plan of this elegant old house in Venice Beach. She's been living here for a little more than a year, ever since she left the university. She rented the place because it had a high-peaked ceiling, and because its tongue-and-groove wall boards painted glossy white reminded her of the clean ribbing of a scallop shell. Because there was orchid-colored tile in the bathroom, and arches over all the doorways. Because of the view, however small, of the ocean. And because it was only a short walk to the strand going in one direction, and in the opposite direction, only a short walk to Main Street, where the grocery stores and thrift shops and bus stops were. And finally, because she could afford the ninety-two dollars a month for rent. She was sure she could sell enough paintings and drawings on the weekends at the street gallery to make that much and more. She'd have money left over.

No Chain-Link Fences

1971, June 21, Monday:

Yesterday was the day of days for me. I went to the Renaissance Fair. Rumsey dropped Frances and me off there in the morning. We begged him to come along with us, but he insisted, "You've been to one, you've been to them all." This was the first time Frances and I had gone.

Frances wore a wine-red velvet quilted jacket that used to be her grandmother's. And I wore a full-sleeved blue blouse, and a black velvet vest I had found in a thrift shop. I embroidered a blue silk heron on the back of it for the occasion. For jewelry all I wore was my gold earring. After seeing so many beautiful long skirts, we both wished we hadn't worn jeans. We felt like ranch hands who had wandered over the hill and into another century.

Neither of us had eaten breakfast, so after the opening pageant, we strolled around sampling food from the food stalls: falafel, corn on the cob, warm beer. We ate some aromatic seeds that a man in a white robe and turban gave us. "He looks like a wizard," said Fran. "Maybe we shouldn't have eaten them. We'll disappear." Fran found her boyfriend at his candlemaking booth, and so I wandered around by myself, which didn't bother me at all.

I got my fortune told by a kind-looking woman wearing a lavender sari and lots of silver bracelets. Her tent was so low I had to crouch to enter it. After she laid out about half of the cards in her hand, she put her fingers on two of them and said something like, "There is someone who has been like a devil for you in the past. This is no more a problem for you."

Then she laid down two more cards, put her pointer finger on one of them, and said, "You never have to think about money. There is always enough for you.

"Here." She pointed to another card. "You don't want no one to be boss over you."

She was silent for a while. I had time to look at the lapis lazuli stones in her bracelets, and the large opal in her ring, which looked like a miniature ocean.

"It is not very clear." She closed her eyes. "There is something about water, there is much water." She moaned a little and frowned. "But see here, you have nothing to worry about." She turned over the last card and changed her tone. "There is much sunshine coming to you. You got a strong spark inside you. You going to live a long long time. You don't worry." She patted me on the back of the hand, and all her bracelets jingled. I laughed. I guess I must have been looking worried. I wish she had said something like, You're a wonderful painter . . . you make beautiful paintings.

I gave her all the money I had in my pocket: only two dollars, and one of the bills was almost torn in two. She smiled at the money and then at me. The sign outside her tent read: "Fortunes Told by Cecilia, Donations." I wished I had more to pay her. I have no idea what a person should pay for a fortune.

After that I wandered around in a booth hung with yards and yards of tie-dyed velvet, a maze of drapes. Some kids were playing hide-and-go-seek in there. Tie-dyed velvet is not quite my style, and yet when I came out I was smiling so hard my cheeks were aching.

I saw Frances and her boyfriend a ways off. She was hanging

onto his arm, and they were rocking with laughter, watching a Renaissance game: two fellows with feathers in their caps clambering up greased poles.

I watched part of a play. I didn't get there in time for the opening, but I think it was from *Midsummer Night's Dream.* The longer I watched, the more I felt as if I were witnessing someone else's dream. The characters seemed to move with a weightless grace. Each gesture and every word felt significant, though only a little of the meaning came through to me, and I remained silent, awkwardly so, as people all around me were jeering, cheering, tossing flowers, and mocking lines. I think now that these people at the edge of the stage were members of the theatrical troupe and an extension of the play.

After the play I hung around the stage waiting for the flamenco dancers to come on. A delay was announced by a mime in jester's costume. As I turned away, a young boy wearing a harlequin's suit danced up to me, playing a silver flute. He spouted a few feathery notes, gave me a feigned demure look, and passed on.

Then the sort of second chance that is supposed to come seldom, if ever, came to me.

I looked up and saw Matthew sauntering down a hill, coming through the tall dry grass. He had emerged from the deep shade of a huge live oak, his hair flowing back over his shoulders like an Apache's. It looked as fine as black silk floss in the sunlight. He was swinging a bottle of wine in his hand as if he had forgotten he was holding it. He looked a little wild, or reckless maybe, but not rough or warlike.

He saw me for sure. I know because when he was a couple of yards away he stopped and just stood there staring, waiting to see what I would do, I think. Those same black, gleaming, mischievous eyes. He was wearing a blue denim jacket, and beneath that, a white shirt too bright to look at.

I walked toward him. I walked up to him. Still he just stood there, looking taller than I had remembered. His jeans looked just washed. He tucked his hand in a pocket and gave me this sly, inquisitive smile.

"Matthew?" I asked. I guess I wanted to make sure it was him after all, and not his double, or a hallucination, or a specter.

He took a quick swig from his bottle and held it out to me. I took a sip and handed the bottle back to him. Then he turned and walked away, swinging the bottle as if it were a purse.

The warm red wine went down easily. I felt like my tongue had slipped down my throat, too. He doesn't want me like he used to, I told myself. Then I asked myself, What's holding me back? What am I—in high school still? There aren't any bells or padlocked doors or chain-link fences anymore. At that moment my passion for Matthew felt both old and new.

I ran after him, toting all the regrets of my prismatic past, like a marbleized balloon, so big and so full of helium that I had to tug at it. I took hold of Matthew's arm so that he had to turn around and face me.

"Matthew," I said, "I've missed you. I've never forgotten you." I wanted to keep looking at his face, but I couldn't. He was staring at me as if I was a mannequin.

I searched in my purse for a scrap of paper. I wrote my address on the back of a grocery receipt. Then I stuck it in the chest pocket of his jacket. I felt a little crazed doing that. But what did I have to lose? What do I have to lose?

I walked away from him without waiting for a response. He had all the information he needed: a lunatic wants you, and here's where she lives. All the information he needs from me. Maybe more than he wants.

After that I felt like going home. I hitched a ride, the first time I had ever hitched a ride by myself. It was from a nice elderly lady who has a home in Pacific Palisades. She talked all the way about her cats, one of which was in heat, about her cactus garden, which was in bloom, and about getting her grand piano tuned twice a year because of the damp ocean air.

She took the coast highway. It was a scorching day and the public beaches were thickly patched with beach towels. Some of the people held the towels in place with their bodies while others stepped carefully, as if they were taking small stitches around the edges of the colorful patches. They traveled back and forth over the sand to the margin of the foam. Sometimes they raveled out farther and looked like bright thread mixing with white cotton. A few went even farther out and like specks of lint were swept back onto shore by the waves. Beyond that there was nothing but shimmering water, and I watched it as the old lady continued to talk. Twice I thought I saw Matthew trying to thumb a ride, but she didn't stop, and it wasn't Matthew anyway. Just some lean boys with dark hair standing on the cliff side of the highway.

After telling me to be careful who I hitched a ride from, she let me off on Main Street, way out of her way. I said I'd like to pay her for the ride, but I had no more money on me. She laughed. She said she likes to drive on Sundays.

Matthew didn't show up last night. I wasn't too surprised. I'm not discouraged. Maybe he already had engagements. Maybe he didn't want to appear too eager. Maybe he passed out. I don't have to start thinking he set fire to the slip of paper I gave him. I don't have to think that he's already attached to someone else.

There have been a few knocks at the door. I hate spying, but what are peepholes for? How can I open the door and tell friends to go away? I don't want to think about anyone but Matthew now. I don't want to see anyone except him.

No one looked desperate, like they were on the verge of suicide. No one was slumping as if they were depressed. Rumsey shrugged his shoulders after knocking twice, and then walked away as if he couldn't care less.

I saw a magnified glimpse of another male in my life. Of all those I've been with, none were right for me for one reason or another. I've made some mistakes: the flutemaker from Seville, the out-of-work actor, the waiter who wants to write but is afraid to, the unkempt poet, the alcoholic photographer, the student brain surgeon, the one who thought he was in Tibet when he was only in Venice Beach. I started muffing up way back with Phil. And with Matthew. I guess that's one reason why I'm going to keep waiting for him now.

Tuesday:

Matthew still hasn't come. Maybe he works all week and is exhausted at night.

No one knocked on the door today.

I've had lots of time to think, to mold stories. I can't stop thinking of him. I can't get him out of my head. I'm not even going to try to.

> Where can you live acres of life in a cubic inch,
> years of life in an hour, or less?
> Without light from the sun?
> Without lifting a finger?
> In a dream, that's where.

I have been out of bed. I haven't been sleeping all the time. I've spent quite a few hours painting, but when I paint I go right on thinking about Matthew, Matthew from every angle.

When I paint I feel as if I'm drawing. I'm drawing with a brush. I feel as if I'm back in Timpanelli's class with a pencil in my hand, and Matthew is standing beside me, working, whistling softly, casting glances at me.

I've been working on a painting of two figures. They are running through the darkness. Their bodies are composed of wisps of flame. Flying sparks trail behind them. I haven't gotten to the sparks yet.

Mother-of-Pearl

After the ceremony she was in the school gym with the rest of her graduating class. She took off the cap, and the gown, and as she was folding it over her arm she looked up and saw that Matthew was watching her. She didn't know what to say to him. She wanted to throw her arms around him. She wanted to close the gap. But she couldn't. There was nothing she could do with him. She eased forward and asked him if he had a senior picture of himself he could give her. He shook his head slowly, and then, much to her surprise, he fished around under his robe, and pulled one out of his shirt pocket and handed it to her. He gave her his glinty smile—just like the first time she had ever seen him—as if they shared a sad secret, a sad secret joke, and he wouldn't tell if she wouldn't tell. Then they walked away from each other as if they had important missions to accomplish at opposite poles of the earth.

She didn't see him again until last Sunday at the fair.

They were strangers, really.

Flora woke with these thoughts. During the day she had to live with the truth of them. She pulled the bedsheets over her face.

What did she do in the twelfth grade? It might as well have been a blind spot in her past. She took another dance class with Pazetti, American literature with Langtry, physiology instead of physics. She had the bedroom all to herself. Janice had gone to Scripps Institute and was studying marine biology. The privacy didn't feel as good as she had thought it would; the room was too empty. She went out with different boys now and then, with no one in particular. She even went out with Phil a couple of times. He was a pre-med student at UCLA, studying hard and nervous about doing well. He wanted to see more of her, but most of the time when he asked her out, she turned him down. Many weekends she just stayed home. She was still in love with Matthew. They no longer shared an art class. She usually saw him only from afar. Sometimes he surprised her by appearing up close, putting his arm around her, grabbing her books and carrying them for her, tugging on her hair —something, anything, enough to keep a desire for him burning in the pit of her.

She turned on her side and curled up in a ball, all twisted up in the sheets. That summer after their graduation, she saw nothing of him. He and his father and Stella moved off Jericho. She recalled what she had done after they had turned away from each other in the Big Gym. She had consented to go with Phil to a graduation party at Stan's house. It was either that or go home and spend the night alone. But it was a mistake to say yes. Phil took it as a sign she'd rather be with him than anyone else. With summer lying before them and the pressure of his studies put aside for a while, Phil was persistent and persuasive. He wanted things to be as they were when they first dated. "I love you, Florey . . . Don't go out with anyone else." She said yes to him more and more. By the end of summer she was pregnant. He wanted to marry her, but instead she got an abortion. Her father ordered Phil to stay away from her. He didn't give Phil a chance to knock on the door. He met him out on the porch and said, "You have a lot of nerve creeping around here." "But Mr. Jackson, sir, I only wanted to know if Flora is all right." She could hear Phil's sorrowful voice through the door. "That's not your concern—never was, and never will be. And if I see you around here again, I'll . . ."

She saw Phil only once after that. One of his fraternity brothers picked her up as if they were going on a date and took her to the fraternity house, where Phil was waiting for her. They drove around in his sports car, not knowing where to go. They ended up parking on Mulholland Drive. He put his arm around her and kissed her. She kissed him, but not like a lover. Like a mother might kiss her dead child—with a numbing sadness and a sense of loss for something that never really had a chance to be. She started crying and he told her not to cry, not to feel bad. "I could use a rubber from now on," he said. She told him it wasn't that. It was no use. There was nothing left. No feeling. And then he was crying, too. She told him she hated herself for not being honest with him, for not telling him everything. "But you do tell me everything, Florey." He shook her hands as if to shake her back to her senses.

"No, I don't," she insisted. "I never even told you I don't like to be called Florey." He looked at her, truly shaken. How could she tell him about the hidden love she had for someone else? She didn't tell him then, or ever. She let him go on thinking she was incapable of devoting herself to one person. She let him think she merely wanted to be free. "We've always gotten along so well together, Florey—Flora." Instead of touching her, he crossed his arms over his steering wheel and wept. "Please, Phil," she said. "You'll find someone a lot better than me. You'll find someone a lot better." And she placed her hand on his back.

That fall she started going to UCLA, as a humanities major. The title sounded large and remote and noncommittal. She read books like *Moby-Dick* and *Anna Karenina.* Her father said, "You're wasting my money and your time. What's a humanities major going to get you—a job in the Peace Corps?" But he didn't push any science major, like biology or geology. He knew that she and chemistry didn't mix.

Though she and Phil were going to the same school, she never saw him. He was at one end of it and she was at the other. And then she heard that he had let himself get drafted. He didn't devise a scheme for staying out, as lots of college students did. And he didn't bother to tell her good-bye. He was shipped to Vietnam. Tess said so. "It's true," Tess told her again over the phone. "Stan knows. He said Phil wanted to go." She could hear Tess's baby blurbering in the background. Tess said, "Say hello to Auntie Flora, Vanessa." There was a wet sucking sound and some syllables. Tess said she had to go to work.

Tess's parents helped take care of Vanessa. And Tess worked for her parents in their catering service. Tess was a mother with a job and an apartment of her own. Flora herself was still a student then, wandering around with a pile of books, still living at home. She and Tess rarely communicated. Only bad news linked them together.

She unrolled herself from the bedsheets and got up. She pulled the curtains aside. It was a foggy morning. The fog was thick against the window. And it was quiet, as if cotton had been stuffed in the ears of everything. She wandered into the bathroom. In the shower, she turned around and around slowly and let the hot water pound down on her from all angles. That old Stones song "Heart of Stone" started playing in her head. She hummed it, and after a while the words came out—something about a heart never breaking. Her voice ricocheted off the tile walls and rang in her ears. She sang until she wore the song out.

She looked down around the bottom of the shower and saw that her rock and shell collection, even when wet, looked dull. She picked up a stone. It was covered with a film of gray mildew. She started scrubbing it with the brush she usually used for getting oil paints out from around her fingernails, and her thoughts drifted far back to the times she had gone with Phil on his surfing trips. When he was out catching waves, she'd go for walks and pick up rocks and shells. The piece of obsidian she held now didn't come from one of those trips, though. She couldn't remember where she had found it. She scrubbed away the fog and it glistened again, like black patent leather. She set it back down.

That summer with Phil—why couldn't she have said no to him from the start? Graduation night was a nightmare. Stan's parents had vacated their house for the evening, and everybody was too shocked to do anything forbidden with all that instant privacy. They had sat there on the couches in Stan's family room, drinking but not getting drunk, telling and retelling stories of all the outrageous things they had done over the past few years—any crazy thing, from swimming in a municipal fountain to sneaking down to Tijuana. The stories had sounded remote and bizarre to her. She had not been a part of Phil's group of friends for a long time. Phil had his arm around her as if they had been going together all along. She should have stayed home alone and spared him the illusion.

And yet she had gone out with him again soon after that, and then again and again. She let the water hit her in the face. After that summer, all those nights making out with him in the front seat of his car—on hilltops, in alleys, in the back rows of drive-ins, along the coast highway. Wishing she were with Matthew. After all those wrong turns. After one pregnancy, and one abortion. Her mouth was open. She was crying, wailing silently into the rush of hot water. After all that, she didn't feel like being with Phil ever again. Why couldn't he understand?

She bent down and picked up an abalone shell. With the water drenching her back, she scrubbed the shell until the mother-of-pearl shone again. An old Portuguese sailor on Malibu Beach had given it to her. She had watched him carefully scrape the animal out of the shell with his knife. She had been awake during the operation, staring at the bright light overhead, listening. That same sound, a rhythmic scraping, slightly gritty, and muted, as if under water. And then, very soon, nothing but an empty shell. She held the abalone under the shower head and watched the water stream out of the row of holes, largest spout to smallest, and thought of all that had been lost, washed down a drain and sent out to sea. She cried for the baby that would have been, and she cried for Phil, wherever he was.

If she stayed in the shower any longer, the landlady, whose bedroom was below the bathroom, might think she was drowning, or at least using up more than her share of water. She turned the faucets off and reached for a towel. She remained standing in the shower with the towel pressed to her face. With Phil, it had been a painful or at best an uncomfortable experience. The only thing that had given her pleasure, she figured now, must have been the feeling of being desired and useful. If she let him do what he wanted to do, he would feel good. She stepped out of the shower and finished drying off. She pulled a pair of jeans out of a drawer and a pink blouse out of the closet, and put them on mechanically. She felt dazed and sapped of strength. Her hair was wet, but she didn't bother to dry it. She draped a towel over her shoulders, went and lay down on the bed. She stared at the crease in the peak of the white ceiling and heard Phil saying, "I love you, Florey, I love you, Florey," so many times over that it sounded like a tape recording. It felt like a tapeworm coiling around and around in her belly. She put her hands on her stomach to quell the uneasy feeling. He told her he loved her, and she believed he did. For that she had been willing to do what he wanted. Her stomach continued to growl.

She tried to remember way back to when she had first met him. Had she been drawn to him at all, or merely pushed? Yes, there had been a slight tug at her heart at first. She had had his scent and the image of his face in her mind, and a feeling of suspense gripping her in the ribs, on those first Friday nights when she knew he would be pulling up in front of the house, and she was ready and waiting for him. But that sensation had passed so rapidly. As if she had impaired vision, the sight of Phil became obscure. His image was followed everywhere by a more intriguing ghost image. No, it was more like a shadow that did tricks of its own when Phil went out a door or downstairs or around a corner. And that shadow was Matthew. And once after art class, that shadow had actually asked her what she saw in Phil. He glided along beside her, waiting for an answer, and when she didn't give him one, he made a sharp turn away from her and went down another path. She closed her eyes. She wished she could erase the mistakes.

She thought of how Matthew and she might have gotten together and squeezed her eyes shut even tighter. Struggling with him in the dark, in his bedroom, and crying to get away—that was as close as they had ever got, that night he kidnapped her from an open party. She wondered if it could be called kidnapping. She hadn't struggled, really, not until he was on top of her.

She got up and pulled the blue curtains shut.

Pastels

Wednesday:

In spirit, I think Matthew and I got very close to each other, with our easels side by side in Timpanelli's class. In his drawings I got an eyeful of something that never showed up in my own. There was a heat in his lines, a liquid sensuality that was enticing. I could tell by watching him that he was in love when he drew. He loved what he was drawing. Sometimes I envied Tess for being the figure he could draw from.

But I was afraid to feel, afraid to accept what he was showing me. And he knew all along what I was feeling and that I was hiding it. He knew I was loving him in my dreams.

That was our sad secret joke.

I'm sure he left that drawing of the figures rising from the blue flames on his easel one day to see if I would dare to take it, and I did.

Flora inscribed these thoughts in her notebook. Then she pulled the curtains back and swung the window open. The fog had burned off. It was going to be a brilliant day. She went over to her easel, removed the oil cloth from her palette, and unscrewed the lids on the turpentine and linseed oil cups.

Again, like so many times before in the last couple of days, there was the sight of Matthew's drawing scattered in shreds in her mind —just the way her father had left it, all over her bed. Just the way she had found it. A warning back then. A bad omen now? She wasn't going to let it be. Matthew would show up.

She recalled how he had made little corrections on her drawing, such as the addition of nipples. And how he had written messages in the margins. *I'd like to brush your clouds away.* She had tried to answer him with lyrical phrases too, but her messages were always a disappointment in the end. To his invitations she was always saying *No,* or *Impossible.*

Once he had brought her a box of oil pastels from the supply closet. They had worked in color together. Her drawings had changed. They had become bolder and more alive.

He had teased her, back then. And tempted her daily, with his comments, his drawings, his offerings, his eyes. She thought about his eyes as she worked on her painting. She needed to see him again, face to face.

The curtains were whipping in and out. The wind had come up. She shut the window and pulled the curtains closed.

Thursday:

I was attracted to Matthew the first time I ever saw him. He was standing on the opposite side of the gully, and the look in his eyes was startling. He was the only boy in Hazelton High that ever gave me a shiver. I didn't know what an orgasm felt like. But by looking at him, I thought I could imagine how it might feel.

I never let him show me how, how it might be done, how it could really feel.

He came into Timpanelli's washroom once while I was in there washing my hands. He locked the door and tried to kiss me. I struggled against him as if he were a vampire and my life depended on not getting kissed. I wouldn't let him touch me.

Now he haunts me.

Jasmine Tea

Flora was awakened by the wailing of an air raid siren—one rude way of being told that it was ten o'clock, the last Friday morning of another month. She put a pillow over her head, and when the noise had gone away she sat up. She shook the sheet until it lay smoothly over the entire bed and her lap. It was impossible to make the rest of the bed from that position, so she crawled out of it. She found the madras spread on the floor, floated it over the bed, and then, using her hand like a trowel, smoothed away all the wrinkles and tried to take the curves out of the stripes.

There was a trill of laughter from down below. She peeked out the window. A girl in a bikini and a boy wearing nothing but blue jeans were passing through the narrow side yard. He was holding her around the waist and trying to kiss her on the ear or neck, and she was pulling away from him and laughing. Flora felt a pang, a twinge of heat, pass up through her. She drew back from the window.

She whisked some incense dust off the velvet cloth on her nightstand and picked up her notebook. Sitting at the edge of her newly made bed, she wrote:

Matthew and I never rendezvoused at a school dance, never retreated to the hills, to his old house for the evening. He did move onto Jericho with his father, however. I wish that had never happened. It was an unbelievable move. My father hated his guts without ever meeting him.

Someone knocked on the door, and Flora slapped her notebook shut.

"Yoo-hoo, Flora."

Flora tiptoed to the door.

"I see a big green eye in the peeky hole," sang Fran. "Open up," she demanded.

Flora obeyed.

"Why didn't you answer the door the other day? I saw Rumsey on the beach and he said he saw you in the window, but you wouldn't open the door for him either. You hole up in here like it's some kind of mausoleum." Fran dropped her purse on the floor and settled back into Flora's overstuffed chair.

Flora went over and stood beside her easel as if she'd been painting. "I've just been feeling out of it." She wiped her hands on a paint rag.

"Into a new painting. I like it—looks like flames. Rather erotic. What I really want to know is, what happened to you on Sunday?"

"I saw someone I hadn't seen in a long time." Flora headed for the kitchen. "Would you like some wine or tea or something?"

"Some tea, please. Do I know him?"

"I doubt it. He's someone I had a crush on in high school." Flora switched the flame on under the kettle and watched it.

"Oh, that one, Phil Ridley?" Fran got up and came into the kitchen.

"No, someone else." Flora appreciated the way Fran didn't jump up and down and throw a fit at every disclosure. Fran gave her a smart smile now.

"Well, is Romeo tall, dark, and handsome, or squat, pale, and ugly?"

Flora kept taking the lids off and on tea tins.

"Let's not drink any of that kind that puts you to sleep," said Fran.

"How's jasmine?"

"Perfect. So . . . out with it."

"Well, he's on the tall side. Taller than an easel." Flora nodded over at her easel.

"Is he blue and wiggly like those figures?" Fran pointed her finger at Flora's painting.

Flora laughed a little. She poured sputtering water from the kettle to the teapot and some of it missed the pot.

"Your hands are shaking. I bet you haven't been eating." Fran opened the refrigerator and saw nearly nothing. She closed it. "You haven't been eating. Either that or you ate everything."

"I haven't been in the mood to eat." Flora was holding a teacup in each hand and staring into the main room as if she could see Matthew standing there by her easel. "I guess he's kind of pale. Pale and straight."

"Taller than an easel, pale, and straight. So where is he now?" Fran relieved Flora of the cups.

"He has very dark eyes. Not brown. Black. So black you can't see where his pupils end and his irises begin." Flora sighed. "I don't know where he is. I wish I knew." She leaned against the door frame.

"Did you put any tea in this pot?" Fran peeked in the pot.

"Oh, I forgot." Flora turned back to the kitchen.

"Well, does he know where you live, at least?" Fran sniffed the jasmine. Then she measured out three teaspoons.

"I told him on Sunday."

"What I don't understand is, why were you dating other guys when you had a crush on this fellow?"

"Matthew. Because Matthew lived on my block and my father didn't like the looks of him. For some uncanny reason my father knew I'd be attracted to Matthew. He banged my head against the wall for the crimes he was sure I was committing with him."

"Ouch. Poor baby."

"Well, how would you like to be punished for sins you didn't even have the pleasure of committing . . . yet?" Flora had drifted back out to the main room. She lifted the oil cloth on her palette. Some of the paint was toughening up. With the handle end of a brush, she poked at the globs; it was like bursting little egg yokes. "Anyway, it doesn't matter now."

"No, really, Flora, it must have been awful. It's a wonder you didn't just run away." Fran set all the tea things on the little hexagonal table between the big chair and the bed. She sat down to pour.

Flora plopped down on the bed. "I guess I should have. I thought about it, believe me. But you know how it is—it would be like skipping all the steps. I wanted to graduate, and go to college, make my parents proud. And my father was running the show. So I obeyed him. I went out with boys I thought he'd think were respectable. Or else I just stayed home."

"No pleasure in that." Fran spun some honey around her spoon.

"Thing is, my father didn't like any of the boys I dated. He didn't even like Phil. But he never accused Phil of anything, except speeding, until my sister informed him that I was pregnant with Phil's baby." Flora looked in her cup and saw a beige bloom floating there. She swished it around with her finger. "Phil was the only one who talked about marriage. He didn't want to see anything die—he didn't want anything to die between us."

"Well, what did you want?" Fran looked worried.

"I wasn't in love with Phil. And I was terrified of becoming a mother. I was still a child myself. Making a decision about anything was beyond me. My father made all the arrangements. And when it was all over and Phil came to see how I was, my father met him on the front porch and told him that if he ever caught him within a mile of me again, he'd call the police and make a citizen's arrest."

Flora took a sip of her tea. "So anyway, my father complained about anyone I went out with. But nothing like the fits he had just imagining Matthew and me together. If he'd ever found out that we were in the same art class, he would've yanked me out of there."

Fran set her empty cup down and sank back in the chair. "Geez, you'd think he'd get sick of chasing boys out of your life."

"Well, finally he just got sick. He had some tests taken on himself during my second year of college, and they came out positive, positively bad, that is. He had stomach cancer. Janice and I were there when the doctor told my father the news. In this little office with no windows, and my father was patting his belly as if to console it. That did it. I fainted in Janice's lap." Flora was feeling queasy now. She lay back on the bed. "When I was a kid I used to wish he'd die of cancer. Sometimes I imagined he *was* cancer. I

thought he was eating away at my life." Flora took a deep breath.
"I never knew what to say to him. I'd go to see him in his hospital ward—he looked so old all of a sudden, and a little frightened—lying there in a white bed, and I'd start advising him to eat yogurt and forget about meat, foolish things like that, things too late to say. He'd just blink at me. Or else he'd complain about something, such as how filthy the chrome bars were on his bed. He'd make me take a close look at them. Sometimes he'd ring for a nurse and make her look, too."

Fran covered her face with her hands and gasped, half laughed.

"And still, even then, he'd tell me what a slut I was, what a hippie freak. He'd say I had no respect for the family." Flora sat up straight. "I'd tell him I had no intention of living in a commune and that I didn't take drugs. I just wanted to live by myself and paint. His response to that was, 'You love to breathe those turpentine fumes. You're fuzzy in the head. You're sadly mistaken if you think you're going anywhere,' and so on. He had all kinds of phrases. It only occurred to me a year or so ago that I couldn't possibly ever turn out to be a 'prune picker.' Prunes don't even grow on trees. Plums do. He really had me rattled." Flora laughed a short regretful laugh.

"You're really going to make it, Flora. Your father would flip in his grave if he could see how well you're doing."

"Maybe he would if he could, but he was cremated."

Fran didn't know what to say to that. Her brows were scrunched together.

"I was surprised. But then, he never liked the idea of anything rotting—not plums, or anything."

There was a brisk rap at the door. Fran jumped up to answer it. Flora sat on the end of the bed, stark still, and waited.

A young man who looked nothing like Matthew followed Fran into the room.

"He says he wants to buy that drawing of the hand sticking up out of the river rocks." Fran went over and sat on the table next to Flora's easel.

"I couldn't make up my mind out on the street, but now I'm sure I want it." He stood with his hands in his back pockets. He looked a little like Phil: tanned and blond, with a perfectly ironed plaid madras shirt, too. He was wearing dark sunglasses.

"Thank you for coming up," said Flora. She held her head and wandered around, trying to remember where she had put the drawing.

"It's probably in that stack," said Fran, pointing to some leaning up in the corner. She was swinging her feet.

"I didn't want to interrupt you when you were working," he said. "I just wanted to get it before it was sold to someone else."

"No problem," said Flora. She found the drawing where Fran had said it was. "I'm glad you like it."

He held it out before him. "It's perfect," he said. "Will you take a check?"

"Sure," said Flora. She couldn't remember what price she had put on the drawing.

"Is it all right if I pay you fifty now and thirty next Friday at the street gallery?"

"Sure, that's fine with me." Flora took the check. "Thank you," she said, barely looking at it. She never felt as if she had earned a payment of any amount.

"Wow, this is incredible." He was looking at Flora's blue flame painting. "Must have been a far-out mescaline trip." He took off his sunglasses and stepped up for a closer look.

Fran puffed herself up and placed one hand gingerly on the edge of the canvas. "This is the product of a pure dream vision." She used a polite instructional tone.

"Well, I'd like to see it when it's finished." He put his sunglasses on again and started moving toward the door.

"She'll be putting the finishing touches on it this week. Two weeks for drying and the varnish. It should be ready for showing in about three weeks." Fran liked to take on the part of Flora's manager. When he had left, she said, "Are you going to show your paintings tonight?" She started gathering up the tea things.

"I don't think so." Flora was sitting on her stool, staring at the painting that Fran had said would be finished and dry in three weeks. "Maybe I'll show them tomorrow night, depending . . ."

"Well, Stephen's still working at the fair. So I told Rumsey I'd come and clap for him at the Marina tonight. He's playing drums with that group again, Beyond Repair. Would you like to join us?"

"I'd like to, but I think I'd better stay here."

"Why?" Fran picked up a spoon she had dropped.

Flora sighed.

"Oh—Matthew," Fran quickly answered herself. "Your new flame, or should I say old flame. Do you still think he'll show up?"

"I don't know, but if I'm not here, I'll never know."

The Eraser

Flora stopped painting and rested her fingers on the edge of her easel. She was thinking about all those storage rooms, all those hidden creases in Hazelton High's anatomy, imagining that she and Matthew were opening the door to one of those forbidden rooms and stepping inside. There were so many of those doors, every one of them stenciled OFF LIMITS in black paint in a blocky lettering style that suggested pestilence or radioactivity. Flora smiled sadly, with one side of her mouth turned up and one side turned down, as Matthew would. She picked up her brush and made several little undulating strokes. She hoped someone had made good use of those rooms.

During the summer between her junior and senior years, the old school was demolished and the new school was built. One went up as the other came down. Several afternoons, she had left the house without telling anyone where she was going, and she had ended up at the border of the old school. She walked the length of its chain-link fence and stopped here and there to watch the growth of the wasteland. Splintered lath, chunks of plaster, and everywhere torn plaques of gray-green asphalt roofing lay scattered in the dirt.

She had been watching on the day they tore Timpanelli's room apart. She half expected to see spirits fleeing from it, but all she had seen was a white cloud of plaster rise up as the walls collapsed. She watched an iron ball on the end of a chain slam through the walls of the washroom. Bits of gaudy-colored Sheetrock and wood went flying in all directions. One of the pieces read *Flora and Matthew Forever.* Matthew had written it as a sort of joke, knowing the room would be destroyed soon.

She hadn't cried at all. She felt as dry as the plaster, as hot as the sidewalk she was standing on. Everything was ruined. Even the giant eucalyptus trees had been cut down.

She took a sip from the water glass on her worktable and continued to paint. She was working on the sparks behind the figures —minute dashes of cadmium red light mixed with cadmium yellow.

Hall after hall, classroom after classroom was smashed to the ground until it looked as if the old army hospital had finally been bombed. The destruction was immense and complete. Crows weren't even interested in the debris. They flew right on over without looking down.

She strained to twist the cap off an old tube of paint. Anyway, one of the things they taught me in those rooms was to accept disappointment. Let the old school go. Why linger over it? The cap came off, but now the tube had a tear in it and purple paint was oozing out.

A big Siamese cat leapt silently onto the windowsill of the house across the way from Flora's room. She set the paint tube down and moved slowly over to her own window. The cat saw her, but he wasn't interested. After a glance, he began bathing himself, licking his shoulders, and his chest, his armpits, sitting way back on his hips and licking himself between the legs as if no one were watching.

Flora continued to gaze at him. She wondered what had become of Timpanelli. For all she knew, Timpanelli had disintegrated along with her classroom. She didn't show up in any of the new ones. Flora couldn't picture Timpanelli sitting at a slick desk in a room full of vinyl tables, metal storage cabinets, stainless-steel sinks—a room built of concrete blocks, painted gray, with high horizontal slits some architect said were windows. And even if Timpanelli had stayed on at the new school for the next year, or any year after that, Flora wouldn't have gone back to visit her. She would have been too embarrassed to. She watched the cat lick his paws and wipe his brow. She had never done enough drawings in class, or out of class, to satisfy Timpanelli. And yet Timpanelli had never given up on her. Flora could still feel her encouragement. The woman was a silent, invisible being standing behind her as she drew, as she painted—approving of what she did, of what she was doing.

Flora recalled the course she had taken her senior year in place of Life Drawing. It was called Scientific Illustration. The instructor had a morbid bent. He would sometimes show her photos of birth defects and accident victims from his collection of medical texts. She had worked for weeks doing internal and external views of a cat—skeleton, organs, muscles, fur coat—from all angles.

The Siamese stopped what he was doing and looked at Flora. Without the slightest hint of what he would do next, he leapt back into the shadow of his own room. Flora went back to her easel.

She had hated that year at the new school. Everything was so stiff and regimented. There were no secret places. No hideaways. All the possibilities of hiding away had been blotted out along with the old school. "But what did it matter to me?" Flora challenged herself out loud. "I was afraid to be alone with Matthew anyway. No. I was too afraid of my father to get close to him." She took a swipe at her painting and then regretted it. We should have run away together, she told herself. But we didn't. Even he stayed on to the very end. She cleaned her brush in the turpentine and tried again. We got ourselves obediently graduated. Accepted our fake diplomas from the smiling Mrs. Baines, and paraded off the athletic field as if we were well-trained dogs.

She stood back slightly and looked at her painting. Then I asked him for a photo of himself, and he shook his head at me and handed me one. She shook her own head now. So many mistakes needed to be corrected.

Friday:

> My souvenir, my consolation prize.
> Better than nothing.
> I got what I deserved for my timidity.
> I still have a picture of his face in the bottom of my chest.

The painting didn't go so well today. I feel a little shaky. He just slipped away. I have no one to blame but myself. I wish I could see him again. I'm so tired of working and reworking my life as if it were a canvas of wet paint.

After writing this in her notebook, she got up off the bed, went to the side table, and took out several pieces of stationery she had been saving.

Dear Mrs. Timpanelli,

I hope I am writing to the right one. If you were *not* my Life Drawing teacher at Hazelton High, I'm sorry to have bothered you, and please disregard this letter.

I never knew your first name and I didn't save my school annual. When I had my first art showing I sent invitations to all the Timpanellis in the phone book. A Timpanelli did show up, a Giovanni Timpanelli, with his violin and his seeing-eye dog. He rode all the way from San Pedro on the bus.

I hoped he was a relative of yours—your grandfather, maybe—but he wasn't. Anyway, he played his music, which sounded like romantic crying, sweet and far-off, like a girl singing at the end of a breakwater. I told him how I was searching for you, and he told me I should search harder, that I should stop pretending I was trying to find you. As he was leaving he said, "When you are ready to find your teacher, you will find her."

So after that I wrote to a high school friend. Do you remember Tess Duban, the model? She said you had passed away, but she went ahead and gave me the addresses of several other students of yours. One wrote back. He said your number wasn't ever listed in the phone book, but he had visited you in Santa Monica about three years ago, and he hoped the address he was giving me now was the one you were still at.

I'm sorry I've taken so long to write.

If you are the Mrs. Timpanelli I've been trying to reach, I'd like to tell you, of all the people who helped me when I was young, you are the one who inspired me the most. This is too simply put, I know, but my father thought he knew when I needed to be "straightened out." My mother knew when I needed to be cuddled. But you, you knew when I needed to be pushed. You told me I'd better draw or I'd shrivel up. Just the kind of warning I needed back then. And when you smiled at my drawings, it was like flipping open the top of a brand-new box of forty-eight Crayola crayons and seeing a splurge of beautiful colors.

Every so often I have a dream where you are still my teacher. You're standing beside me, nodding and smiling as I paint. Or else you are scowling at me because I can't seem to get started—there's nothing on the easel! Once I dreamed you handed me a white eraser the size of a brick and said, "Why don't you try again?" In the last dream I had, I sat down on a bus bench, and there you were, next to me. You were feeding corn chips to a pigeon that was pacing back and forth on the curbstone. Then the pigeon changed into an alligator, and I gasped. "Don't you like alligators?" you asked. "Not really," I said. The alligator was nudging me in the knees with his snout. "Well, you have to have the patience of an alligator"—that's what you said. "Do alligators have patience?" I asked. "I don't know," you said. And we laughed so hard we missed the bus. It roared right past us.

I can't really figure out this dream. All I know is, I'd very much like to see you again, in person, and I hope you get this letter. I hope you are well.

Still Your Devoted Student,

Flora Jackson

P.S. I don't have a telephone. My address is: 22-C Leeward Court, Venice Beach

A Night for Leaving the Windows Wide Open

Flora woke up on her back with her hands clasped together. She pulled her hands apart and looked at them. Her fingers were ringless. She had stopped biting her nails after moving away from home, but now they were short again, freshly nibbled.

Matthew had given her a black sapphire ring, but she had given it back to him. After that, he mocked her by slipping cigar labels on her finger, or handing her the aluminum rings from pull-top cans, giving her coiled pipe cleaners to wear. Childish versions of a ring. He wrote her a love letter, too. But she couldn't answer it the way she wanted to, so she didn't answer it at all.

She let her hands fall back down on her chest, back down on the sheets. "I'm living inside a shell of a room, between some glossy white walls, beneath a glossy white ceiling." Her eyes roamed around aimlessly. "I'm still only a dreamer," she whispered. "All I've got are these fantasies laid down over my everyday life like layers of tracing paper over the base drawings."

She looked at her notebook, set against the black velvet of the nightstand. Cupid was always leaping from the bed of Psyche. She picked it up and read her last entry:

Looking back, Matthew, I know I loved you deeply from the start. All those hours I stood beside you in Timpanelli's Life Drawing class, I loved you.

Last year I sold that painting of your calling on me at my house, my father's house. I sold it to a woman who said it matched a vision she had had. I never thought I'd see you again. So many times I saw you knocking on that door in my dreams. And I ran away with you in my dreams, but what does that matter now? I'm still alone and you're still somewhere else. Our flight to Mexico was only a mirage. You used to say, "Let's run away, Flora. Let's go to Mexico." And I'd say you were crazy. And you'd say you were going to tie me up and force me to run away with you. Then you'd wink and go on painting.

I've wasted a lot of time being afraid, so why shouldn't I dedicate a week or two out of my life now, just waiting for you, trying to set something straight?

She stopped reading and looked at the paintings hanging along one side of the room. Some of them were crooked, as if someone had been tampering with them during the night. She got out of bed and straightened them. Then she got back into bed and wrote:

If you don't come to me, I'll go out and look for you. I'll take a bus, or maybe hitchhike if I have to. I'll go back to the fair. You might be there again on Sunday.

Maybe all I need is one long night with you, and then the spell will be broken, or else sealed for life.

I'm old enough to know that it's hard to make anything last—a day, a friendship, one's own lifespan—but I wish I could have another chance with you.

If I knew your address, I'd write to you.

Do you remember the bomb? The bomb shelters? The bomb drills? We crawled under our desks. We were like children playing hide-and-seek, hiding in the most conspicuous places.

Matthew, I'm not trying to hide from you at all now.

It must be Saturday because the air raid siren went off yesterday. "I wish I could spit on it, and thereby extinguish it." Mr. Langtry said that once while the siren was still blaring, and everyone laughed.

It's unbearable to think about wars and the world blowing up. During our last year of high school, the boys were invited to go to the new auditorium during lunch hour and listen to recruiting officers from the different armed forces give their pep talks on how good it is to serve your country and further your education.

Did you go?

What they wanted were volunteers for the Vietnam War. Some boys returned to the lunch area with a new aura about them. They had committed themselves somehow, signed their names to something maybe. They looked like they felt important, but they looked fuzzy around the edges, too—as if a part of them had already been shot up and left lying in a swamp.

That's not exactly how I saw it at the time. More likely I was annoyed because most of the boys in the school had been lured out of the lunch area on that particular day, leaving all the girls with nothing to do but wait for them to return.

But they didn't get you, Matthew. That's one of the thoughts I had when I saw you walking down the hill at the fair. You're still alive.

A couple of years ago Tess wrote me more bad news. Floyd had been hit and killed by a train in boot camp. I tore the letter up and threw it away. I couldn't believe it. Had he been joking around and the joke had gotten out of hand? I pictured him roped to the tracks as in a silent film. Or had he intended to get hit, like Anna Karenina? N. C. Wyeth's car stalled on a train track. But accidents don't just happen. Aren't they encouraged? What did Tess mean, "got hit by a train"? I wrote her a letter back asking her. She wrote me an eight-page letter in return. She said Vanessa was three years old and liked to wear little black leotards. Tess said she was going to marry a Denver man with a nine-year-old son of his own. And she was going to move to Denver because he owned and managed a ski shop there. Nowhere in her letter was there any mention of Floyd.

Floyd *got hit by a train.* Phil *went to fight in the war.* It's the kind of thing that makes me jolt up in bed in the middle of night. Is that the end of their story? Where have they gone? Where are they? I want to know.

Then I start wondering, Am *I* doing everything right? Or anything right? Not offending anyone, not offending fate?

The sun had sunk on Saturday, and still Matthew had not appeared. She hated having to switch the light on over her easel. The sun has abandoned me again, she said, even though she knew that was nonsense.

She was supposed to be showing her paintings at the street gallery tonight. She hadn't shown them last night either. But she didn't want to leave her apartment, not even for an hour.

She thought maybe she should confide in someone at this point. She could think of no one but Fran. Fran would understand, but Fran had already lent an ear. In the last week, her other friends had stopped knocking on the door. She didn't blame them in the least for giving up on her.

Yesterday, without knocking or calling out to her, someone had slipped a disturbing note under the door. It read:

> Flora,
> Your silence is a fault that blots out all your charms.
> I'm tired of wasting my time on you.
> You might as well be a mute beast. Locked up.

She picked the note up from the table and stared at it again. It wasn't signed. It wasn't from Matthew. No, it couldn't possibly be from Matthew. It must be Theo on one of his poetic rampages. She crumpled it up as she wandered into the kitchen. She hadn't eaten anything in two or three days. She wished she never had to bother with eating. She looked around the kitchen. Its utter orderliness left a blank in her mind. Cooking makes a mess, and eating takes time, was all she could think. But she didn't want to faint. If Matthew knocked on the door she wouldn't even be able to hear him. Maybe he'd sense that something was wrong, break the door down and revive her. But it would be more like him to just go away without doing any damage. Matthew was not a destructive person. She never saw him kick a hole in a wall—a show of defiance and virility performed by many of the boys at Hazelton High. He had never even unbuckled his belt.

"I'm getting a little carried away." She spoke out loud. She decided she'd better eat something. She opened a cabinet and took down a box of oatmeal, poured some in a pan, added hot water from the tap, and put the pan on the stove. She turned the knob and blew on the burner to get the flame going.

She stood there stirring the oatmeal, around and around—it seemed to take forever. She started singing a song she had heard on the strand:

> Well all right, well all right,
> Oh, we'll live and love with all our might.
> Well all right, well all right,
> Our lifetime love will be all right.

She sang it over again. That was the only part she could remember. She had asked the old black man who was playing it on his guitar where the song came from. "Oh, ways before you was born, sugar." And he had sung one of the lines again, something like, "Those foolish kids can't be ready for the love that comes their way." She stopped stirring and carried the pan, with the spoon stuck in it, back to the easel. She spent the evening painting. Before going to bed, she made another entry in her notebook:

What did he do last night? Where is he tonight?

It's warm and clear out. People are still coming out of their houses, letting their screen doors bang, and walking to the beach. They are playing drums and singing up and down the strand. I think I can hear the waves soaking into the sand even. It is a night for leaving the windows wide open. Next door someone is playing a saxophone, the same couple of measures over and over again, bending and sliding the notes. Now and then, he breaks off playing and sings the words with surprising frankness:

> I saw your name, baby,
> In the telephone booth
> And it told all about you, mama,
> Boy, I hope it was the truth.

Matthew, please come.

Two Candles

Early Sunday evening, Flora drew a hot bath and sank into it. She lay there very still for a long while, just floating. She gazed up into the palm tree. Her father had given it to her when she left home. Actually, he had let her take it from the windowsill in the kitchen. It had been a scrawny little thing in a pint-sized pot. "Let's see if you can make it grow," he had said, challenging her. Now it was nearly too big to be indoors. The point of the newest frond was bent against the bathroom ceiling. Something hooked into her and tugged hard. *He never even got to plant his avocado trees.* The water in the tub was glassy still. Drips from the faucet made loud, hollow-sounding dents. She watched them fall, one after the other.

Suddenly she sat up and pulled the plug. Matthew might arrive and she'd be all wet. She dried herself in a hurry and put on the floor-length robe she had bought at Goodwill, an orchid-colored silk, brocaded into an unending garden of pines, peacocks, and reflection pools. It made her think of an elegant, sad-eyed lady from Peking who might have married an American, come to Los Angeles, and cast off the kimono in favor of American clothes. She closed the windows in the bathroom. The evening fog was rolling in. She brushed her hair, in a rush to dry it.

She walked into the main room and switched on the light over the easel. She felt so lightheaded. She took one look at the overstuffed chair and sank into it. The hot water had made her feel boneless and dreamy. She passed into sleep without feeling any friction.

When she woke she found herself looking at the painting on the easel. The only light in the room was shining on it and not much else. It's not so bad, she thought. For a moment she wondered whose painting it was. Then she reclaimed herself as its creator. As far as it's come, it does look like a vision made of flames, figures painted out of flames. She made a flourish and saw that the hair-brush was still in her hand. She brushed her hair with it.

Her father used to say how everything would burn. "Everything in sight. Either the bombs will do it or the blacks will do it, one or the other. Just mark my words." But he never said anything about burning love. She felt something like a hot heavy rock pressing on her chest, and lower down, lower than her stomach, she felt the seering pain of emptiness. She wished Matthew were rubbing against her. She felt senseless to everything else. She saw the sparks of his eyes. How easily she could have him. He was on top of her, pressing her down into the overstuffed chair. But then, as she was about to yield to him, the sensation was shut down with a terrifying jolt. It arose from the thought of the entire world being burned or blown to blackness and no one being able to hold anyone, no future for anyone to share.

She gripped the arms of the chair and searched into her past. What had she done to help? Some of her friends, and some of the people she met on the street, asked her if she would paint posters against nuclear this and nuclear that. Someone had said, "If a bomb was dropped on Los Angeles and Flora had time to see it, she'd be admiring the colors of the sky." She had done a few posters, but thoughts of war, thoughts of the end of the world, made anything else seem pointless. She wanted to think about Matthew now. She tossed her head back against the chair, and bounced forward. She didn't want to think about Matthew. She wished she could forget him. What was he anyway?—just one human being out of billions.

She got up and went over to the chest, lit the candle in front of the mirror, stood back and looked at it. With a flick of a match there are two candles, two flames. Two for the price of one, she mused. One is real and one is reflection, and who can tell the difference unless they actually try to touch them? Then they'll know which one drips hot wax and which one only gives back a cool, flat image.

She regarded herself in the mirror. The kimono drooped over her shoulders and hung loose. In the dim light, its orchid color was muted to gray. She looked like the maid who dared to try on the empress's clothes. She almost disappeared beneath them. Too thin, always too thin, she thought as she turned sideways, and then away from the mirror. A big drop of wax landed on her mother's doily.

She went into the kitchen. There was a bottle of red wine on the shelf. She opened the refrigerator and looked in the crisper. She ate an apple. Then she looked at the fruit bowl on the counter. She peeled an orange and ate it. Then she peeled a very ripe banana and ate that, too. She felt like a tropical bird on a binge.

She took down the bottle of wine and stuck a corkscrew in it. The cork came out with a wholesome plucking sound: no ragged wounds along its length, no clogs in the throat of the bottle. She smiled and poured herself a glass. She held the glass by the stem and carried it tenderly, as if it were a rosebud, into the main room. She set it down on the worktable and seated herself on the stool in front of her easel.

"Just open a bottle of wine and get back to work; he's bound to show up." She spoke this oath as she folded back the oil cloth from her palette.

She picked up her paintbrush and looked at the painting. She let the brush land in the first patch of paint on the palette and then brought it to the painting. It was the wrong color. She went to dunk it in the turpentine cup and bent the bristles. She looked down and saw that she had forgotten to remove the lids from both the turpentine and the linseed oil. She cleaned the brush, making long wavy streaks on the paint rag, and straightened its bristles with her fingertips. She dabbed the brush in the right color, a blue, the color at the head of a match, and touched the tip of it to the canvas.

She took sips of wine in between strokes without knowing that she was, and forgot about the interruptions she usually got without wanting them, and the one she did want and didn't get.

There was a rapping at the door—one followed by three quick ones, like an indecisive woodpecker. Flora dropped her brush, rushed to the door, and opened it wide.

Her landlady was standing there in her quilted satin robe, her beaded slippers. She always knocked with the tips of her nails. Flora should have known.

"Is anything wrong, dear? No one's heard a sound for days." She gave Flora a quick once-over.

"I'm fine. I've just been working hard . . ." Flora tried to focus, tried to concentrate. "Earning the rent, food, pocket money, you know." She tried to sound lighthearted. She nodded her head and got the landlady to nod her own head in rhythm with hers.

"Putting paint on canvas?" asked the landlady as she took a peek over Flora's shoulder and could see no life beyond.

"Yes," Flora assured her and started to close the door.

The landlady said, "That's nice, but if you need anything, come see me. Don't think twice." She was convinced that everyone was crazy, but some were dangerous and some weren't. She didn't think Flora was a dangerous crazy.

"I will. Thank you," said Flora from a crack in the door. She knew that Mrs. Weiss liked to have her tenants pay visits to her own apartment. Mrs. Weiss considered herself the brood hen for all the tenants. Every time Flora felt the hot air puffing out of the wall vent, which it often did, even in the summertime, she imagined it was Mrs. Weiss fluffing up her breast feathers.

Flora had been Mrs. Weiss's guest on only one occasion, the day she had rung the bell at the ground-floor apartment to ask if there was a vacancy. Mrs. Weiss had invited her into her parlor, as she called it, a dim and dingy-looking room. Its most outstanding feature, after the heavy brocade drapes and the lamps that were lit in the middle of the day, was the sour steamy air. It smelled as if Mrs. Weiss's bedroom slippers had been simmering on the stove all morning.

Flora closed the door as quietly as she could so as not to reattract the old woman, who was already click-clacking back down the hall. It was the contented sound of someone who had done her duty.

Flora's heart was thumping hard and fast. It sounded like a dog thrashing at fleas, pounding his hindquarters against a hardwood floor. She went back to her easel. The paintbrush had rolled across the palette. There was no point in cursing the landlady; it wasn't her fault. Flora wiped the mess of colors off the handle and went back to work. She would keep right on painting. She must keep on painting.

The points of fire trailing behind the figures seemed to flicker as if they were being blown out. She looked over to the row of finished paintings along the wall. Her eyes filled with hot tears. "My life, my life"—she took a harsh stroke at her painting—"feels like a bad mixture of oil paints and turpentine—beautiful dreams thinned out with toxic facts."

She squeezed some titanium white onto the palette and mixed it with ivory black, added a touch of yellow to make gray, the gray of soot, and cinders, and smoke.

There was another knock at the door, not made with the tips of the fingernails this time. She dropped her brush again and froze.

There was another triplet of knocks. Lots of people knock like that, with their knuckles.

She moved toward the door and stood there in front of it for a moment without drawing a breath. She considered peeking through the peephole, but decided against doing that. She tightened the sash on her robe and opened the door slowly.

Matthew was standing back a ways in the dark hall. He was smiling with his eyes and his mouth. He stepped slowly forward and held out a bunch of wildflowers.

Flora looked at the slightly wilted flowers and then clutched them to her chest. Matthew handed her a long rolled-up piece of paper.

She held the flowers and the paper in one hand and uncurled the paper with her fingertips. She kept staring back and forth from Matthew to his drawing.

"May I come in?" Matthew cocked his head in a gesture of polite jest.

"Yes!" said Flora. She stepped back a little and tripped on her robe. If she was dreaming, she hoped she wouldn't wake up.

"Am I too late?" asked Matthew, wondering now whether he had awakened her.

"No. No, not at all," said Flora, regaining her balance. "Please come in." She took hold of his hand.